To: Hal + Dieta
Fellow colleague
in the fight against
Communism in Berlin,
& Elsewhere
Barry Kelly

"Lies are a trap,
not a deception."

bk

To Hal - a true warrior

JUSTICE WITHOUT MERCY

Barry Kelly

Pp
ProsePress
www.prosepress.biz

Justice Without Mercy

Comments: davidbarrykelly@hotmail.com

ISBN: 978-0-9851889-1-7

This material has been reviewed by the CIA to prevent the disclosure of classified information.

All characters in this book are fictional.
Any resemblance to actual persons,
living or dead, is entirely coincidental.

Published by ProsePress
Pawleys Island, South Carolina
www.ProsePress.biz

Cover Illustration by Barnie Slice
Contact: bjslicejr@sc.rr.com

Cover Design by OBD
Contact: proseNcons@live.com

My thanks to all our uniformed men and women who defend this great nation. I cannot forget those who serve and served sub rosa. May you always be there.

Acknowledgments

Since I write primarily from personal experience, enlivened by an active imagination, there are literally scores of people whose lives and adventures have contributed to my store of knowledge. I can't thank them individually and most wouldn't want to be singled out. None of my characters are molded after anyone I ever knew. My characters develop slowly and, then guide me through the story.

My first novel, Justice Beyond Law, *took me more than ten years to complete, with time out for two major cancers, a heart problem and a seemingly endless search for an agent and publisher. I learned about the trade of storytelling in that drawn out period. This novel was written, edited and published in less than one year. I hope my readers find some improvement in my storytelling. If the truth be known, the second novel would never have been written without the encouragement of a growing band of readers who wanted more of the characters created in the first novel. I hope they will be pleased and pass on their comments to me. Who knows? Maybe there is a third novel waiting to be born.*

Linda Ketron again was the midwife in bringing Justice Without Mercy *to life. She is the proof of the wisdom in seeking out the busiest person you know when something needs done. Linda and Annie Pott worked to sprinkle commas and apostrophes throughout the manuscript as well as remind me, even in fiction, the same person cannot be in two places at the same time and that vehicles do not change color in the turning of pages. Barnie Slice created the art work for the cover. Anne Malarich graciously worked her camera magic. My friend and publisher, Bob O'Brien of Prose Press, was, is and, I hope, will be a source of encouragement and advice in the promoting of my novels.*

Thanks to my many friends and relatives that encouraged me to write. My younger brother, a retired professor and marine officer, I can always count on for encouragement and support. My daughter, Beth Ramsey, and Maggie Ward helped market my novel by guiding me through the protocol required by social networking.

Anyone married to a writer knows how selfish we can be in following our own priorities. While my wife is an excellent editor and writer, she left me to my meandering journey in the land of fiction while she maintained our home, managed all financial areas, dealt with the training of our new Bouvier ~ all the time letting me think what I was doing was important.

Barry Kelly

Prologue

Five years ago Joel Hankins, known in the camps as Mohammed Abu Moussa, finished his training at the camp for foreign fighters in Afghanistan. He learned to handle most small arms and explosives but was near the bottom of his trainee group of twenty. His strength and toughness were not equal to the rest of the trainees. The camp was above nine thousand feet with very little vegetation. They lived in caves and were never really warm at night in the winter months. The people they lived among were incredibly poor. Every disease in the mountains of South Asia was visible in the small village near the training site. Even so, his experience at that camp was the highlight of his life. He was someone, someone special. He wasn't the loser everyone said he was in Pittsburgh. He had even met Usama Bin Laden.

Just before he left the camp, he was given an important mission. His leaders told him they had been searching for months to find a westerner of the true faith to help carry Jihad to America. Joel wasn't sure of the true faith, but he did pray at least twice a day and spent another hour each day reading the Koran. He had grown comfortable with the teachings of the Prophet and was proud to be a part of the holy war to establish a Muslim Empire that someday would include the United States.

His leaders knew they were not strong enough to have their own sovereign nation in the face of the forces aligned against them. Control of territory was necessary to recruit and train followers. In Joel's training group, there had been students from Saudi Arabia, Jordan, Iraq, Palestine, Egypt, Pakistan, Indonesia and several western nations. If the Taliban could not hold Afghanistan, where could the faithful train and plan damaging attacks against the infidel nations? Joel was happy he had been assigned to help locate a place within the United States where faithful Jihadists could find safe haven.

Before he left Afghanistan, he was taken to a compound in Peshawar and left in the care of a Palestinian trainer. This man was an expert with real experience in clandestine operations. The trainer told Joel that in the next three weeks he had to be ready for his assignment in America. He was told to forget his Muslim name. While he was in America, his name would be his own, Joel Hankins from Pittsburgh, PA. When his training was over, he would return to Pittsburgh and tell his family he was done traveling around the world and wanted to prepare himself for a career in business. At first Joel objected to this plan but his mentor, a powerful man with intense dark eyes, told him there was no room for dissent. He had been chosen and he would follow orders, or he would never leave the compound alive.

Joel never doubted that Hakim meant every word he said. Putting on his most respectful look, Joel said he would obey and carry out any mission assigned to him.

During the next three weeks, Joel was given intensive instruction in the methods of planning, supporting and carrying out terrorist activities in the United States. He had always been good at detail and soon reached a level of competence that surprised Hakim. In the last week, Joel learned how to deal with hostile interrogations and to prepare cover stories for everything associated with terrorist operations. His first mission was to establish a rug merchant shop in Charleston, SC. The necessary money would be deposited in his name in a Charleston bank.

After Joel satisfied Hakim with his ability to use the tradecraft of espionage, he was delivered to a Taliban supporter in Peshawar who operated a rug manufacturing and export business. Another two months were spent learning how to appraise and sell rugs. From time to time, Hakim would drop by and give Joel a mission to accomplish. Joel never knew whether the mission was for real or practice.

When Joel left Peshawar, he had lost all the trappings of a devoted Jihadist. His thin blond hair was cut short in the style of young Western businessmen. His beard was gone and his new clothes tailored to his scrawny build. With his light blue eyes, wind-burned acne face and wearing his first tailored suit, he was ready to return to Pittsburgh where he had a personal mission and then on to Charleston. His long stay in Pakistan was covered by his learning the art of dealing in Oriental rugs. A hundred rugs were sent in his name to a holding address in Charleston as further evidence of his status as a rug dealer.

It had been two years since Joel left Pittsburgh for Pakistan and Afghanistan. Getting off the Greyhound bus at the downtown terminal on a sunny October day, Joel decided he wasn't going home. His mother died while he was with the Taliban. He hated his father and only wanted to see him one more time – to kill him. Killing didn't require any talk. Joel also had a mental list of girls he knew in Schenley High School who had laughed at his advances and talked about him behind his back. Shirley Bronson and Sally Hartley were the worst. Joel planned to look them up and see if they could still laugh when he was finished with them. His growing lust to kill young women was one thing he had never disclosed to his Muslim contacts. Now that he had the killing skills and the training to avoid being caught, he was ready to start.

Joel took a local bus out to a poorer section of Oakland and paid cash for a room at a rundown boarding house. No questions asked. Just cash in advance. Two days later he paid cash for a high-mileage 2000 model Dodge van. He wouldn't kill his no-account father on this trip. No sense in giving the cops something to work on by getting the Hankins' name involved. Four days later, he had killed both girls.

It was easy. They were both students at Pitt and lived at home with their parents. In two days he had their after-school schedules down pat. Both worked in the University's library week nights and walked home together just after ten o'clock. His first try failed. Too many bystanders were close to his selected ambush site. He had learned patience. The next day Joel parked his dark blue van at another site along their route home. When the girls passed his parked Dodge van laughing and talking. Joel slipped out of the shadows behind them and slammed their heads together. Holding them up, he used his remote to open the side door and shoved the stunned girls inside. There were no lights on in the van. Pulling the right fuses had fixed that. In the darkness after gagging them, he put cloth bags over their heads and duct taped their hands and legs.

Just before midnight, Joel dumped their naked bodies in a wooded area of Schenley Park. He kept their clothes. Along with the photos he took while torturing them, he had a good start on his collection. With both girls his clumsiness caused him to miss the moment of death. The next time he would do better.

Early the next morning he got in his van and left for Charleston. He loved the news coverage. The killings made the front pages of the Pittsburgh papers and the evening news on the networks. With his new knowledge and training, it was easy to outwit the police. There was no evidence he had returned to Pittsburgh, and he left no evidence behind. Those feel-good murders were his business. His al Qaeda leaders didn't need to know.

Two years later, Joel's rug shop in Charleston was making a little money. He had found an ideal place for the shop in a rundown building on the western end of Meeting Street. It had an apartment above the shop and a two-story, three-car garage in the back with space on the second level for two bedrooms, a bath and kitchen with a small sitting area. It was enough to house four or five people for short periods.

Three or four times a year, an al Qaeda courier stopped in his shop to deliver instructions and wait for Joel to write a response. He had no electronic communications with al Qaeda. They used a simple code based on a particular edition of the King James Version of the Bible.

Life was good. Joel continued the training regime he learned in the camps and joined a shooting club. At least twice a week, he took private Taekwondo lessons. Within a few months he would test for his blue belt. He was no longer the scrawny kid that left Peshawar two and a half years ago.

Joel made time for his passion for thrill killing, but he never killed in Charleston. His training had taught him the importance of patience and attention to detail. He set no pattern in his kills, except that his victims were all attractive young girls. No weapons were used to kill them. Joel never killed in any city more than once a year. He was addicted to the feeling of power he got from killing. He would take his prey his own way while he was young and alive. There was no rush like watching the light fade in his victims' eyes. No one would ever have these bitches. In a few cases he had been lucky enough to catch the moment with his digital camera. Too bad he had to keep the images hidden. Rug business trips provided all the cover he needed for visiting other cities. The urges were becoming stronger. It was about time he made a hunting trip to Myrtle Beach.

One

Jack Brandon, on his way to run some errands, paused on the porch of the mountain cabin he inherited from his father, and looked out over the thousand acres of Pennsylvania's Allegheny Mountains that came with the cabin. His father, Peter Brandon, built the cabin, two hours east of Pittsburgh, as a final hiding place, in his struggle to escape a vengeful KGB. Forty years ago, his father, a KGB officer on the fast track, opted for freedom in America but on his terms. He stole all the operational funds the KGB provided for his mission in America. Assuming the name Peter Brandon, he eluded the KGB hunt. The team hunting him found and killed his wife and infant daughter. Only Peter and his young son Jack escaped. For the next three and a half decades, Peter Brandon extracted his vengeance by working with a CIA officer to destroy a Cold War espionage network of Soviet undercover agents living in America. During the last year of his life, Peter revealed his story to Jack, who joined him in his mission to protect America from foreign terrorists' threats. Jack's background as a Marine Recon Officer and detective in the homicide department of the Pittsburgh police gave him the know how to pick up his father's mission after al Qaeda killed Peter Brandon in his McLean, VA home. The hideaway mountain cabin now housed Jack, Kathy and Shadow, Jack's beloved Bouvier des Flandres. Kathy had been an up and coming CIA case officer, who joined the Brandon Group to escape the increasing bureaucracy of the counter terrorism office, and the money covered her mother's medical bills.

Shortly after Jack's father was killed in his home by terrorists, the FBI and local police, acting on information supplied by the group, took care of the remaining elements of the terrorist network. The identities of Jack and Kathy were exposed to al Qaeda during a deadly showdown in New Delhi.

A few more days of rest, then they would have to decide where they would set up next. Some place where it would be difficult for any revenge seeking terrorists to find them. Jack was still running over some options in his head as he drove back from his short trip to Somerset, PA. Besides the need for some groceries, he made a few phone calls. Using cell phones from the cabin was not done. Pay phones were getting scarce but there were some in Somerset. On the way back, he'd decided he would take Kathy and Shadow for a visit to his old home in Pittsburgh. Jack was so focused on the details of a trip to his old haunts, he nearly missed the turn into the overgrown lane to the cabin.

Shadow, the 100-pound plus black Bouvier, came bounding up the quarter mile one-lane entrance to the cabin and jumped into the front seat with Jack when he opened the door. Shadow liked few things better than to sit up front and hang his head out the window as he surveyed his domain. Jack pulled into the small parking area below the cabin and was welcomed by Kathy with a big hug when he got out of the Cadillac SRX.

"Hey, I've only been gone for a few hours. Don't look so worried."

Kathy pushed him back so she could see Jack's face and said, "It's just that we've had so many close ones in the past year. I don't think you worry enough and that attitude scares me to death. In the almost a year since I've been sharing your bed, I thought for sure I had lost you more than once. I don't want to change you, but could you just please take fewer risks. First, Recon Marines, then a homicide detective and, even worse, picking up your father's crusade against terrorists. There, that's my speech. I just had to get it out."

"Kathy, I know I'm not immortal and believe it or not, I intend to cut down on the risks we take. How about we go to Pittsburgh for a few days? We could stay in my old house. It's sitting empty. Or we could stay at a hotel. I want to show you my alma mater, the University of Pittsburgh, a real northern city university."

Kathy said, "Good! Some city living would be good and I'd like to see your old house. Maybe we'll live there someday."

"I'm not sure Shadow will be happy there. He never liked my ex-wife and despised the small backyard. Anyway, he can come with us. He's spent too much time in kennels recently.

"I want both of us to have dinner with my friend and the Assistant Chief of Investigations. I worked for him in the homicide unit. He's a great guy and like a father to me. Okay? Let's get packed. We'll start with a visit to my old house. It's still furnished with what I could afford on a cop's salary. The place is probably dusty as hell. We can be there in three hours."

Kathy said, "So let's get started. We don't need much. We do need new wardrobes after losing all our stuff in India."

On the way west on Route 30, Kathy questioned Jack about the house, neighborhood and details of his previous life as a detective in the homicide unit of the Bureau of Pittsburgh Police. She told Jack she was having trouble with his financial status as a police detective one day and a near-billionaire the next. How did he deal with that? Jack told her it wasn't hard. He was the same person, or almost the same person. He knew that one day his father would leave him some money but had no idea of the extent. The size of his father's estate took his breath away when Lee Jensen, his father's attorney and friend, revealed the figures to him, as well as the terms of acceptance. To accept his inheritance, Jack had to agree to work full-time, using the wealth his father accumulated from the seed money taken from the KGB when he escaped, to enjoy and protect American freedom.

Kathy had been with Jack and Anita, her best friend and fellow team member, on their mission of the past year to track down and kill his father's murderers. Kathy knew she and Jack had been lucky. Anita gave her life to save Jack's. She accepted that hazardous operations meant casualties had to be expected. Luck was also involved in her meeting Jack. She'd never met a man like him before. Kathy thought Marsha, Jack's ex-wife who wanted to be rich, had dumped Jack and run off with a divorce attorney. Too bad for her. Jack was spoken for now.

Two

Driving down the familiar streets of Oakland, a sense of déjà vu swept over Jack. Shadow sat up straighter and stared out the window. Rush hour was nearly over and minutes later, Jack pulled into the driveway of a small detached house just off Forbes Avenue. The house looked abandoned. It was more than a year since he loaded his old Cherokee station wagon with his few belongings and Shadow and headed east to McLean, VA, to take care of his adored ailing father. A lot had happened since then. He could barely remember what his ex-wife looked like. He was certainly a different person than the young, naive man who had lived here. Everything seemed smaller. The violence and stress of the last year marked him. If he had ever feared death, he no longer did. He knew he was a killer when his loved ones or country were threatened. Few people could do what he now did routinely. His senses were always on near-maximum. A feeling of confidence flooded through him. He now loved a woman who loved him in return and was willing to share the danger. Shadow's nudging brought him back to the present.

Laughing at Shadow's antics, Jack opened the door and let him out. He watched Shadow stretch and relieve himself on the small strip of grass in front of the house. Marsha had yelled at Shadow every time she caught him urinating on the grass. Kathy got out after examining the house from the car and headed for the front porch. Shadow looked at Jack, gave his Bouvier smile and ran up beside Kathy. As they moved near the front steps, Shadow stopped, stepped in front of Kathy and growled deep in his throat. Jack never questioned Shadow's instincts. He called to Kathy to stop.

She said, "What's wrong?"

"I don't know but I always trust Shadow's warnings. Follow us around to the back."

Jack put his hand on Shadow's back and led him to the back of the house. Shadow sniffed and continued to growl quietly. In the backyard, a slanted double trap door, typical of houses built in the 1930s, led to the cellar. Taking the key to the padlock from its hiding place behind a crack in the German siding, Jack opened the lock and eased one-half of the door open.

Little of the late morning sunlight reached the basement. It was too dark to make out the interior. Jack could just see the four steep cement stairs leading into the gloom. With Shadow leading the way, Jack and Kathy moved quietly down the stairs. Shadow had stopped growling and stood at the bottom of the stairs leading up to the kitchen, sniffing the bottom step and the surrounding area. Jack picked up a flashlight he had left on the cluttered work bench and giving a small prayer to the makers of modern batteries, switched the flashlight on. Its beam cut through the gloom in the windowless basement. Examining the basement area quadrant by quadrant, he could find nothing out of place until he turned the beam upwards and almost immediately saw a small, partially concealed shape fastened to the inside of one of the rough-cut ceiling joists. A closer look showed a black insulated line running from the shape along the joist and then up through the old pine floor.

"Kathy, what do you see up there?"

She took the flashlight, looked intently at the dark object snuggled up to a ceiling joist and said, "That has to be a bomb of some kind. I don't see a triggering mechanism."

Jack was no stranger to explosives or booby traps. His years in Marine Recon had trained him well. He was not going to try to disarm what could be a very sophisticated triggering device.

Jack took Kathy's arm and said, "I don't see one either, but disarming bombs is beyond me. Let's get out of here."

Rubbing Shadow's head, he led the big dog back to the SRX. Jack drove around the neighborhood streets, while Kathy used her counter-surveillance skill to make sure they were not being followed. She gave Jack an "all clear." He parked a block away from the house, pulled over and got his cell phone out. Jack dialed the number from memory. Captain Shorer's secretary immediately recognized Jack's voice and put him right through to his old boss.

"Captain, I thought you would still be at lunch."

"Jack, how in the hell are you, and what brings you back to your old haunts? Football season is here and the Pittsburgh Panthers could use you, if that old knee would hold up."

"It's holding up well, but my football career is over. I've been out of the country for a while and trying hard to get my father's estate shaped up. I need to see you tonight, if possible. I went back to my old house in Oakland and found a booby trap in the basement. I might have triggered it, if Shadow hadn't made me be careful. He growled when we approached the stairs to the front porch. I took his warning, went in through the basement door and found the bomb attached to a ceiling joist."

"Christ, Jack! What have you been up to? I better get the bomb squad out there immediately. I have no choice. The damn thing may be big enough to kill a few neighbors."

"I'll meet the squad at the house. Can we do this without the sirens and lights?"

"Okay! I'll try to treat it as a suspected gas leak but that won't last. We have to talk. I don't like people trying to kill my best detective, even if he is on a leave of absence."

"You got it! I have a long story to tell you. But the story has to stay between you and me for the time being. You'll understand when I give you the details. How about dinner tonight? I want you to meet my significant other. She is a gorgeous and dangerous lady."

"You're on! I'll pick the place. Now let's deal with the bomb."

"You pick next time. I know you like the Fish Market, and we'll be staying at the Convention Center. I'll see you in the restaurant tonight. Seven-thirty, okay?"

When Kathy asked what was going on, Jack told her the bomb squad should be arriving there any minute, and he had to show them what he found.

Kathy said, "Damn those people. How many of them do we have to kill? I am really angry. Thank God for Shadow. I love that dog. How did he know?"

"I'm a bit puzzled. Dogs have sensory capabilities that aren't understandable by humans. Shadow is very intelligent and doesn't miss anything. He wasn't trained as a bomb sniffing dog, and it's doubtful he could have caught the distinctive odor of the explosives from outside the house. His reaction must, in some way, be tied to the recent attack on my father's house in McLean."

Two full-time housekeepers and Jack's father died in the attack, but not before Shadow gave the alarm and killed one of them. Two additional intruders were killed in the house. The attack team was made up of members of a renegade KGB sleeper team based in Charleston, SC.

Jack said, "I wonder if a surviving member, motivated by revenge for the death of one of his family, may be responsible for the bomb. Shadow may have picked up the scent of an old enemy."

Ten minutes later, as the light was beginning to fail, a police cruiser glided past the house and parked down the street. Jack recognized one of the officers and, leaving an unhappy dog in the car, he and Kathy went to meet them. Don Esposito saw them coming, "Hey, Jack, how ya doin? We don't need you drumming up business for us! You never were boring! Whatcha got here? The Captain said it was a bomb situation. Is that right? And aren't you going to introduce me to Miss America?"

"Don! Give me a chance to get a word in! I missed you, too. Yeah, some package nestled up to a joist in the basement with a wire running out of it. Being the smart detective I am, I told myself not to fuck with it but to wake up Esposito. He's getting all that hazardous duty pay for telling the bomb squad where to go. Kathy, say hello to Mr. Esposito so he can get to work."

"Hello, Mr. Esposito. I hope you're good at this bomb business."

"I'm not too bad. Glad to meetcha. If you tire of this bum, call me. I can be available. Jack, how about you show me where this suspect bomb is lurking?"

"Okay, suck it up and follow me. Kathy, please keep Shadow company. He hates to be left out of any action. Hey, Esposito, remember, please don't touch the damn thing until I get out of there. I'm not drawing the big bucks for bomb squad duty and, besides, I'm on leave-without-pay. Follow me and I'll show you my bomb."

Jack led the two officers around the back to the outside stairs and opened the cellar doors. Once inside, Jack used his flashlight to point out the bomb. Esposito took a quick look and said, "Okay, I see it and it sure looks like a bomb. That wire running out of it may mean that it's not set up for remote detonation or that this bomber is damn smart. Who in the hell would want to kill a poor dumb detective on leave-without-pay? Who've you been hanging around with? Never mind talking. Let's get out of here. I think I heard the real bomb squad pull up."

After talking to Esposito, the bomb squad Lieutenant set about directing his growing on-site force to evacuate every house within two hundred feet. Jack knew that action would take at least an hour, and there was nothing he could do to help. He waited until the Lieutenant was finished issuing his preliminary orders and introduced himself as the owner of the house. Esposito chimed in to add Jack was a homicide detective on leave. Jack then offered to give the entry team the house keys and a briefing on the layout of the house. Jack could see the Lieutenant was giving him his undivided attention now that his bona fides were established. When the officer asked him who was on his suspect list, Jack told him he didn't know. He didn't want to pass out any more information before he had a chance to talk with Captain Shorer.

When Jack slipped into the car with Kathy and Shadow, she told him the newspapers could have provided enough information for the bomber to find his old Pittsburgh house, who then placed the bomb in an attempt to kill him or someone he cared about. She doubted it had anything to do with their killing a room full of al Qaeda mid-level cadre in Kathmandu.

Jack said, "I believe you're right. Maybe the bomb forensic guys can give us something. Now let's get Shadow checked into his old kennel and ourselves in a hotel."

Three

Joel finished his visit to the major Oriental rug store in Georgetown, SC. The two rugs he now had in the back of his 11-year-old Dodge Town and Country pleased him. He could mark them up at least seventy-five percent in his Charleston shop. His next stop would be Surfside, just fifteen minutes south of Myrtle Beach on Route 17. He might stay in Surfside. There were many motels that wouldn't demand a credit card, as long as you paid up front with cash. Joel had no intention of leaving financial forensic trails to document his movements. His instructor in Peshawar, Pakistan, drilled into him the rules of playing the espionage and terrorist game. His instructor would be proud of him. There were many places along Route 17 up the Carolina coast where he could change license plates. Earlier in the year he'd stolen plates from an Ohio car. Even if by some miracle the motel manager checked license plates against his register, there would be no audit trail back to Joel Hankins. Too careful? Not the way he had been trained. You could be too tentative, but never too careful. Success came from dedication and attention to detail. Maybe tonight he could find a young woman. Although the tourist season was not at its peak, Myrtle

Beach was a good hunting area. Tourists and young teenage girls, away from home for the first time, hadn't had time to develop the street smarts to protect themselves. They desperately wanted a good time and didn't believe people like Joel were out there hunting them.

In the early evening, just after dusk, he'd select a shopping mall and quietly sit in a parking space until he spotted a young girl pulling into a parking spot. At this time of year the girls weren't wearing much, and he liked to evaluate his target before the attack. If possible, he would move his van next to her car and wait for her to return. All he had to do was slide open the van's side door, grab his prey and pull her inside. A little chloroform on a small towel held over her face for thirty seconds would end the struggle.

He wasn't interested in sex. His joy and excitement came from the kill and watching the essence of life escape. That was real dominance. Joel had improved his skill but still struggled to collect the exact moment of death.

The same modus operandi worked on most of his captures. For sure it wasn't always as smooth as he would like. Sometimes he had to take the risk of getting out of the car or moving the van up beside his victim, pretending to ask a question or flirt, until he could use his chloroform-saturated towel to trap his catch. How surprised they all were when they regained consciousness and found themselves helpless. He had to be careful not to beat the girls too badly or to torture them until they lost consciousness. Once he had made that mistake and she died while unconscious, depriving him of the joy of watching and recording the magic of life leaving her. Her selfishness put him into an uncontrollable rage, and he beat the girl's body until it was almost unrecognizable. He wouldn't do that again. Rage leads to mistakes. He had burned everything he had on to get rid of the traces of blood. The inside of his van was also splattered and needed new mats and some of the upholstery replaced.

The victim he selected at the mall wasn't as young as he first thought, and she put up a strong fight before the chloroform put her out. He took great pictures of her face as she died. Some of his skin might be under her fingernails, even though he did his best to clean them. Maybe the cops would be careless and miss their chance to get his DNA. Not every police department had a crack forensics team. Joel took no time in disposing of her. He dumped her naked body along a deserted road to the beach.

Four

Just as Jack and Kathy were getting settled in their suite at the Convention Center, the phone rang. Captain Shorer was calling to tell Jack that it was a bomb and it had been disarmed. The bomb was rigged to explode when a pressure switch under the rug in the small foyer was depressed. The technology was old, but it was clear the bomb had been placed by a professional. A forensic team was searching for prints and any other traces the bomber may have left behind. The bomb squad searched the entire house. No other explosives were found. So far, interviews with the neighbors had failed to turn up anything. The press would carry as much of the story as they could collect. You can't do evacuations and question neighbors without getting some unwanted publicity. Jack thanked the Captain for calling and said he had reserved a table in the dining room of the Fish Market for seven-thirty.

Before going down to have dinner with Captain Shorer, Jack briefed Kathy. He told her he trusted Captain Shorer completely, but they had to remember, he is a police officer and bound to follow the law, so no discussions about their killing a number of terrorists in the US, India and Nepal. The Captain will wonder why someone put a deadly bomb in Jack Brandon's Oakland house. A detective on leave-without-pay should not be a target for a professional bomber.

Jack decided the best cover stories used part of the truth. He planned tell Captain Shorer he believed it was the same people who killed his father. Shadow killed one of the attackers, and his father and the Vietnamese staff killed two more. Now the terrorists affiliated with al Qaeda had Jack's name and photo. Maybe the bomb attempt was related to al Qaeda trying to even the score. Kathy asked Jack if he thought that story would fly.

Jack said, "Captain Shorer is too seasoned and wise in the ways of the world to question the story. If you don't want the answer, don't ask. Chime in at any time during dinner, just stay with the broad outlines of the basic story. Before we get too deep into dinner, I have a couple of checks I want to give the Captain toward his favorite charities."

Jack ushered Kathy into The Fish Market restaurant at seven twenty-five, knowing that Captain Shorer would be there precisely at seven-thirty. The hostess had their table ready in a secluded alcove. The mention of his suite number when making the reservation must have carried some weight. At seven-thirty Jack saw the Captain coming their way behind the hostess. Jack introduced Captain Shorer to Kathy.

Captain Shorer said, "In this place, after duty hours, I'm Paul to everyone except the best detective I ever had. He can still call me by my title, otherwise I won't be able to control him."

Kathy smiled and said, "We share that problem. Jack is not easily controlled. I wish I had a magic awesome title."

Captain Shorer laughed and Kathy said, "My mother told me good men are not controllable."

Paul took her hand and said, "Anyone as beautiful as you are can get along without an awesome title." Their drinks arrived and after they toasted the Pittsburgh Police Bureau, Jack said, "I have something that will give me great pleasure, if you will accept my offering?"

Captain Shorer looked at Jack and said, "You have my full attention. What are you offering?"

"It's no secret that you have almost single-handedly kept the Policemen's Fund for officers' families in need due to injuries or death in the line of duty in the black. Please accept my check as a donation to the fund."

Jack then reached into his jacket pocket and passed an envelope to his Captain. Captain Shorer said, "Thank you, Jack" as he opened the envelope. Seconds later he looked up at Jack and said, "Is this for real?"

"Yes, it is. You see, I inherited far more money than I was expecting, and I can't think of a more deserving place to spend some of it."

"Jack, this is the first million dollar personal check I have ever seen. Are sure you want to do this?"

"Yes, but one caveat. I want to remain anonymous. Please make up some story about where the money came from if you need to. It's all done legally."

"I can do that. This money will let me do more for some families who really need help. Any more surprises before you tell me about the bomb?"

"Yes. One more. You see, I also know about the program for children you operate through fund-raising events. So here's another contribution."

Captain Shorer opened the envelope, looked at the check and said, "Anytime you want to have dinner with me, I'll come even if I need to be carried. Two million dollar checks in one evening are too much. I assume the same caveat applies?"

"Yes, if that's okay with you."

"Jack, I will never forget this evening and I haven't even had dinner yet. Your money will do a lot of good in the city of Pittsburgh. Now, I do need another drink. Maybe even a double."

Everyone ordered another drink. Jack said, "This is the Captain's restaurant, and I propose asking him to order for us. Okay?"

Kathy laughed and said, "Go for it, Paul."

Over dinner of steamed mussels, grilled flounder covered with a caper sauce and sautéed asparagus accompanied by a few bottles of Cakebread Chardonnay, Jack told Captain Shorer the story he had earlier tried on Kathy, adding details when he could. Jack gave the full story about the attack on his father's house and all he had learned from the local police. Captain Shorer said he would ask the police for a copy of their report to include in the file about the bombing attempt on Jack's house.

Jack was sure the local police would cooperate. They had a high opinion of the Pittsburgh Police Bureau and the Captain in particular. Jack then asked Kathy not to be embarrassed, but he was going to give the Captain a summary of her background. After he finished, Captain

Shorer said they made an awesome team. He would like to have them working for him.

After dessert, Kathy asked to be excused. She was sure the men had some things to talk over, and she also needed a good night's sleep. After she left, Captain Shorer ordered some more coffee and said, "I have something to talk to you about. Do you have the time?"

"Captain, you know I do."

"I need some help. You know how I hate unsolved homicide cases. Well, I have one that is almost ready for the cold case storage locker. First, let me tell you about the case and what few facts we have. Almost three years ago, two Pitt coeds were murdered on their way home from the University's library. Their naked bodies were found in Schenley Park by an early morning jogger. Their families had called 911 around midnight, two hours after the girls should have been home. Normally, you know, we wouldn't have done anything about two college girls being a couple of hours late coming home. Lieutenant Arrington knew one of the families, and alerted a couple of black and whites to cruise the area. They found nothing but did verify that the two coeds had left the library together about nine-thirty. They should have been home within 30 minutes.

"Of course, once the bodies were found, we put resources on the investigation. Forensics, in cases like this, usually gives us quite a bit of data. I have never seen a sex crime that produced so little information. No semen was found on the bodies. They were killed elsewhere and dumped in the park. No special positioning of the bodies. They were just dumped. The lab said both died from broken necks. Bruises on the bodies indicated their heads had been smashed together with considerable force, as if someone came up behind them and banged their heads together. Traces of duct tape were found on both bodies. Legs, arms and mouths had been taped. No signs that either one put up a struggle. Other than the fact they were found naked, there was nothing to indicate that this was a sex crime. Both necks were broken the same way. Most likely by a right-handed person, who had some hand-to-hand combat skill. The captives, we believe, were killed within an hour of their abduction.

"In the next four weeks we did everything we know how to do, ask for public support, neighborhood canvases, backgrounds into the lives of the victims and their families. No one could name any enemies. No stalkers were noticed. Classmates were questioned. Both girls were attractive, popular and dated frequently. Everything was tracked down. No hits. Trying a Hail Mary shot, I had every boarding house that provided short-term rooms for cash within ten miles queried for the night of the murder. We were able to track down nearly all the short- term renters that checked out within twenty-four hours of the murders. One possible suspect was found. A young man, early twenties, gave a probable false name, left shortly after dawn the day after girls were taken, no one saw him go, but the owner remembered he drove a dark blue Dodge van with temporary tags. We canvassed all the used car lots where cash can buy a car without much, if any, check on the identification of the buyer. Again, we found one lot that after some pressure was applied, the manager remembered a sale to a young man. The salesman's description of the buyer and the one of the boarding house owner were hard to reconcile. The resulting police artist's sketch was not of much use.

"The investigation in Pittsburgh has run its course. We've been looking at crimes in other areas that bore a similar M.O. A few have. Our search criteria included any killing of young women, where the cause of death was not from some sort of weapon and where none of the usual earmarks of a sex crime were present, like semen, mutilation of the bodies or ritualistic positioning of the corpses. Over the past two years, five incidents fit our search parameters. All occurred in the southeastern states. All five were within two hundred miles of a center point, the city of Charleston, SC. None was within fifty miles of Charleston. All took place in urban areas. Forensics indicated all the victims showed signs that they were beaten before their necks were broken. Also all showed traces of the use of chloroform. The Pitt coeds were bruised but no trace of chloroform was found."

Jack said, "Interesting, but that's not enough to conduct a serious investigation. Do you have anything else?"

"There is one thing, but it's so tenuous, even my own detectives think I am grasping at straws. And it's not enough to put on the police wire. I'm even a little reluctant to mention it."

"Chief, you have always thought outside the box, and many times, you have been right on. So go ahead."

"Two weeks ago an out-of-work, old mill worker was found dead in an alley behind a Garfield bar. What little money he had was still in his pocket. Medium- priced watch on his wrist. No signs of violence, except that his neck was broken in the same pattern as our two coeds. The bartender recognized the victim and said he was a frequent customer and there was no trouble or argument between the victim and anyone in the bar.

"I've asked several other police departments to send us x-rays of their broken neck murders. I expect them to start arriving next week. In the meantime, we just finished a background investigation of the victim, his family and friends. The man's only family member was a son, who showed up briefly for the funeral. The only real asset the victim owned was a rundown bungalow in Garfield. Not enough to murder anyone over. The son hadn't seen his father in the last five years. There was no relationship. The son said his father was a mean bastard who mistreated his mother and him. I checked with the police in his home area and the son was seen in his Charleston shop the morning of the murder."

Jack said, "Captain, come on, what you are holding back?"

The Captain chuckled and said, "I see you can still stay ahead of me. Okay. Here is my outside-the-box analysis. In talking to the son, you could see he hated his father. Our background check on the son showed he dropped out of Schenley High School in his senior year and disappeared for the next two and half years. He has a passport that, according to State Department records, was used to go to Pakistan the year he dropped out of school. He was in the same high school class as the two murdered Pitt coeds. No record of his being in Pittsburgh at the time they were killed. But he was back in the country by then. And he now lives in Charleston!"

"Do you know what he was doing in Pakistan and how long he was there?"

"According to his passport entry from Pakistan, he was there for a little more than two years. We have no idea what he was doing, but suspect he was being trained in an al Qaeda camp inside Afghanistan. Now you know as much as I do."

"Your hunch is worth checking out. It's a long shot but what else do you have. I would like to see the x-rays of the broken necks. But first, tell me why you told me this tale."

"I don't know what you are doing, but it occurred to me while I was listening to your briefing about the bomb in your old house and wondering what you weren't telling me, that you might be able to help with this case. I could give your badge back and a letter confirming your affiliation with the Pittsburgh Police. I could also provide a legal umbrella for the rest of your group to work with you. Gun permits and the works. It just happens that the Chief of Police in Charleston is a personal friend, and I know he would allow you to work for me on this investigation if he were kept informed, especially since I can tie this to the bomb attempt to kill one of my officers."

As Jack started to respond, the Captain said, "Sleep on it. I think this guy may still be working for al Qaeda. He is now operating a small Oriental rug outlet in Charleston importing rugs from Pakistan and Afghanistan. Does that strike you as a perfect cover job or what?"

"Okay, Captain, I'll think on it, talk it over with Kathy and call you sometime tomorrow."

"Jack, I want you to do this but I'll not push it. I am still in shock over your very generous gifts. God bless you. Now, I must go and so must you. Never keep a beautiful woman waiting too long."

Five

Jack waited until breakfast the following morning before he discussed Captain Shorer's proposal with Kathy. He told Kathy that Shorer wanted them to help him with a possible serial killer case that started in Pittsburgh three years ago. Kathy said she was interested in the part about them being legal and having real law enforcement credentials. She wasn't quite ready for another intercontinental battle with terrorists just yet. A bit of detective work sounded just fine, and Charleston was a great small city.

"You may think I'm being macho, but I'm going to tell Captain Shorer that we will help him with the investigation of his serial killer, but without the knowledge of the Charleston Police Chief. I'll accept the badge, but no other credentials. I'll also use our Pittsburgh address on any documents the Captain gives us. He has to know, sometime during our work in Charleston, we will do things outside the law that will upset any police department.

"Prosecutors couldn't use any evidence we provided, and we could get Captain Shorer in trouble. I'll agree to keep him informed. I want to go after this guy for his possible connections to al Qaeda. Captain Shorer can always deny any authorization of our activities on his part. Okay?"

"Okay. I'm ready to go with you, but let's be as careful as we can. Charleston is not Nepal where we could go in with guns blazing. Now that we are outside the law again, I want to make an unauthorized visit to a crime scene. Is the tape still up at your house in Oakland and have all the bombs been removed?"

Jack laughed and said, "Captain Shorer is all about thorough. He had his guys go through every inch of that house. I'm sure the crime lab guys are done by now. How come you want to go there?"

"Two reasons. First, I want to see why your ex hated that house so much, but mostly, I want to see what the bomber could have learned about you from searching your house. You remember I am a trained CIA case officer and see things through different eyes. So swing by on our way back to the cabin and let me do my thing."

"Okay. Let's plan on going back to the cabin the day after tomorrow. That will give us some time to visit my alma mater."

Jack pulled into the curb near his old house and said, "Well, here it is. Let me get Shadow out, and I'll give you the tour."

"Jack! No! You and Shadow stay out here. I don't want all the distraction that follows you two about. I won't be much more than an hour. I'll give you the all clear and then you guys can come in."

Using the key Jack gave her, Kathy unlocked the door and stepped into the small house. She wrinkled her nose at the smell of mildew associated with closed up houses. She started her slow walk through with the downstairs, small living room and a smaller dining room off a Pullman kitchen that needed upgrading. A door to the cellar from the kitchen. No bath downstairs. A staircase with a landing and a right angle turn, led upstairs. A small bedroom in the back of the house, and a larger one in the front with a Jack and Jill bathroom between them. Kathy, talking to herself, said she could live here. The bones are okay. The house just needs some care and a bit of money to open it up, and it would be a good in-city house for a couple getting started. She opened the door to the backyard and walked over to the outside cellar door and examined the lock.

Now that she had done her get-oriented walk through, Kathy went back to the living room to check out the small desk sitting in an alcove off the living room. One by one Kathy took out the drawers and went through the contents. In the center drawer, she found Jack and Marsha's social security numbers, birth dates and pictures. Jack's college transcripts were in another drawer along with a small address book containing his father's telephone number and address. Bills from Jack's attorney, assorted utilities, vet bills and signed charge card imprints were in another drawer along with bank statements and car repair bills. Another document disclosed Jack's badge number, work phone and address.

After checking all the downstairs closets and kitchen cabinets, she went upstairs to the bathroom. Opening the medicine cabinet, she found several nearly empty prescription bottles, mostly for Jack's ex-wife. Kathy went downstairs and stood quietly in the living room while she put her findings together. All in all, any trained intruder could collect the same information. She didn't know if the intruder had taken anything with him.

It was time to get Jack inside for some questions and a look at the basement. Shadow bounded up the steps and started growling as soon as he came through the door. He ran all through the house sniffing the floor and growling. When Jack opened the kitchen door to the cellar, Shadow charged down the stairs. Jack hurried after him, assuring him it was okay and rubbing his head until Shadow stopped growling. Jack turned to Kathy and said, "There's no doubt in my mind that our bomber is related to one of the men who killed my father. Might even be a brother to the attacker Shadow killed."

While Kathy nodded her head and continued prowling around the cellar, Jack thought, she is bothered by something. Not wanting to break her concentration, he waited until she turned to him and said, "Jack, there's a real problem here. You say the outside cellar door was locked with a padlock, and it's unlikely that anyone could have found the key. The lock shows no signs of picking, and the back door was locked on the inside with a dead bolt. So how did he or she get in and out of the house?"

"Well, he could've gone out the front door and relocked it with his picking tools."

"I doubt a professional bomber, which this person was, would take a chance on stepping around the pressure-activated bomb trigger placed under the foyer rug. The space there is really small. One misstep and it would be all over. No, the intruder had another way out that we haven't found yet."

After a careful window by window search, Kathy pointed to the dog door in the kitchen. Any opening big enough for a hundred pound dog provided enough space for a small man to squeeze through. The rough edges of the dog door held a few small blue threads. Kathy told Jack it had probably been pulled closed and latched with a thin wire loop. Jack laughed and said he couldn't wait to call Captain Shorer.

Kathy said, "You know the bones of this little house are not bad. A few changes and I could live here."

As Kathy was looking around the kitchen for anything she could add to the cooking tools in the cabin, Shadow went through the dog door into the small backyard. Lost in thought, Jack barely heard the front door ease open with its customary slight squeak. Without even thinking, he pushed Kathy down behind the kitchen counter that divided the kitchen from the small dining area. The intruder leveled a .38 Magnum at Jack and said, "Finally, I get to kill you. My family swore we would find and kill you. First, I want you to know why. Then you are going to wish that the bomb had killed you."

As he was telling Jack that his family and his dog had killed two of his brothers, Jack felt Kathy slip a heavy butcher knife into his hand below the counter. Watching the killer's eyes, Jack could tell he was getting ready to shoot. Just as the magnum steadied, Shadow came charging through the dog door with a roaring growl. The killer's gun switched to the bounding Shadow, giving Jack time to position and throw the heavy butcher knife. Six inches of the knife buried itself in the attacker's chest just as Shadow's charge crashed into the killer, knocking him to the floor. Jack vaulted the counter and threw himself on the downed gunman before he could bring his weapon up against Shadow's chest. Shadow had fastened his huge jaws on the man's throat. Kathy came sliding up against the killer from his other side and plunged another kitchen knife into his kidney. Jack took control of the magnum revolver and pulled a growling Shadow off the attacker.

"I hope you had enough, you son-of-a-bitch. If you aren't dead, you soon will be."

Jack had to hold Shadow's collar as the huge black dog wasn't sure his adversary was finished. Kathy checked the shooter's carotid pulse and said, "It's okay, Shadow, this bastard is really dead."

She knelt beside Shadow and hugged him with tears running down her cheeks. "How can we ever thank him for saving our lives twice in two days? This dog will never ever do anything wrong."

Jack pulled out his cell and called Captain Shorer. When he answered, Jack said, "Captain, I need a homicide squad at my house. We have a dead man who came into the house with a .38 Magnum to kill us. He has three lethal wounds and is lying where Shadow's charge knocked him down. All the weapons are here, and it's a clean crime scene."

"Good Lord, Jack, you certainly know how to stir up the unit. I'll have a squad there in five minutes. Sure there's no need for an ambulance?"

"No, this perp is dead three times. Just the forensic guys, the morgue wagon and a homicide detective to take our statements."

When Jack saw the first squad car pull up and cut the siren, he saw an old friend, Dan Reilly, get out of the black and white. Jack called out, “Hey, Danny, better come in the back door. The front entrance is pretty messy.”

Reilly and his partner came through the back door took one look at the scene inside and said, “Jack, what the hell are you are up to? A bomb one day and a murder attempt the next day. Is everyone here all right?

“Yeah, we’re all okay. Dan, this is Kathy and you know Shadow. I think both of them still have their warrior blood up. So forgive any lack of hostmanship. I think you will find three possible causes of death, the knife in the chest, the torn throat and the knife thrust in the kidney.”

“Jack, why didn’t you just shoot the bastard? It would have been much neater.”

“We weren’t carrying. That’s something I am going to change as soon as you finish here.”

“Jack, this perp gets the drop on you with a magnum and, before he can shoot, he gets a kitchen knife in the chest and kidney and his throat ripped. And he had you covered from 15 feet away? You gotta admit that’s something you don’t see every day. My partner, Bill Rogers, will take your statements while I put the crime scene together. I think the forensic guys are here now. Okay?”

A few minutes after the forensic team started on the crime scene, Captain Shorer came striding through the back door. He took one look at the dead body and bagged weapon and said, “Jack, what the hell is going on? Are you all okay?”

"We're all okay. A bit of adrenalin still pumping, and Shadow is still looking for another bad guy."

"I was told on the way here that no shots were fired. How did you take this guy down from 15 feet with no firearms?"

"Pretty much instinct, reaction and luck. When the shooter came through the front door, he focused on me. He never saw Kathy on the floor behind this waist high counter. I pushed her there as the door was coming open. The guy had a speech he wanted to give before killing me. He could have easily killed me, if he had come in shooting. The delay gave Kathy time to slip a knife in my hand and when Shadow charged through the dog door, the shooter swung the magnum to Shadow. That's all the time I needed to throw the knife. Shadow and the knife arrived almost simultaneously. The shooter went down. By the time he hit the floor trying to defend himself from Shadow, Kathy and I were on him. She put another kitchen knife into the shooter's kidney and we called you.

"I think Shadow heard the front door open, the strange voice, and charged in. This is conjecture, but I believe Shadow recognized the shooter's scent. When my father and his staff were killed in Virginia, Shadow was shot by one of the attackers but still killed him. I think the guy on the floor was connected with and related to the man Shadow killed. During the shooter's speech, he said something about the family hunting me down."

"Okay. Leave that part out of your statement. No use letting the shooter's family know that we are on to them. The press would love to play up that angle. Until this thing is solved, I insist that both you and Kathy carry badges.

You can supply your own firearms and the documentation I give you will cover you. Do you agree?"

Kathy hugged the Captain. Looking at Jack she said, "I don't know about him, but I will happily take the badge and gun offer. No more scenes like this. I felt so damned helpless."

"When you're finished here, give the key to Reilly and come to my office. I want to go over a few things with both of you."

Jack looked at Kathy and when she nodded, he said, "Captain, we'll be there in an hour. All right if we bring Shadow in with us?"

"Jack, that dog is welcome any time. Wish I had one like him."

As they watched the Captain's car pull away, Jack put his arm around Kathy and said, "Well, what do you think?"

"I'm worried. We've been lucky. We could have been killed twice in the last two days. I don't mind living close to the edge, but this is getting ridiculous. A gun and badge will help, but we must make some changes to our lifestyle and our security. The bad guys know who we are and we don't know who they are. That's not a good picture. Frank will want us to continue helping him run down domestic terrorists for the CIA, but that will be very difficult if we don't deal with the people who are trying to kill us. We need to have a meeting with Frank soon."

"As usual, the lady from the CIA speaks with clarity and resolve. I share your premise. Let's agree to cooperate with Captain Shorer on his possible serial murder case. Then, after we meet with Frank, we can use our new police credentials to find and deal with the people who are hunting us."

An hour later, after giving their brief statements to Dan Reilly, Jack, Kathy and Shadow pulled into the Bureau of Police parking lot at 1203 Western Avenue. The guard at the door was waiting for them and even said, "Hello, Shadow, anytime you want a change, come to my house. Much less excitement. Go on in, Jack, the Chief is waiting for you."

Mildred, the keeper of the Captain's inner sanctum, smiled and said, "Jack, when are you leaving? You're causing far too much action and confusion in our world."

"It's good to see you again, Mildred. May I present my partners, Kathy Grayson and Shadow?"

"Kathy, you will never know how many broken hearts your man left behind when he went to Washington before the ink was even dry on the divorce certificate. Keep him on a short leash while you're in town. The Captain has coffee ready for you and I'll bring in a bowl of water for our hero."

Mildred ushered them into the Captain's office. He hugged Kathy and Jack and said, "I hope you both know how lucky you are, and Shadow, you are the best cop of us all."

Shadow knew he was the center of attention and, with his stubby tail wagging, looked like he was wondering what's the big deal. Captain Shorer led them over to a conference table and told them to take a seat and help themselves to the coffee and pastry. Kathy said, "I was always told the only pastries allowed in a cop shop were doughnuts."

The Captain grinned and said, "She is not only deadly and beautiful but has a deep understanding of police work. Now let me get bureaucratic and serious. I'm concerned about the efforts some unknown revenge seekers are making to kill you. You are a police officer on leave without pay but still under the protection of this office. I've professional and personal reasons to end this. I need your help to do so.

"I want both of you to go undercover to find these killers. I'll give you solid credentials and badges. You can provide your own weapons. You'll report only to me and Dan Reilly. I'll check out two encrypted iPhones for your use. From what you've told me, I think your search will take you to Charleston. Certainly my suspected serial killer is there. So, two separate operations for you. You will be modern day versions of dollar-a-year people. No expenses. That's not a problem, is it?"

"No, money is not a problem. But, I've other issues to discuss."

"Okay. The floor is yours."

"I can't tell you everything I'd like to, because of security issues that I don't control. I think I can tell you enough for you to see the potential problem. It has to be off the record. Kathy and I have been doing some covert work for the government in the field of counter terrorism. It's the problem of national security issues taking precedence over law and order. I think you used to call it justice divided when the Feds played their trump card in a Pittsburgh case.

"We've one high level contact that we report to infrequently. We get no money, only instructions and information. If we get caught, we're on our own. I'm sure we can handle your work and what we do for the government, as long as you know we won't always be able to tell you everything that's going on. I'll promise you, if dual responsibilities gets to be a problem, we'll tell you. Kathy, what say you?"

"I agree and thank you, Captain, for your trust."

"I can't believe I'm doing this. It seems right even if it sounds a bit wacky. So far I don't feel I have to brief the Bureau Chief or any of his staff minions. I'll tell Dan only what I think he needs to know."

"Kathy, let's get to work. Captain, can we read your file on the possible serial killer?"

"Sure, as soon as you raise your right hand and I swear you in and give Kathy a badge. Jack, unless I'm mistaken, you still have yours."

"Yeah, I do. Occasionally I get it out and look at it. Life was much simpler then. In fact, the badge is in my bag."

"Good because you'll need them to pick up some weapons at your favorite gun shop. You can read the file right here. It won't take long. I have to go to a meeting now, so I'll say goodbye and good hunting. Just leave when you're finished. Do you need any more coffee?"

Kathy said, "No, we're good. I hope the next time we see you, we'll have some good news. Thank you for your help."

Captain Shorer was right, there wasn't much in the file. The x-rays of the cause of death indicated a right-handed person or persons with some combat training and strength killed all the victims. When she finished reading the file, Kathy said, "I don't believe in coincidences. The fact that this elderly mill worker, killed in an alley with no robbery evidence, exhibits the same neck fracture as the young females puts this Joel Hankins person square in my sights. He was connected to the two Pitt coeds, the old mill worker was his father, and now the other killings are centered around Charleston where Hankins has an Oriental rug store. All we need is some evidence that will stand up in court. So let's get started."

"Come on, Shadow, you heard the lady. It's time to get up and go." Shadow got up, stretched and followed them out to the car. On the way out Mildred rubbed the dog's head and handed Jack a small box containing two iPhones. As they were leaving the parking lot, Jack said, "Before we start back, I'm going to stop at the gun shop most cops use to get us a couple of handguns."

"Great. I already feel more secure. Real creds and a weapon. Never again do I want to feel as helpless as I felt on the kitchen floor in your house when the shooter burst in. I'm a little surprised the forensic team was not able to identify the shooter. That should tell us something. Like maybe these people are careful to stay under the radar and pay close attention to detail."

Jack pulled into the small parking lot outside the Wilkinsburg gun shop. Leaving the windows open for Shadow, they went into the nearly empty shop. Jack led the way up to the counter and said, "Hey, Charlie, got any old rusted handguns priced high for your cop friends?"

"Jack, haven't seen you in months. What happened, lose your weapon?"

"No, just need a good backup for myself and my new partner. Kathy, come on up here and meet Charlie. He never saw a cop he couldn't sell his old stock to."

"Hello, Kathy, what are you looking for?"

"How about the SOCOM, Mark 23?"

"Good choice but expensive. I've five or six in stock. They run $637 without the 10% police discount."

"Kathy, show the man your badge and Charlie, we'll take two SOCOMs with four mags each and 100 rounds. Throw in shoulder rigs and behind-the-back belt holsters. Don't forget our 10% discounts."

"How could I forget with you high IQ homicide guys looking over my shoulder?"

Twenty minutes later, the SRX pulled out of the parking lot on the return trip to the cabin in the Pennsylvania mountains. Kathy set to work loading the magazines and fitting the SOCOMs into the belt holsters.

Kathy hadn't finished loading the magazines when Jack said, "Kathy, when Anita died in my arms, she asked me to take care of her sister's daughter. Then she said, 'her daughter is my daughter.' At the time you thought she was drifting away, and I didn't understand her. But, what if I did? Could she have had a child while she was in high school or early in college?"

"You're suggesting Anita had a baby when she was in her late teens or early twenties and gave the baby to her older sister to raise as her own daughter?"

"Yes, don't you think that could have happened?"

"Of course that's a possibility, assuming her dying words were as you heard them. It's not a unique solution to an unwanted pregnancy. Where does that leave us?"

"Her sister's home is on the way back to the cabin. Call the number she gave us for her sister and see if we can stop and see her. We can be there in 45 minutes."

When Kathy mentioned Anita's name, her sister, Marie, agreed to see them right away. She lived on the corner of Foster and Mace Streets and said they would see a blue Cherokee parked in the carport. Jack gave Onstar the address and 40 minutes later, Kathy spotted the blue Cherokee, and Jack parked along the curb next to the mail box that said Marie Kowalski. The houses were small, mostly dating from the 40s and 50s. The lawns were trimmed with small but attractive gardens.

Marie saw them pull in and came out on the porch. She greeted them and after introductions, said, "Come on in. I have a Pit Bull mix in the house, so I think that black bear in your car should stay there. I'll bring him some water and, with the windows open, he'll be fine today. If he needs a walk, a small park is just down the street."

Jack signaled Shadow to stay. He gave his disgusted look but lay down on the back seat. Jake, the Pit, looked them over carefully as they entered, but when Marie said "these people are friends," Jake relaxed and came over to have his head rubbed while he sorted out Shadow's scent.

"I want to hear about Anita but first, can I serve some tea and scones?"

Kathy said, "We don't want to cause any extra work, but I can't turn down a cup of tea, especially accompanied by a scone."

"Nonsense! You are friends of Anita, and I'm grateful that finally someone has come to see me. I miss her terribly. I'll be back in a few minutes."

"Kathy, do you see any similarity between Marie and Anita?"

"Maybe in mannerism and a little bit in the eyes, completely different body style and skin tone. Marie is much lighter in color than Anita. Anita had that distinct Mediterranean coloring. Also Maria is taller and much heavier. She doesn't have Anita's graceful movements. Sometimes sisters are not carbon copies. I wouldn't have identified them as sisters based on appearances. It will be interesting to see the daughter."

"Depending on what we learn here, I'll have Lee Jensen's law firm draw up some legal papers dispensing Anita's estate including a monthly payment from us. Marie will have to sign a non-disclosure agreement stating that she can talk to no one about what we tell her. And remember no true names here, first names only. Follow my lead on the circumstances of Anita's death. I'm going to include an intense fire that made body recovery impossible."

Kathy heard Marie coming from the kitchen and got up to help her manage the tray loaded with scones, butter, jam and a large teapot. Marie made a second trip to get the tea cups. When she came back and all were seated, Marie poured the tea. Kathy noted that Marie was probably using her best china service in their honor.

Jack said, "Marie, this is too much. But I, for one, very much welcome the elegance and homemade scones are a rare treat."

During tea Marie asked, "What can I call you? I know Anita worked in the don't-talk-about-it-world. I'll appreciate anything you can tell me."

"You can call me Jack and my partner will answer to the name Kathy."

"Oh, yes. Anita said she had a good friend called Kathy."

"Anita and I worked together and were very close. I will always remember her and admire her. She saved our lives more than once. She gave her life to save Jack's in a shootout with some terrorists halfway around the world."

"Will I be able to bury her?"

"We're so sorry, Marie, but that won't be possible. The fire fight was followed by an intense fire that was not extinguished. No bodies were recovered. We have a few suitcases of Anita's things which we'll ship to you in the next week. Anita wanted her estate to go to you and her niece. You will be getting a letter in a week or so explaining Anita's estate. Will that be okay with you and the rest of her family?"

"Yes, I don't see any problem. My husband, Harvey, left when Kelly was still an infant. He has never been back to see Kelly or send any money. I kept his name but there aren't any Kowalski's involved in our life. I have no idea where he is or even if he's still alive. If he thought I had any money, he'd be at the door in a heartbeat. Without Anita, I would have been in trouble. She sent me enough money each month to help me get by."

Kathy asked, "Tell us about your daughter. Anita often talked about her niece."

"Kelly cried for days when we heard Anita had been killed. They were always close. She has her own apartment in Oakland. Not too far from the University. She's trying to follow her aunt's career. Her grades would be better if she didn't work so much. She has two jobs. When she comes for a visit, she is either studying or sleeping. You know how it is with some mothers and daughters. Kelly and I are not as close anymore. I think she resents me telling her to forget college and get a good job."

Kathy nodded and said, "Do you mind if we talk to her?"

"No, of course not. She's 22 and on her own. I'll give you her address and phone number, and you can call and ask to see her."

Marie said she would be back in a minute with Kelly's number and address.

Jack waited until Marie had left the room and said, "When she comes back, let's make our goodbyes. I want to go back to Oakland and see Kelly. Our house should be safe for a quick visit. I'll tell Captain Shorer we are going to spend one or two nights in the house. The crime scene tape should be gone by now."

Kathy replied, "I feel a lot safer being forewarned and armed, but I don't think we should take the risk, even if it is slight. We just don't know if the guy who tried to kill us is alone. If he wasn't alone, his partner or partners could easily have set another bomb, maybe hidden better than the first one. I doubt that your police buddies have put a 24/7 watch on an empty house. I'll find us a hotel or motel that is pet friendly. Shadow can sleep in the bedroom with us. He won't let anyone get close. It seems we have nearly worn out our welcome. I'm ready to go."

Marie came back with Kelly's address and cell number, and Jack told her to expect a letter from an attorney in a week or two. Jake was the only one showing any warmth as he wagged his tail at the door. Marie shook hands with them and closed the door.

Kathy said, "What happened? We were doing okay until we said we wanted to talk to Kelly."

"Money happened. She's afraid Kelly will get the bulk of Anita's estate. And she got that right. I don't think all is good between mother and daughter. When we get on Route 22 West, try to reach Kelly on her cell. It's not too late to take her to dinner. If you have to push her some, do it. Use Anita's name and say we've some serious things to discuss with her."

"Hey, don't forget I'm the case officer/agent handler on this team. You're just a recon marine with some cop experience and a nice guy to have around. And being rich helps and I'm still on your payroll and you are still the boss. Boss, do you agree about finding a hotel or motel?"

"Yeah, it makes sense. No use pushing the envelope when we don't need to. Now try to reach Kelly and get us a room somewhere in or near Oakland."

Six

Kelly picked up on the first ring. When Kathy mentioned she was a close friend of her Aunt Anita, Kelly agreed to see them for dinner. Kathy explained that Anita's friend and boss would be with her. She asked Kelly to pick a nearby restaurant where they could talk. Kelly said she would be at Joe Mama's restaurant on the corner of Oakland Avenue and Forbes at seven o'clock. Kathy said they would be there and, if Kelly got there first, to get a booth or table where they could talk. A private room would be perfect.

Kathy looked over at Jack and he said, "Perfect. We don't have time to check into a hotel, so Shadow will have to stay in the car. He'll be okay as long as he gets a walk and something to eat. I'll pull off on the first country road. We can stretch our legs and Shadow can do his thing. Break out his kibble and water bowl."

Ten minutes later Jack turned off onto a secondary road that led to the small town of Delmont. A few minutes later they parked off the road under a large maple tree on the edge of a corn field. Shadow was glad to get out and bounced around like the puppy he still could be.

Jack knew Oakland well and had eaten several times in the restaurant Kelly picked. He pulled into the small parking lot just after seven, cracked the windows for Shadow who settled down in his first class compartment in the back of the SRX. Kathy looked at her watch and told Jack she bet Kelly was already here.

"We'll soon find out," he said as he opened the door for Kathy. Kelly saw the couple getting out of a Cadillac from her seat in a booth and was sure they must be the people her Aunt knew. She moved toward the front door to meet them. Just inside the door, Kathy hesitated and stopped, staring at the young woman coming toward.

"My God, Jack, she's a good bit taller but is the very image of Anita."

Jack said, "She has to be Anita's daughter. Add 20 years and she would be Anita. I can't believe the likeness."

Kathy, with tears running down her face, hugged Kelly and said, "I may never let you go."

Jack joined them and kissed Kelly on the cheek. Kathy laughed, still hugging Kelly, "He really doesn't do that much. His middle name is stoic, no emotion here. Kelly, you look so much like Anita. Let's get out of the center of the floor. I want to sit down and hear all about you."

"Okay. But you must start by telling me about Anita. I still cry when I think of her. I loved her, more like a mother or older sister than an aunt. We had a special bond and I'll miss her forever."

On the way to their booth, Kelly said, "I hope you like this place. The food is very good. The service, a little less so."

Jack said, "Don't worry, we're here to see you and I have eaten here several times in a former life with the Pittsburgh Police Bureau."

"No kidding! You were a cop here?"

"Yes, and I lived less than five minutes from here. I graduated from Pitt. So we have some things in common besides Anita."

"I can't believe this. Here comes our waiter. Let's order drinks before he gets away."

The waiter came up to the table and started his spiel. Jack interrupted him and said, "Carlo, never mind the speech. Bring us three Rolling Rocks."

Carlo looked at Jack and said, "What a rotten night. God's gift to the homicide squad is here. How the hell are you, Detective? I'll take personal care of your order. Cash only. No credit."

"Be careful and you'll get the same big tip."

"Some things never change. Three beers coming up."

Kelly said, "I guess you really do know this place. Carlo has been a fixture here. Kathy, Anita told me about you. I know very little about her work except that she avoided my questions."

"You know that Anita was an army major in the Special Forces. She was wounded in Iraq before she retired from the army and joined the CIA. She couldn't tell anyone about her work there. I worked with Anita in the counter-terrorism group. She was very good. She wasn't an analyst or a desk jockey. She was an active field operations officer and a very talented shooter. I don't think I ever knew anyone who was better in a real shooting situation. Anita and my friend here were taking down a room full of al

Qaeda terrorists when Anita was killed saving Jack's life. She died in Jack's arms. Her last words were about you."

Kathy saw that Kelly was struggling to hold back the tears and changed seats to sit beside her. With Kathy's arm around her, Kelly let the tears flow. When she got under control, she excused herself to fix her face.

When she was gone, Jack said, "How can we not tell her that Anita is her mother? Who will that hurt? Marie has already written her off. As long as some money arrives, I don't think Marie will cause any problem."

"I agree but first let's probe Kelly's feelings about her mother. Also, while there is nothing wrong with the name Kowalski, I'm having a hard time attaching it to Kelly who is really a Marino. Kelly Marino has the right sound."

Kelly came back just as Carlo was setting three Rolling Rocks on the booth table. Jack took her hand and said, "Why don't you order for us? It's been a couple of years since I've been here."

Kelly handed the menus back to Carlo and said, "Bring us an order of eggplant Parmesan with linguini and one of garlic crusted chicken. We'll start with a plate of crispy calamari."

"Hey, Jack, my friend, this lady ain't no cheap date."

"No problem, Carlo, I've invested my cop salary very wisely."

Kathy said, "We'll answer any questions you have, the best we can. Now will you tell us about Kelly? Her plans, dreams and hopes."

"Right now I'm sort of adrift. Anita was my only anchor. It's because of her I'm in school. She sent me money directly to help with my education with the understanding that I wouldn't tell Marie. I could have gone to any school in Pennsylvania but I wanted to follow Anita to Pitt. I want to do athletics but I just don't have time with my part-time jobs and class work. I'm not happy with my grade level but I'm dropping one job to bring my grades up. During the few times she came to visit when I was grown, we would go to the local high school track and compete. I could take her in the 100 meters but anything longer and she just ran away. I couldn't believe it. She was old enough to be my mother. Nobody that old should embarrass me on the track."

After Carlos delivered the calamari, Kathy laughed and said, "Anita was special. She could run away from both Jack and me. She was awesome in the water. Come to think of it, she could outshoot both of us. And this big guy here served in Iraq with the Marines as a sniper. So don't be embarrassed. Anita was better than most of the world."

Jack nodded his head and said, "Anita was a true warrior. We can't tell you everything but I want you to know that Anita died in my arms after saving my life. We both owe her."

"Did she say anything when you were holding her?"

Jack looked at Kathy and nodded. Kathy said, "I'm going to tell you something you should keep to yourself for now. Don't even tell Marie. Can you do that?"

"Yes, I can. Especially with her. She's like a newspaper. Whatever she knows, she tells."

"This will be hard for you. Anita asked Jack to take care of her sister's daughter, since she was her daughter. Jack and I believe she was giving us a clear message that you are her daughter and her sister raised you as her child."

Kelly put her hand up to her face and said, "Oh! I knew it! When I got older, I looked so much like my aunt that people were always commenting. And Marie's husband, Harvey, made it clear I wasn't his kid. Why didn't she tell me? I'll never get to tell her how much I loved her and wished she were my mother? Is there a grave site anywhere?"

"No, there was an intense fire following the firefight, and no bodies were recovered. Maybe someday Kathy and I will take you to the place where she was killed. That's the best we can do. Know that she always loved you and did what she thought was best for you. I believe she would've told you the truth when she could be available to you full time."

Kathy said, "How are you going to deal with Marie?"

"That's easy. She has written me off. She doesn't want me to finish my education. When we heard Anita was dead, she said, 'What good did her fancy education do for her or us? Don't you see people like us have to live in the real world? Get a job, find a husband, have kids and grab what little else you can.'

"I hated her for saying that. Only the thought of Anita kept me going. So, for Marie and me, nothing will change. Except I've never felt comfortable with the name 'Kowalski,' so I'll start the legal process to change it to Marino after my grandfather. Kelly Marino sounds good to me."

Jack raised his glass and said, "From now on, you are Kelly Marino."

Over the eggplant and chicken, Jack and Kathy outlined some changes Kelly could make in her life. Kathy started by saying, “We can help with the name change. That will be easy. Jack has a very good attorney. I think Jack has some other possibilities he wants to discuss with you.”

“If you agree with my proposal, you will have no more money problems. You can quit your jobs and work full time on being a student. Starting now you are an employee of the same organization Anita worked with. Your salary will be $250,000 per year with benefits. After graduation, if you decide to continue working with us, your salary will double. If not, you will get a lump sum payment large enough to carry you until you get work elsewhere. In return for the backing, we will require you to keep us informed of your progress, including your selection of university courses and a successful completion of some other training we assign. As you successfully complete both aspects of your training, we will be able to tell you more about your mother’s career. Also, this arrangement must be kept secret from everyone, unless we tell you otherwise. Any questions?”

Kathy thought, Jack is really testing her. He wants to know now if she has the stuff to be part of what we do. If so, that’s one course of action. If not, then he will see that she gets a good start on her new life.

“I’ve a few. But I don’t know enough now to ask all the right questions.”

“Not to worry. Ask the few you have. There are no wrong questions, only wrong answers. I won’t give you any of those, so go ahead. You have the floor. The first person to see Carlo, signal for three more beers.”

“May I call you Jack?”

"That's an easy one. Yes, you may."

"Okay, Jack, why are you offering so much money to a girl you don't even know?"

"Ah, but I do know you. Kathy has known your mother for years and I trust her judgment. She doesn't believe you have fallen very far from the tree. Secondly, Anita's daughter is someone I would bet on sight unseen. Thirdly, I'm pretty good at judging people and I like what I see. And, lastly, I admire your discipline in sticking to your goals when Marie and, I suppose, others were telling you to forget your dream. I believe the money will be well spent and, incidentally, I can afford to invest the money. Next question."

"I have one more year of study for my B.A. I'm majoring in history with a strong minor in criminology. My grade point average is about 3.3. Are you recommending any changes to my program?"

"What are your extracurricular activities?"

"Outside of the R.O.T.C. program, I'm not active in anything else."

"Yes. I have some recommendations, but you don't have to accept them. I want you to get on the track team and to start martial arts training in Hapkido. A friend of mine runs a good Dojang in Oakland, and I'll give you a letter to him if you decide to accept my recommendations."

"What do you want me to do on the track team?"

"That's between you and the coaching staff. I want you in a good conditioning program, and the track coaches will lay it out for you. Don't hesitate to tell them about your mother's records at Pitt."

"Why the kung fu stuff? Is it for real?"

Kathy said, "After your first week, you won't be wondering whether it's for real."

Jack laughed and said, "Hapkido is a very tough and deadly martial arts, not a sport. You don't spar seriously. It's too dangerous. In the Dojang, no questions or tentative moves by the students are expected. Your instructor will be in total charge."

Kathy added, "We aren't fixated on GPA ratings. Our interest is in how well you can think, react and execute. At least half of what you have learned should be forgotten. The trick is knowing which half."

"Okay. Kelly, do you have other questions? We'll give you contact phone numbers for us. Call at any time. I have a check for you to deposit. Your tuition, board, books and some reasonable car are some of the things it will cover. Kathy will send you an iPhone that will be charged to our company. Do not let anyone else use it under any circumstances. The phone has some special capabilities Kathy will explain to you. Just so the record is straight, there are no second chances. Anita made that rule and it has served us well. This check is for $75,000. Deposit it and use it as necessary. There is nothing for you to sign, and we don't need or want any receipts. The money is yours. It is not a loan. You are in charge."

Kelly looked at the check and said, "I've never even seen a check for this much money. It is for real, isn't it?"

Kathy said, "Yes, the check is real. Jack has money, but he doesn't waste it or spend it on ostentatious items. We want to see how you handle these changes in your life. There will be more, if you and we get through a sort of probationary period. Remember you can opt out at any time and so can we."

Jack said, "I've another point to make. If you get a phone call from us, email or text message asking you to go somewhere, just do it. Don't think about it. All your expenses will be paid, including special tutors to make up for missed school. Your Hapkido instructor will understand. You need not explain yourself. For a while and only when necessary we'll give you a reason you have to travel. If that happens, stick to the story. Have we frightened you?"

"No, but it makes me think I just might earn the money you're paying me. When will I see you again?

"In a month or so. Jack or I may ask you to come to Washington or Charleston. You should receive a letter from our attorney within days on the issue of your name change and your employment situation. We all have to pay taxes."

"Okay. We have to go now. Your training starts right now. You never saw us, and no one can know about our arrangement. Please stay at the table for five minutes after we leave. I'll leave enough cash for the bill and tip. Kelly Marino, I'm very glad we met you, and I hope you will feel the same way before too long."

Kathy hugged Kelly hard and whispered, "It will be okay."

Seven

On the trip back to the cabin the following morning, Kathy and Jack talked about what the intruder could have learned in the house before he planted the bomb. Kathy looked through the papers she took from the house, and told Jack the bomber now had a very thorough description of him. "He has your social security number, the transcripts of your education, records from the Marine days, sports awards, bank records and employment with the Pittsburgh Police Department. He also knows your ex-wife's name and the name of her lawyer. If that isn't enough, the stuff left in the medicine cabinet provided doctors' names, addresses and some treatment history."

Kathy said, "Altogether too much information to ignore and hope for the best. I bet forensics won't give us much about the person who tried to kill you. We have got to take this very seriously. I saw nothing that would lead to the cabin, but our next move has to be well planned. I'm almost sure these people will try again."

"Okay! So let's get ready for them. First off, we're going to get you acquainted with more basic weapons and a deeper exposure to Hapkido. We can work on the weapons at the cabin. Then, we're going back to McLean, and my old friend Paul Kim is going to teach you some basic defense and attack moves. That is, if you're willing to spend a number of hours in the Dojang. Once you get started, I can add to your repertoire. Paul is one of the best there is. What say you?"

"Jack, remember that long flight from Delhi to Honolulu, I was still recovering from the shock of having to kill that al Qaeda gunman who was going to shoot you in the back. I knew then I need to improve my reaction time and use of weapons if I'm going to hold my own. So, yes, I'm ready to commit to some serious training and conditioning."

"I'm glad to hear you say that. You're already very good. We just need to make some small improvements. Mostly, improving reaction and shooting discipline. The gunman who came out of the kitchen closet in Ali's house is a good example. Two things, you were a little slow to shoot, and then you emptied your .38 revolver into him. In a perfect redo, you would shoot as soon as he stepped out of his hiding place, and you would have saved at least three rounds for a possible other immediate target. Okay?"

"Yes, I can see that now. I guess I can't expect to be lucky every time."

"Luck is good, but tomorrow we begin a bit of weapons training. First, I have a story for you."

"Great, I like stories. Is this a good one?"

"It's a story I've wanted to tell you when I first fell in love with one Kathleen Grayson. It's a story you need to hear before you marry me. My father told me this story when he knew his heart condition was terminal. In case he died before he could tell me, he made a recording and put it in a safety deposit box for me to find later. Now I want you to hear the same story."

When they had unloaded the car at the cabin and finished a very late lunch, Jack led Kathy out to the porch and asked her to listen to his father's story. Before Kathy put on the earphones, he said, "Please, no questions until you've heard the whole story and, to take away the temptation, Shadow and I are going for a walk."

Jack knew he had to give Kathy the privacy and time she would need to deal with his father's unbelievable story.

Kathy adjusted her earphones, slipped the DVD into the small player and heard a deep raspy voice of a man she had never met. She could hardly believe what she was hearing. Jack's father was a KGB agent who was smuggled into the country across the Canadian border when Jack was not much more than an infant. As she listened further, the story became even stranger. Jack's father built his financial fortune from money he stole from the KGB. Neither he nor Jack was a legal US citizen. She heard this disembodied voice telling her how they had escaped from KGB teams sent to hunt them down. My God! Jack's mother and baby sister were killed by the KGB. That explains a lot. This hidden cabin with the incredible supply of weapons, the hidden escape tunnel and the training in the form of games that his father put Jack through. No wonder Jack is so attuned to impending dangers. He grew up with it. His father's relationship with Frank goes back decades. He has been working for the CIA the entire time he's been in the US. This has got to be one of the best kept secrets. Talk about deep cover, this family is deep cover. Now I see why Jack wanted me to hear this story before I make any legal commitments. I don't know whether I'm angry or honored that he is sharing this history with me now.

His father's relationship with Yuri, the terrorist killed last year, extends back to the time they were both up and coming KGB officers. Yuri led the team that killed Jack's mother and sister. No wonder he was so focused on killing Yuri and his entire network.

As Jack and Shadow walked along the mountain trail, Jack remembered how much his father's story had shocked him. He hoped Kathy would be able to handle this situation better than he had. To find out that he had been using a false name his entire life and was not even a citizen of the country he served shook him badly. Not to mention his father was a former KGB agent, still on their wanted list. Maybe CIA could cope with these facts but the FBI would slap both he and his father in the lockup at the first opportunity. He loved and admired his father and was proud to be an American. After all he was no different than the millions of illegal aliens living in the US, many of whom earned their citizenship by serving in the armed forces. He wasn't a spy or a counter-intelligence agent but he was a damn good cop. He had no doubt he could continue his father's legacy.

Nearly an hour had passed. Shadow had grown tired of romping in the small brook. Jack gave Shadow the signal to move out. Arriving back at the cabin, he saw Kathy was still on the porch. She looked up, saw Jack and ran down the steps into his arms. "My God! Jack, what an incredible story! You've known this for over a year. Why tell me now?"

"My dad thought this story was better forgotten. He almost decided not to tell me. I trusted you from the beginning but believed it was unfair to ask you to marry me without telling you this story. So I did. Are you angry?"

"At first. I got over my hurt feelings as the story unfolded. Your father essentially lived the life of a deep cover agent and carried his story to the grave. I suppose you and I can carry it on. The best way to do that is to follow your father's wish and just forget it and live a normal life. I don't see how his story can ever be uncovered. Let's destroy the evidence now. I'm sure Frank made no records of your father's past. Is this DVD the only record?"

"As far as I know, but we had better search all the files in the hidden room in this cabin."

Jack and Kathy spent two days in a complete search of Peter Brandon's secret files. They found three documents that would lead a reader to suspect a further search was needed. Those documents were destroyed along with a number of outdated files.

Eight

Kathy sat on the porch of the cabin, looking out over the valley where she had improved her conditioning and weapons skills. She had spent six hours a day for a week, training to use small arms and building up her stamina running on the mountain trails. Jack, with years of experience and Special Operations training, dramatically improved her hand gun skills and reaction shooting. Kathy knew she was rapidly becoming more than proficient with her SOCOM .45 caliber, Mark 23 Mod0. Jack suggested they buy at the gun store in Pittsburgh and after 30 minutes of practice, she told him it felt right. Another two days on long-range marksmanship with the Stoner SR-25, and she completed the Brandon school for shooters. Finally, Jack told her she was good to go.

While Kathy was working on her conditioning with long runs on mountain trails, Jack spent hours on the phone with his attorney, Lee Jensen, getting the legal work done to change Kelly's name to Marino and setting up her employment with a schedule for salary payments and a post office box for business communications, as well as a phone line in Jensen's office that answered to East/West Consultants, a nominal company set up by Lee to protect the Brandon business. Jack arranged for $50,000 from Anita's estate to go to her sister Marie Kowalski, with the remaining $25,000 of the estate to be sent the following year, also from a front organization managed by Lee Jensen. Jack told Lee he could expect trouble from Marie and to handle her firmly. The insurance program Jack provided to Kathy and Anita was a Brandon self-insurance program, because Jack suspected that proof of death might be impossible to provide to an insurance company. Kelly would get the entire $500,000 but not yet. In the interim, the money would be invested for her.

The next day they packed a few suitcases and locked up the cabin. Kathy would be sorry to leave this cabin, where after months of fighting terrorists, she had found a sense of peace and security in the mountains. She told Jack she regretted their short vacation was ending.

She was sitting on the porch waiting for Jack and Shadow to come back from their afternoon walk. Kathy met them in the parking area said, "I think I could stay in this cabin for a long time. Don't ever sell this place. It means too much to me."

"Don't worry. The cabin is my last physical tie to my father. It's a keeper."

Jack said, "We'll set up in the McLean Ritz Carlton Hotel, where we first met. They'll accept Shadow as long as we use the back elevator. Tomorrow, I'll introduce you to my old friend, Paul Kim. Paul's dad willed him the Dojang a year ago. He is a real martial arts fighter and a very good instructor. On the Dojang floor, he is king. Just do what he says as well as you can and quickly with no questions."

From that point on, her training and conditioning program was brutal. Five full days each week for three weeks, studying Hapkido in Paul Kim's Dojang in McLean, had taken all her athleticism and dedication to get through each day. After the first week she knew how to fall and learned basic footwork. After several awkward mistakes, she understood that footwork is the most important part of martial arts fighting. Paul had specially designed ten basic moves for her to work on. Now she could do all of them without thinking. There was poetry of motion in Hapkido, emphasizing flowing body movements that focused the power of the entire body at the point of impact. After learning the basics, she was now working with Jack to add to her repertoire of moves. She could escape from nearly all common holds. Jack told her it was unlikely she'd be fighting trained martial arts fighters. An untrained fighter would have little to no chance against her, once he and Paul were finished with this phase of training.

Tomorrow morning they would be driving to Charleston. She would be the driver. He may be the martial arts specialist, but she was the driver. Jack was too slow.

After two days in Charleston, they bought a place on Johns Island with a five-acre lot bordering the marsh and rented a condo in Charleston proper. Shadow loved the open space. Jack showed him the boundaries knowing he would stay within them. Both properties were put in Kathy's name. Jack didn't want to give a possible survivor of the Charleston terrorist cell any advantage. The bomb in his Pittsburgh house and the shooting attack focused his attention. To staff the Johns Island house, he coaxed out of retirement a Vietnamese husband-and-wife team with weapons skills his father had hired years ago.

Jack suggested Kathy call an interior designer to help furnish the house. She could learn a lot about Charleston by running around the city with a professional decorator. It also gave them excellent cover for all parts of the city. Their primary target operated a rug shop. If the owner was who Captain Shorer thought he was, Mr. Joel Hankins would check them out when they went to his rug shop. Jack was sure Hankins would find that they were furnishing a house and put them in his potential customer category.

Nine

A Year Ago

A small group of ranking al Qaeda members were holding a critical meeting in Karachi, Pakistan. Since the destruction of the twin towers they hadn't been able to bring Jihad to America. Their leader, an Egyptian who had been educated at Princeton University and lived almost twenty years in the United States before joining the movement for Jihad, was the undisputed theoretician in al Qaeda. Today he was using the name Mustafa al Faraq and traveling on a Jordanian passport. To his followers, he was known as the "Professor." The group filed back into the meeting room after prayers. When everyone was seated the Professor said, "I must tell you now about the enemy, and how we are going to defeat the most powerful nation the world has ever known. With the defeat of America, the Christian world will dry up, leaving the followers of Allah to inherit the Earth. When you are looking for a weakness in an enemy, you must look at their strength, for that is where you will find its weakness.

"America's strength is in the unprecedented freedom of its citizens and the diversity of cultures, races and religions that function freely and unfettered in the so-called

New World. Most Americans pride themselves on the tolerance they show each other in the face of vast differences in attitudes and beliefs, emanating from the multi-ethnic and religious fabric of their society. Within that fabric there are many threads that have never been tightly woven. It is our task to find those threads and pull on them until the fabric of national unity comes apart. We shall fray that fabric so badly that it can never be woven back together again. The melting pot that mixed races and religions will boil over and spill its stored up hatred across the Great Satan's land. Do not think that the American people are weak or afraid. They are a powerful warlike people that cannot be defeated on the field of military battle. Even though many of them blame their country for all wrongs and believe that talk, negotiations and compromises can solve all problems, we cannot defeat them. They must be led to defeat themselves. That is our challenge and it is why we are here today. We must take the battle to America.

"As long as the battleground is on our sacred soil, we are losing the war. On our land, the Americans and their allies use their soldiers with all their awesome firepower and reconnaissance capabilities against us. Within their own country, they send police, lawyers and courts to fight us. They don't realize that the location of the battlefield doesn't change the struggle. It is all part of the same war. One does not send lawyers, judges and politicians to war. In America, the politically correct way to fight the war we are going to bring to their shores is to use 'law and order' techniques. This approach will never work against our disciplined Jihadists who are willing to sacrifice their lives.

"Now, let me discuss their other weaknesses. There are hatreds between Blacks and Whites, between Blacks and Hispanics, between Muslims and Christians, among Protestants, Catholics and Mormons. Jews and non-Jews. Southerners and Northerners. Irish and Italians. Puerto Ricans and Blacks. Germans and English. Illegal aliens and citizens. The rich and the poor.

"We must act as the catalyst that fans these historical differences into an open flame that will consume our greatest enemy. We have seen this strategy work in Iraq by exacerbating the anger between Sunni and Shia. On the battlefield, we are no match for the Americans. But, by using the long repressed hatreds of the people against those of different races, religions and beliefs, we will triumph. That is the theory. Now, how do we make it happen?

"Many Americans are already angry with Muslims, so it should be easy to make them take out their anger on moderate Muslims by planting a bomb to explode in a city with a large Muslim population. The Soldiers of Allah, a title I just made up, will take credit for the bomb. A single action may be enough to drive some of the angrier anti-Muslims to take violent action. If not, we must have patience and try again. The Koran does not require haste. It only requires faith and sacrifice.

"Over the last five years, we have trained a number of Americans and sent them back to America to await our call to action. We now need them to attack America from within. Burn Black churches by a revived racist group, the Ku Klux Klan. Burn White churches in the name of Black revenge. Attack Jews, in the name of Muslim organizations. Attack Hispanic illegal aliens in the name of a mythical right wing American group. Blacks attacking Asians. Poor attacking the rich. All these attacks will be believable. Your job is to provide the money and the martyrs necessary to keep the attacks going. This is our most important project. I will be going to America soon to get this Jihad begun."

Ten

Jack and Kathy were enjoying their third week in Charleston. To operate in a city, you have to know the city. Each day Jack and Kathy walked and drove through its neighborhoods. Life was a little slower than in McLean. Or maybe, Jack thought, there was just less wheel spinning in this southern jewel. During their meandering, they located Joel Hankins' Oriental rug store. Kathy stopped in a few days later to case the shop and its owner. She bought an interesting five-by-three-foot tribal rug from Pakistan and spent almost an hour looking through the stacks of rugs and chatting with Mr. Hankins. Later she told Jack that Mr. Hankins was one creepy guy who didn't like women very much. She could easily believe that Captain Shorer's suspicions about his being a serial killer could be right on. Kathy sketched what she had seen of the shop and the next day checked in at the courthouse to gather more data about the property. The courthouse tax records showed that the property included a two-story garage attached to the rug shop.

While she was doing her research, Jack scouted the neighborhood to find a place where they could observe the shop. He found a location that looked good and, using a cover company set up by his attorney, Jack contacted the realtor. Later that day, he rented a vacant two-story building with a good view of Joel Hankins' shop. It was across the street and about fifty yards east of the rug shop.

Joel was restless. He thought how long can I fuck around all the damn day with these rugs? There is not a lot of money to be made. It's been three months since an al Qaeda courier had stopped in his shop. The courier said that he should expect an important visitor soon and that big things would be expected of him. He had been on a high for the first month. After that he decided his superiors had changed their minds again. He really wanted to go out and capture another young girl but knew he had to keep his urges under control. Maybe next month he would go hunting again. Tonight he would put one of his flash drives into his notebook and look at some of his best images of young women being tortured and killed. The several gigabyte flash drives were easy to hide. The hard drive on his notebook contained nothing that could get him in trouble. He stored his al Qaeda notes the same way. At times he was tempted to share his art and research, but he knew that would be almost certain suicide.

In two more hours he would close the shop and go for his one-on-one training session in Taekwondo. His test for the blue belt was coming up, and he needed to work on some of his open hand forms. As Joel was mentally going through his most difficult form, the door opened and a well-dressed middle-aged man walked in. Joel said, "Hello. May I show you some rugs?"

The man looked around and said, "You have done well. I am the man from Herat. Perhaps you have been told about me."

Joel was shocked. He had never had an important al Qaeda visitor before. He said, "Yes, I have heard you were coming. What can I do for you?"

"Do you have a place we can sit and drink some tea?"

Joel hung the closed sign on the shop door and ushered his visitor up to his living quarters above the garage. The small area was spartan but functional and clean. While Joel was making a pot of strong black tea, he asked his visitor what he should call him. The visitor laughed and said, "Whatever you want. My name is not important but my mission is, and I will need your help."

Joel sat down at the small table and waited for the man from Herat to talk. After sipping his tea he said, "I see you learned how to brew a good cup of tea. Do you remember what else you were taught in Peshawar?"

"Yes, but I haven't had much opportunity to use it."

"That will change. The time has come. Once before conflict between Americans began in South Carolina, and I see no reason why another one should not start here almost in the shadow of Fort Sumter."

Joel leaned forward in his chair, staring at his visitor and said, "I am sorry. I don't understand."

"Don't worry. I will tell you what you need to know. First, what I am going to say, you must never tell anyone. Your life and mine depend on it. You may ask some, and I repeat some, questions but I probably will not answer most of them. I will stop in often enough to keep your instructions current. The first questions you might have are, who am I, and where am I from? Those questions I do not answer. You have already guessed that I am no stranger to America and its history. I am not a citizen of any country, only a loyal worker for the cause, as you are. Now, your first task is to ready this place to keep three or four people out of sight for a few days. Buy the supplies you need but do not call attention to yourself by your purchases. Make sure you have put prayer rugs here for my people. Do not be surprised when you are excluded from some of my meetings up here. The others will be leaving. You have to stay here and the less you know, the better off both you and our cause will be. You must be prepared to carry on your activity here for at least the next year. We have a lot to do together. We are sending you some help. Within the next two weeks a man, whose name is Joseph Green, will come to the shop. He will give you a message from me. Hire him. He has been well trained and told to take orders from you. Pay him enough to rent a room and buy his meals."

With that the man from Herat finished his tea and left, just as the afternoon traffic was picking up. Joel was both excited and frightened by his visitor. The man's cold gray eyes cut right through him. Whoever he was, he was used to people following his orders. Joel had no doubts about doing exactly what he was told to do.

Eleven

The Vietnamese couple, the Minhs, did more than run the house. Although beginning to show their age, they were still very fit. Both were veterans of the war in Vietnam with the Quang Tri Provincial Reconnaissance Unit. Jack briefed them on the bomb attempt on his Pittsburgh house. The Minhs listened carefully and asked Jack to provide them with two 12-gauge pump shotguns and night vision glasses.

With the Minhs on guard, Kathy and Jack felt free to live a near-normal life in Charleston. Kathy loved to churn laps in the heated pool, hoping she could shame Jack into a race. Jack was a strong swimmer with a lot of in-water experience, but Kathy still beat him in the sprints. It didn't matter how hard he tried, Kathy always beat him. She told him he should stop fighting the water and move through it. Maybe someday he would figure it out.

Kathy hoisted herself out of the pool, one full yard ahead of Jack. In deference to the Minhs, she was wearing her bikini. Kathy was addicted to skinny dipping and was delighted with the large pool and total privacy, so she could indulge herself. By the time Jack had settled in the heated cabana, Betty Minh appeared with two cold Yuenglings, homemade chips and a salsa dip.

Kathy had spent the early afternoon in their surveillance post across Market Street from Joel's rug shop. Jack asked her if she had learned anything from watching the rug shop.

Kathy said, "Your serial killer is not doing much business. Maybe four people visited the shop all afternoon. Nothing special about any of them, but one was well dressed. He stayed an hour and left walking. He looked and walked like a European, maybe from a Mediterranean area. I decided not to follow him, even though I thought it was unusual someone so well dressed was walking in an area that was not all that good. There were a number of more convenient parking spots closer to the rug shop. I did get some photos of him that I think are pretty good. We need to send them to Frank. Maybe some of his counter-terrorism analysts can identify this visitor.

"Captain Shorer told you this rug dealer was trained in the al Qaeda camps in Afghanistan. If he is part of a support network, any visitor he gets may be a terrorist. The well-dressed visitor looked to be in his mid-fifties. It is possible he is a pro and was being careful, looking for surveillance. Following a subject walking from a meeting some blocks to a parked car gives a surveillance team real problems. I think we should set up a remote motion-activated camera system aimed at the door of his shop. There is not much traffic in and out, so it shouldn't give us a logistical problem to check the tape once or twice a week."

"I think we might need some help. Watching a suspected serial killer is a job we can do. Adding the task of watching a possible terrorist site compounds the problem, for we must be alert to all the visitors to the shop as well as Hankins himself. The two of us cannot do that."

Kathy said, "Look, I know about you cops and rules of evidence, but we need to break some rules. We need to look inside that shop before things get more complicated."

"I suppose that means you go in."

"You got that right. I am the spook who can pick locks, search computers, look for entry traps and generally be a lot smarter about clandestine entries and searches than a handsome, well-trained cop who is, by the way, an excellent lover. So you watch your perp and I'll do the dangerous, highly skilled work. Okay?"

"Put like that, what choice do I have?"

"Okay. I love it when you agree."

"Never mind the gloating. We need to do some planning."

Their past random surveillance coverage of the rug shop indicated Joel Hankins seldom left the shop for more than an hour. On Tuesday and Thursday evenings, he went to a small Taekwondo Dojang at 9:00 and stayed there until 10:30.

At 8:30 on Thursday, Jack was parked down the street from the Dojang watching the front and only entrance. At 8:45, Joel appeared. Jack waited until he saw Hankins come out on the Dojang floor in his uniform before he called Kathy and told her she could go into the rug shop. Kathy had studied the lock when she visited the rug shop a week ago. She was confident the lock itself wouldn't be any problem. She has also sure there was no technical intrusion alarm in the rug shop, but Hankins may have trapped the entries to his shop and living quarters to reveal any entry after his departure. It had been cloudy all day and the night was unusually dark and threatening rain. Kathy stepped up on the narrow wooden porch and, with a quick glance around the door's edge for traps, dropped on one knee and began to pick the lock, being careful not to leave any tell-tale scratches on the lock. Twenty seconds later she was in.

Snapping on her small beam hooded flashlight, Kathy went up the back staircase to Hankins' living quarters over the three-car garage. Her light showed a clean orderly bedroom, bath and small sitting area that opened into a Pullman kitchen. The freezer and storage cabinet were stocked to overflowing with frozen dinners and staples. Heavy drapes covered the windows. Kathy used her digital camera to shoot pictures of the entire area. She wanted everything to be back in place when she left.

There were two other small bedrooms furnished with two cots and sleeping bags in each one. The windows were covered with heavy black drapes. The only sign of indulgence on Hankins' part was the high definition TV and the Oriental rugs on the floors of all the rooms. A desk was centered on the wall opposite the bathroom under a black-draped window. A notebook computer was on the desk. After checking for any traps, Kathy sat down at the computer and hit the power switch. She checked all the internal drives and then went to files on the 'My Computer' area of Windows 7. She found no hidden files or files protected by a password on the hard drive. Checking the desk drawers she found no DVDs or CDs. The access slots to the two DVD drives were dusty. She then checked the most convenient USB port and found signs of routine use in the small scratches around the port. So, she thought, he makes use of flash drives to store his data. I guess that makes sense for a traveling merchant who wants the ability to showcase his wares. Except that they are nowhere to be seen and surely he wouldn't have taken them to his Taekwondo lesson. Multiple gigabyte flash drives would be easy to hide. If he uses them a lot, the hiding place should be close to the desk or in the desk.

For the next ten minutes, Kathy searched the desk drawers. She took each one out and examined their interior and exterior. Finished with searching the desk and not finding a flash drive, she leaned back and thought, surely his hiding place has to be nearby. She thought, wait a minute, girl, the guy uses a notebook and, if his flash drives are not for the rug business, he could move the notebook anywhere, so maybe the flash drives are hidden where he could relax. There was nothing under or in the mattress. She checked the drawers in the bedside stand and, taped to the back of the bottom drawer, she found three flash drives. She knew there wasn't time to open any of the drives, so she put them in a USB port on her notebook one by one, and thirty seconds later all the data they contained were transferred to her hard drive.

She just finished when Jack called and told her Hankins had left the Taekwondo Dojang and appeared to be heading back to his shop. She had three minutes to clear the shop. With a quick look around, Kathy saw nothing out of place. She hurried down the stairs and after pausing to check the area outside the shop entrance, slipped outside. Kathy picked the lock closed. She was just entering the side door of the observation post when she saw Hankins' dark blue van coming down the street. She thought, that is just a little too close.

She watched Hankins park his car in the garage. A few minutes later a sliver of light escaped from a window in the upstairs living area. As planned, she headed home to meet Jack.

Kathy thought, from idea to execution in two days. Not bad. No red tape or approval chains to climb. No endless briefings and hand holdings of nervous superiors. No struggle for funding. There was something to be said for freelancing. But, it was clear they needed some help. A two-person team was too limited, and pushing beyond your resources is a proven formula for failure.

Jack saw Kathy pull into the driveway and waited for her on the back patio. The late January weather certainly was better than it was in Pittsburgh. He could tell Kathy was in her cool state waiting to tell him what she had. Jack hugged her, handed her a cold beer and said, "Okay, what did you get while I was babysitting Mr. Hankins?"

"Well, we have a picture layout of the shop and living quarters and some computer files. We don't have any coverage of the garage. Ran out of time. Let me walk you through the visual layout first."

She covered the shop area very quickly but paused in the coverage of the living area. "First, the living quarters are laid out and furnished to house at least six people. The kitchen is stocked with enough food for several days. Most of the frozen dinners are suitable for a South Asian or

Middle Eastern diet, including basmati rice and pita bread. Probably from that Whole Foods store in Mount Pleasant. It looks to me as if Mr. Hankins is expecting some visitors who plan on staying for a week or more. No sign that any women are staying there or have been there."

"Anything else?"

"Yes, let's see what I copied from the flash drives I found taped to the bottom drawer of his night stand. I didn't have time to open any of the files, so I don't know what's on them. From the care he took in concealing them, they must contain something he wants to hide."

Kathy opened the files she copied to her hard drive. The first several frames contained pictures of rugs with prices and descriptions. The next frame brought gasps. A naked young girl, not much beyond her middle teens, lay on her stomach. Her neck was wrenched around so her blank eyes were staring up. Her body was covered with welts. Each frame seemed worse than the one before. Kathy could feel her stomach churning and ran into the bathroom. Jack could hear her heaving and thought, no wonder, this is sick stuff, real sick.

Kathy came back looking a little green but said, "Okay. I want to see the rest of what this sick son-of-a-bitch has been doing."

There were a total of ten young women tortured and murdered. All with their necks twisted, except for one whose face and body was so badly beaten, she might have died before he could break her neck.

Jack stopped his pacing around the room and said, "I would like to go over and kill this guy right now. I'll leave the flash drives in his pocket. We can't let this sick bastard kill again. All of these sexual predators need to be put away for life."

Kathy said, "We have a big problem, the standard conflict or divide between the law and national security priorities. If we take this guy down, it will scare off al Qaeda contacts who may intend to use the rug shop as a staging or training area to kill several hundred Americans. If al Qaeda knew their support agent is a serial killer of young women, they would kill Hankins themselves. We'll have to keep close track of our sick rug merchant and try to keep him from killing anyone else. We'll get him as soon as we talk to Frank and he gives us the go-ahead.

"I see no pattern here except that the women are all young. Nothing else sets them apart. Not hair color, body type, racial or ethnic background. We know he doesn't sexually assault them. There is, according to your old boss, Captain Shorer, no DNA from semen, blood or anything else. Why does he do this?"

Jack said, "Three years ago I was working with a small task force in Pittsburgh, trying to get a serial killer of young girls, even younger than this nut is killing. Again, little or no forensic evidence. This was before the routine use of DNA. We finally trapped this guy and killed him in a shootout. Before he died, an officer asked him why? The killer said, 'The eyes! The eyes! I love seeing the light go out and the soul depart.' Maybe that's what we have here."

Kathy said, "You know, I was wondering why the eyes were always open on his victims' pictures. You may be right on. That also means he doesn't keep his prey alive very long and he doesn't play with them. He beats them, breaks the neck and shoots his pictures. This guy must be stronger than he looks and well-coordinated to break their necks and get his camera ready to shoot before they die. I hate to say this but we have a few more files to look at."

The rest of the files had to do with the rug business and a copy of the King James Version of the Old Testament. The business files listed the towns and cities Hankins visited buying and selling rugs. Jack realized the need to correlate the dates and places of Hankins' travels, with the homicides of the young women with the same M.O. Trouble is, if he gave this information to Captain Shorer of the Pittsburgh Police, he would be off and running to gather the evidence and arrest Hankins before Frank and the counter-terrorists were ready.

Would they have to let this monster walk the streets in order to stop an unknown terrorist plan? The cop in him said, hell no! But after battling with al Qaeda, he knew they were capable of bringing a major terrorist attack to the United States again. Kathy had the floor and was waiting for Jack to focus on the files, especially those associated with the Old Testament. Finally, he looked at Kathy and said, "Why in hell does this monster have the Old Testament on file in his computer?"

"Well, it's not for religious purposes. There is nothing religious in his living quarters. No religious books or pictures. This bastard doesn't belong to or go to any church. In the time we've had him under surveillance, he hasn't gone near a mosque. Before the science of cryptology became technologically advanced after WWI with near random generated codes, intelligence agencies used books to code messages. The code could be made up of a substitution code based on a pre-designated line or lines on a page of the book. The page of the book used for a message would not be used again. So each message would have a different substitution code."

"So, you're saying we can decrypt any message Hankins gets from al Qaeda."

"No, I'm not saying that. Without the page and line numbers, we can't break his code. NSA probably could but not fast enough. I doubt that he gets any messages by radio or via the Internet. They are more likely to be hand-carried or mailed messages. So, what we have doesn't help us."

"Okay, so much for that, I have a couple of ideas how we can stop this nut from killing again. It will require some help to keep track of him 24/7. We'll need to put a beacon on his van. It's the only vehicle he has, and I don't think he will rent a car to go kill someone. Anytime he moves the car, we'll have a team standing by to follow him.

"It's time to call Frank and see if we can go see him."

Twelve

Before Jack could tell Frank he and Kathy wanted to come up for a meeting, Frank said he would be in Charleston tomorrow to see them. Jack got the flight number and arrival time and told Frank one of them would meet him.

The next day Kathy met Frank as he came through his gate at Charleston airport. Kathy smiled to herself as she picked Frank out of the passengers streaming out of the gate. No one seeing Frank would even imagine how important he was to their safety. He was the kind of dedicated CIA officer who did his job quietly and efficiently. Mild manner, not quite. He was very tough when needed and wasn't big on second chances. She remembered once in the Counter Terrorism Center when a pompous middle level manager was stating that his unit had met all their objectives and had no failures to report. Frank stared at the officer and said, "That's not quite true. You have just failed as a leader. Meeting all of your goals means to me that you have deliberately set the bar too low. Managers often do that. Leaders never do. When good people fail, it means to me that they are pushing the envelope. Taking justifiable risks. Not playing it safe to look good. I expect to have your request for a transfer on my desk within the hour."

Kathy said, "Everyone at the table got a lasting lesson in leadership."

An advertising sign partially screened her from Frank and she waited until he was walking past her before stepping out and taking his arm.

Frank said, "I see you haven't lost any of your skills and you look great. All that action over the last year hasn't aged you a bit."

"No, but it made my hands sweat a few times and I still miss Anita."

"Yes. So do I. While I'm here I want you to brief me on Anita's sister and daughter."

"You knew Kelly was Anita's daughter!!"

"I suspected but didn't know until now. Thank you."

"Frank, damnit, are you always going to be a step ahead of me?"

"I hope so. Where are we going to meet?"

"Jack has set up our house as the meeting site. It's isolated and quiet. We'll be there in about 40 minutes, depending on traffic."

Shadow came running up as Kathy pulled into the circular driveway. Frank said, "I finally get to meet the famous Shadow. I hope he likes me."

"You don't know the half of it. Shadow saved us twice last month when Jack took me to see his old house and to meet Captain Shorer of the Pittsburgh Police Bureau. That's a long story that I'm sure Jack will cover."

Jack met them at the front door. "Frank, welcome. I now have a better appreciation for your world than I did when we first met. Come into the dining room. I've set us up around a table. The Minhs have left us the fixings for lunch. Sweet tea and coffee are ready and almost anything else."

"Sweet tea is good. Let's get to work. Tomorrow I need to be back in Washington, and there is a lot to cover."

As they seated themselves around the table with Shadow lying in his customary spot between Jack and Kathy, Frank said, "If you agree, I want to take the floor first."

Jack nodded and Frank began, "Your first year was phenomenal. Your small unit was successful beyond any expectations on my part. Tracking down and killing those al Qaeda cells in America, with some help from the FBI, I expected you would accomplish, but when the trail led to India and Nepal, you were just as effective. I know Anita was killed and I grieved for her. She was a great warrior. You must put it behind you. Anita wouldn't have it any other way. I'm not finished but I want you to tell me about Anita's family, especially her daughter, Kelly."

"Jack, why don't you tell the Pittsburgh story while I get lunch on the counter?"

While Kathy was showing her domestic side, she could hear Jack telling Frank about their Pittsburgh adventures. She noted he left out some parts regarding his own actions and his instincts in following Shadow's lead. She would fill in the blanks when taking Frank back to the airport. Kathy tapped a spoon on a glass and said, "Thanks to the Minhs, lunch is not only served but it quite good judging from my grazing. So everyone, serve yourself, please."

Frank noticed that both Jack and Kathy were never very far from the out-of-sight but quickly retrievable handguns. He thought, that is good. These people don't take security for granted. I hope they will agree to my proposal. I need them.

Over a cold lunch of sorrel soup, potato salad and sandwiches of rare thin-sliced sirloin with Vidalia onions, sliced tomatoes and a mustard-touched horseradish dressing, Frank began his proposal.

"I want to bring you in a little closer. Without using any names or events that could identify you, I got general approval to enlist contract agents, as long as there were no identifiable costs to the CIA. No paper trail will exist. As usual this kind of relationship has one important rule – don't get caught. As in the past, you will only report to me. Anything I ask you to do will be voluntary. You will take all the risks and bear all the costs. I will provide information and some non-specific CIA equipment when required. Neither your accounting nor CIA's can show any links to this relationship. For starters I want you to add a few more people to your team. I have some suggestions, mostly people Kathy knows. Unfortunately, none of them will be as well qualified as Anita. Comments or questions?"

Jack said, "When we were in Pittsburgh, Captain Shorer asked us to check out a suspected serial killer who began his spree in Pittsburgh about 18 months ago with the brutal killing of two Pitt coeds. The suspect was trained in al Qaeda camps in Afghanistan and Pakistan and is now running a rug shop in Charleston. Captain Shorer gave us badges and weapons permits. But we asked him not to inform the Charleston Police, so from a legal standpoint the badges are not of much use in Charleston. Kathy made an entry into the shop while I watched the subject. She found and copied disgusting pictures of dead naked young girls. All were killed by a counter-clockwise twist of the neck. None of the 11 kills left any recoverable forensics evidence. We had no subpoena, so the evidence will not be useful in a trial setting. A further complication is that we think the rug shop is now active as an al Qaeda support base or, as you guys say, a safe house. Kathy photographed a well-dressed foreigner leaving the shop and walking some unnecessary distance to his car in a questionable neighborhood. She thinks he may be a player."

Reaching into his briefcase, Jack slid three black and white 8x10 photos across the table to Frank. Frank shuffled through the photos and then asked for a magnifying glass. Peering intently at the side view of the visitor, he said, "My God! This man is the 'Professor' AKA Mohammed Al Naziri. He was in the graduate program at Princeton the same time I was there.

"He is very high on our capture or kill list. His looks are deceiving. He is a highly intelligent planner and a cold-blooded killer. The Professor comes as close to anyone I've ever heard of who can kill innocent people without remorse. He is very dangerous and wouldn't be here unless something big was in the planning stages. This is a very big deal. Let's work out our approach, starting with the premise that the Professor is your number one priority. You can deal with Captain Shorer's serial killer after we deal with the Professor. Agree?"

Jack looked at Kathy who had clenched her jaw, and Jack knew she was going to tell them her position.

"Frank, I recognize national prerogatives, but I want to show you some pictures. I'll wait until you've finished your lunch."

"Go ahead, Kathy. I've finished. So show me the take from your illegal search."

Kathy handed Jack a flash drive and asked him to show Frank the pictures in their office while she cleaned up lunch.

After seeing the pictures, Frank said, "I see why Kathy is upset. This guy is really sick, and he surely will not stop on his own. Left alone, however, the Professor will kill dozens or more innocent people. He has to be our priority. He's so disciplined that he will close up shop here and move elsewhere at the first indication there is a possible compromise of his security. In any event, he won't completely trust this untested rug merchant and will be watching and testing him the entire time. He'll have his own people watch the rug shop now that he has made contact. If we're lucky, they may not have set up in time to see Kathy pick the lock."

"How do we know they didn't see her?"

"We won't until we see the Professor again. If they saw her, he will be long gone, leaving the rug merchant to take the fall."

"So I leave Captain Shorer out of the loop and let this sick bastard kill more daughters, sisters and wives."

"Yes. If you try to trap him, scare him off or beat him to death in some parking lot where he's waiting to catch his next girl, the Professor will run. He's too important to jeopardize over a serial killer. As much as the rug shop owner disgusts me, we must leave him alone. It will take all we have to try to keep track of the comings and goings at the rug shop. Call Kathy to join us. We have some work to do."

When Frank told Kathy about his decision making the Professor their top priority, she said, "Look, I understand that national priorities trump local serial killers, but I don't have to like it. When you give us the go-ahead on our sick serial killer, he is going down either legally or otherwise."

The rest of the afternoon was spent in a long planning session. Frank thought the observation post Jack set up was necessary, but they needed to move a real business into the space, a business allowing people to come go during the day and for the owner to work long, irregular hours. Kathy suggested a computer or a camera services and repair shop. She even had the perfect person to act as the owner/operator. She remembered Lou Washington, a former FBI surveillance specialist with very good technical skills, from working with him on a joint FBI/CIA operation in Washington, D.C., and he only lived twenty minutes from Charleston.

When Frank asked how well she knew him, she said, "It just so happens that I worked with Mr. Washington a few years back on a domestic surveillance problem with foreign implications. Lou is a retired FBI officer who was the expert in street surveillance operations. He now owns a camera service and repair shop in Mount Pleasant with his daughter. I'm sure he wouldn't mind picking up some extra cash.

"He's the best I've ever seen at all kinds of surveillance. He saved me once from an ugly situation. We were running a surveillance operation in a bad part of Washington. Three street thugs cornered me. They were just moving in when Lou arrived. He told them to move on, but they didn't take his advice. He broke the lead guy's knee, pushed him into the closest attacker who went down. Lou grabbed the third guy's arm, pulled him close and hit him with an elbow strike to the side of the neck. He took my arm and we just walked away. He said later that the only difficult part of the fight was being careful not to permanently maim or kill one of them. He is not as skilled as Jack is, but he is a dependable fighter. If you agree, I'll call him and see if we can go out to his shop."

Kathy wondered what Jack would think of Lou. He was an impressive man, at least fifty-five and still moved like a predator. Lou and Jack were alike in many ways. Both carried themselves like warriors. No bravado or tough guy acts. People just stayed out of their way. Jack was a little taller and heavier than Lou with twenty years of Hapkido training. Still, something about them made her feel they were pretty equal.

Frank said, "Before I run to the airport, let me summarize my thoughts. First, my plans to expand your little unit have to be put on hold. The Professor is too important. Taking him down has to be our number one priority. Only add more people if you need them to monitor the rug shop. If he shows up again, call me immediately. Use the term 'Princeton' for this activity in your reporting to me. Don't send any information regarding the Professor to the FBI. I'll take care of any necessary notification of other Agencies. Lastly, no more entries to the shop or mobile surveillance of anyone coming and going from the shop without my okay. This man is one of the best professionals in the business, and I don't want him even to get a sniff that we have picked up a thread to his operation. I can't even go to any of our foreign intelligence liaison sources for help. I believe the Professor has his agents inside all of them, especially the Pakistanis. Any questions? Okay, I see we are all on the same page. This is a great lead and we've been lucky to get it. Good work. Now, Kathy, can you take me to the airport?"

Thirteen

Following the Professor's detailed instructions, Omar, the Black Muslim leader of the bikers, led the four motorcycles across the bridge from Mount Pleasant into the outskirts of Charleston's historical district. Then, with a final check of readiness, he passed the word to take out their assigned targets.

Holding one bike team in reserve, Omar and his sidecar rider sped off to attack Kahal Kadosh Beth Elohim, the historic Jewish Synagogue on Hasell Street. The other two teams headed for the Roman Catholic Church next door to the synagogue and the Congregational Church on Market Street.

All the attacks were planned to take place in a three-minute window. The Professor liked to keep operations simple. All the teams were trained to use the same M.O. The saddlebags of the bikes were full of homemade Molotov cocktails, glass quart bottles filled with a mixture of gasoline and liquid soap with a cloth wick. Simple, but quiet and effective.

After getting the bikes as close to the targets as possible, each team member dismounted with three fire bombs each and ran to opposite sides of their targets. Two fire bombs through the basement windows and four through first floor windows. The fires would start slowly and then gather strength. Before the bikes were out of sight, fires were raging. The three motorcycles hit their targets within their three-minute window.

At a wooded site, little more than a mile from the Hasell Street bombings, they loaded the bikes into a waiting truck that headed south to Savannah. The men got into a van waiting nearby. No problems were encountered at any of the targets. As the van drove west on Highway 26 to Columbia, the sounds of sirens from racing fire trucks could be heard.

The van driver called the Professor and told him the work was completed, and they expected to be at their dispersal site on schedule. After receiving the report of success from his team leader, the Professor sent an email through three other destinations before it was sent from Atlanta to the network news centers in Charleston saying:

"THE BLACK MUSLIMS OF AL QAEDA HAVE RETALIATED FOR YOUR ATROCITIES AGAINST ISLAM. THIS IS ONLY THE BEGINNING. MORE DESTRUCTION WILL OCCUR. NO AMERICAN CITY IS SAFE AND NO AMERICAN IS SAFE. YOUR GOVERNMENT OF 21ST CENTURY TEMPLARS CANNOT PROTECT YOU FROM THE WRATH OF BLACK MUSLIMS IN AMERICA. THEY HAVE BEEN WELL-TRAINED AND WANT REVENGE. AS THE CRUSADERS DID IN JERUSALEM WITH MUSLIM BLOOD, CHRISTIAN AND JEWISH BLOOD WILL RUN LIKE RIVERS IN THE STREETS ALL THROUGH THE LAND OF SATAN."

Fourteen

It was late the next afternoon before the Charleston attackers all made their way separately to Columbia, SC. The Professor listened to their separate debriefings from behind a screen and sent them all to Myrtle Beach to await further commands.

The Professor had two groups waiting for him in Myrtle Beach, one group of young White Aryans and the other of more Black al Qaeda recruits. All Americans were recruited in the US and trained in Somalia. His plan was simple. The Aryans, dressed to look like the old KKK, would attack and burn a number of Black churches between Georgetown, SC, and Savannah, GA. The Black al Qaeda group would retaliate for the burning of the Black churches by attacking white churches and wealthy white residential neighborhoods. Each attack had to be quick and decisive. No one could be captured. The Black al Qaeda team, using motorcycles, would hold their attack until the White KKK group in pickup trucks finished their work and the news media focused on the attacks. The Professor picked one man in each group to be the enforcer. Anyone in danger of being captured would be killed. Now he had time to prepare his two suicide car bombers.

The Professor checked into a three-star motel near Broadway at the Beach in Myrtle Beach. Here he could use one of his American aliases. The constant coming and going of tourists provided him with a perfect background. There was no real security check. He was amazed that the possession of any credit card and, in some cases, a driver's license was all that was needed as long as one had enough cash. In the Great Satan, profit ruled. It was simple. If you had credit, it trumped any need for cumbersome background checks, especially for prosperous Americans.

The Professor was an excellent language student and his American accent was flawless. He took steps to protect his American alias. No one associated with his great plan would ever meet him where he was staying. In two hours, just after dark, he would meet his two male drivers. The young girls of Muslim faith from good Palestinian families were the actual suicide bombers. The families would be well rewarded after the incidents. There would be no questions. The girls would be martyrs and Jihadist heroes. They would follow the instructions of his two drivers.

His second in command arranged for the logistics needed. All the girls had to do was take over the driving of their cars for the last half-mile. Their handlers would get the girls behind the wheel with their left wrist handcuffed to the steering wheel. The handlers controlled the timing of the detonation. Timed right, the explosion would cause damage and deaths within 100 feet. The car bomb attacks were scheduled to occur within a five-minute window in different parts of the city. After the Professor prayed with the martyrs, he sent them and their handlers to the rug shop in Charleston under escort of Joseph Green, the man the

Professor had instructed Joel Hankins, the owner of the rug shop, to hire.

Fifteen

After returning from an in-town dinner, Jack and Kathy were watching late news when news of the attack on churches broke. Jack called Frank and asked Kathy to get on the extension. Frank answered his home phone on the third ring. Jack gave him a quick brief, with Kathy adding some details she knew he would want. Frank responded that he was sure the Professor was behind these attacks and that he was just starting. He told them he was heading into the office and asked them to call him in an hour.

By the time Jack and Kathy got Frank on the phone, he had been briefed by his own people and was ready to get down to work. First, he wanted to get the observation post overlooking the rug shop up and running 24/7. If Jack had trouble staffing the OP with vetted people, he would send three people from his office tomorrow. Frank emphasized that burning of the churches was the Professor's work. Much more would be coming. The Professor wasn't taking the risk of personally running operations in America for small stuff. Something much bigger was in the works. Right now their only lead was the rug shop and its owner. Jack said he would call tomorrow with his plan. In his usual style, Frank hung up before Jack could say goodbye. The conversation was over, why waste any time with goodbyes. Jack smiled at Kathy and said, "Are his telephone manners part of CIA protocol."

"No. He's always been that way. I've never been able to figure out where it comes from. It is definitely not part of CIA manners."

Jack said, "Go meet this Lou person and get him to come here now and to bring anyone else that you and he agree would fit in. Offer him whatever he needs, including covering any business losses he might have by coming here. I also think that we can use Kelly. She can make up whatever course work she misses later. This is a good opportunity to get her started. Can you call her and ask her to come in the next few days? She can stay at our house for now."

"Okay, that leaves you alone to man the OP."

"No problem. I've spent hours as a sniper and a cop manning an OP. Just get back as soon as you can."

Sixteen

Kathy called Lou Washington's photo shop in Mount Pleasant. Lou was delighted to hear from her and agreed to a visit the same afternoon. Lou's storefront was in an older mall on the ocean side of Route 17. There was some traffic in the mall, but Kathy had no trouble finding a parking place right in front of the shop.

Lou was waiting for her. "My God, Kathy, you look wonderful. I'll have to watch myself. I could fall in love with you. I'm vulnerable. I just finalized my divorce from my third wife last week."

Kathy hugged him and said, "I don't know whether to congratulate you or give you the 'poor baby' treatment."

"Actually, I could use some of both. Come inside and meet my daughter and tell me what brings you to this dismal place."

One look at the shop window and the dingy interior, and Kathy knew business was not going well. Lou reversed the "Open" sign on the door and led Kathy into the back of the shop. Working at a computer work station was a beautiful black woman Kathy judged to be in her middle twenties. Lou said, "Storm, I want you to meet Kathy, an old and good friend. Kathy, Storm is my daughter from my second wife and my only daughter. You can see she gets her looks from her mother."

"Dad, come on. Praise my skill in keeping us afloat, if you need to say nice things. Kathy, as you can see, our photo shop is not making us rich."

"Hey, Storm, she just got here. Let's give her a cup of coffee before we share our business plan."

"Plan! What plan? Never mind. Kathy, can I get you a cup of coffee? The best thing we do here is to make our own blend of coffee. My dad is a coffee fanatic."

"Sure, if it's that good, let's have it black."

"Kathy, from your body language, you don't have a lot of time. Your trademark impatience is showing through."

Lou cleared a space on the work table and pulled up a chair for Kathy.

"I guess I'm obvious. I never could wait very well."

She could hear Storm making coffee and whispered, "Can we talk in front of Storm?"

"Yeah. She never tells anyone anything. She knows what I did for the FBI. Her specialty is hacking. She's very good and, if the truth be known, her hacking ability keeps the shop door open."

Storm returned with three steaming cups of black coffee in English china cups. Kathy said, "Wow, not only is the coffee great but I expected stained shop style mugs."

"Not here. Dad may brew the coffee but I supply the cups. I love the thin edge of good English cups. Some of these cups cost more than a number of our cheaper cameras. Dad, this has all the look of a serious meeting, and I don't think it involves romance. Do you want me to go for a walk?"

Lou said, "No. I want you to stay and speak up when you have something to say. Okay, Kathy, you have the floor."

"My significant other runs a small team of counter terrorists. Lou, you remember Anita Marino. She was one of the team. She was killed last year in a firefight in an Asian country. I tell you that because there is and will be risk involved. The money is exceptional. For example, you each would get something around $250,000, plus expenses. Jack will also cover any business losses incurred. In fact, if he believes your business would be useful, he may offer to buy it from you. There will be no contracts, and you can opt out or be fired at any time. There are no second chances when it comes to carelessness or security lapses."

Storm asked, "How and when is the money paid?"

"Any way you want it. Standard practice is half up front, the rest monthly."

Lou looked at Storm and asked, "Okay, daughter, what do you think?"

"Dad, there's not much future here. If we can get our investment out, let's go for it. I'm bored and ready to take some chances to make some money. I don't want to be sitting here five years from now."

Lou reached over, took Kathy's hand and said, "We're ready. What's next?"

"Close this place up and follow me to Charleston. I'll put you up in a hotel for the first couple of weeks and then see if you need more permanent quarters. I want you downtown because the trip out here takes too much time. Are you buying or renting a place now?"

Lou said, "Renting."

"Then keep it for now, until we see what develops. Now go pack a few bags. Be ready to go to Charleston in an hour. If you both have wheels, bring them for now. Give me a cell number, and I'll tell you what hotel I've arranged. After you're checked in, call me and I'll set up a meeting with Jack."

When the door closed, Storm said, "Is she always like this? I like her style."

"Daughter, the woman is a warrior with no give and not too much of a sense of humor. But, you can trust her with your life. I know."

Before Lou opened the door to his apartment, Kathy called and told him to check into the Marriott Courtyard Charleston, 125 Calhoun Street. She had reserved two suites in her name. Kathy made the call as she was crossing the bridge into Charleston. She knew Jack would be in the OP. Once Jack said okay, she would pick Lou and Storm up and bring them to the OP. Meanwhile she would have time to brief Jack.

Seventeen

The hours passed slowly as they always did in a static stakeout. Jack finished his thermos of coffee, made a trip to the head and resettled behind the "scope" watching the rug shop. A single white male in his twenties stepped up on the porch and went to the rug shop. Well, at least something was happening. Ten minutes later the same man came out of the shop, posed momentarily for good photos as Jack clicked away, and then walked west on Market Street.

Before he was out of sight, Jack saw the garage doors behind the shop open up. Focusing on the open doors, Jack waited, camera ready. His patience was rewarded as he saw two cars ease down the alley way and nose into the open garages. The doors closed immediately, and he was cut out from any more views of the cars or their passengers. He noted the license numbers as they pulled into the garage, even though he was sure the photo surveillance caught both plates. Both cars were older models. One was a blue Mercury sedan, the other a gray Honda van. It looked as if there was one passenger in each front seat. The passengers might have been females, judging from their size and clothing. Jack was checking the digital images when Kathy used her key to open the door.

"First, gimme a hug! I just recruited Lou and his hacker daughter to join us."

"And what else?"

"They will be in the downtown Marriott in an hour and will call us from there. I think we should bring them both here and brief them on the OP rules you will make up as you talk to them. They are hurting financially and want the work. I believe his daughter, Storm, is also a little bored working in camera shop. Oh, there is another rule. Jack Brandon is only allowed occasional random glances at Miss Storm. She is unattached, quite beautiful and very intelligent. She is quick and probably has good street smarts, as well as hacking skills. I like her. But, remember, touching is not allowed without my express permission and that will never happen."

"Anything I shouldn't say?"

"I didn't tell them about our contact with Frank. I wouldn't use any names or organizations. Just let them know we take direction from the good guys. Now, what can you tell me?"

"Just before you came in, we had some action across the street. Two cars came down the alley and pulled into the double garage attached to the rug shop. I'm not a hundred percent certain but I believe five people, including two females were in the cars."

"My God! Jack, they must be getting ready to set off a couple of car bombs soon."

"Yeah, I thought that was the most likely option, especially with the two females. And those two cars are the only ones we have ever seen going into the garage. Hankins leaves his van on the street."

"This must be almost a done operation. The cars wouldn't be here unless they were loaded with explosives. The females will be the drivers and martyrs. The men will handle all operation details and get the women ready. Most likely the cars will be detonated by remote signal. At least that is the M.O. al Qaeda has used in the past. We have very little time."

"I'm going to call Frank now."

When the call was answered, Jack was put through to Frank. After bringing Frank up to date, he said, "I'm sure you and Kathy are right. The logistics have been completed. They will want a daytime attack to kill the most people. They will move tomorrow. We have very little time. We cannot let the car bomb attack succeed, and we cannot tip off the Professor. Your thoughts?"

Jack said, "I'll call you back within the hour."

Eighteen

Joel Hankins was visibly irritated when a young male customer entered the shop. Single young men were not rug buyers, and he didn't feel like dealing with a walk-in who may want to just look around. Joe Green didn't give Joel a chance to brush him off.

"My name is Joseph Green and you know who sent me. We have work to do right now. Open the garage doors. I have two cars to move inside immediately. We can talk later. I'll be with the cars in the alley in less than five minutes." Before Joel could ask him anything, his new employee was out the door.

Joel was in the garage when the cars pulled in. He was astonished to see two young girls get out of the cars. He was ready to host five people but never thought two of them would be females. With the limited space of his living quarters, he wouldn't be able to avoid them. The sound of their voices, their smells and all the female characteristics would be on open display. He loved hunting them but couldn't stand being around females, especially young girls. Maybe he could stay downstairs in the shop. Still stunned by their presence, he led his visitors into the shop and upstairs. The limited baggage was stacked in a corner. Joel showed them the bath, the kitchen with supplies for meals and the TV. Joe Green asked him what was wrong. Joel realized he was repeating himself and his confusion must be apparent. He took Joe by the arm and said, "Come down to the shop with me."

Downstairs Joe said, "What's wrong? You had plenty of notice, and it looks like you have the necessary stuff to house them for a few days."

"It's not that. I wasn't expecting any females, and my quarters have no privacy."

Joe looked at him, laughed and said, "That's no problem. The girls have their minds on other things than privacy and comfort. They, too, are warriors for Allah. Forget about them. They, along with their escorts, will all be gone in a day or two. Anything else?"

"Yes, why are they here? This is my shop and I want to know what the risks are."

"That attitude and talk could get you killed. I don't know the details, and if you ask the men upstairs, they'll kill you without a second thought. Now show the girls the food stores and anything else they will need to get a meal ready. We are all hungry."

Joe Green paused, thought for a moment, and said, "For your own protection, do not argue with the two men. They are Palestinians as are the girls and, to begin with, they don't like you or our country. So do what they ask without question. They are with the man from Herat, and he does not want any questions. I think he told you that when he was here."

Nineteen

Jack looked around the room strewn with cardboard boxes. An overflowing box of fast food wrappers filled one corner. The only organized, clean area was where the optical surveillance equipment was set up. He said, "Kathy, I hope your mind isn't as cluttered as this pig sty. We need to come up with a plan. It's damn clear we can't let those car bombs be set off tomorrow in downtown Charleston. That's the first priority. The second is to stop them and not spook the Professor. I believe we must destroy the bombs where they are and then be prepared to follow a bomber. At least one of them will be reporting to the Professor. If we fail, we lose our only link to the Professor. It will take some air assets. When we can get a plan together, I'll call Frank to arrange for the resources to trail the bombers when they leave Charleston."

Kathy said, "Okay, I agree that's the strategy, but we'll have to destroy the cars where they are with a fire. The explosives in those cars will probably burn. I doubt they will explode. If they do, better in their garage than in a populated area of Charleston. And I don't want Hankins to get away."

Jack said, "We need some immediate help. Call the hotel and get Lou to come now. Give him directions to park in the back of our building. When you get off the phone, I'll call Frank and tell him our approach and see if they can handle the surveillance problem."

After making the call to Frank, Jack was studying the garage through the tripod mounted scope, when Kathy said, "Lou and Storm are on the way. I think we can talk about the problem with them. Lou was one of the best B&E guys in the business. He broke into dozens of places and dealt with a bunch of problems. Usually he had to make it look like there had not even been an entry. In this case the fire will cover our tracks. I didn't see any signs of an alarm system when I was in the shop. I doubt there will be one in the garage. But we can count on someone being on guard in or near the garage."

After several hours of planning, they had a plan everyone accepted. Kathy brought in a bag of Big Macs, fries and coffee. It was now eight o'clock. Five hours from the kickoff. Everyone was resting in their own fashion. Responsibilities and communications were clear. Jack and Lou had the actual entry. Kathy volunteered to put a beacon on Hankins' van, parked on the street almost in front of the rug shop. Storm was left to monitor activities from the OP.

If all lights in the upstairs section of the shop were off, 1:00 AM was the start. Limited-range, hand-held, two-way radios were the choice. Jack didn't want cell phone activity in the area of the shop before the fire started. Cell phones were a start for fire investigators and the police. The explosive bomb residue will kick any fire investigation into high gear.

A few minutes after 1:00 AM, Jack and Lou, wearing black, slipped out the back door carrying some limited equipment and crossed Market Street a block east of the rug shop. From there, they worked their way back to the alley running behind the garage. A narrow trash-cluttered passageway ran between the garage and the next building. Their planned entry point was a window about seven feet above ground level. It looked as if it hadn't been washed for several years. Jack crouched under the window, giving Lou a platform of his back to examine the window.

Lou whispered, "I can't see through the window. I'm going to remove a pane. The caulking is nearly gone. I'll only need a few minutes."

"Do it. I can hold you."

"Reach up with your left hand. I'll hand the pane down to you."

Jack thought this guy is good. I never heard a sound.

An instant later Lou stepped down and said, "I had a good view inside and didn't see any guards. They may do periodic checks. What next?"

"Give me a boost. I'm going to check out the interior with my night vision gear. If I see anyone inside, I'll take them out. No one upstairs will hear the silenced shot from my .22 High Standard. When I step down, I'll give you a back to spray our two-gallon can of gasoline on the cars inside. Our hand pump sprayer should reach both cars. It should not leave any acceleration track for the investigators. Make sure you leave a trail of gas near enough to the window for a burning wad of newspaper to set off the fire."

"What were you, a cop or an arsonist?"

"You'd be surprised what cops learn about the dark side."

Sixty seconds later, Jack stepped to the ground and said, "No one inside. Your turn."

Lou sprayed the two gallons of gas inside the garage, making sure to douse both cars and the entryway to the shop. He stepped off Jack's back and said, "Just drop the burning newspaper inside the window. The gas trail starts there."

"Okay. You take all our stuff and move now. When I drop it, I'll move fast. The gas vapor may have filled the garage and give us an almost an instantaneous explosion. The shortest path for me is to go immediately behind the building at our back. I'll meet you at the end of the alley. Then we'll split up and make our separate ways to the OP. Okay."

"I'm gone."

Jack gave Lou 20 seconds, quietly broke the glass pane Lou removed, lit the newspaper torch and shielding the small flame with his body, dropped it in the window. By the time he took three steps behind the adjacent two-story abandoned brick building, he heard a soft woomp and the darkness vanished as the fire shot out the window behind him. By the time he joined Lou halfway down the alley, the fire was engulfing the entire building.

Twenty

Inside, Joel felt the building shaking slightly. He then smelled smoke and shouted, "Up! Everyone up! The damn building's on fire!! Down the stairs! It's the only way out!" Without checking behind him, Joel grabbed his notebook and ran down the stairs. The flames closed behind him, and he heard the shrill shrieks of the girls. As he reached the outside shop door, something crashed into him from behind. It was the flaming, screaming body of Joe Green thrashing on the floor. When Joel opened the front door, the draft of fresh air fueled the fire into an inferno and he knew no one else would make it out. Behind him in the short hallway, he could see Green's still-thrashing body burning.

Joel ran to his car. Now he had to get out of Charleston. The fire inspcctors would discover the residue of the car bombs and he would have no explanation. My rug inventory is gone. I can't collect any insurance and my bank account will be off limits before I can get to it. The first thing in the morning, I have to get to my safety deposit box in Georgetown to pick up my survival money and a new identity. Thank God, I followed my training and planned for an escape. Certainly by tomorrow afternoon, the cops will be hunting for me. I’m really leery about trying to use my recontact instructions.

Twenty-one

From the OP, Kathy and Storm saw the fire blossom and a minute later watched Joel Hankins run out the shop door and drive away in his van. Kathy, turning to Storm said, "I just got back from putting our tracker beacon on his car. Now we can track that murderous bastard." Using the secure cell Frank had given them, she called him and said, "The rug shop killer is on the move in his car. Tracker beacon is in place. Everyone else in the rug shop must be dead. I can hear the sirens coming. We are all okay here."

As Kathy hung up, she heard Jack knock on the door. Storm opened the door and looked startled when she didn't see Lou. Jack said, "Don't worry, he is only a minute or so behind me."

Kathy ran over and gave Jack a hug with tears of relief running down her cheeks. She wiped her eyes and said, "I've called Frank, and he has his airborne tracker up and searching for Hankins' van. It shouldn't be a problem. I think we need to get Lou and Storm out of here. Our cover story for being here and not calling in the fire is marginal at best."

"Okay, send them back to the hotel. We'll contact them tomorrow. After our neighborly curiosity is satisfied, we can also head home. Tomorrow we'll find out what we can about the fire investigation and go from there. If we are very lucky, the bomb residue may not be too apparent, and it will be classified as an accidental fire of unknown origins. A burned down rug shop won't incite a first class investigation even with the five bodies, unless they are identified and have suspicious records."

"Frank won't want this fire linked to a failed terrorist attempt. He'll be thinking maybe the Professor will buy that the fire was caused by a faulty bomb mix. No one can tell the Professor differently. Our sick serial killer won't know and the others died in the fire. We still may be able to use our rug merchant to find the Professor. I think he will stay in his comfort zone along the southeast coast. He must have some way of contacting al Qaeda. Maybe through a personal ad in a local paper."

"Call Kelly and tell her there is no longer an emergency but to come anyway. I believe the Professor had more of a reason for beginning his terror campaign in Charleston than the fact he had a rug shop safe house in town. If he continues here, we have to be ready for him and right now our team is ragged. We need to get it together. Maybe we should keep this OP location, even if our former target is now burning to the ground."

Kathy said, "I agree the Professor will keep his focus here. I think he has more than a safe house in the area. He must have at least ten people working with him and a lot of past homework. We might as well keep this place. Lou and Storm can set up here, maybe with a camera shop cover."

Twenty-two

Joel was keeping within the speed limit, even though he desperately wanted to get north of Georgetown on Route 17 before the State Police would be looking for his car. Once there he could decide where it would be safest to stop for the night. He had some minor burns on his neck and arms that hurt like hell. Joel had no feeling for the people who died in the fire. Just the feeling that he had lost his capital and the hard work he put in to build his business. Thank God, he had saved the images of the young girls in their moment of death. Those couldn't be replaced. Each one was unique.

He had enough of al Qaeda. If all they could do was destroy his business in a failed bombing attempt, he was done with them. Take their money and disappear. He didn't care if he ever touched another rug. He would find another way to support himself and his real work of hunting and killing young women. His research was much more fulfilling than selling rugs and acting as a boarding house keeper for occasional terrorists. Let the man from Herat try to find him.

When Joel's van parked in the rundown Vision Motel in Surfside, the CIA helicopter that had tracked him from his rug shop in Charleston reported his position, and a ground surveillance team vectored into the location took up position around the motel. Frank had instructed the team to maintain discreet surveillance but do not lose the target.

The next morning Joel drove over to the Citizen's Bank of Surfside. After going through the identification procedures, he emptied his safety deposit box of two different identity packages and $100,000. Now he was equipped to disappear. Using his new identity as Robert Huxley, he bought a five-year-old gray Ford Explorer in good condition with 40,000 miles. It was a cash deal in a small used car lot that was hurting for business. No questions were asked, and he drove off with dubious temporary plates.

His old blue van was parked two blocks from the used car lot. Getting rid of it would not be a problem. Parking the van in a nearby strip mall with the keys in the ignition and no plates would attract some of the clientele hanging around the cut rate shops. Pulling up several slots away from the van, Huxley AKA Hankins removed the van's plates, took his reserve of stolen plates from under the back floor mat, and drove off in his Ford Explorer. The temporary plates would last 30 days.

When Joel's car was out of sight, one of the three surveillance cars pulled into the mall and parked beside Hankins' abandoned car and removed the tracking beacon. Frank instructed his surveillance team to remove the beacon Kathy had placed behind the grill and not to install it on another car. The Professor was far too street smart. He'd check Hankins' car for beacons at the first opportunity.

Twenty-three

The early edition of the Charleston newspapers and TV news carried the story of the fire on Market Street. There was very little information for the Professor to analyze. The fire burned the rug shop to the ground. Five badly burned bodies were found, three males and two females. No identifications were being released yet. The article reported that the hulks of two cars were found in the garage. It is not known if the shop owner, a Mr. Joel Hankins, is one of the bodies. The car registered to the shop owner has not been located. The cause of the fire is yet unknown. Charleston fire department forensics personnel are still investigating.

The Professor put his plans for further violence on hold until he had time to decide if his operation was in some way compromised. If no one reported back to him, he would assume that the shop owner escaped and the people he sent to Charleston to carry out the car bombing all died in the fire. For now, he would wait for the rug merchant's personal ad to appear and see if the Charleston authorities discovered the residue of explosives in the burned cars. No matter what, his plan to spread terror and chaos in the Charleston area would continue. Joel Hankins was not an important part of his plan. But, if he did not use his contact procedures, the Professor would conclude he was now a liability and send someone to find and kill him.

Frank, at the Counter Terrorism Center (CTC), decided that it would be impossible to control the investigation of the fire. The explosive residue in the cars would surely be revealed, but he doubted arson would be suspected. Most likely the evidence would point to faulty mixing or storing of the explosive since there was no explosion. For now he was going forward with tracking Joel Hankins and hoping a lead to the Professor would emerge from observing Hankins. He knew Jack Brandon was strengthening his team and could follow up on any action required in the Charleston area. Thank God, Jack's team had uncovered and destroyed the car bombing plot.

Kathy met Kelly Marino's flight from Pittsburgh and used the drive back to their house to bring her up to date. Kelly said, "Now I see why you pay such big salaries. I guess I'll have to earn mine. I'm ready to get started. I can keep up with my studies with the University's online program. I hope there is a place I can continue with my Hapkido training. I really like it and seem to have an aptitude for the moves. I remember Jack telling me to concentrate on the movement of the feet. Boy, was he ever right. Some of the higher belts haven't figured that out yet. I'm getting ready to test for my blue belt in the next month."

When Kathy pulled the SRX into the driveway, she saw that Storm and Lou Washington were already there. She gave Kelly a short rundown on the father and daughter on the way to the deck where Jack was waiting to begin a planning session.

After introductions, he briefed them on the fire scene, "Shadow and I walked along Market Street past the burned rug shop. There were a few firemen and police officers at the scene and yellow tape everywhere. We stopped and one of the firemen came over. I think he wanted to see Shadow. Not many Bouviers walking around in downtown Charleston. He asked so many questions about Shadow that I felt free to ask him about the fire. So far they haven't determined the cause. Arson hasn't been ruled out. The building was burned so completely that the investigation is very slow. The five bodies all appear to have been killed by smoke inhalation and burned beyond recognition. There were no smoke alarms, and it looks as if the people were surprised and waited too long to get down the only exit from the second floor.

"After the fireman walked away, Shadow nudged my leg and gave a low growl. I think he was remembering the attack on my father's house that killed my father, his two friends and house staff, and burned the house down. Shadow was badly wounded in the fight but managed to kill one of the attackers. Still, his reaction to the fireman was out of character for him. He's usually good with people and very laid back."

At that time the Minhs came out with a heaping tray of sandwiches, sweet tea and soft drinks. When everyone had settled down, Jack said, "Counting Shadow and the Minhs, we are a group of eight, a small group with a big job. We don't sign secrecy agreements and have no legal penalties for leaking information. But there are always consequences. I do not give second chances for carelessness, stupid risk taking or not following orders.

Most times you will have an opportunity to voice your reservations and offer changes to plans. I want that. But, so much is at stake, including our lives, that there is no room for tentative actions or varying independently from the plan. You can count on having some kind of communications in every operation, so no need for acting without informing. Even with everyone doing their best, bad things can happen. On our last foreign venture, Kelly's mother, a true and highly trained, dedicated warrior, was killed saving my life. All of our operations are based on the volunteer principle. Before I go any further does anyone have questions or want out? Now is the time."

Kelly said, "I'm a newbie but count me in. In the short time I have been a member of this group, everything they told me they would do, has been done."

Storm spoke up, "My dad tells me I can trust you people. That's enough for me. But, I would like to know a little about what you expect from me when we leave your house."

"Fair enough. Tomorrow morning I want you and Lou to get a couple of bikes. Your job is to infiltrate biker groups, especially those with a radical Muslim ideology, and try to get a lead on the bikers that torched religious buildings in Charleston last week. If we can identify one of them, we'll have a chance of finding the Professor and ending his terror plots.

"The bikers may be hired help. They could attract attention by spending too much money. Work the areas where biker organizations exist within 200 hundred miles of Charleston. Kathy will give you money for expenses. Don't be too careful about letting people know you are not hurting for money. Come up with your own cover scheme. Again, Kathy will support you with some flash documentation. Use cash. No credit cards. This house will be manned 24/7 until we get some leads. Use your new cells and leave messages on the house phone, at least once a day. Don't hesitate to leave small bits of information that may seem unimportant.

"Kathy and Kelly will concentrate on Joel Hankins, the rug shop guy and serial killer. He must have a way to get in touch with the Professor or his people. We now know where he is and can track his car. Remember, this guy is a monster. He has killed a number of young girls. Our job is not to bring him in or stop him if it means alerting the Professor to be even more careful. In this case national security trumps criminal cases, no matter how heinous. Kathy has some good contacts in the world of national security and will use them to help us. Okay, let's finish up the food and everyone get a good night's sleep. Kelly will bunk here for the time being."

After Kelly left to go to her room, Kathy put her arms around Jack and said, "Well done. I knew there was some reason beyond your money and good looks that make me want to crawl in bed with you. Before I seduce you, I need to tell you I'm worried."

"What could be worrying you?"

"Your dog. That's what. I was almost shaking when you were telling us about Shadow's reaction at the fire site. That dog has never, never been wrong. I trust his instincts more than my own. He gave your father warning when Yuri's team attacked his house. He killed one of the attackers, he warned us of a bomb in your old Pittsburgh house, and he played a big role in saving us from the gunman in the same house the next day.

"We have evidence that Yuri's attack team came from Charleston to kill your father. We know Yuri's cells were often made up of family members. It's probable that the Pittsburgh gunman came from the same family in Charleston. And now some fireman at a Charleston fire site asks a number of questions about Shadow, and Shadow's reactions to him were definitely hostile. The easiest way for that family or cell members to find you is to look for a Brandon who owns a big black Bouvier. Now I know that is all probable and stretches of logic, but I trust that dog. One more thing, I suppose that you gave the fireman your name if he introduced himself."

"Yeah, I did. Your thesis is a bit farfetched, but we have to act on it. The risk of ignoring your analysis is too great. I'll brief the Minhs right away. They'll know a few people from their days in Vietnam who can help us. By tomorrow noon our security will be improved. I have a weakness for trusting people in uniform for what they represent. I need to crank up my suspicion level. I hope you're wrong but you have my attention."

"Okay, now that we've solved that issue, let's go play the mating game." One of the many things Kathy loved about Jack was his interest in giving pleasure to her. In their lovemaking Jack had learned she didn't like prolonged foreplay or teasing. She liked her sex uncomplicated. Hard and fast. Taking his hand, she led him back to the master bedroom.

Twenty-four

Formerly Hankins, now Huxley knew he wasn't going back into the rug business. The man from Herat could find him in a week or less if he did. No, his new business had to be very different. And it had to be in his hunting area. He knew this coastal area from Mount Pleasant north to Myrtle Beach. Before he had driven five miles north on Route 17, he decided to make a U turn and go south to Georgetown, a perfect place for many blue collar service jobs and an area he could hunt from.

Georgetown was perfect. Robert Huxley would be a house interior painter. He knew paints from his high school jobs and working with Oriental rugs gave him a sense of color coordination. Almost no start-up costs. Just a one-man business operated out of a small rundown garage or warehouse. His Ford Explorer could be his work vehicle. The roof rack could carry all the ladders he would need. No paid advertising, just word of mouth and maybe some hand-delivered flyers in mail boxes. People would hire him because he was low cost, neat and showed up on the job as promised.

His good-for-nothing dad did make him develop a work ethic, and he learned the value of keeping your word and showing up to do good work, especially the finishing. All that was necessary was to put up a good front.

While he drove, Huxley worked on his new identity, oblivious to the two surveillance cars a quarter-mile behind him. As surveillance jobs go, Huxley was easy. He showed no signs of being conscious of anyone following him. His sudden U turn did make his followers back off a little farther. Once he stopped and got out of the car, it would be different, small town foot surveillance is difficult. Strangers do not blend in easily.

Maybe, just maybe, he could go hunting in the next few days.

Twenty-five

Jim Beasley, the fireman Jack and Shadow met at the fire site, couldn't believe his luck. The man they had just missed killing in Pittsburgh was in Charleston with his damn dog. They weren't able to get many details about his brother's death, but they did know the dog had saved Brandon and his wife. What the hell were they doing in Charleston, especially at the fire site? When he got home, he would call for a family conference. Brandon would soon learn that the ways of the South were not dead yet. Revenge for killing family members called for, no, demanded revenge. No mistakes this time. Brandon was on Beasley turf. His older brother, Jake, was a former cop who was now selling real estate. He could find out where Brandon and his dog were staying. Damn, he would soon be a family hero! God is good, an eye for an eye. That's the Bible's way.

Twenty-six

Kathy told Lou to keep their hotel rooms for now. On their way back to Mount Pleasant, Storm said to her father, “Well, are we living high on the hog or what? Our new employer either has real money or he doesn’t care about it.”

Lou replied, “Yeah. I think both. He has money and doesn’t mind his people going first class. But, don’t take that for softness. I was with him when we fired the garage. He is one cool and deadly guy. Kathy told me he had killed a knife fighter with a single blow to the chest. That’s how he got the scar on his upper left arm. I know something about street fighting but Jack is a trained killer. All I know about Hapkido is that it is a Korean martial art and a very deadly skill. When it comes to killing, the Koreans are serious. Kathy said Jack was trained by the best. She’s also had some Hapkido training. Did you also see that they are never without a weapon on them or within reach? No mistake, we are with some very serious people. Three of them went on a mission last year. Two came back. What we’re doing with them is very dangerous. On the plus side, they are very good people and won’t expect us to take any risks they wouldn’t take.”

"I agree, but there is another thing. The pay is very good. In six months, I will be out of debt. I'll risk my ass under those conditions."

"Okay, daughter, but stay very focused. Jack said to pick up a couple of bikes. We'll use my bike. I know what it will do and it's comfortable for two people. Some of these bikers will be hard. I'd like for us to stay together. Bikes can get separated all too easily. Besides I'm proud of my bike. I've kept it in good condition and for a thirty-year-old Harley, it does okay."

Storm said, "If we are going to be showing money around, we need to get some newer biker clothes. I also assume we'll be carrying."

"You got that right! We'll take those two 9mm Brownings I got from my dad. You've fired them several times. I think you're pretty good. They're untraceable and we have permits. Problem is they don't match the fake IDs we'll be getting from Kathy."

Lou asked, "What do you think of our assignment? Any ideas about approaches?"

"Yes, when we get set up in a motel or wherever, I'll get working on collecting info on local bike clubs and do some discreet hacking into police files and suspect clubs. If radical Muslims are behind this violence, then there has to be some connection with a Mosque or Muslim organization. We can hit the local biker hangouts from Myrtle Beach to Columbia, maybe Atlanta. I can pose as your lover. No father would be parading his daughter around in some of the places we'll be going."

"Okay! But, how about the other question I asked? About how you feel about our job?"

"First off, we need the money. I'm tired of dreading picking up our mail and answering bill collection calls. We need to do better. This is a chance to get a stake. That's the upside. Downside is that I'm scared. These are nice people, and they're treating us very well. I even like them, but make no mistake, these are hard people with little or no give. I have never killed anyone or even come close. I don't think Jack or Kathy lose any sleep over killing. My God, there were six people in that building. Five of them burned to death. I know you helped set the fire but how do you handle what you did?"

"I've been involved a few times in the past with operations that resulted in people getting killed. Killing marks everyone. I don't care how cool they seem. It stays with them. I'm sure Jack and Kathy handle it by knowing they did the right thing. Wouldn't it be worse if we had let the car bombs go off in downtown Charleston? How many innocent people could've been killed and/or maimed for life? Where is the moral certitude?

"A very senior citizen who served in Vietnam as a civilian contractor told me a story that helped me understand personal responsibilities. He said that he was in direct control of a few Vietnamese hunter/killer teams that patrolled the jungles within rocket range of major cities. A subordinate had given rules of engagement instructions to one team that prevented them from firing on groups carrying 122 millimeter rockets within launching range of civilian targets, if women and children were part of the group. He told me that he countered that order because the people carrying those missiles had some choice, however slight, not to follow Viet Cong orders. The innocent civilians sleeping in their homes had no choice when death from the skies fell on them. Where is the morally right decision? In my mind, our responsibility is to protect the innocent. That's what we did in starting the fire in the garage hiding two car bombs.

"Remember we may get into a situation where I'll expect you to cover my back. If you feel you can't do that, please tell me now."

"I think ..."

"Not good enough. You can't think. In an emergency, action moves too fast for you to think. You must react. There's no time for thinking, analyzing or reflecting. When going into action, leave the thinking behind. Just react. Shoot and we'll sort it out later. In the meantime we will both be alive. Don't try to wound or disable the shooters. Aim for the body mass and shoot, just the way we did at the range. "

"I can protect your back but help me to get ready. I just don't have your instincts. I don't see all the variations you see all the time. Our heads are different."

"Seeing the threats and possible fighting moves will come to you with a bit of experience. Some people never get it. You will! Being constantly ready, knowing what's going down and what your role is will guide your actions without any mental hesitations. Now let's get our bike out and serviced and get ourselves packed. I think we'll also visit the range before we start out."

Twenty-seven

After the one day meeting with the other members of the team in Charleston, Kelly was told to go back to Pitt and make arrangements for an extended absence. Three days later she was on her way back.

Kathy parked in the short-term parking at Charleston Airport and took up a position at the baggage carousel. She had been there ten minutes watching the approach to the baggage area. Kelly's flight landed some 15 minutes ago, according to the overhead monitor. Kathy was beginning to think maybe Kelly missed her flight, when she noticed a well-dressed young woman approaching her.

Kelly smiled and said, "What's the matter? Don't you recognize me?"

Kathy laughed and hugged Kelly. "Aren't you suited and booted? You didn't have a wardrobe like that the last time I saw you. You look wonderful. Anita would approve. I know I do. Can't have you looking like that around Jack. I know he really liked your mother and, if anything, you are even more beautiful. I'm suddenly motivated to go shopping."

"I'll join you. All I have is this carry-on. My other stuff wasn't worth hauling around. It is really great to be earning enough money that I can buy a few things without getting a headache about the cost."

On the trip back to Johns Island, Kathy briefed Kelly on the car bomb event and the need to keep track of the one person who escaped the fire. Jack wanted them to pick up watching Hankins as soon as they were told where he settled. She would have a few days to get ready for her first assignment.

Kathy told Kelly that Jack asked her to check out her shooting and Hapkido skills first thing tomorrow morning and to give her some basic tips on surveillance and tradecraft. "This briefing is the beginning of your training. You must remember what I've told you. After a few days, I'll expect intelligent questions and comments."

Kelly said, "Great, it's about time I start living up to my Marino heritage."

While chatting with Kelly on the way home, Kathy thought this is more than awesome. Here I am talking with Anita's daughter just like I used to talk with her. I'm only about seven years older than she, but I feel like I'm her mother. You can believe I'm going to watch over her. Don't worry, Anita, I have her back. I more than owe you for saving Jack's life. Kelly is a great kid. She looks so much like you that I almost called her Anita. You can be proud of her. She turned out well. If I ever have a daughter, I hope she can be like Kelly.

As a special treat, Kathy and Shadow brought Kelly coffee in bed on her first morning in the Brandon house. Kathy said, "Just so you know, this is a one-time event. Although Shadow may come in to say good morning, he does not served fresh brewed French roast. Also for you

Pittsburgh people, this is a very old South Asia custom, to serve bed tea or coffee to honored guests. Now you have one hour to have breakfast before we head to the shooting range Jack and I have been using."

"Okay. I'll be ready. But, tell me, why do you and Jack still practice at the range? I thought you both were already very good."

"Very good is not good enough. We are better than very good, Jack especially. To stay sharp you need regular practice and the weapon needs to be constantly checked for small deviations in performance. Most of the time, the deviations are the operator's fault.

"After the shooting session, I'll checkout your Hapkido progress. This afternoon we'll do some surveillance training. Consider this as a fast forward boot camp. Do not ask questions during the exercises. Just listen. You can ask questions later when we go over your performance. You now have 55 minutes to get ready. Time to roll. Let's go, girl!"

Kathy left but Shadow stayed with Kelly, who asked, "Is she always like that. I guess the honeymoon is over."

Shadow put his big front paws gently on the bed and wagged his stubby tail while Kelly sipped her coffee and rubbed his head. The bond between the two was instant. Jack told her Shadow, in some way, knew she was a friend because of Anita. He couldn't explain it other than to tell her dogs were a lot smarter than people believed. If you are open to them, you will learn that they can communicate.

After a breakfast of soft poached eggs on toasted raisin bread, grits, smoked sausage and two more cups of coffee, Kelly thought maybe the honeymoon wasn't quite over. The Minhs were excellent cooks. In the car on the way to the shooting range, Kathy told her that the Minhs were warriors and their primary role was to protect the Brandon house. Two friends of Jack's father who were also his house staff were killed when a terrorist cell from Charleston attacked and burned the Brandon house in Virginia. Shadow was badly wounded in the attack, but sounded the alarm and killed the man who shot him. Don't judge the Minhs by their appearance. They are old but still formidable fighters with experience in fire fights.

Before leaving the house, Kathy picked up a High Standard .22 with a six-inch barrel and a .357 revolver Dan Wesson model with a six-inch barrel. The .22 to check Kelly's form and accuracy and the .357 Magnum to test her skill with a heavy caliber high recoil weapon. Both weapons, among an assortment of others, were in the oversized gun cabinet in the Brandon house.

Kathy started with the man-sized paper target at a 15-foot distance. She checked Kelly's grip and form and made a few small adjustments. She told Kelly to fire the entire magazine into the chest area with a tight grouping.

Kelly put all her shots into a six-inch grouping in the left side of the chest area. Kathy said, "Not bad. I see you have your mother's genes. She was very good with a handgun and outstanding with a rifle."

Moving the target silhouette to thirty feet, Kathy told Kelly to reload and to focus on head shots, using the same steady firing rate she used at the 15-foot range. All but two of the rounds were in the head.

Kathy commented, "Very good. It seemed to me that you missed your first and next to last shots. The first miss was because of an improper setup to begin. Your weight was a little too much on your back foot. The second miss looked to me that you had lost focus momentarily. Let's try that again at 35 feet. Same drill. Concentrate. In this case there is only one target."

This time Kelly put all 10 rounds into the target's head. Kathy said, "Not only good. But very good. That was excellent shooting. Jack will be pleased. Now let's move up to the big stuff. Don't think that the .22 High Standard is not a very effective and deadly weapon, especially when loaded with .22 long rifle hollow points. It can also be fitted with an effective sound suppression system."

For the .357 Magnum, Kathy moved the new target back to the 15-foot range. Kathy watched carefully as Kelly loaded the heavy revolver and brought it up to her firing position. The revolver was near the top of the line for recoil. Indoor shooting with this weapon required good ear protection. Unfortunately, when you had to use it in a real situation, especially inside, ear protection was not standard practice. Using a slow cadence, Kelly put all six shots in a 14-inch circle. Using rapid fire, two of the six missed the target.

Kathy said, "Not bad! The .357 Magnum revolvers are not made for beginning shooters to score well. Practice is necessary. Now that we have tried both ends of the recoil scale, try my .45 caliber SOCOM. It manages the recoil better and has a 12-round magazine. I noticed that our hands are about the same size. This weapon should feel good in your hands. As you can see, a sound suppressor can be easily attached. Give it a try. Fire the entire magazine, and then insert the second magazine and continue firing. The target will be at 30 feet. Fire when ready."

After firing the .357 revolver, the .45 automatic seemed easy to control. Kelly fired two magazines and put all her shots in the chest and head of the silhouette. Kelly cleared her weapon, turned toward Kathy and said, "I love that gun. It felt like an extension of my arm. I didn't fight the recoil."

"We have one more in our cabinet. You can have it. I want you to get a concealed weapon permit. The man who runs the range will help you with the applications and requirements. Use our address. The house is in my name. Let's get some lunch and after that we'll run a surveillance exercise."

Twenty-eight

The Minhs reacted quickly to Jack's request for some additional help to guard the house. They called upon some of their old comrades who had served under Minh in the Quang Tri Provincial Reconnaissance Unit (PRU) that was run by the CIA during the Vietnam War. The two men who arrived the next day were skilled landscapers.

No one would suspect that these elderly landscapers were clearing lines of fire, laying out distance markers, installing remote cameras, motion detectors and manual switches for perimeter lighting. They also put in a pergola and plantings that blocked line of sight for long-distance rifle shots, especially at night. Inside, Jack and the Minhs positioned weapons and ammunition at strategic locations. Jack wasn't sure there would ever be an attack, but he was taking Shadow's and Kathy's warning seriously.

If an attack happened or seemed likely, his plan was to slip on his old ghillie suit or black clothing and take out the attackers in the marsh grass that bordered the property. This time the only surprise was for the attackers. There would be no law and no quarter.

Jack, Kathy and Kelly were sitting around the breakfast table savoring the last of the morning coffee. Kathy was telling Jack about Kelly's progress. Her

Hapkido needed much more work but her shooting skills were good, and she quickly picked up the procedures and nuances of surveillance operations. Yesterday Kathy picked out targets as they were walking downtown Charleston and told Kelly to trail that person unobserved for one hour and report back to the starting location, prepared to brief her on what she had observed.

After Kelly followed two subjects, Kathy said, "Okay, now let's have an afternoon tea while we talk about your experiences today. First, tell me what you've learned."

"Following someone takes patience and stamina. Being constantly alert and finding a way to blend in, while waiting for your target to move on, is mentally and physically tiring. Several times I felt like I was totally exposed. A couple of bystanders came over when I was standing around and asked me tourist type questions. One guy was hitting on me. Acting normal, while you're focused on an entryway or a subject getting into a car or meeting someone, is difficult. Once I convinced myself I had to go into a clothing shop after my subject. Not a good idea. The shop wasn't crowded, and both the clerk and the target looked over at me. I said I was just browsing and left. From then on I was really careful that the subject didn't see me again. I remembered you telling me the only way a target can spot a surveillant or a team of surveillants is by seeing the same person in two or more locations. In your world, there are no coincidences. My experience in the clothing store made an impression."

"I wanted to start you out on unsuspecting targets before we complicated the exercise. Tomorrow Jack will be our subject. In real life situations, working against someone skilled in street operations, you'd be briefed on the target. Those types are always checking for surveillance. I was checking today while we were walking downtown. Jack is very good at surveillance. I'm better at detecting people trying to follow me. They are different skills. Learning what problems the followers have will help you detect people trying to follow you. Those skills involve discreet actions to make surveillants show themselves, and the really difficult task of losing the people following you, without their knowing you took evasive actions to get away from them."

"Kathy! I had no idea this stuff was so complicated or serious. Will I ever be able to learn it all?"

Kathy laughed and said, "I felt just like that at one time. Like all skills some people are just better surveillants and intelligence officers. I'm not sure everyone can be taught to be exceptional at this skill. I think you're a good student, and I like what I saw today. You see, I was following you the whole time."

"You weren't! I never saw you!"

"You weren't supposed to. I'm glad you told me about your mistake at the clothing store. Not everyone would have. Remember, it's not a matter of looking good but of being good."

Twenty-nine

During dinner Kathy told Jack how well Kelly had done on her first surveillance exercise. Kelly chimed in saying, “The more I think about it, the worse I feel about screwing up.”

Jack said, “Try to keep your thoughts positive. When Kathy says you did okay, you did okay. Think and analyze before and after the action. During the action, don’t think or analyze too much. Just react, you will do better. Fall back on your training. Thinking when in action means you had too little training or you don’t trust your training and instincts. The result is tentative responses that can lead to you or someone on your team getting killed.

“Maybe now is a good time to make sure you know what to do if this house is attacked. I see you are thinking, ‘what’s he saying. Surely I didn’t hear this house might be attacked.’ I hope not but Kathy and I were having dinner at the Ritz Carlton in McLean when my father’s house was attacked. My father was killed along with his house staff. Shadow was seriously wounded. Shadow gave the alarm and my father, his servants and Shadow killed three of the attackers. I really don’t expect the same thing to happen here, but I want to be prepared. You should know that

Kathy believes there is a higher likelihood of an attack than do I."

"You got that right. You didn't expect a bomb or an attack on us in your Pittsburgh house either. Yet it happened."

"Yes, you're right, and that's why I want to bring Kelly up to speed now that she is living here. Let's start with the weapon. I believe Kathy gave you one of our SOCOM .45s. That's good. The weapon will fire nearly the same as the one you fired on the range. After dinner load four magazines, chamber a round and keep it under your pillow. I believe you should make having a loaded weapon handy a rule, as long as there is a real threat. I have, ever since the night my father was killed.

"If an attack happens, your area is to cover the inner hallway outside your room and the windows in your room. Stay away from the windows unless you have to get outside or need to take up a firing position at the window. Don't hesitate to shoot but know that the two Vietnamese landscaper/guards will be outside with me. I don't want us all trapped inside the house.

"The attackers don't want a 911 call response, so they will have to complete their mission in less than five or six minutes. They could plan on using explosives to burn the house with us inside. At the first sign of trouble, Shadow and I'll be outside. We will all have radios and Kathy will call 911 and be in the laundry room/ops center watching the video coverage from our cameras. The Minhs, armed with shotguns, will have primary responsibility for the front and back doors. If we are overrun, go out the back through the pool area to the woods behind the house. Get into a good shooting position and stay put. Move only if you have no other choice."

After the sobering dinner conversation, Kelly did as suggested and put her weapon under her pillow. Extra magazines and the radio went into her cosmetic case. She smiled at the thought of exchanging her beloved lotions for three magazines of .45 cartridges and an iPhone-sized radio. She had never been anywhere close to a firefight and wondered what her mother would do if she were here? God, she hoped she had her mother's warrior genes. After checking out the different routes out of the hallway and the night view from her bedroom windows, she gave in to exhaustion from her day's activities and, with the sound of gently falling rain, dropped off to sleep.

Kelly awoke suddenly, first to the sound of Shadow's barking roar and then to the sound of breaking glass and gunfire from the front of the house. She grabbed her handgun and bag of magazines and leapt off the bed toward the hallway where she dropped to the floor and looked both ways down the hall. From the front door she heard more gunfire and saw a man coming down the hall firing into all the rooms. He was still 20 feet from her room. She rolled on her right side and fired three times into the mass of the attacker. He went down and almost slid into her. Kelly shot him twice more in the head and raced to the front door. Mrs. Minh was on the floor with her husband tending to her, while he kept his shotgun trained on the broken front door. He looked up at Kelly and motioned for her to get to the back of the house. She sprinted to the sliding glass door leading to the pool deck, slipped outside and crouched behind a long three-foot-high cement planter. She hardly noticed the cold falling rain on her bare skin. Putting in a fresh magazine, she heard Kathy calling her on the radio. She gave Kathy her position and a report of what she saw.

Kathy said, "I don't how many there are. Jack and Shadow are hunting outside in the marsh grass. I haven't heard from them. Hold your position. I'm giving you perimeter lights. Stay undercover. The Minhs have the front covered. Her wounds are not life threatening. She's a tough fighter."

"Okay! I have good cover and can hold here. Let me know when help is arriving. I have to get something on. I'm totally naked."

"Never mind. Just stay focused. This isn't over yet. I can't see any movement on my screens."

Jack and Shadow were motionless in the high marsh grass. They were almost invisible. Shadow's wet black coat and Jack's black tee, black baseball hat, and a mud-darkened face and arms reduced their image to a mottled dark spot. Jack called for Kathy to turn on the perimeter lights on the marsh side. The light was no threat to them. It produced faint mottled shadows. The January rain was picking up with a rising wind, masking the sound of moving through the marsh grass and diminishing the effectiveness of his quadrant search for the intruders. Fortunately, he only had to search the area in front of him. Shadow was standing with his attention fixated at a point directly in front of Jack, who was kneeling with his back to the light coming from the house and scanning the marsh with night vision glasses. He knew somewhere in front of him one or more attackers were concealed. He could wait. His experience as a Marine sniper in the beginning of the

Iraqi war guided his every movement and plan. Instead of the heat and dryness of the desert, he had the mosquitoes, mud and wetness of the marsh. All his senses were on high alert.

Shadow was quivering with repressed energy. Jack knew one word from him, and Shadow would be on the attackers and would probably be killed if there were more than one. He heard Kathy and Kelly on the radio and felt they could control the house. Kelly must have some Celtic blood to go into battle naked. The two Vietnamese guards were on the other side of the house. Jack trusted them to hold their flank.

Just then Jack saw the grass move. It could not have been the wind. These people were clumsy. Concentrating on the area of the slight movement, he could make out the shapes of two men. Flipping his M-16 to full auto, he fired an entire 20-round magazine into the area. Slamming in a fresh magazine, he fired again into the spot where he could now hearing thrashing and someone calling for help. Reloading on the run, Jack and Shadow quickly covered the 100 feet and charged into the area. Two men were down. They both looked dead. Jack told Shadow to stay and checked carotid arteries. Both were dead. Neither of them had any ID.

Wondering if there were any more, Jack called Kathy. Before she could answer he heard rapid firing from the back of the house. One of the weapons was a SOCOM and that must be Kelly. Jack and Shadow ran to the back of the house.

Kathy told the two Vietnamese guards to pull back to the house, but be careful, there may be more. Shadow beat

Jack to the pool and leapt upon the man trying to drag himself away from the house. Kelly ran up and pulled a growling Shadow off the dying man. Jack saw that the man Kelly shot would not live until the medical help arrived. He heard the sirens coming and knew it was time to wrap up. Jack looked at Kelly and said, "Very well done. You probably saved Kathy's life." Kelly was standing holding Shadow who was still growling. Jack thought he had never seen a woman or a man so natural in their nakedness.

Kelly saw Jack looking at her and said, "I guess I better get something on before the cops come."

"Before you go, are you okay with killing two men?"

"Yes, but I don't know yet. They were shooting at me. I had no choice. I just did what Kathy taught me. It worked. I hope Mrs. Minh is all right."

"I don't know yet. The police will want to split us up for questioning. I may not be able to stop that. Just tell the truth about the attack but don't mention we were ready for it. The two Vietnamese the Minhs brought in can just disappear. Their truck is parked a few streets away. No reason for them to be involved. I'll take care of that now. Take Shadow with you and get dressed. Give me your weapon. If they ask, tell them you and Kathy were shooting today, and you borrowed the handgun from me and just hadn't cleaned and returned it yet."

By the time the police cars slid to a stop in the driveway, everything was in place. The Vietnamese guards disappeared with their weapons, Kelly was dressed and Mrs. Minh was insisting she was not badly hurt and didn't need to go to any hospital. Kathy blocked off the hallway crime scene and Jack made sure the weapons of the two dead men in the marsh had been fired. Jack told Kathy to get her badge out. He hoped their badges, even from out of town, would cut them some slack with the Charleston cops. He knew he could count on Captain Shorer to stand by them, especially since this attempt on his life was another part of the Pittsburgh attack. His gun and Kathy's were registered with the Pittsburgh police. And Kathy's 911 call would help them with their plea of self-defense.

Jack, Shadow, Kathy and Kelly met the police cars in the driveway, displaying their badges. When the leading sergeant saw the badges, he slowed down and took his hand off his holstered Browning nine millimeter.

"We got a 911 call about shots being fired. Do you want to tell us what happened?' Looking closer he saw the badges were issued by the Pittsburgh Police Department. "And you might include an explanation about the badges. Are you with the Pittsburgh police?"

Jack said, "We're both on special assignment. Captain Shorer will vouch for us, but first the 911 call. A number of armed men attacked our home and wounded a woman inside who should have medical care."

The sergeant called for his partner, who was near the patrol car to call for an ambulance. Jack said, "You also should call for a crime scene team. There are some dead men. Three outside and one inside. They were all armed. I don't know if there are any more. I think we finished them."

"What! You're kidding me."

"No. Wish I was. Come inside. We can start there."

As Sergeant Wilson stepped up on the porch, he saw the broken glass and blood-stained floor. Down the hall brass rounds, drywall dust and shot-up doors lined the hall floor surrounding a pool of blood and a dead body.

"What the hell happened here? Jenkins, bring everyone up on the porch and get some backup in here. Get a roadblock set up. Nobody comes in but officials that need to be here. No tramping around until the crime scene team arrives. And don't use your radios. Call in with a cell. Let's keep the media out as long as we can. Looks like a damn war went on in this house. Send someone to the back of the house. Be careful, there may be more attackers out there."

Jack said, "Your officer will find a body back by the pool deck. Two more are 50 feet or so out in the marsh."

"Who in hell killed all these people?"

When Jack moved toward the pool deck, Kathy stepped in, still holding her badge, and said, "Sergeant, we did. Me, the Vietnamese house staff, Jack and Kelly, our houseguest. I'm Kathy Grayson, the man you were talking to is Jack Brandon. Over there," pointing to Kelly, "is Miss Marino. Mr. and Mrs. Minh are staff members and Shadow, the big black bear-like creature, is the one who gave the alarm and tracked the two in the marsh."

"We'll need statements from all of you. But for now we must secure the crime scene area. I think you'll need to find another place for a few days. Can you do that?"

"Of course, we'll help in any way we can. We have a condo in town that will hold us until you're done here."

When Sergeant Wilson left to walk back to his squad car, Kathy took advantage of the opportunity to talk privately to Jack. She found him back by the pool. He was just finishing a heads-up call to Captain Shorer and was starting to call Frank when Kathy came up. He put his arm around her and said, "You done really good, managing all the pieces of the attack. And we didn't lose anyone."

"I told the Sergeant that we killed all those men after they attacked us and introduced him to all of us. He asked if we could find some place to relocate until the crime guys were finished. I told him we had a downtown condo."

"Good. Our stance here is one of maximum cooperation without saying too much. Nothing about Hankins and the rug shop, or Frank. I think we'll be okay, though the local chief may want to yell at us for a bit. Our answer is to ask how this could occur in a major southern city. Is our neighborhood safe?

"I'm not sure, but I think one of the attackers Shadow and I killed in the marsh was the fireman who asked so many questions at the rug shop fire. Killers on the city payroll. The media will love it. Your instincts were right again. You're almost as good as Shadow."

"High praise, Mr. Brandon, but no human is as good as Shadow. Thank God for that dog. Call Frank. I'm going back to talk to Kelly. She was wonderful. I saw just bit of a stark-naked Kelly lying on her side, pumping .45s down the hallway. What a sensation that would be on YouTube. We could make her famous. Seriously, she may need some TLC. She's tough but shooting her first two people, even in self-defense, is going to give her some sleepless nights."

Kelly had her mother's genes. Three days after the violent attack, she told Kathy she was okay and sleeping well. She could call up the memories but her head was okay. She said that she was still in awe that she had been part of a team that stopped a surprise attack by four armed men and only Mrs. Minh had been hit in the arm requiring some tricky surgery. Fortunately, Charleston had quality medical care. She was with them now working with one arm in a sling and muttering about the scratch everyone was upset about. In her days with the PRU, she would have been on the next mission.

Jack was very pleased that they had escaped without legal problems. A phone call from Captain Shorer to Chief Lowell got them treated like active duty officers. The fact Jack and Kathy were not doing any active investigative work in Charleston eased all budding turf problems. They had weapons registered with Pittsburgh police because Jack, a Pittsburgh police sergeant, was on leave without pay while taking care of his father's estate. Jack's father was killed in by a team that may have been from Charleston. When the man who attempted to kill Jack, Kathy and Shadow in Pittsburgh was identified by the Charleston police as being a former city policeman fired for corrupt activities, Chief Lowell dropped all pending charges and said they were welcome to stay in Charleston as long as they wanted. The police force, to a man, admired the defenders of the Brandon house, and when they learned Kelly killed two of the attackers while naked, every bachelor cop and some who weren't, wanted to date her.

The media coverage was intensive for three days with pictures of the house and occupants, especially Shadow and Kelly. Jack believed that their stay in Charleston was limited. With all the notoriety, he didn't see how they could help Frank at CTC, and surely Joel Hankins would never come back to Charleston. Kathy had been in close touch with Frank, who felt the Professor was not through with Charleston and wanted them to stay in place for a few more months. Jack put his misgivings aside and agreed.

Next week Frank wanted Kathy and Kelly to take over watching Hankins. It seemed he relocated to Georgetown, SC. Kathy knew it would be a tedious, boring job but a good way to get Kelly some field experience. After seeing the images of Hankins' killing of young women, Kathy was anxious to take him down. Before they left for Georgetown, she intended to show Kelly the images so she would know this guy was a real serial killer and to be extremely careful. Frank didn't want to expose any of the Brandon group to his inside agents, so he sent all the surveillance reports and images to her MacAir notebook. They were scheduled to pick up surveillance of Hankins tomorrow at 1100. He had moved into an apartment over an empty garage on the west end of Highmarket Street in Georgetown. The reports had seen him put his gray Ford Explorer in the garage. Therefore, he must also be renting the garage.

Jack hated to see Kathy and Kelly disappear for an indefinite time, even if it was only 90 minutes from Charleston. He could tell Shadow knew Kathy was going away. The big black Bouvier had bonded with Kathy from day one. He had to contact Lou who would now be reporting to him. If there was no sign of activity from the Professor in the next two weeks, he might be in the wind. At least they had stopped his car bombing attack.

Thirty

For days after the fire at the rug shop where the Professor's car bombing teams were hidden, he waited for word from Hankins who, he knew from the media coverage, had escaped the fire. He searched the news tirelessly looking for the bit of information that would give him a basis to judge if it was an accidental fire or something more sinister. He had a lot invested here. Even at his level, he had to produce results. Not everyone had bought into his plan to stir up the American "melting pot" to weaken the Americans by turning them against themselves. He had had a good start but the car bombing fiasco hurt.

Tomorrow his white Aryan bikers with KKK hoods would be turned loose on Black communities. Some would be in pickups, the others on motorcycles.

As dedicated and disciplined as most were he couldn't keep them sitting around waiting for action. Myrtle Beach was a perfect place for bikers to gather at any time of the year. This time his raiders would be armed. If they had to fight to escape that would be good. Being captured at a road block along Route 17 between Murrells Inlet and Mount Pleasant was a real possibility, if the police were alerted to use their radios and block a few roads. Some of his soldiers would die, if not this time, certainly on the next attack. If captured, there was not much they could tell under interrogation to endanger him. They were all good Jihadists. Capturing them would not be easy.

The attack was scheduled for 8:30 PM. By then it would have been dark for nearly three hours. No one will confuse the attackers' organization. They will be wearing Aryan emblems on their jackets, KKK hoods and dropping racist Aryan pamphlets. Two pickup trucks and four bikes in all. Trucks north of Charleston and bikes to the South. Columbia and Savannah were the designated recovery points. The raiders had picked, studied their own targets and done drive-bys. No one left their ride. The passengers throw gasoline and soap cocktails. Both drivers and passengers shoot targets of opportunity. Speed and surprise were a must.

Secure in his upscale motel suite, the Professor was intently watching the TV news on two separate channels. He also had a local news station on the radio. 8:30 passed, 8:45 and still nothing. At 8:50, a TV news flash stated they had reports of burning churches and gunfire along Route 17 north of Mount Pleasant. Good, the party had started.

By ten o'clock it looked as if the attacks exceeded his best estimate. Six churches were badly burned. The fire fighters were stretched very thinly on the burning route. No one had died in the fire, but ten people were killed by small arms fire and 25 more wounded. The content of the Aryan pamphlets, dropped by the attackers, was displayed on the news channels and talking heads were running to the ramparts to explain what all this meant.

The police engaged two of the motorcycles in a running gunfight north of Mount Pleasant. Two attackers were killed in the fight. Three police officers were in critical condition in local hospitals. A wide manhunt was underway for two of the attackers who escaped on foot after their pickup crashed. The attackers along Route 17 south of Charleston seem to have escaped. The number of attackers, all reported to be white males, is uncertain at this time and the police are asking the public to call in on the displayed hotline with any eye witness reports of the attacks.

The Professor smiled to himself and went to bed. Tomorrow would be a busy day. By morning the authorities should have more complete reports. Two days later, school buses between Georgetown and Mount Pleasant would be the targets. These daylight attacks will strike terror into every parent with a kid in school. He gave some thought to moving up the attack of school buses but decided to stick with his first plan.

Thirty-one

When the news of the attack on Black churches first broke, Jack called Frank at his office. Frank was also watching the news unfold. He immediately said, "Jack, this is undoubtedly the work of the Professor. You can be sure more will follow. Unless his rug shop guy gets in touch with him, we will have a hard time finding him. Do you have anything from Lou Washington?"

"No. Not yet. I'll call him as soon as we're finished. Kathy and Kelly checked in. They are sitting on Hankins right now. It's hard for two people to do a 24/7 surveillance."

"I know, but I'm afraid of using more people. Kathy is one of the best I've ever seen. She won't be tempted to be too aggressive, and she won't make stupid mistakes. It's also more than probable that Mr. Joel Hankins has no intention of recontacting the Professor. After the fire, he may have had enough. He's more interested in killing young girls for the thrill than being a true Jihadist for a cause he probably doesn't believe in. I'll give him two more weeks and, if there's no attempt to contact the Professor or al Qaeda, you can take him down. Tell Kathy she can put a beacon back on Hankins' car. That should make it a bit easier to keep track of him."

Jack knew the conversation was over when he heard the dial tone. Frank is consistent. His telephone manners hadn't changed.

Kathy picked up on the first ring. She was also watching the breaking news of the attacks along Route 17 just south of where she was in Georgetown. The nearest burning church was just south of the Santee River within 20 minutes' fast driving. Jack told her of his conversation with Frank.

She said, "Okay, only understand that sick bastard is not going to kill any more young girls as long as Kelly and I are sitting on him."

"Just don't jump the gun. The professor is still our number one target. And get Shadow and me a room. We're coming up Saturday."

"I hope that's a promise. Kelly can do double duty for a day. She's really doing well. I almost believe Anita is guiding her daughter. She was the best. See ya soon."

Kathy put her iPhone in her pocket and went next door to tell Kelly what was going down. Frank suspected an al Qaeda high official called the Professor was the mastermind of all the recent terrorist activity, including the failed car bomb plan. Kelly asked, "What if the Professor comes tonight, while we're resting in our motel?"

"Two reasons I don't want him to come tonight and, with everything going down, the Professor is not going to come calling Mr. Hankins. We can't cover him 24/7 by ourselves and, if we did, the target might make us or the Professor would for sure. Switching cars and clothes makes us harder to spot, but not impossible. If Hankins and the Professor make contact, it won't be a one-time thing, unless the Professor kills him. I believe the emergency contact procedure is a personal ad in a local paper. That's why I've been scanning them every day."

"How will you know the ad, if you see it?"

"I'll be able to smell it. The ad will be a little different in language. It will be innocuous and the phone numbers and addresses will be bogus. So, if I suspect an ad, we'll have more work checking it out without spooking the bad guy."

"Kathy, can anybody learn all this stuff?"

"Not everyone can. But I'm your teacher and Anita is your mother. You'll pick it up. I'm counting on it. Remember, I didn't teach that naked shooting stuff. If you had taken the time to grab some clothes, both of us could be dead now. Mission first."

Thirty-two

Robert Huxley, formerly Joel Hankins, was growing more comfortable with his new surroundings and identity. His apartment above the three-car garage was old and rundown, but it was better than where he grew up. He must have been nuts to get involved with al Qaeda. Very serious people with no sense of humor. Set up a good business cover for them, and they trash his business and him. His growing Oriental rug business was over. He hoped changing his name and car would be enough to keep those scary people from finding him. If they knew his main interest in life was hunting and killing young girls and not living the life of a Jihadist, he would be dead.

In just a few days, he had found work as a painter. It didn't pay much but it was a start and he didn't need much. He still had thousands of al Qaeda dollars. Too bad he couldn't collect the insurance on his shop and contents. Well, it wasn't worth his life. The cops were just as far from catching him as the Muslims. No fingerprints on record. No credit cards and no social security. Robert Huxley would just have to make it alone. With the Jihad business out of the way, he could concentrate on his research of the instant of departing life. He had to keep away from his study of martial arts for a while. That scary old dude from Herat would be looking for him when he didn't see the recontact personal ad in the local papers. Tonight would be a good time to go hunting. Help get his mind off his worries. He had always been lucky on Thursdays.

Just a block away in a parking lot with a clear view of Hankins' apartment, Kathy and Kelly were sitting in one of the two cars they were using today, and talking about their target. The file Frank provided contained Hankins' daily Georgetown activities, pictures of people he met, and locations of his painting jobs. No one had been inside his garage or living quarters. There were a number of other pictures of his apartment, car and restaurants he frequented. Nothing to indicate he was trying to get in touch with al Qaeda. Kathy believed Hankins was frightened and wasn't cut out to be a mainline Jihadist.

Before they left the condo in Charleston, Kathy showed Kelly the pictures she found in Hankins' apartment of dying or dead young women. Kelly was just as angry as Kathy was when she and Jack first saw the pictures. Kelly said, "At the first opportunity, let's get him. The little weasel shouldn't be breathing the same air."

At six o'clock, Hankins backed out of his garage. Kathy gave the Explorer a block lead and pulled out behind a small red sedan. Once he headed north on Route 17, she dropped back another quarter mile. Other than a few gated housing developments, there was nowhere he could go until he got to Pawleys Island. Hankins' right taillight was brighter than the left one making the car easier to track at a distance. Kelly also had the car in view through her binoculars. As the traffic increased, Kathy moved up. For the next 45 minutes, they cruised along fifty plus yards behind the five-year-old gray Ford Explorer. Kathy mentioned during a stop for a traffic light, "This surveillance is, so far, as easy as it gets. Hankins isn't even checking for anyone following him. When he parks, be ready to get out quickly and follow him, while I find a good place to park our car. Keep in touch with your cell. Remember, no eye contact."

Kelly said, "He's driving like he isn't sure where he's going. He's heading toward the bright lights just ahead."

"Yeah, he's going to Broadway at the Beach, a big tourist area. You know, the bastard may be hunting again. He barely got settled in Georgetown. The creep's hormones must be flowing. Get ready, he's turning into the parking lot beside that upscale hotel. I'll drop you just past the entrance to the parking lot. I'll go on down and come in from the other direction."

Five minutes later Kathy parked in a space near the area reserved for valet parking. She had a clear view of the front entrance and got her camera ready. Looking out through the windshield she had a perfect view of the front entrance. Kelly called in and said, "He's sitting in the bar nursing a drink. I can see him through the glass window. Don't think he can see me."

"Okay, where did he park?"

"Just to the left as you come in the entrance. There were several open spots facing Route 17. Not a good place for him to do his chloroform stunt and drag some young girl into the Explorer. Not enough cover. He must be doing some recon or what do you call it."

"We intelligence types call it casing, my dear."

"Hey, Kathy, I'm trying. What do I do now?"

"What do you think you should do?"

"Come back to the car?"

"Yes. I'm parked just to the left of the valet area."

As Kathy was watching for Kelly to come out, a black Cadillac CTS pulled into the valet area. Kathy was admiring the car when she had a full front view of the driver emerging. She was astounded! Training took over and she snapped several pictures. She couldn't be mistaken. It was the Professor. Was he here to meet with Hankins? She called Kelly who answered on the first vibration and said, "Don't leave yet. Find a place where you can disappear, if Hankins comes your way. There is an older, well-dressed gentleman in a dark suit, no topcoat or hat coming in now. I'm interested if he and Hankins meet or see each other. Be very discreet. Okay?"

"Got it."

Kathy called Jack and said, "Get Frank on the line right now. We have the Professor under surveillance in Myrtle Beach at the Beach Combers Hotel on Route 17 at Broadway at the Beach. He just entered the hotel. Hankins is there at the bar and Kelly is in the lobby, watching to see if they meet. I got several good pictures of him as he got out of his car. I'm sending them to you now."

"Stand by, Frank is coming to the phone."

Seconds later Frank was on the phone. He said, "Kathy, are you sure it's the Professor?"

"One hundred percent. You should have the pictures soon."

"What are you doing in Myrtle Beach?"

"Kelly and I followed Hankins up here. We thought he was going hunting. He showed no sign of checking for a tail. I'm going way out and say I don't think this is a planned meeting. I just don't think it's the Professor's M.O. to risk meeting a dingbat like Hankins in a hotel lobby."

"All our tradecraft lore tells us this cannot be a coincidence, but you may be right. Let's see what Kelly has to report. Try to find out if he is staying in the hotel. I'm sending a team right now to Myrtle Beach. I'll tell you where they locate. I want you to brief them before you go. I know it will expose you. Try and keep Jack and Kelly away from them. I don't want them exposed as well.

"The pictures have just come in. No doubt you caught the Professor. Kathy, that is wonderful work. Now keep him under surveillance until you can brief the team, and then you get some rest."

Jack was still on the line and said, "Kathy, it's great to be very good and very lucky as well. Looking forward to Kelly's read. Remember, Hankins knows what you look like. I'm coming up tomorrow with Shadow. There is nothing we can do here right now. Okay?"

"Great! I really want you to come. I'll bribe the motel guy to let Shadow in my room. Kelly is just down the hall. See you later, depending on what the Professor does and when Frank's team gets here. Love you, bye."

Kelly called Kathy and said, "The Professor got in an elevator by himself. The elevator went nonstop directly to the fifth floor. He did not meet Hankins. I don't think they could have seen each other. The Professor wasted no time. He went directly to the elevator. Hankins never left the bar and his back was to the Professor the entire time. What now?"

"Stay cool and out of sight. When Hankins leaves, we stay here and make sure the Professor doesn't vanish."

Thirty-three

When Kathy cut off, Jack called to check on Lou and Storm. After a couple of rings, Lou picked up. Jack said, "Can you talk now?"

"Sure, go ahead."

Jack asked, "What do you think of the Aryan attack? What are people, especially biker folk, saying?"

"Storm and I've talked about these attacks over and over with several bikers and have some general insights but nothing specific and no leads. We have been to and talked with bikers in Atlanta, Myrtle Beach, Surfside, Savannah and Columbia. They're all talking about the raids and who could be doing it. These people aren't cold-blooded killers. No way would they be part of burning churches and killing innocent people. We believe the attack bikers aren't from or part of organized biker groups or gangs. Sure, some of them are hard people, some have records and they won't be pushed around but killing innocent people isn't them. We think the attackers are their own group with a political objective justifying the unprovoked violence. None of the people we talked to would send a note to the media justifying the attacks as revenge for the actions of Templars during the Crusades. This has to be a Muslim political fringe group behind these attacks. I don't think we can do any more running around on my bike. We've given out a phone number to a few people to call if they hear anything about the biker raids. Jack, I think we might as well come in."

"Yeah, I agree. It sounds right. Come on in. Check back into your hotel rooms. You may be needed by Kathy in the Georgetown area to help with covering a few people. Call when you get a decent sleep and are settled in."

Thirty-four

Kelly and Kathy were sitting in their car focused on the front entrance of the hotel. Kelly said, "How are we going to make sure the Professor doesn't leave by another exit?"

"With two people we can't. But, being the smart operatives we are, we have located his car. I can see it from here. It looks like he's playing the role of a well-to-do businessman. If I'm right, he's locked himself into that role. He wouldn't be slipping out another entrance into another parked car or going out an entrance to the rear parking lot and walking around the front to the overnight valet section. Hotel people would notice that. Not in keeping with his cover. A good cover is necessary but it also has some built-in problems, such as required behavior. Knowing the behavior required allows hunters like us to predict some of the target's actions. Unless he suspects some hostile group knows where he is, he will not leave the hotel dressed as a cowboy or a golf-playing tourist from Minnesota. So be patient and watch the front door. Of course, we don't want to miss Mr. Hankins' departure. If he doesn't come out in the next 20 minutes, you will have to check if he's still in the bar. We also have his car in sight."

"What if Hankins leaves and kills some young woman?"

"This is a tough business. We have to try to prevent the greatest threat. And right now that's the Professor. He's already killed more Americans than Hankins ever will. If the car bombs had succeeded, dozens or more could have been killed or badly hurt. We were lucky that time. We need to be a step ahead of the Professor. We don't need to build a legal case against him. He's an enemy combatant trying to kill us. If we can pin him down anywhere, he'll be picked up, interrogated, and imprisoned or executed under the jurisdiction of a military tribunal. All we have to do is keep him located until he can be grabbed. No one will be reading the Professor any rights. There now, do you have any more short questions that need long answers? If not, go check on our pervert."

Kelly was barely in the lobby when Kathy saw her come out and hurry back to the car. She opened the car door and said, "Hankins was paying his bill. Look for him to come out any minute now."

"Okay! When he drives away, we're going inside. I want to have a drink in the booth he just left. You go first and make that happen."

When Hankins' tail lights disappeared going back toward Georgetown, Kelly and Kathy walked into the lounge. Kelly asked the hostess for a booth and pointed to the one near the back of the lounge. Once they ordered drinks, a soda and bitters for Kathy and a draft light beer for Kelly, she asked, "Why are we sitting here?"

"Two things. I want to see what he could see sitting where I am now, facing away from the entrance the way you said Hankins was facing. I want to check the seating area, just to be sure he didn't leave a note, mark or signal of some kind for the Professor. When the waitress left, I checked the underside of the table and the edges of the bench."

"I didn't see you do that."

"You weren't supposed to, nor was anyone else. I don't see how Hankins could have seen the Professor or the Professor him. And nothing was left in this booth. I doubt Hankins used the men's room. You would have seen him. So now I'm reassured this was a coincidence, not a scheduled meeting of any kind. Also I assume Hankins did not use a cell or hotel phone while he was here. So now let's get situated so we can watch the lobby for the Professor."

Just after midnight Kathy signaled for the bill. She explained to Kelly that it was unlikely the Professor would be coming down to the lobby to meet anyone, and they were too exposed to hang out any longer in the lounge. Back in the car, Kathy said she would take the first watch and for Kelly to get in the backseat and get some sleep. If any cops came by when Kelly was on watch to wake her, and she would use her badge and tell them they were okay.

Kathy's cell vibrated at 6:30 AM. It was the head of the unit Frank sent to take over the coverage and taking of the Professor. She agreed to meet them right away in the Piccolo Coffee Shop near the hotel.

They had pictures and a brief on the Professor from Frank. Kathy briefed them on the Professor's car and its location. She didn't know the room number or what name he was using, only that he was probably on the fifth floor. Kathy asked if she and her partner were needed any longer. The team chief said no, they would take over from here. When Kathy asked if he wanted to go over his plan, he acted as if she wasn't cleared and told her she could go now. They had to move quickly.

Kathy and Kelly were on their way back to Georgetown within the next five minutes. The Professor, following a lifelong habit of getting up at five AM and was now enjoying a cup of dark French Roast coffee on the terrace off his sitting room. His one light bag was packed. This morning he planned to leave the Cadillac CTS in the valet parking and take the VW Passat he kept stashed in the shopping center parking lot in the next block. From long practice he constantly scanned his surroundings. He was just finishing his most recent check of the front of the hotel, when he received a cell call. The caller told him to leave immediately, a team of counter terrorists knew where he was and would soon surround the building. Looking from his balcony, he saw a group of young men in suits come out of a coffee shop and walk directly toward the front of the hotel. In all his checking of the hotel environment, he had never seen a group like that. They surely weren't tourists and, if they were well-dressed businessmen, they would not have had breakfast or even coffee in a place like that. No, trust his instincts and his inside source. It had been a few years, but he knew his spy was dependable. He had used this source for years.

Without another thought, he picked up his small bag and walked down the back stairs and across the back of the hotel parking lot to the shopping mall and drove off in his VW. In his business, there was no such thing as over-reacting. There was only being alive or being dead. Always take the safest action and forget convenience or inconvenience.

Twenty minutes later, Frank's team rushed into his room only to find it empty. A frantic search of the hotel and grounds turned up nothing. Not even a fingerprint was found in a short check of a few of the usual places fingerprints are always left in a hotel room occupied by normal guests. A housekeeping maid on the floor said, when questioned, she had seen a guest carrying a small bag go down the back stairs about 30 minutes ago. She looked at the Professor's picture and said, "Yes. That's the man. He was a good tipper and had very good manners."

A check of the hotel's surveillance cameras confirmed the maid's report. There was no question the Professor went down the back stairs as the team from Frank's office was coming in the front of the hotel. The team chief called Frank at CTC and told him the Professor was gone. Frank was furious and asked, in an icy tone, what had happened? The team chief said he didn't know. The Professor must have been scared off by something the two women, who were sitting on him, did.

Frank said, "The woman you talked to has more experience than your whole team combined. She is the best I have ever worked with. I'm sending her back to the hotel to find out what happened, since you can't tell me. Report immediately to my office. You and your team get the next flight to Washington."

As usual, the team chief was left with a dial tone.

Frank called Kathy when he cut off the team chief. Kathy and Kelly had just arrived back in Georgetown to eat, rest and resume coverage of Hankins.

Frank asked her what could have happened to make the Professor disappear.

Kathy said, "Frank, I'm surprised. I can't tell you what happened. The team leader refused my offer to help. I offered to go over his plan and he blew me off. He is without a doubt one of the most condescending son-of-a-bitches I have ever run into. I was surprised at how they were dressed, all in dark suits and ties. They looked like a Government team in a sea of tourists, beach people and golfers. It's hard to find a group of young men in suits at Broadway at the Beach. That's about all I can say. Is the Professor's Cadillac CTS still there?"

"I don't know. Please go up there, show your badge, make it a criminal law thing and find out what happened."

"Okay. I'm on my way."

"Kelly, you have to cover Hankins on your own. Frank wants me to find out how and why the Professor got away from his team. Remember no risks, no confrontations, and do not get made. It wouldn't hurt to use a different car."

"Got it. Call me if I can help."

On the way back to Myrtle Beach, Kathy wished she had a siren. This speed limit driving was making her crazy. The return trip took her 40 minutes, not bad considering traffic conditions. She left her Ford Taurus in valet parking and flashed her badge at the attendant and told him to keep it handy. The front desk was clear when she walked up, flashed her badge and asked to see the manager. The manager came right out and asked her to come into his office. She showed her badge again, along with a picture of the Professor coming into the hotel.

Kathy said, "This is important but no need to upset the routine of your hotel or its guests. This man had a room on the fifth floor. I want to know what name he used, how long was he here and whether he had been here before. Also what ID he used. After that I want to see his room. Please put it off limits for a few hours. Lastly. I want to know what our team did when it came into the hotel early this morning. I'll need all the relevant camera coverage, starting with this man coming into the hotel last night and going up to the fifth floor. Coverage of him leaving by the back staircase is especially important."

Kathy smiled her sexiest and told the manager she didn't want to take much of his time. He called an assistant manager and passed on Kathy's requests and told him to make it his top priority.

While she was waiting, Kathy went up to the fifth floor, checked camera coverage and walked down the back stairs. When she opened the outside door, she saw the route the Professor must have taken. He wouldn't have stashed a second car in the hotel lot, but in the shopping strip mall adjacent to the hotel lot. She walked over and checked camera coverage. It was not extensive but, if operating, it should show cars coming and leaving, as well as foot traffic in most of the parking area. Again flashing her badge, she checked in with the small rent-a-cop mall security office.

"Sure you can see our camera take. We record over it every other day, so if you want today, you got it."

"Show me starting from 6:30 this morning."

"Can do. Just sit over there at the other monitor. Tell me if you want to stop or blow up a frame."

It took a few minutes for Kathy to orient herself to the camera angles. There were a few overlaps but more gaps than multiple coverage. Right at 0655, she saw a figure entering the southeastern edge of the parking lot. She had Terry blow up the image. It looked like the Professor to her. She then tracked the figure to a green car two rows in from the street. Blowing up the image, she saw it was a VW Passat with a South Carolina license plate. She watched as the car started out and got a license number. Thanking Terry and getting him to make her a copy of the tapes, Kathy went outside and called Frank.

Kathy told Frank, the Professor had a clear view of the coffee shop used by the team that morning from his balcony. The doorman told her all the suits came in together. Kathy told Frank there was a half-full coffee cup and a burned down French Gitane cigarette with the full ash intact. Kathy said she believed the Professor was sitting there early this morning, having his coffee and a cigarette when the team came en masse across the street. It looked like he left abruptly. The hotel camera time confirmed his departure. She added, "I visualized the route he must have taken. The natural escape route led to an adjacent strip mall parking lot. I checked with the security office regarding camera coverage and now have coverage of the Professor walking along the edge of the strip mall and getting into a late model green VW Passat, South Carolina plate SIT 301. I don't think he'll keep the Passat very long. Finding the Passat quickly is our best shot at locating this slippery bastard. One more thought, if we can keep the whole affair quiet, the Professor won't be sure the danger was real or just his paranoid instincts kicking in. If he isn't sure, he may keep to his schedule."

"Kathy, that is a first class bit of police work accomplished in an amazingly short time. I wish you would come back and work for me."

"Frank, thank you. It's nice to be wanted. Anything else I can do before I head back to Georgetown and Mr. Hankins?"

"No. But I want you to know that I'm sending your pompous friend back from whence he came when he shows up. I pulled you off because I didn't want you getting mixed up in a possible high profile arrest with all the media coverage. This administration is so hungry for positive press that they will leak anything that makes them look good. I'll be in touch."

Thirty-five

Every hour on the network and cable news stations and channels, the attacks on churches in South Carolina were covered with new, but mostly speculative, reports and analysis. The most riveting were the interviews of eye witnesses to the violence. In one instance a man talked of attending the A.M.E. Church near McClellanville. He said, "I was just coming out of the church with my family, when a pickup truck roared up the driveway to a skidding stop in front of church. I was so close I could see the eyes of the attacker through the holes in his hood. The letters KKK were clear.

"My grandfather told me stories of these people. I pushed my kids and wife down behind the azaleas bordering the driveway. The man in the bed of the truck started throwing gasoline bombs at the church and at cars in the parking lot. A shotgun was poking out the passenger window. It swung my way and the KKK guy screamed, 'Die, you black bastard.' Before he could shoot, I jumped at him and jerked the weapon from his hands. The truck never stopped moving. I swung the shotgun up and emptied that pump gun into the truck. I know at least one of them was hit. When the cops found the wrecked truck, there was blood on the front seat at the passenger window. I'm a veteran and no KKK punk is going to threaten me or mine. No way, not anymore!"

Going north on Route 17 after his escape from the hotel, the Professor heard the report on CNN radio, when he was scanning to see if anything was being reported about what he thought might have been an attempt to capture him. He wondered if other American victims of his attacks had the same aggressive attitude. Both good and bad. Good, if he could channel the aggression inward, but bad, if it was channeled toward the attackers specifically and not generally against another racial group.

He missed not having some of his best people with him. Operating alone was even more difficult than he remembered. If the attempt was real, how could they have known he was there? As long as his source in the Counter Terrorism Center survived, he had a decided edge, even though he couldn't call his source but had to wait for him to call. How did they find out he was even in the country?

He decided to step up his time schedule, but he would be even more careful. When the scheduled attacks in Charleston were underway, he'd move to the next phase of his plan and attack the capital of the land of Satan. Leesburg, Virginia, your Confederate past is coming back. It was also time to begin the blog campaign. One blog would copy the words and traditions of the KKK. The other blog would argue for Muslim rights in the name of The Warriors for Allah. The Muslim blog will be supported by pamphlets distributed during attacks. The KKK audience needed no support. Every Black in America knew about the hooded racists. The Professor was sure the media would pick up and replay the KKK propaganda. He planned the Muslim blog to be centrist enough to be acceptable to the Mosques of America. Here the media would follow the lead of the law enforcement/counter-terrorist forces in following the Muslim blog. The messages would be simple, consistent and pounded repeatedly, following Goebbels' big lie theory, "Tell it often enough and people will believe it."

He wasn't worried about the cyber security of the blogs. His expert knew how to disguise the places of origin. His blogs were already written and had different themes, servers, domain providers and protection for followers and commenters. Modern revolutionaries had to use the new cyber techniques. Tonight he would make the phone call to start the blog publications. He didn't expect instant results, just sow the seeds of discontent and religious intolerance.

His attack teams were ready. In five hours, just after dusk, targets in and around Charleston will be hit hard. This will be the last direct mass attack. The next phase will be random sniper attacks, spreading to other cities. Sniper attacks were very cost effective. Two or three snipers could tie up a city. They didn't have to be great marksmen. In this kind of attack, even misses caused havoc. The snipers have full freedom in the selection of targets. The more random, the better. The goal is not to destroy but to terrorize the general populace.

Thirty-six

After talking to Kathy, Frank made the decision to put out an immediate APB notice through the FBI to locate the Professor's green Passat, license South Carolina SIT 301, last seen on SC Route 17 headed North in Myrtle Beach at 7 AM. He made it clear the requirement was not to apprehend only to locate and immediately inform the FBI, who would take over the surveillance, under strict instructions to follow discreetly, using air assets when possible.

The Professor crossed into North Carolina and was making his way to I-95 and Richmond. He knew his training protocol said he should change cars now. Changing cars always carried some risk. He decided he would abandon the car in Richmond, breaking the chain of ownership and renting or buying another one somewhere in the area. Using his iPhone, he sent an innocuous text message that gave the final go for the Charleston attack. He and his followers knew few, if any, of them would be alive tomorrow. They were Soldiers of Allah who were proud to die in his name.

Jack Brandon had just finished a long call to Kathy when the first reports of gunfire were reported as a news flash. Within the next 45 minutes, there were reports of attacks in nearly all Charleston areas. A car bomb had been exploded in the Medical Center of South Carolina University. More reports of gunfire and fire bombs were flooding the news services. The Emergency Rooms of the major hospitals were jammed with the injured. Every fire company in the city was out in full force. The airport was closed. The State Police were blocking airport access roads to trap the attackers who smashed through the gates and used gunfire and gasoline bombs on aircraft loading or unloading passengers at the gates. Casualties were climbing. The Mayor called for police and firefighters from the outlying areas. The Governor asked for federal help and issued orders to call up units from the South Carolina Guard. Homeland Security promised swift help. Shelter announcements were constant. Anchors and officials were struggling to keep panic from their voices. Charleston was in chaos.

Jack knew the action was beyond anything they could help with, but decided to bring Kathy, Lou and Storm back to Charleston tomorrow afternoon. Kelly had to stay in Georgetown to watch their serial killer. Kathy was certain that Hankins was not interested in getting in touch with the Professor. The little snake just did not have what it takes to be part of the Professor's team. Kathy told Kelly to keep a very loose watch on Hankins. Drive-bys to check on the activity level at the garage would be enough. If Kelly saw him leaving Georgetown to follow, but very discreetly. And no static stakeouts to watch his apartment and garage. Too much risk without any backup. Kathy had emphasized her concerns, but on the drive back to Charleston she had the feeling that Kelly didn't think Hankins presented much of a threat to her.

The following afternoon, when Lou, Storm and Kathy arrived and gathered in the Brandon condo, the news was full of the extent of the attacks. People killed numbered 37, injured 115. Property damage estimates were not all in, yet calm was returning to the city. The immediate attack was over. By early morning the last of the attacker holdouts had been wiped out. Southern resolve was reasserting itself. The people's view of Muslims had shifted from one of tolerance to a hardened watchfulness.

Most of the attackers traveled in pickup trucks. The number of attackers was not known yet, but 22 had been killed in gunfights with the police. Several of those were killed at roadblocks set up by the State Police. There were no reports of any captured attackers. Pamphlets carried by the attack teams stated they were Soldiers of Allah and the war was just beginning. Before it was over, Charleston would be Cordoba of the South, named after the Muslim cultural city in Spain that was the high water mark of the Muslim invasion of Europe.

Late in the day Frank called Jack and said, "You have now seen the Professor's work. His fingerprints are all over this attack. With 20 odd fighters, he brought a major American city to a momentary standstill. His weakness is that he cannot sustain an effort like the attack on Charleston. He just doesn't have the manpower and cannot get it. Although we won't get any credit, we won this engagement. Just as we won the Vietnam battle of Tet in 1968 in military terms. I'm not sure what the long-term political effect will be of this miniature engagement. I hope and suspect that the American people are much smarter and tougher than the Muslim strategists believe. If the intent of the KKK symbolism and attacks by the Soldiers of Allah in American cities is to terrorize the population and to turn faction against faction, it will fail. But, this is not over yet. It won't be until we capture or kill the Professor."

"Do you have any instructions for us? It seems to me this has escalated beyond our capabilities."

"I may need your group when we locate the Professor. In the meantime you could deal with your serial killer. National security issues no longer protect him. Justice can take its course."

Thirty-seven

Hankins looked at his watch. It was 7:00 PM dark and cold. He was bored with his new life in Georgetown as an indoor house painter. It paid less than his Oriental rug store in Charleston and the work was much harder. His urge to kill had grown until he couldn't think of anything else. His last foray to Myrtle Beach produced nothing. But, he never looked beyond the hotel lobby. He felt he had graduated from taking any young woman available. He wanted to kill someone whose disappearance or death would make the national media news scene. In the past he had worked like a trapper, setting the trap and waiting until a young woman came close enough to be grabbed. Now he was going to be the hunter. He would search an area until he saw someone with class and money. The type of car, the dress and the shops the potential victim visited now defined his search criteria. He was going tonight. The urge was strong, but he must not settle for anything less than he deserved.

Kelly, following Kathy's instructions about keeping only a casual watch on Hankins, missed him leaving his garage. The light was on in his apartment and she assumed he was there. He was now sitting in his Ford Explorer watching the front door of the well-lighted shop. Hankins had noticed a fashionable jewelry shop in North Myrtle

Beach on a previous hunting excursion. From his parked car, Hankins could clearly see the interior of the store. His plan was good. He had only been in place for 30 minutes, yet had seen two very desirable targets. Now he was watching a young woman of his dreams shopping for what looked like diamond earrings. He had seen her park her car a half-block from the jewelry shop. She went into a high-end dress store near where she parked and was now in his hunting area. A car moved from a parking place next to her Lexus. Hankins didn't even think. He just slid the Explorer in next to the Lexus on the driver's side.

He could still see the front door of the dress shop but not the interior. He knew she was alone. All he had to do was wait. He decided to use his cane and a shopping bag of empty boxes as props. Hankins was waiting in a secluded spot three cars away from the Lexis. He saw her leave the dress shop with an armload of packages. When she walked between the cars with her purchases, Hankins was only a few steps behind. As his prey approached the driver's door of her Lexus, Hankins stumbled, dropping his packages between their cars. She turned around, saw the man with a cane trying to retrieve his dropped parcels, and bent down to help him.

Muttering apologies, he took his ether-loaded cloth out of his bag and pressed it tightly against her face. No one saw the short struggle. In less than 30 seconds, she was on the floor in the back seat and under a blanket. He put her packages in her car, closed and locked the Lexus door, and drove slowly out of the shopping area onto the service road. He found an isolated spot and bound his victim with duct tape. He hated handling duct tape while wearing gloves.

This one was too good for his usual routine of torturing his catches and then quickly killing them with his signature counterclockwise neck twist, while he shot images of the moment life left. Dumping the battered bodies was a mere housekeeping chore. He never gave it a thought and never went back to the dumping place. He had his digital images to awaken his memories.

This one would be different. He was going to take her home. He knew it was dangerous, almost madness. But, the urges were strong, stronger than ever, and she was special. Even her looks. Blonde with a page boy haircut, the stylish black skirt, white ruffled blouse and black short jacket. Good legs in stockings and high black pumps that showed them off. It was the eyes that surprised him. He had never seen more beautiful eyes. They were almost violet. He needed another look. The pictures would be sensational. Maybe he would have to post them someway.

Home was only 15 more miles. The plan was coming together in his head as he drove. He heard some stirring in the back. That was okay, she couldn't shout or even move about. He planned on driving straight into the garage. Thank God, it had a remote opener, a decrepit one but it worked. She would stay in the car until he readied a place for her upstairs. If she would be quiet, they could talk. He wanted to hear all about her. For a while she could remain dressed, and he would be nice to her. If she refused to do as he asked, the rules would change. He would have to make that clear. Otherwise, it wouldn't be fair.

He realized he hadn't even thought about the man from Herat or his work with the terrorist. He heard the news reports on his TV about the violence in Charleston and knew who was responsible. He was so lucky. If it hadn't been for the fire that burned his shop and killed five of the terrorists, he would have been involved in that mess and would now be dead. They would never find him, and his woman would help him not to worry about them.

Thirty-eight

At 9:30 PM, Kelly was driving toward Hankins' apartment for another check, when she saw the gray Explorer pulling into the garage under his apartment. She continued for another block, then pulled into a strip mall. She could see the lights in the apartment come on. Kelly wondered about the change in Hankins' daily pattern. Other than the time he drove up to the hotel bar at Broadway at the Beach, he had not been out at night since they had him under surveillance. Could that sick bastard have been out hunting? It was dark at 6:30 PM. He had barely time to hunt a subject, torture and kill her and get back to his apartment in three hours. Maybe he struck out again. Maybe he was just doing some scouting. She decided to watch the apartment for another hour. His lights were always out by ten. Kelly thought she would stay until Hankins turned his lights out. At 2:30 AM, his light went out. What could that squirrel be doing so late at night? Kathy said he wasn't a reader and didn't seem to be a devoted big screen TV watcher. He didn't drink. He was up and on his way to work before eight in the morning. Kelly planned on being in a stakeout position before seven tomorrow morning. Kathy had told her that when a subject changes his or her pattern there is a reason. She would find it out tomorrow.

Hankins had no trouble getting his prey up the narrow stairs into the small, dingy apartment. She was still groggy. He guessed she only weighed about 115 pounds. He was so pumped her weight was nothing. He dumped her taped up body on the unmade double bed. Wondering who she was, he opened her purse and took out her wallet. She was Sally Ann Bradford, age 25. He noted her ring and decided she must be Mrs. Bradford. Her driver's license was from Durham, NC. Apparently she was here as a tourist. Unless her husband was also here, maybe no one would be looking for her for a while. Her car parked in front of the dress shop would alert the police. No pictures of kids in her wallet or in her iPhone. She had a checkbook, a couple of credit cards and $500 in cash.

The woman opened her eyes and tried to scream. Hardly a sound escaped. Good, he could leave her in the apartment when he went out. With her hands and feet secured, she would be helpless and couldn't make any noise. Hankins walked past the bed into his orderly kitchen and picked up a serious cutting knife. Coming back, he showed her the knife and said he was going to take the tape off her mouth. If she screamed her face would get cut. A scar to remind her of their date. With panic in her eyes, Mrs. Bradford nodded she understood. He ripped the tape off, messing up her makeup. The knife blade was nearly touching her face. Hankins saw she was trying to talk. Finally he understood she needed some water. He put a hand under her head and gently tipped the glass. After drinking she tried to talk again, but he stopped her. Going into her purse, he found lipstick and blusher. Telling her to be still, he patched up her makeup. Standing back, examining his handiwork, he thought, this one is special. The best I have ever captured. I must be careful not to destroy this opportunity. He also thought, I must be crazy to have brought her here. I want to talk to her, but if I wait too long, fear, stress and tears will take her beauty away before I can capture the moment of death.

Just having her here gives me problems I've never had before. I want to keep her for some days but she will have to eat, use the bathroom and even bathe. It'll be risky to leave her alone for more than an hour or so. If I kill her tonight those problems go away. I'll still have to get rid of the body. That means keeping a dead woman in my apartment until after dark tomorrow. It was now 2:30 AM and he still hadn't made up his mind. Even as frightened as she was, he enjoyed talking to her. It's surprising what you can learn about someone in a very short time, if they are motivated to answer all your questions. He even answered some of her questions. She asked if he was going to rape her. He laughed and said no, he wasn't interested in sex. He could tell from her eyes that his answer made her more frightened. He wanted to tell her that real power was the power to decide between life and death, including how and when. That was purity. Death was clean. No shades of gray. No judgments about good or bad. In comparison, sex was tawdry, full of delusions and illusions. Hankins was certain she would not understand. A discussion like that could ruin the moment and beauty of death.

Just after 2:30 after giving her another drink of water and helping her to the bathroom, he used his ether pad and put her to bed using the last of his duct tape. Tomorrow he had to get some more and a couple of frozen or carryout meals. Nothing else was on his agenda.

Thirty-nine

Kelly was in a perfect place to watch the Hankins apartment just before 7:00 AM. The garage door was an easy target to watch. She calmly drank her Starbuck's instant Morning Joe coffee and munched on a couple of Kudzu's glazed donuts. She laughed at herself, in a stakeout drinking coffee with a breakfast of donuts. Was she a real cop or what? She kept telling herself this guy is dangerous. Was she really planning on searching his apartment after he left? Why not? He never went back to his place until after 4:00 or 5:00 PM. She had plenty of time. She could search his tiny apartment in less than an hour.

When the garage door went up at 8:05, Kelly was so focused on her entry plan, she nearly spilled her coffee reacting to a rush of adrenalin. The gray Explorer backed out of the garage, waited for a break in traffic and merged into the westbound traffic on Fraser Street. Kelly waited five minutes and walked the half block to the garage. The people door on the side of the garage was partially screened from the street by a large oleander shrub. The hinges were rusty, and she was sure they would protest being used. No problem. No one was home. The lock may be a different problem. It had a patina of rust and tarnish.

She wasn't really good at lock picking yet. Kathy had coached her but she was a long way from being proficient. This deadbolt lock was old and wouldn't have the newest technology. Sweat was dripping down her sides as she struggled with her two picks. She was sure she was using the right procedure. The damn lock was just corroded. Five minutes later, with a curse and an angry twist of her top pick, the dead bolt slid back into the door. Taking a firm grip on the doorknob Kelly pulled and, with a protesting groan, the slightly warped door opened.

She quickly stepped inside and slowly closed the door but did not even try to pick the double-keyed lock closed. Light from one very dirty window allowed her to make out objects in the garage and the corner staircase. Giving her eyes a few minutes to adjust, she moved across the garage and started up the steps, staying close to the wall where stairs were always the sturdiest and less likely to squeak. She reached the small landing. Kelly tried the knob. The door wasn't locked. She eased the door open just far enough for her to slide through.

Kelly had no way of knowing Hankins hadn't gone to work. He was less than a half-mile away in the paint supply area of Walmart buying duct tape and a few other items for his painting business. After that he was going to pick up some frozen meals. He wanted to hurry back to Sally. He should kill her today. Why then was he thinking he needed several meals? Using her name was also a mistake. It made her more of a human to him. He had been lonely for so long. Hankins knew she couldn't stay, and he couldn't let her go. It was only a question of time and impulse. Sally had to die.

The first thing Kelly saw when she eased through the door was a fully dressed woman in a rumpled bed. She even had her shoes on. The duct tape across her mouth, around her legs and wrists was a frightening contrast. Kelly was at the bed in three strides and in seconds had the tape off her mouth. The woman was gasping so fast her words where jumbled. The cry for help came through. Kelly hurried into the kitchen and came back with a knife to cut the tape off her legs and arms.

The woman clung to her and gasped, "Hurry, get me out of here! He'll be back soon! He's crazy! He'll kill both of us!"

Kelly said, "Are you hurt? Are you able to walk?"

"No. I'm not hurt, just terrified, and I don't know if I can walk or not. Help me up."

Kelly got her up but she couldn't walk by herself. The tape around her legs had been very tight. As Kelly was mostly carrying her to the door, she was berating herself for not bringing her handgun. Kathy had told her not to go anywhere without a weapon. You either had it all the time or you would find yourself unarmed when you need it.

Hankins finished his Walmart shopping and was driving back to the apartment, staying within the speed limit. When he was in sight of his garage door, he keyed the remote opener. The door failed to open. He knew the batteries were low and needed to be replaced. Outside the garage, he tried again. The door went up with its usual creaking rumble.

Kelly was just starting down the steps when the door started up. She spun around and pushed Sally back inside the room.

Sally cried, "He's back! He's back! God! Help me." Kelly grabbed her and said, "Be quiet! Get on the bed. Stick some tape across your mouth! Hide your ankles and wrists! No time to call 911. Don't say anything and do not look at me! We need the surprise."

Kelly could hear the garage door closing and Hankins' footsteps on the stairs. He would soon be opening the unlocked door. The door swung open and Hankins with his arms full of packages saw only something moving incredibly fast. Kelly hit him chest high with a textbook side kick to the chest, packages partially deflected the kick but the force sent him tumbling to the garage floor where he bounced up against the Explorer. She didn't know if he was carrying a weapon or not. She didn't want to give him any chance to get back into the apartment and Sally. Kelly decided to fight him from the small landing outside the door.

Hankins rolled over and got to his feet. The light wasn't good and he was sure that was a woman on the landing. He had no idea Sally could fight like that. He had just taken the hardest kick in his four years of studying martial arts. He started up the steps. The woman was wearing jeans and sneakers. It couldn't be Sally. He called out, "Who are you?"

"Your worst fucking dream. Come up these stairs and I will kill you. You sick pervert."

"What do you want?"

"We came for you."

"Who?"

"You know. The Professor, your boss, sent me to find you. He wants you for running away after the fire. We didn't expect to find a woman here. You have some explaining to do. I don't like your chances. My assignment is to keep you here until others arrive. You don't have enough time to get past me, and I don't think you could. I'll kill you if I have to."

Hankins paled when he realized the man from Herat had found him. He was without mercy. Dying at his hand would be terrible. He had to take this woman first. If he could get past her and get his notebook and hidden flash drives, he might have a chance. Escaping from al Qaeda, just to have the cops all along the East Coast searching for him, was not much of a tradeoff. He gathered himself and started up the steps.

Kelly knew from Kathy's briefing that Hankins was a Taekwondo middle belt with four or five years of one-on-one training once a week. She felt confident she could hold her own. Jack had arranged for her to study Hapkido. Hapkido was not a sport. It was about killing and levels of hurting. Her instructors were very good. She was a beginner but she had some basic moves, especially the kicks that pleased her instructor. She saw Hankins get off the floor. Get out of his jacket and slowly start up the steps.

This time, when he was halfway up and planning his attack, Kelly launched herself down the staircase, catching him in the face and chest with her heels. Hankins crashed to the floor. Kelly's thrust carried her on to the hood of the Explorer. Before Hankins could get up, she had leapt back onto the stairs and was waiting for him at the top again.

"Hey, rug guy, you want to try that again. I don't want to hurt you too badly. The boss won't like it. Please don't make me kill you. Believe me, I really want to."

Kelly knew she was messing with his mind, and it had bought her some time. There were only three outcomes to this standoff. He would jump in the Explorer and escape, kill her and Sally, or she had to kill or maim him. If he believed she was from al Qaeda, and the Professor and others were on the way, he just might opt to escape. She could not stop him.

Kelly glanced at her watch, only 9:15 AM. It seemed like hours had passed since she picked the lock. If only she had brought her gun. She saw Hankins get up and walk over to the workbench. He searched for a minute, then picked up a hammer and started back up the steps. In some ways that was helpful. She now knew what kind of an attack he would bring. It had to be a downward or a level blow from the right side. She didn't plan her counter-moves. She would take whatever opening he gave her. React, do not think, is what Kathy told her. Kelly saw Hankins making moves to get in close where she would have trouble using a kick against him. He feinted with a right-hand hammer strike and when she focused on defending the expected strike, he hit her on the right side of her head just below the temple area with his fist. Kelly staggered back toward the open door. Dazed and sight impaired, she regained her balance and when the hammer strike came from the right, she blocked it with a rising left forearm block and smashed his face with a powerful right elbow strike. The elbow strike surprised and hurt Hankins. He temporarily lost his balance and forward movement, giving Kelly the opening she needed to deliver a front snap kick to his groin. Her kick missed his testicles but was delivered with enough force to knock him down the steps.

She knew he was badly hurt, but she was still having trouble with her vision and nausea. If he came back quickly, she would be in trouble.

Hankins got up and said, "You bitch. Now I have you. I'm going to hurt you before I kill you."

Smiling he started up the steps again, switching his hammer from hand to hand. As Kelly was gathering herself for a death fight, Hankins suddenly flew backward and lay still. Kelly heard a voice saying, "Hey, little sister, thought I would lend a hand. Are you okay?"

"Kathy! Where did you come from?"

"Later. You okay?"

"Yes. A bit woozy. The son-of-a-bitch caught me with a solid punch to the head. I had him, you know. But, am I ever glad to see you. Is he dead?"

"No. I think he'll come around. I just slammed his head on the cement. Are you focused enough to bring me something to keep our little perp still? You know, I don't think he outweighs you by much."

"I'll bring you some duct tape."

Kelly stepped back into the sleeping area and was surprised to see Sally on her feet holding a large kitchen knife. "That's the spirit, Sally. It's over now and you're safe."

"Thank God! I peeked and saw most of the fight. You were wonderful. What are you, some kind of ninja? I was praying for you. What happened to him?"

"My boss is what happened to him. She could handle three like him. He's unconscious. Hand me the duct tape. He's going to see what it feels like. Put some hot water on. I badly need a cup of tea."

Kelly told Sally to stay up here while she and her boss got her attacker wrapped up. Hankins was still out. Kathy said, "The bastard is still alive. He is going to have a monster headache. Let's tape him up while he's not squirming around. Make sure his mouth and eyes are taped."

Five minutes later he looked like he was encased in a cocoon. Kelly asked, "What are we going to do with him?"

"While you were upstairs, I called Jack. He was just on the outskirts of Georgetown. I got a little earlier start than he did. I don't want to talk anymore around Hankins. He may be awake. Follow me over near the garage door. If we are quiet, I don't think he can hear us. Okay, we have another more immediate problem. What do we do with your friend upstairs? Is she in decent shape?"

"Yes, she doesn't seem physically hurt. Her arms and legs have recovered from the tight tape bindings. Mentally, I don't know. She seems strong but she had an awful experience. She looks and sounds like she is a classy woman with money and a decent education. Probably well connected. I guess the problem is that she has seen or soon will see both of us. We don't want to be part of a criminal investigation, court appearances or publicity that could be all over Hankins' case, even without the al Qaeda involvement."

"Well, you got it. Smart girl, if I overlook the bad judgment of coming here alone and unarmed. Right now I can't. Let's get on with the show. Jack will be here in about 10 minutes. He'll park near your car and come in by the side door. Incidentally, I thought for sure you were on stakeout when your room was empty and the car gone. Lo and behold, your car was parked and locked in a very good place to watch the garage door. When I examined the side door, I saw your lock pick tracks.

"Using all my considerable analytic powers, I deduced you were inside. Opening the unlocked door and seeing your flying ninja act, I was sure. It was then that I realized junior G-girl had come to the party unarmed. When Jack gets here, I'm sure he will have thought the problem through. My suggestion is that we talk your friend into keeping the whole thing to herself. I doubt she will want the smarmy media speculating on what happened to her in this sordid place. I doubt she wants to sue anyone and surely doesn't want to testify in court. If our sick perp is dead or locked up in some national security place, her overnight horror story will not be front page. Anyway, we have to get her out of here now.

"Take her out to your car. No names or story. This case has some nasty sides to it that could embarrass her and even put her life in danger. You can flash my badge, and I mean flash, and tell her we try to protect people like her from consequences they don't deserve. Tell her the attacker is not working alone. Her name should be kept out. We can do that, if she'll cooperate. She will not be needed in the investigation. We don't even want a statement. Go! Do your thing."

Kelly ran up the stairs. Her vision was almost back to normal. A couple of Advil would be great. She was carrying Kathy's badge in her hand. She flashed the badge at Sally and said, "Get your stuff. All of it. We're outta here."

After a quick check, Kelly led the way down the stairs and out the side door to her car. Sally was quiet but when the car left Georgetown and crossed the Waccamaw bridge on Route 17 north, she asked, "Where are we going?"

"We wanted to get you out of there before local police show up. I'm part of a special federal unit that deals with serial killers. We have enough to send this guy away for life. We don't need your testimony but, if you want, you can be part of the witness parade and have your story all over the news. I figured you didn't want that and my boss agreed. So it's your choice."

"You mean for me this whole thing is over, and I don't have to tell my story to the whole world?"

"That's right. I could see no upside for you to be involved in a long drawn out legal case. But, it is your choice."

"No! I just want to forget the whole thing."

"You won't be able to forget it, but you'll be able to deal with it. Part of this procedure is that you do not talk to anyone about what happened. Otherwise, some defense lawyer will be handing you a summons. Understand?"

"Yes. How can I thank you?"

"You have. You stayed alive until we got there. I couldn't stand another dead young woman. Just do something good for someone in need and live a full life. Remember, you've been given a second chance. Not many people get one. Use it well. Now, where is your car? I want to help you with a believable story as to why your car was left wherever all night and where you were. It's possible someone called the police to check your car or to tow it."

It didn't take long for Sally to make up an alibi for her absence. She wasn't sure anyone would have missed her. She had her own rented condo and lived by herself. She was working her way through a messy breakup of a long-term relationship. Her car was where she left it. Kelly hugged her, and Sally said, "You know I'll never forget you, especially your mother tiger act on the landing. If you do this kind of thing all the time, please be careful. It's strangely comforting to know there are people like you looking out for the rest of us. Thank you."

Forty

By the time Kelly returned to the crime scene, Jack and Kathy were quietly talking in the garage. Kelly joined them and Jack told her that they were going to interrogate Hankins, who they now knew was using the alias Huxley. His apartment had to be made to look as if he just left. His car would be gone and with any luck the police wouldn't even be called. Whoever owned the apartment would put a rental sign up and that would be the end of the story of Mr. Hankins, alias Huxley. Jack said, "Okay, crew, let's get to work. Put on latex gloves and wipe down the areas you think or know you touched. All signs of Kelly's friend must disappear. Kelly, you take charge of doing the upstairs. Take your time. I'll need at least 30 minutes with our killer of young women."

After Kelly went upstairs, Jack and Kathy set to work improvising a water-boarding interrogation capability. It didn't take much, a towel, bucket of water, an incline board of some kind and restraints. Jack searched the garage and found a six-foot-long 2x8 that once was part of a rather well-built workbench. In ten minutes they were ready to use the killer's duct tape to firmly fasten him to the 2x8. With one end resting on the back cargo space of the

Explorer, Jack was ready. He said, "Kathy, you handle the questions and I'll motivate him."

Together they carried a trussed up Hankins to the back of his Explorer and taped him to the plank Jack found. His mouth and eyes were taped. Jack leaned down close to Hankins and said, "This will be very unpleasant. I don't care if it kills you. When you get a question, answer fully and correctly. Any lies will be punished immediately. I'm taking the tape off your mouth. Any screaming or shouting will get you taped up and the questioning period will be over. Cooperation is good. Resisting is bad. Understand?"

Hankins nodded and Jack ripped the tape off his mouth. Kathy moved in close and asked him to describe his training in the al Qaeda camps. Hankins hesitated and Jack put a dry towel over his face and said, "Breathe now. It will get harder."

Hankins jerked as Jack slowly saturated the towel with cold water. He was soon struggling to breathe. Jack added more water. Waited another 20 seconds and took the towel off his face. Hankins gasped for air. Kathy gave him a minute and asked the same question again. Hankins said nothing for the next 5 seconds and Jack put the towel over his face again and said, "When the question is asked, you begin answering immediately. No thinking. No answer, no breathing. Understand?"

Hankins nodded several times. Kathy asked the same question again. He immediately began to talk. Jack recorded it all on his iPhone. The interrogation lasted an hour. Jack had to use more persuasion only one more time when Kathy asked how Hankins communicated with his al

Qaeda control, what was the recontact plan, and what encryption system was used.

Kathy said, “Okay! I’m done here.”

Jack drew her off to one side and said, “Get Kelly out of here. Check and see if she’s done upstairs. If getting rid of this killer gets nasty, I don’t want Kelly mixed up in this mess. She needs a little protection from some parts of our work for now.”

“Agreed, but what are you going to do with him?”

“I’m working on it. The problem is getting rid of the body. It’s possible that Frank may be willing to take him for further interrogation or for use as bait. But, we must not leave a trail back to us. When you and Kelly leave, I’ll call Frank and see what he has to say. Does Hankins’ laptop have his killing pictures on it?”

“I haven’t checked it yet. We do have the photos I copied off his flash drives. I could put them back on his machine and backdate the download.”

“Do that. If Frank agrees, I’ll make sure Captain Shorer gets the pictures of the young women this creep killed. I keep forgetting all the illicit skills you learned at the CIA, or was it UNC?”

“Actually, both.”

Jack finished re-taping Hankins’ mouth as Kathy and Kelly left the garage to go back to the motel and check out. Jack went upstairs for a final check and to call Frank on his cell. He was put straight through. Jack said, “We have Hankins and have interrogated him. Kathy got some interesting stuff. If you’re ready, I’ll download the audio now.”

It took Frank a few minutes to scan the tape. Then he said, "Yes, we can use this, especially the encryption data. Our Afghan field guys can use the info on the camps and his training in Peshawar. I don't want Hankins. But, it's worth a try to use his recontact method. The Professor might respond by sending someone to checkout Hankins. Picking up whoever he sends may help us find the Professor. Your team is now big enough to dangle Hankins and see who bites. Work up a plan and tell me what you think. The only alternative is to make him disappear today."

"All right. I don't think the Professor will send one person. I'll bet he sends a team of shooters to get rid of Hankins. I don't think he has a place in his scheme for him."

"You may be right. Give it a try. There is no real downside. Unless he takes Hankins alive and interrogates him, he won't be sure we were involved. I believe he has so much at stake, he will continue with his plans."

Jack was going to comment but found he was now listening to a dial tone. He grinned, that guy is certainly consistent. He never says good-bye. Sure doesn't waste words.

He dialed Kathy and when she picked up, Jack said, "Frank wants us to dangle this guy by activating his recontact plan and see who shows up. I'm willing to try it for a day or two, period. We'll need Lou and Storm. Please send for them. See if they can arrive today. Kelly can arrange for their lodging."

"Okay, but you know this is going to be a mess. Keeping the perp captive for that time is going to be a witch."

"If it gets too hard, I'll get rid of him. For now I don't want to leave him alone. I'll take the first four-hour watch. Tell Kelly to get some rest. She's on next. I'd like to get the personal ad in the Myrtle Beach Chronicle in time for tomorrow's edition. Can we do that?"

"Yes, I'll get right on it. That means we have to be ready to deliver him to the recontact site."

"Have Lou and Storm in our room when I get there, and we can put a plan together."

"Got it. I'll pick up some food. Want your usual?"

"Yes! If you can find a good Reuben and pick up two cheeseburgers for Shadow, hold the vegetables and ketchup. He needs a treat for being so good cooped up in my car. See you soon."

Forty-one

The Professor was enjoying his drive north up Route I-95. It had been years since he had cruised American highways as a graduate student. Even now, he was still impressed by the extent of the national highway system. The Americans are certainly the Romans of our time. They are a formidable enemy. The sheer size of the land mass and the technical know-how of their population present great problems to any would-be conqueror. To defeat them, we must make them defeat themselves. Their own political leaders are already preaching class warfare. I believe that kind of rhetoric is our strongest ally. Rome fell apart from internal strife, so will America. I can only pray I live long enough to see it happen. I've devoted my life to destroying the American Empire.

Keeping within the speed limit and carefully following all traffic signs, he was now within 5 miles of the primary Richmond exit. He could not afford even a routine police check of his documentation. He had some familiarity with Richmond from the past. He liked the City and had read extensively about Richmond as the capital of the Confederacy. It was past time to change cars and this was an ideal place. His plan was simple. Drive to the Richmond Airport, park in a lot, and take a taxi to the

Jefferson Hotel on West Franklin Street. He liked the Jefferson and had stayed there many years ago. There was no chance anyone would recognize him now. At least one night in luxury would be good. He had perfect alias documentation that would pass close inspection. After getting a good rest, the Professor planned to visit one of Richmond's used car lots and buy a two- or three-year-old car for cash.

The next morning when he checked out of the Jefferson, paying cash, he was almost sorry to be leaving. After all the hiding and hard living he had endured the past decade, there was something to be said for luxury and tranquility. He was a committed Islamic Jihadist but he could feel the allure of Western culture. This was indeed the land of the Great Satan, if even he had to resist the pull of western decadence. When he got to his destination, he promised to spend more time in prayer and meditation.

Now, he had to focus his attention on buying a used car in a way that would not leave a paper trail. The Professor took a taxi from the hotel to a used car lot he selected from the newspaper ads at the hotel. His selection advertised a number of late model cars and trucks. He had been using luxury cars. It was now time for a change. He got out of the taxi at a restaurant a block from his destination. When the taxi was out of sight, he shouldered his light carry-on bag and walked to the car lot.

He was immediately approached by a salesman who asked, "May I help you?"

The Professor, using his New England accent, said, "I'm interested in looking at a pickup truck in good condition I could use on my small farm." When asked about his price range, he said, "I'll pay cash and want to pay no more than $20,000."

When the salesman looked surprised that he was going to pay cash, the Professor told him, "I deal in land sales and just collected my share of a mid-sized deal and don't want to run the money through my account and my wife's lawyers. Is that a problem?"

"Not at all, and I think I have just what you are looking for. I can bring it up or you can walk through the lot with me."

"I'll walk with you in case I see something else I like, and I'm in a bit of a hurry to get on the road."

Forty-five minutes later, the Professor had handed over $21,000 and signed a stack of documents that made him owner of a white 2006 Ford F-150 4x4 XLT with 41,032 miles on the odometer. Where he was going, the F-150 would blend into the surroundings and the 4x4 capability might prove useful. If, in some way, the authorities had managed to pick up his trail, this change in vehicles will throw them off. It would take an outstanding bit of police work to make the connection between his Passat left at the airport and the Ford truck with dealer plates.

An hour later he pulled into a rest stop and made a phone call to a number in Baltimore that would be bounced to Falls Church and which instructed one of the many al Qaeda support workers to post a personal note on an obscure Facebook page. Al Hasani would see the comment and know what to do. He was perhaps the best sniper the Professor had ever seen in all his days of Jihad. Hasani had been very hard to convince he must travel to America and wait for the signal to begin his own war against Americans.

Checking into his complicated communications system that included the social media, three web pages and two blogs, the Professor learned that Hankins had placed a personal ad precisely as called for in his recontact plan. He made another call, ordering the death of Hankins, the rug merchant he never trusted, especially since he was the only person to escape the fire that destroyed two well-planned car bomb attacks. He knew the odds against the explosives causing a fire were minimal. Several dedicated Jihadists were killed in the fire. He wanted Hankins to pay for his failure.

Forty-two

All five members of the Brandon team were in Jack's motel room. Lou and Storm had just arrived. While they were eating a late carry-in lunch, Jack brought them all up to date. The mission was to capture one of the expected al Qaeda team they expected to kill or kidnap Hankins. Kelly briefed them on the layout of the garage apartment where Hankins was living. He was now securely tied to his bed.

Lou asked, "What do we do with Hankins?"

"Good question. We don't want him. The Feds don't want him and I don't think al Qaeda wants him. My first concern is that nobody in this room gets killed or injured. By now I believe even our newest member, Kelly, realizes it is much easier to kill than capture. Capturing a Jihadist is not going to be easy. Better to let them have Hankins than to risk one of us getting killed. According to Kathy's interrogation of Hankins, the recontact plan calls for Hankins to be in the extreme northwest corner of the Walmart parking lot at the junction of Route 17 and Route 544 in Horry County. We need a plan to get him there like a staked-out goat in a tiger hunt. The people coming for him will be pros. They will reconnoiter the scene before committing. Their attack will be fast and deadly. I really don't have a plan to capture one of them alive. These people will not surrender and we cannot get into a shoot-out, especially in a public place. The only thing I can think of is to hit one with a long-range shot and then prevent their carrying off or killing the wounded person, and I don't like it. Too many opportunities for things to get out of control. Comments?"

Lou said, "My comment is, I don't like the scenario. It puts us in a constant reaction mode. How about we stake out the scene and take the first opportunity to grab one of them before they attack. They won't be checking out the place in force. One or two will be deployed as scouts. The scout or scouts will seek out the best observation spots and check out the overall area from there. We pick the likely spots in advance and set up our ambush. Leave your perp to deal with al Qaeda on his own."

Kathy said, "I like the approach. It keeps us in the driver's seat. Worst case, except for one of us getting killed, is that we get nothing and the bad guys get Hankins. Good riddance. It also gives us the option of doing nothing and following one of them to a place where the odds are definitely in our favor."

Jack was silent for a long moment and then said, "The truth is that we don't have the resources for this or the authority to endanger a number of innocent bystanders. There is also the problem of the Professor learning we know something of his operation. I don't think the Feds would like that at this point. My plan is to set up video coverage of the recontact scene and see if they will provide the surveillance coverage to follow the people that pick up or kill Hankins. Kathy, please deal with your Fed friends. You speak their language. Lou, check out the scene and pick the most likely observation posts. Storm, please select and set up the equipment needed to get coverage of the northwest corner of the parking lot. Lou will help you after he picks out the most likely observation points. Kathy, Kelly and I will move Hankins into position two hours before the recontact schedule of 5:00 PM. Remember, it will be getting dark by 6:00 PM. Okay, let's go."

Jack waited until Kathy talked with Frank, who gave his okay and said he would have two surveillance teams in place. The teams would depend upon them for car descriptions, direction of movement and a departure alert. Jack and Kathy went in one car to within a block of Hankins' apartment. Jack entered the apartment first, Kathy and Kelly followed at three-minute intervals. Jack stepped inside the side door to the garage with his SOCOM pistol in his hand, round chambered and safety off. He moved silently across the garage floor and up the staircase. Hankins was still tightly wrapped on the bed. Tape over his mouth and eyes. Jack checked the small apartment, put the SOCOM under his belt in the small of his back. Taking ear plugs from his pocket, he forced them into Hankins' ears. He no longer needed to speak, see or hear. Kelly and Kathy arrived and they began prepping Hankins. Jack pulled the tape from his mouth, jerked him to a sitting position and jammed the neck of a bottle of blended whiskey into his mouth. By the time they got over half of the fifth into him, Hankins passed out and reeked of Four Roses.

The three of them carried Hankins down the stairs and into the passenger seat of his own Ford Explorer. Jack could have easily carried him down over his shoulder but didn't want to take the risk of Hankins throwing up and drowning in his own vomit. It was too soon for him to die. Everyone wore latex gloves and there was no reason to wipe down the apartment or Hankins' car. Jack drove the Explorer. Kelly and Kathy with Shadow followed in their own car. With all the duct tape removed and the residue scrubbed off, Hankins looked like a sleeping passenger, held in position by the seatbelt.

It was only a 30-minute drive from Georgetown to the Walmart at the junction of routes 17 and 544. Jack noted where Kathy parked and temporarily parked nearby. He gave Hankins two sleeping pills and forced another several swallows of Four Roses down his throat. Then he drove to the nearly vacant northwest corner of the parking lot. He shifted Hankins to a position behind the wheel and left the nearly empty whiskey bottle on the seat. As a last measure, Jack put the loaded .38 revolver Kelly found in Hankins' chest of drawers in his lap to convince al Qaeda the passed-out Hankins wasn't part of a setup. He had been in the northwest corner of the lot for less than three minutes.

The lot was filling up with after-work shoppers. On the way back to where Kathy and Kelly were waiting, Jack checked in with Lou on his cell. Lou told him he hadn't seen any sign of anyone lingering in the observation points he located. He and Storm had a good view of the Hankins car from a less obvious surveillance post and the telescopic camera lens was sighted in. Storm was ready to video the site when the people coming for Hankins were seen.

Jack said, "Great! I'm going to wait here until you spot them. We'll give them scheduled time plus an hour before we move Hankins."

Jack climbed in the back seat with Shadow and brought Kathy and Kelly up to date. When he finished, he said, "We might as well relax a bit. We could be here for two or three more hours. With Lou's experience on the street with the Bureau, he's not going to miss anything. My main worry is that alcohol and sleeping pills affect people differently. It's possible Hankins will surface too soon."

At 3:30 Jack's cell awakened. Lou's voice said he saw two men at a high point on the bank overlooking the parking lot using binoculars. They were checking the entire lot but seemed to focus on the northwest corner. No cars were headed to that position, and no one was walking near the Explorer. Lou's voice got more urgent as he said, "Jack, I see movement in the Explorer and the two guys are coming down the bank toward the Explorer. The driver's side door is opening. The bait is awake. Storm has the video running. The two men have split up and are approaching the Explorer from both sides. Your perp is out of the car but hanging on the door. He's seen the two men. He's got a gun."

Hanging on every word, they heard three distinct gun shots, then two more. Lou said, "The perp fired first and put the guy closest to him down. The other one fired twice at Hankins. Hankins is down. The only one standing is now right over both of them. My God! He's tapped them both in the head from close range and is now running down the parking lot toward the main entrance."

"Lou, you and Storm try to get a good description of the car he gets into. That's more important than getting good images. Can you see plate numbers at your range?"

Storm said, "I'm watching him through good optics. I can see plates. He's getting into a late model blue Ford, four-door sedan. One other man in the car driving. They're headed out the main gate to Route 544. Plate number is BBC 497 South Carolina plates."

Kathy was relaying the information to the CIA surveillance teams as she got Storm's report, including that shots had been fired and the bait and one attacker were down and presumed dead.

Lou, holding his position, said, "I see no evidence of any police or local security. A guy parking his new car 30 yards away saw the bodies and got his cell out. He's still talking into it. It's time for us to leave. You especially, before the entrances are locked down."

Kathy didn't need any encouragement. Her rental was already headed out the main entrance. The surveillance team, deployed along 544 west, checked in and said they had the target car. The make, color and plates matched the description.

Storm called in and said she and Lou were headed south on Route 17 to Georgetown and would see them there.

Kelly said, "Where'd Hankins get a gun?" Jack replied, "A little bit of staging on my part. I put Hankins' loaded .38 in his lap, figuring the fact he had a gun would make it look less staged. I didn't think he would regain consciousness that soon. Sometimes little touches work better than planned."

Kelly said, "Will I ever think like that?"

Kathy said, "I'm just beginning to follow Jack's thinking. Maybe in ten more years. I don't know about you. You are already in a crash course and, I think, doing very well. Jack may not agree, but the process goes something like this. Don't close out a plan. Always stay with it and add things that improve it. Think what the plan will look like to your enemy as it unfolds. Do not make decisions until you have to. There is no rule that early decisions are a good thing. Knowing when not to make a decision is important. You will never have enough information to make a perfect decision. People, like Jack, with great operational minds, have a feel when to make decisions irrespective of the information on hand. There now, I'm sure I've added immensely to your education in the Brandon School."

"I think I'm sorry I asked."

Forty-three

Frank called the moment they unlocked the door to the motel room. Kathy answered her cell. She started to brief Frank but he cut in and said, "I've been informed by the surveillance team. They are now sitting on the two shooters who left the scene. We've deployed a capture team and should have them under interrogation by tonight or tomorrow morning. That's not why I called. The Professor's Passat was just located in the parking lot at the Richmond Airport. A forensics team will soon be on it. I gave instructions that nothing else be done until you get there. I don't have anyone else who can put themselves in the head of the enemy as well as you can, or as quickly. The investigative job you did in Myrtle Beach still has my staff scratching their heads. The know-it-all you had to deal with at the hotel fiasco is no longer with us. Go to Richmond as soon as you can. Use your police badge. Call me direct, if you run into any trouble. The contact instructions you will need for the forensics team are being downloaded now. Put Jack on. I need to talk to him."

Jack took the iPhone from Kathy and said, "Go, I'm here."

Frank replied, "I need Kathy in Richmond as fast as she can get there. And I need you and the rest of your team up here by tomorrow afternoon. I'm convinced that the Professor stopped in Richmond for a travel break and to change cars. He is on his way here. I know him, and this is where he can do the most damage. Early in the Iraq war, he ran several al Qaeda sniper teams. He was very good at it. We deployed a number of teams to wipe them out. You didn't know it, but I now know you were part of this operation as a Marine Corps Officer. The record tells me that you were a highly skilled sniper and were very effective in counter-sniper operations.

"I'm convinced the Professor is planning such a campaign in the Washington area. Last year we almost caught an al Qaeda operative, known as Al Hasini. He is an exceptional sniper. He slipped through the Minneapolis Airport before we could get deployed. No question that he was there. The facial recognition software identified him. I've seen the pictures. There is no doubt. He will be casing set-up areas for sniper operations. I need you to also pick areas you think he might use. Your whole team will be needed."

"Got it! I'll need some equipment. We can all stay at my house in McLean. It has just recently been rebuilt, everything but the landscaping. I'll call you when we get in. I remember that guy. I missed him once. It's good to have a second chance."

Jack knew the conversation was over but waited a second for the dial tone, Frank's signature good-bye.

Kelly drove Kathy to the Myrtle Beach Airport for a timely route to Richmond. Storm and Lou drove back to Charleston to pick up the clothes they would need and to check out of the hotel. Shadow stayed with Jack. He would be going to Washington in the back of the Cadillac SRX. His own first class compartment. Two hours later Jack, Kelly and Shadow were on the road. Kelly was driving. Jack said, "I hope Kathy didn't teach you how to drive her style."

"No, I'm not as good as she is but I've been practicing, especially high speed passing while checking my six. She also showed me how to pick and use a good pace car. Let the pace car get the ticket is her mantra."

"No more, please. I'm already terrified. I'm going to try to sleep. Wake me when you need a break."

Kelly could hear both Shadow and Jack were in a deep sleep. Driving in the tunnel of her lights, she thought, I've never felt more alive and at peace with myself than I am right now. I'll bet my mother felt like this. How else could anyone do what she did for so long? I wish I knew more about her. I know Kathy and Jack know more than they've told me. I'm sure they'll tell me more when they feel the time is right. I feel closer to them than anyone I ever knew, except maybe Anita. Too bad I didn't know sooner. Someday I want to trace her last mission. I think Jack and Kathy owe me that much. I wonder why they aren't married. It's easy to see they are very much in love. I don't know Kathy well enough to ask her. I know Jack was married once. Maybe they're afraid the ritual and commitments of a marriage will damage what they have. I know Jack does not have a wandering eye. A girl can tell when a man sees her stark naked, and there's not even a glimmer of want in his eye. If I didn't know better, I'd be doubting my own sex appeal. This career doesn't leave much opportunity to find a companion. But if my mother could find a relationship in this life, I can.

Forty-four

By the time Kelly drove past the exit to downtown Richmond, Kathy had already been on the ground working for hours. After identifying herself to airport security, an electric car took her out to the forensic team in the parking lot. She didn't know any of the team. It was obvious they had taken their briefing seriously. Their only question, was she the agent who found the Professor in Myrtle Beach. Kathy said, "Yes, now what can you tell me?"

Jackson, the team leader said, "We found his prints and some hairs on the headrest that should give us DNA. No documents, papers, maps, rental agreements or even food wrappers were found in the car. From the time he left the hotel in Myrtle Beach until he pulled into the parking lot, according to parking lot cameras, four days ago, Friday at 1:25 PM, the timeline indicates no stops along the way. He probably stayed within the speed limit. At 60 mph the driving time matches the time available between his departure and arrival here. He didn't use the car phone and the nav system is not like Onstar. We cannot back-track his movement. We found some slight scratches on the back of the mirror that may have held a rental sticker. We're running the VIN number against a number of databases and should have something soon. We know where he's been but don't have a clue to where he went in Richmond, and we are not likely to find any clues to his current whereabouts in this car.

"We haven't worked the airport camera coverage. Our very clear instructions were to leave that to you. We'll hang around Richmond until you clear us to go back to Washington. We're putting up at the Jefferson. If you need us, one of us will be on call in the hotel. We haven't checked in yet, but I'll give you my cell number. I'll be listed under Bill Jackson in the hotel records."

Kathy thanked the crew and turned and walked back to her security-provided jitney and driver. The driver took her back to the Chief of Security, Oscar Connor. Kathy said, "Before we check passengers on every flight leaving here to anywhere during a four-hour period. I have some very clear photos of the wanted man and a definite time period. Using our deduced time, standard facial recognition software and your judgment of what route he would have taken from his car in the lot to a plane or exit, we should be able to find him. Can you spare a couple of your best people to help me?"

"Sure can, and I'm one of them. Let's get started. Grab a cup of fresh coffee, and we'll head down to the monitor room. My assistant will join us there."

Kathy outlined the problem to the monitoring supervisor. "A green Passat entered the parking lot last Friday at 1:25 PM. I need you to determine the routes from his parking spot to buying a ticket, boarding a plane or exiting the airport. Then, using a timeline, narrow the video search. I have a clear photo of the man to enter into your facial recognition program. Is that enough for you to get started?"

"Yes, that's a lot more than we usually get. Give me a few minutes to lay out probable routes and to get the photo scanned into our search parameters."

In ten minutes the supervisor was ready to go. He found the car entering the lot immediately and was able to follow it to its current position. The image of the man exiting the car wasn't good enough for facial recognition, but they could follow the man walking to a parking lot bus stop and getting on board at 1:35 PM. The cameras picked him up getting off the bus. Here the facial recognition software gave them a hit. The cameras lost him in the crowds. Kathy said, "This guy is a pro. He knows about cameras. Check your imagery of the major ticketing area, boarding areas, security check processing and exits." It wasn't until they focused on the exits did they get another hit. This time he was still carrying his one bag with his topcoat over his shoulder and wearing a hat and glasses. The Professor could be seen getting into a blue and white Citizens Taxi. The taxi number and the license were clearly visible as it pulled away.

Kathy said, "Great job! Please make a copy of the video footage we found on our subject and give it to Mr. Bill Jackson. He may still be examining the car in the parking lot. If not, he's staying at the Jefferson. Now I need to rent a car. Thank you very much. You certainly understand your facility. It's a pleasure to work with dedicated professionals."

Mr. Conner was obviously pleased with Kathy's praise and called for an airport cart to take her to the car rental section. Kathy selected a Ford Mustang and set off for the Citizens Taxi terminal. On the way she called Frank and told him that the Professor left the airport in a taxi no more than 30 minutes after parking his car in the lot. She promised to call again after checking out the taxi terminal.

Kathy thought her outfit was perfect for playing lady cop. Faded, but not new jeans, a black tee just a little on the tight side, dark leather pull-on half-boots and a tan linen jacket that covered her SOCOM .45 caliber sidearm in a tilted holster far back on her right side. She fastened her badge on the left front of her belt, well removed from any possibility of its interfering with a fast movement to bring her weapon into play. Her inch under six-foot height, shoulder-length natural blond hair and athletic 140 pounds rounded out her image. She wasn't above using that image to help in eliciting information. Her steadily improving skills in Hapkido improved her confidence in handling situations without using her firearm. She was pleased with the way she had dealt with Hankins without even thinking about drawing her weapon.

The taxi terminal was just on the fringe of the 'Fan' area of Richmond. Once inside the smoke-filled entrance area, she went directly to the dispatcher's desk. Her badge and gun were clearly showing.

The nameplate said he was Clarence Fox. Kathy said, "Mr. Fox, I need some cooperation."

Three of the smoking loungers crowded up around the desk.

Turning to face them, Kathy said in her toughest voice, "Go away. If I need you, I'll call."

They laughed and jeered. Kathy stepped hard on the nearest instep and, when the man reached for her, she pressed a nerve on the outside of his forearm below the elbow. He yelled in pain. Kathy moved closer and said, "Now beat it, before I really hurt you."

Holding his forearm, he moved away followed by his friends. Mr. Fox said, "Lady, you are welcome here anytime. Buck is a real problem. I can't handle him and the boss won't fire him. You certainly took him down a few pegs. Watch your back. He'll be thinking about getting even."

"For his sake, I hope not. Now, I've a couple of questions. Last Friday at about two o'clock, this man was seen getting into taxi number 12, plate GHY 617. Can you tell who was driving that cab and where he is now?"

"Yeah, I think so. It'll be just a minute."

Kathy waited, looking around the room that was the terminal for Citizens Taxi Service. This must be a job opportunity for ex-cons, judging from the tats and attitudes of drivers hanging around.

Mr. Fox motioned her over and said, "Got him. It was Bobby Anderson. He's a regular. Pretty dependable. He's nearby, I'll call him in."

Bobby showed up ten minutes later. Kathy was getting tired of being ogled by the creeps and asked Bobby if he would mind stepping outside.

"No, Officer, I'm okay with that."

Once outside, Kathy showed Bobby the picture of the Professor and refreshed his memory about the fare.

Bobby asked to look at the picture again and said, "Yeah, I picked him up at the airport. Light luggage which he kept with him in the back seat. The odd thing was, he gave me no address. Just to drop him off in the historical part of the city. He'd tell me where. He did and I dropped him. He gave me a good tip. I was curious. What well-dressed guy, carrying a suitcase, gets out of a cab in the middle of a street. I was nosy enough to swing back around and saw him going into the Jefferson Hotel. I guess he didn't want nobody to know where he was staying. In this business you see a bunch of strange stuff. Anything else?"

"No. That helps us a lot. Thank you very much."

Bobby went back to his car and drove away. Kathy was parked a half-block down the street. When she got to the Mustang, Buck and one of his pals was leaning on her car, blocking the driver's side door.

Buck outweighed Kathy by 80 plus pounds. A muscular type with bulging tat sleeves on his forearms and a belly gone to fat. He pointed at her and said, "Let's see how tough you really are. Nobody pushes me around. Gun, badge, whatever, it doesn't matter. So if you're gonna call for backup, do it while you can."

Kathy said, "Let's just drop it. I'm sorry if I hurt your male pride. It will be better for both of us if you just move aside and let me drive off."

Buck said, "No way, bitch. I'm gonna slap the shit out of you."

Kathy relaxed, ready to take what opening he gave her, while watching the second man who didn't say a word and looked unhappy. Kathy thought, the second guy wants no part of this. Buck's charge came with surprising speed. Kathy pivoted to her right and side-kicked him just above the knee, stopping his momentum dead. His intended one, two combination never got untracked. He was down, white-faced, trying not to scream and holding his broken knee with both hands.

Kathy called to the second man and said, "Take care of him, and I won't drag you both in. Next time, you both go to the slammer, if you're still alive. Get away from my car, I'm leaving."

The second guy ran inside and Kathy drove off as two men came out to drag Buck inside. She thought, my instructors were right. Stay calm, don't think, take what you're given, strike hard and end it quick. They were also right. The knee is a weak point. I could feel his knee going. He got off easy. Lucky for him neither Jack nor Shadow was here.

Next step is to check into the Jefferson. Haven't been there for ten years. Not since I was a CIA trainee. Doesn't surprise me that the Professor stayed there. He is very well educated, and Frank said he always enjoys fine things, has good taste and has no trouble mixing revolution with luxury. Charlestown, Richmond, maybe this terrorist is old world. Where will he go next? My guess is that he'll continue north to DC and places like Baltimore, Philadelphia and New York. Frank knows him and has a feel for his overall plan. Jack and Kelly will soon be in McLean. Wish I was there now. My memory of Jack's house is of a burning shambles. To be honest with myself, I'm jealous of Kelly being in that house with Jack and Shadow. I trust them both, but that's just the way it is, and I think always has been.

Kathy ended her musing as she drove up to the main entrance of the Jefferson. Before she checked in, she asked to see the Chief of Security. The front desk called him and he came over. Taking in Kathy's badge and gun, he asked, "Officer, what can I help you with?"

Kathy introduced herself and said, "I'm almost 100% certain that this man stayed here for at least one night starting last Friday." She then showed him the picture of the Professor. He took the picture and walked over to the front desk, conferred with the staff on duty and came back to Kathy.

He said, "You're right. This person stayed here Friday night and checked out Saturday morning."

"What name did he use while here?"

"Should I first see a warrant?"

"If you want to be uncooperative in a Federal Investigation you can insist on a warrant. I can call Washington right now and, rather than a low-key inquiry, they will flood the hotel with agents, close off the room he used and question staff and guests. Is that what you want?"

"No need to threaten the hotel."

"Excuse me! That was not a threat. Read promise. I'm tired. You're holding up my investigation. I haven't even asked you how a high-ranking terrorist checked into your hotel under an alias with questionable documents and no credit cards. Check the desk and you will find he paid in cash, and you never even thought that was unusual. Where have you been the last ten years? Now, which way do we go?"

The Chief of Security went back to the desk with a worried look on his face. When he came back he said, "The man you want registered under the name Harold Hollingsworth, and he did pay his bill in cash."

"Okay. Now I want a copy of everything he signed, including his bill. Also I want to question everyone with whom he had contact on the hotel staff. If the room he used is empty, I'll need to see it. How did he leave the hotel? Did he have a car? Call a taxi? Did the doorman call the taxi? Can you make all that happen?"

"Yes, I can, and I'm sorry we got off to a bad start. Can we start over?"

Kathy smiled and said, "Of course."

The room hadn't been occupied since Harold Hollingsworth checked out. Realizing it would probably be a wasted effort, Kathy called the forensic team in to search the room. They were all booked in the Jefferson and were in the room in 15 minutes. Kathy briefed them and then left to interview the housekeeping staff and doorman. The interview of the housekeeping staff only revealed that Hollingsworth was a pleasant man who tipped well and took dinner the day he checked in and breakfast the next morning in his room.

Her interview with the doorman was slightly more productive. The doorman told Kathy he remembered the man in the photo. He turned down his offer to call a cab just after nine o'clock in the morning and walked down the street carrying his bag. Just before he turned the corner at the end of the block, he flagged a cab. When Kathy questioned him about the cab, he said it was one of those blue Citizens Taxis. Kathy thanked him and had the doorman call for her Mustang.

She knew exactly where the taxi terminal was, and 15 minutes later walked into the reception area to see Mr. Fox.

The word had spread. The loungers in the drivers' area got quiet, and Mr. Fox stood up when he saw her come in.

Kathy said, "Good morning, Mr. Fox. I have a few more questions. Can you help me?"

"Yes! Of course I can help you, Officer. What do you need?"

She showed him the same picture and said, "This man got into one of your taxis about 9:00 AM last Saturday on the corner of West Franklin Street and North Jefferson. I want to talk to the driver."

Mr. Fox checked his aged PC and said, "Harry Ingram was the driver. Hey, Harry, come over here. The lady wants to talk to you."

Kathy was amused, Harry was the quiet partner of Buck the taxi driver who tried to attack her earlier. Harry approached the desk in a hesitant manner and said, "I'm sorry about that. I knew nothing about Buck planning to waste you a bit. Doctor said he could begin to use crutches in a couple of days. He still doesn't know what happened."

"I'm not here to talk about our meeting. Give my best to Buck. If he wants to meet again, I have a room for him in the federal pen. He needs to work on anger management before it's too late. Now, a few questions. Mr. Fox, please tell Harry what we need from him."

"The officer wants to know everything you know about the man in the picture on my desk."

"I don't know this guy. He might have been a fare. I just don't know."

Kathy said, "One more chance and then you come with me. I know you picked this man up around nine o'clock Saturday morning near the intersection of West

Jefferson and West Franklin streets. Think before you answer. It is a felony to lie or withhold information pertinent to a Federal Investigation. Do you understand? Answer truthfully and you are home free. Tell me."

Harry said, "As I remember this fare was walking along West Jefferson carrying a suitcase. He signaled and I thought he looked like he was going to the airport, so I stopped. It's a good fare out to the airport and often a better one coming back. He gets in and tells me to take him to the 3000 block of West Broad Street. I drop him there. He gives me a good tip and I drive off."

"Did he ask you any questions or did you talk to him at all?"

"I asked him if he wanted me to wait. He said no, I'm meeting a friend."

"Nothing else?"

"No, I swear that's all."

"Okay, Harry, we're done here. Thank you."

When Harry left, Mr. Fox, the dispatcher, said, "You put the fear of God into these guys and they don't scare easy. When you were walking up to the door, one of them said, 'Be quiet! Here comes fucking Wonder Woman. Do not mess with her.' Coming from them that's high praise."

Kathy smiled and said, "Just doing my job. Thanks, I don't think you'll be seeing me anymore."

When she was outside, Kathy called Frank and told him the Professor used the name Harold Hollingsworth to register in the Jefferson Hotel. His forensic team was now going through the room he used. Kathy said, "He's going north and needs wheels. I have a lead on where he might have picked up a vehicle. I'm going out there now to check some used car dealers in the 3000 block of West Broad. I'll call you when I learn anything more."

Kathy found a curbside parking space on West Broad beside a fire hydrant.

She sat in the car and put herself in the Professor's position. He needs transportation. He has fake documentation but he doesn't really trust it. None of the used car dealers along this street is going to take a check from anyone without checking with the bank. I don't know how much cash he has, but he will have to have it to buy a car. The rental option is nonexistent. It is too controlled. He's not in much of a position to bargain. I doubt he wants to carry his bag up and down Broad Street looking for the best deal. He can't ride a cab into several car dealers. It would call too much attention to him. So he'll want to make a deal in the first lot he tries. His taxi was traveling the same direction I did, and he wouldn't want to cross the street in front of his driver who would remember his strange client. He would also want to use a place that had a large choice of cars and a number of daily sales so his cash purchase wouldn't stand out.

Using her reasoning, Kathy decided to try Commonwealth Auto Sales. It had a big selection of cars and trucks and was on the right side of the street. She pulled into the lot and saw a salesman walking toward her before she was even out of the car. When the salesman asked how he could help her, she opened her jacket, revealing her badge and handgun and then said, "I'd like to see the sales manager please."

"He's over to your left, leaning on the Cadillac CTS."

He waved his arm and called, "Charlie."

Charlie looked up and walked toward Kathy who was moving in his direction.

He said, "Car shopping?"

Kathy smiled and said, "Nope, perp shopping. I believe you sold this man a car last Saturday morning."

The manager looked at the photo and said, "What's this all about?"

Kathy gave him her cop smile and said, "That's not the way it works. I ask the questions. Let me try again. What kind of car did you sell this man for cash on Saturday morning?"

From the look on his face, Kathy knew she was in the right place.

While the manager was making up his mind about what to tell her, Kathy said, "I'm not interested in your operation. When I find out about what this man bought, I'll be gone. If you decide to stonewall me, you will have made your last sale for a few days, while we go over your books, question your staff and search the entire lot. Now, which is it?"

"Your information is good. He was in here Saturday morning, but he didn't buy a car. He bought a Ford 150 4W truck, and he did pay cash."

Kathy said, "Good choice. Now, if you will please get me a copy of all documents involved in the sale, including VIN, dealer plate number, and the truck's description, distinctive marking or damages and history. I notice you have some camera surveillance. I'll want copies of all the tapes that show the man in question, and a short talk with everyone he talked to."

"Okay. Come inside and have a cup of coffee while we get what you want."

An hour later Kathy drove off the used car lot and headed for Route I-95 and McLean. When she pulled onto I-95, Kathy used her hands-free iPhone to call Frank. When he came on the line, Kathy said, "I have some new information. The Professor, using the same alias, bought a used 2006 white Ford 150 XLT 4x4 with 41,032 miles and Virginia dealer plates, DHL 1450 for $21,495 cash from Century Auto Sales, West Broad Street, Richmond. The truck has no distinguishing marks. I've alerted your forensics team to pick up a package containing all the paperwork and some surveillance camera footage. I've no evidence but I believe he is still headed north on I-95. I interviewed everyone at the car lot who had contact with him. Nothing turned up. He was strictly business, no small talk."

"Kathy, great work. Nobody believes you could get so much information in such a short time. You are acquiring a remarkable investigative reputation. Okay, come up and join the rest of your team."

Kathy heard the dial tone and thought, I guess Frank said goodbye. She knew she was a good investigator but recognized she was also lucky. Kathy had expected to have to visit at least a half-dozen car dealers and maybe more. She had reduced the search by some common sense analysis, but lady luck certainly helped. Now it was time to put the pedal down and get home to McLean and Jack.

Forty-five

Just north of Richmond, Kelly pulled off I-95 and into an Exxon station. Jack had been awake for the last 50 miles and, after using the men's room and walking Shadow, he told Kelly he would drive from here. The area was new to Kelly and she was fascinated with the development and heavy, high-speed traffic. Jack told her this was her mother's world. She had spent years in the Washington, DC metropolitan area when not deployed.

Kelly asked, "What can you tell me about my mother's life and death?"

"You know some of the story. I'll include more details. I only knew Anita for the last year of her life. She joined our team just after my father was killed in the house we are going to now. The house burned to the ground. Anita, Kathy and I set up our living quarters in the apartment over the three-car garage. From there we planned operations to take down several terrorist cells run by a renegade KGB officer. Your mother played a crucial role in our success.

"The chase extended to India and Nepal. We located the meeting place of several al Qaeda officials above a shop featuring Tibetan artifacts. Your mother and I charged into the meeting room and found six men and one woman seated around a long table. We started firing and, just when it looked like the shooting was over, the woman, who turned out to be an assassin high on the wanted list, was shooting at me from under the table. She had been hit but not fatally. I yelled to Anita to watch out. The assassin turned her weapon on Anita and shot her high on her thigh. Anita dropped her empty shotgun and pulled her ranger knife from her boot and dove under the table. She was shot again in the chest but managed to kill the assassin with her knife. I got to her seconds before she died.

"Nothing could have saved her. The thigh wound had severed an artery and the chest wound itself was fatal. She was in my arms. She knew she was dying and wanted me to leave her. In the seconds left to her, she said, 'Take care of my sister. Her daughter is my daughter.'

"Somehow a fire got started. There was no way I could carry her body out of the fire and make an escape. We had talked about these kinds of scenarios, and it was Anita who made us all pledge to protect the group. The critically wounded and dead had to be left. As a result none of us was ever charged, and I don't think al Qaeda ever figured out what happened. Your mother saved my life. I will be forever indebted to her."

Kelly gave Jack a moment to get the huskiness out of his voice and to wipe the few tears running down his cheek. She said, "Thank you. I wish I'd had a chance to know her better. Now, another question. How does your past with my mother affect me?"

"It makes you a special person to me. Anita was nearly ten years my senior. There was no romance. I still love her and miss her incredibly. She was the big sister I never had. Having you here, gives me a chance to keep and continue the memory. I could have taken care of you without bringing you into our group, but Kathy and I saw your potential and we needed a replacement. You are still here because of your own skills and courage. You are the real deal. I know Anita would approve. Will I try to protect you? You're damn right I will. You are precious, but you still have to pull your weight."

"Thanks, Jack. I'll try hard to fit in. I have a lot to learn."

"That's a perfect attitude. Look ahead. You thought the traffic was heavy 50 miles back. What you see now is normal DC traffic. There is almost no slack time. We'll soon be in the action capital of the world, and a beautiful city. I never tire of the DC skyline. In another 40 minutes, we'll be in the driveway of the Brandon house."

By the time Jack drove u the last uphill sharp curve, Shadow was sitting up, looking out the window and whining to get out. Jack hadn't seen his father's house since the rebuilding process. His attorney, Lee Jensen, had the responsibility to rebuild the house. Only occasionally had he asked Jack for guidance. Lee forwarded pictures from time to time, and Jack approved the plans before the building started, but he was not prepared for seeing the house. It was magnificent. It was fitted perfectly into the landscape. The planting was in progress. Lee told him that a series of rainy days put the crew behind schedule. They would need another week but the interior was finished and furnished.

Kelly was shocked by the presence of the house. She looked at Jack and said, "My God, how rich are you? I've never been in a house like this. I'll tell you, there's nothing like this in either Greensburg or Jeannette or even in Oakland, PA, the three areas I grew up in." Jack laughed and said, "It is impressive but I assure you, this house can't compare with some of the old mansions in Oakland. You just haven't been exposed to this style of living. I am very lucky. My father made the money. My job is taking care of it and spending wisely. Give me a minute to let Shadow out."

Shadow hit the ground running. He circled the house and came back to Jack's side. He rubbed Shadow's head and said we can go inside now, Shadow's done his checking."

It was almost dinner time. When Kelly entered, she could smell food being prepared. Jack grinned and said, "I asked the Minhs to close up the Charleston house and come up here. You will also notice that the landscape crew we had at the Johns Island house are here. They acquitted themselves well in defending us. They may not recognize you with your clothes on."

"Will I never live that down? Next time there's an emergency, I'll get fully suited and booted with complete makeup."

"Just don't forget your SOCOM."

"Don't worry. I learned an important lesson that night. No matter what you think, always be prepared. Bad stuff can and does happen."

"The house has several bedrooms with attached baths. You can take your pick. You could take your mother's old room over the garage, but that makes extra work for the Minhs and separates the team. This place has been attacked once and it could be again. The last time, besides my father, the terrorists killed the house staff. Only one of the attackers got away. My father killed one. Shadow, though severely wounded, killed one. And the Nguyens killed another.

"Some days later, your mother, Kathy and I trapped and killed the leader and two of his shooters. Those men, who tried to kill us in Charleston, had ties to the same group. I forgot to tell you, the same group tried twice to kill me, Kathy and Shadow in Oakland while we were staying in the house I lived in when I worked as a homicide detective. Shadow saved us there."

Jack settled in the master bedroom, far more elegant than the original had been. Now, besides a large bathroom in soft granite shades, a sitting room with a wall-mounted flat screen TV, computer station, multiple phones, a concealed refrigerator and comfortable overstuffed furniture, with a dining table for two overlooking the heated swimming pool and the small park adjoining the property, was screened from the sleeping area by a tasteful muted Japanese screen of random Kanji pictographs.

After a dinner of stir-fried vegetables, sticky rice and grilled filet mignon, Mrs. Minh showed Kelly to one of six guest rooms, telling her she liked this one the best. Kelly told her, she had never been in such a well-appointed room. Mrs. Minh laughed and showed her how to use the complicated shower, the TV that responded to voice commands, an iMac stand-alone computer, and house intercom system. She told Kelly, tomorrow Mr. Jack would show her the security features built into the house. She also asked if Kelly had her own weapon and did she need any more ammunition. Kelly kept a straight face but was sure that she was in the only house in McLean where the house staff made sure you had a weapon and enough ammo.

Just before leaving, Mrs. Minh said that it is a Brandon tradition to offer bed tea or coffee in the morning at seven o'clock. Actually, she said with a muted giggle, it was Miss Kathy who started it. Kelly was dead tired and decided to watch an old movie, maybe even a Western and get a good sleep. She needed a couple of restful nights. Only a man of her dreams could make this evening better.

Shadow showed up as she was getting in bed. She scratched his cropped ears, he licked her hand and continued on his rounds. As usual, Shadow had the run of the house. He could sleep anywhere he wanted.

Jack finished exploring his new house and went back to the master bedroom. It was only nine o'clock and he knew Captain Shorer would still be up. Captain Shorer answered on the first ring. Jack said, "Captain, do you have a few minutes? I've got a report for you."

"Jack, good to hear from you. I wondered about you with all the action in the Charleston area. Sure I have time. Shoot!"

"Well, to start, you were right on about your Hankins perp. He was killed yesterday by two al Qaeda shooters. The little perp managed to shoot and kill one of his attackers. One of my new recruits, Anita's daughter from Pittsburgh, saved a young woman he had tied up in his Georgetown, SC apartment for later pleasure. She saved the woman and fought Hankins off until Kathy arrived and flattened him. The Feds asked us to stake him out as bait, so they could catch an al Qaeda terrorist. Instead, it ended up in a shootout. We were not involved in the shooting. Kathy found some awful pictures of the young women he'd tortured and killed. Seems he only wanted to get pictures of the moment of death. I'll send you a flash drive with the photos. I'm sure they wouldn't stand up in court. I don't know how to bring closure to the families of the dead women. There was no time for the niceties of due process.

"Thanks to your suspicions, six al Qaeda terrorists are now dead and I believe another captured. Five of those were killed in a fire. They were sleeping in an apartment over a garage. Two cars rigged with big bombs were in the garage to be used by suicide bombers the next day in downtown Charleston. It was impossible to tell all this to the police in Charleston, due to the need to protect an ongoing Federal Investigation. The division of justice between national security and law and order requirements is often weighted in the Feds' favor, but not in this case.

"I had no approval to pass on this information to you, but I know you will handle it carefully. Maybe, at some point, more can be officially released to the pertinent authorities. We have moved out of Charleston and are now back in my father's house, recently rebuilt. I'll keep you posted."

"Jack, my best to you and Kathy. I understand Shadow helped again when your Charleston house was attacked. Keep your badges and weapon authorizations until this thing is over. Thank you for the call. Now I can sleep a little better knowing the pervert who killed those Pitt coeds is dead and will not kill any more young women."

The next morning at breakfast Jack told Kelly she would be on her own for a while, but to stick around the house until they heard from Lou and Storm. He expected them to arrive sometime today. Kathy would be in Richmond at least one more day.

When Jack called Frank and requested to see him, Frank said, "Glad you called. I want to see you today. Can you get a room at the Ritz where we can have a working lunch? I can't think of anywhere else to meet with you and have no one who knows me see us together and begin to speculate. Some people in my office are beginning to realize that I have some damn good outside people helping out. I want to be careful as possible, even if it is inconvenient, to protect you and your group. I think Kathy told me that you favor Reuben sandwiches. Please ask room service to prepare one for me with some black coffee."

"No problem. I can get a room nearly anytime. One of those perks rich folks like. See you at about noon. I'll call you with the room number before then."

Forty-six

Before the Professor reached the outskirts of DC, he received a brief report stating Hankins was dead but not before he killed one of the martyrs with a hidden gun. The other two escaped. No police or people watching the recontact place were seen. Good, Hankins was a security threat just waiting to happen. It could hardly have been a setup. My people are very good at detecting surveillance, and Hankins had a loaded weapon. Who would stake out a trap with the bait armed, unless there was backup in the area to help him? The media reports would have more information. It still amazed him that so much information was given out by the various media outlets. Hankins was now history. He had to move on to his well-planned sniper attack that would shut down traffic in and out of DC. His campaign in Charleston was not a failure, but it was not nearly as disruptive as he wanted it to be. Soon he would be receiving internal criticism and hinted comments about funding. Hasani was the best. He and his people would remove any doubts his peers had about his war on America, in America.

He was going west along 495 and then Route 7 to Leesburg, Virginia. Three years ago he had used Arab money to buy a small, five-acre retreat on the west side of

Mount Gilead four or five miles south of Leesburg on Route 15. He had never been there, but the descriptions of the log cabin and property almost perfectly fit the needs of his small group of dedicated Jihadists.

It was no longer as isolated, but the increased traffic would cover movement in and out of the country roads. He liked historical anomalies. Where better to attack American capitalism than from a former slave cabin dating back to the late 1700s? His Ford pickup truck would fit right in. Hasani should be there now. He loved to sit and talk in front of a big crackling fireplace. In addition to his skills as an assassin, Hasani liked to cook. He planned to enjoy himself on what surely would be his last battle against the West and their Christian God. There was no escape from this battle.

Using the GPS, he easily found his hideaway farm. Driving over a cattle guard up a steep rutted driveway, he parked next to a white Chevy pickup truck. Hasani came out to meet him. They embraced and the Professor let himself show a little emotion. He truly liked this simple talented fighter for Islam. With a thousand Hasanis, the war against the materialism of the West would have been over long ago. Hasani had no personal agenda. He always followed the guidelines given to him. Never complained. Never made special requests. Never questioned his superiors, even when he knew they were mistaken. He was a warrior from times past. He could have been a warrior in Saladin's army, when it defeated the Western forces and the Templars at the battle of Hattin. Hasani would have loved battling the Templars. They had a similar code. Nothing for one's self, everything for the cause.

He knew he was on the American most wanted list of terrorists, but they cannot know I am here within an hour's drive of the White House. Over strong coffee, the Professor discussed the mission Hasani would undertake in two days. The campaign would start with two car bombs, one on the American Legion Memorial Bridge and one on Chain Bridge. Suicides were not required. In truth their only real use was the need to get a bomb near the target in the face of security forces. He didn't have the resources to lose people without gaining an advantage. Two car bombs. Escape is simple, use four cars. The bomb cars are left on the bridges in any lane, and the drivers escape by getting into the getaway car right in front of them. The bombs are detonated by cell phone signals when the Jihadists are out of blast range. The only hard problem was to get the explosions within a five-minute period to increase the political effect. Traffic was always heavy during the morning and evening rush hours, but difficult to time precisely. He wanted the bombs to explode in the midst of heavy traffic. Using cell phones to coordinate timing would help, but there was always the unknown factor.

The car bombs were intended to get the authorities to focus on bridge defense and car bombs, while the main attack would be Hasani's team of snipers attacking motorists on major arteries during rush hours. Since all the shooters could routinely hit a car-sized object at a thousand meters, it would take a while for the defense to catch up. By that time, he would have moved on. Hasani told him everything was ready. The car bombs were in the stable. The eight snipers, all American recruits, had their weapons ready and sighted in. Hasani always used his favorite rifle, the Barrett M82A2, a .50 Browning semi-automatic weighing 23 pounds. His team members were told to choose their own weapons. All elite shooters have a go-to rifle, and using different weapons makes it harder for the enemy to use ballistic forensics to back-track ammunition buys.

The Professor sat in the old part of the cabin made entirely of chestnut logs with new chinking and dabbing. The stone fireplace held a roaring fire, providing the only light in the room. It was against his beliefs, but all men have weaknesses and his was single malt scotch and strong cigarettes. The fireplace warmed the room. Staring into the fire with the flickering light dancing over the logs, he could see his part in the struggle against Western dominance in perspective. His name would not be recorded in the flow of history, but he felt fulfilled in believing he was on the right side in a fight that will last for at least another 1,000 years. He had a very small part to play, and he would play it as well as he could.

Forty-seven

Precisely at noon, Jack heard a tap on the hotel room door. Verifying it was Frank by looking through the peephole, he opened the door.

Frank looked around the suite, saw the table set for lunch with his sandwich under a warmer and said, "It is really very nice to have assets that can afford to pay for their own safe meeting place, not to mention the Reuben under glass, oops, silver."

"My father taught me that, every once in a while, you have to cater to the proletariat. Please be sure to sign the guest book for the record."

"If you remove the silver cover from my Reuben before it freezes, I can eat and pass on words of wisdom."

As they sat down at the table, Frank said, "Has Kathy arrived yet?"

"Not yet. I expect her today."

"She was very good when she worked for me. I'm amazed at how much better she is after 18 months with you. She is by far the best investigative asset I can call on. She has the ability to put herself into the mind of her target and pick up the trail. Once on the trail, she is like a pit bull. Nothing deters her. She just runs over anyone who gets in her way.

"The Professor would be more careful, if he knew how easily Kathy is able to back-track his movements. It's almost as if she can visualize his every action. I can't explain it. She just moves ahead where my other people would report the trail was too cold. You can't teach what she does. That old story, you either have it or you don't. What happened to her the last year and a half?"

"I can't give you a good answer, but the change I've seen is in her confidence level. None of her movements, actions or thoughts are tentative. I thought she was always holding back and leery of committing herself. Not anymore! She has also taken on the mentoring of our new member, Anita's daughter, Kelly. Kelly worships her and is rapidly becoming another Kathy Grayson. During the attack on our Charleston house, she killed two of the attackers face-to-face while she was totally naked. Afterwards she said, 'I just did what Kathy taught me.' I think taking Kelly under her wing has made Kathy even more positive. She no longer has any fear for herself. Anita's death in some ways has strengthened her. You know Anita was her big sister and her mentor."

"That helps. Thank God she's on our side. We're going to need her, if my thoughts about the Professor are correct. Tell me in more detail about the Hankins' story and the shootout at Walmart."

Jack recited the entire story, including the fight Kelly had with the killer, and the water boarding interrogation. Jack asked Frank about the CIA surveillance and capture of the one shooter who ran from the parking lot.

Frank said, "He was captured at a rented condo in Conway, SC. It was all done very quietly. His interrogation took too long for the intel to be actionable. You know, we have certain 'law and order' rules we must follow to ensure these dedicated terrorists are given their full rights. In this case the terrorist was an American citizen but had knowingly engaged in an active war against his country. Anyway, he told us very little. I don't think he knew much. The Professor is a believer in 'need to know.' He compartmentalizes even the most trivial of information. He loses efficiency and initiative, but gains a strong security shield. According to this home grown terrorist, the Professor is going to carry his war to the Nation's Capital, and he has a Jihadist hero to lead his campaign, but most of his soldiers are American-born citizens.

"We know the Professor likes to use sniper teams, and he is quite good about deploying them. We know his best sniper, Al Hasini, came into the country through the Minneapolis Airport last year. We don't know where he went from there. Our facts end there. The rest is analysis from my shop and from my personal knowledge of the Professor and his work. I believe that Hasani was sent here early to get established. Primarily to put together a team of snipers. I guess the number to be less than ten. I also believe they are Americans who have been trained in the terrorist camps. A few of my analysts believe some of them got their training in survivalist camps in the US. A few of these camps have an 'advanced' shooting training. They are hard to monitor and we don't have good information on what they do or who went there.

"I've two areas I want you to cover for me. The first is applying your knowledge of sniper operations and Hasani, in particular. I want you to think like Hasani would in attacking the Washington, DC area. The Professor will pick the targets, but Hasani will select the shooting sites.

"Assume you have 5 to 10 shooters on your team, and your assignment is to severely impact the life and functioning of the city and its people. Also assume the sniper operations will go on for several days. First, select the target or targets and then, the shooting sites for the targets. Use the capabilities of all your people. I can supply you with target information and any technical gear you may need, including ground and air transport. Oh, and I want you to begin now. What do you think?"

"Are you sure this job is hard enough for us? God, Frank, of course we'll do our best, but this is an immense undertaking for five people."

"Yes. I know, but your capabilities are special. You won't waste time taking on the universe. My hope is that you will uncover our city's weakness to sniper attacks and be able to focus on real targets. The professor is pragmatic and has only limited resources and a limited time to damage the well-being of our people. He will spend the lives of his team, including his own. He needs success and world media attention. I've put together an internal Counter Terror Center team to help. They can provide logistics, analytic support, research, satellite photography and whatever information the Government uncovers once the party begins. The Administration, for all its shortcomings on supporting the war on terror, has one clear goal and that is to reelect the President. Letting terrorists cause the population to lose faith in the Administration's ability to keep them safe is not in their play book. You will get my total support."

"Okay. We'll need a helicopter on standby in some easily accessed place that will fly us around the metro area whenever we need it. If funds are a problem, just tell me and I'll pay for the ride. Two pilots should be enough. Can you make that happen?"

"Yes. I'll arrange for the helicopter and two pilots. What else?"

"Two Heckler & Koch PSG1 rifles and 500 7.62 x 51 NATO rounds, 6 x 42 telescope sights, 20-round magazines, sound suppression and the best night vision gear for two two-man teams. Detailed military tactical topographical maps starting from two klicks outside the Beltway and recent satellite photographs of the same area. To start, the resolution does not have to be the best. Add a couple of good imagery analysts to your team."

"You got it. Call me and tell me where to deliver the gear. The chopper will be at the Leesburg Airport in two days. I'll brief the pilots on getting approval for their flight plans and give them a phone number to call in any conflict with the authorities."

"My team should all be at my father's house by now. I'll develop an approach to this operation and keep you informed."

As Jack walked Frank to the door, Frank said, "You know your father would be very proud and impressed with your record. He was outstanding on espionage problems, but I think he would say that your skills in the counter-terrorist arena are better than his. If you weren't so effective as an operator, I'd try to get you to do some training. This meeting place worked well. If you see no problems, we can do this again. Good luck."

Forty-eight

When Storm, who was doing the navigation, saw the Brandon McLean house, she said, "Dad, what kind of people are they? Look at this house. I've never even been inside a place like this. Have you?"

"Only at a crime scene. Notice they never act or talk as if they have real money. Jack is still a Marine and cop and Kathy is a spook. They are very good people, but hard. Jack and Kathy look like they're the all-American couple but they can kill easily. Kelly is now almost there. She killed two professionals in a 15-foot shootout. That is just not natural. She has her mother's DNA whose trade was killing on the field of battle. She was better than Kathy and equal to Jack. I do okay, but in a rare moment of honesty with my daughter, I'm not in Jack's league.

"Remember, they'll never make us do anything. We can always say no. The pay is very good. I believe we are on the side of the 'white hats' and we can contribute."

They had only been sitting outside for a few minutes when Shadow came bouncing out and put his huge paws on the car's roof. Storm took one look and said, "Dad, I think he wants you to come out first."

"Sure, Shadow and I are old friends. That dog is smarter than most people."

Lou got out and was greeted warmly by a sitting Shadow lifting his right front paw to shake hands. Storm said, "Do you think he knows I have a problem with huge black dogs?"

"I don't know. Why don't you ask him? Shadow come on over and say hello to Storm. She's a bit afraid of you. Maybe you should sleep in her room tonight."

"For God's sake, Dad, don't tell him that."

"Why not? A dog that big sleeps anywhere he wants."

Kelly came out and said, "Lou stop scaring her. Shadow hasn't bitten anyone yet this week."

Storm said, "That's not a bit funny, Kelly."

"Well, it's true. Come on in. Kathy's expected by dinner time. I'll show you to your rooms and give you a chance to freshen up a bit. Jack's downstairs in the gym doing an incredible workout. You can join him if you want a workout. He's been helping me with my Hapkido."

Storm said, "No thanks. I'll pass for now. A hot shower is what I want."

"You may change your mind. All the guests' baths have deep soaking tubs with jacuzzi options. Follow me and I'll show you to your rooms."

Looking around her bedroom and attached bath, Storm thought I could get used to this. The entire house looks like it came out of a House Beautiful magazine. Storm was still exploring when Mrs. Minh said over the intercom, "Miss Kathy is here."

While the Minhs were putting her light baggage in the master suite, Kathy ran downstairs to the gym. Jack had just finished his third set of 20 pull ups, when Kathy burst in and threw her arms around him. "I couldn't wait to get here. You can't believe how much I missed you. First, take me up to that beautiful master bedroom place and then walk me through the house. It looks like Lee has done a marvelous job."

"Are you sure you don't want to work out first?"

"Come with me now! No stops for a shower."

After one of the Minh's superb dinners of curried chicken, a Vietnamese noodle soup with shrimp and a dash of nuoc mam, and steamed rice, Jack said, "We'll have coffee in the new command center. I haven't shown the center to you yet. We'll run our new operation from there."

Kelly said, "Tell me, what was that sauce in the noodle soup? It was super. Did the Minhs make it or buy it?"

Jack laughed and said, "Nuoc mam is notorious. People either love it or can't stand it. The Minhs bought it. The sauce is the result of a long process of distilling fish and that's as far as I go."

The command center was a 30-foot by 15-foot room with several flat screen monitors on the walls. Three stand-alone iMacs with quad processors, i7 intel cores and 27-inch monitors lined the far wall. When everyone had gathered around the table with fresh-brewed Colombian roast, Jack said, "I've accepted a very difficult mission. Some background. An al Qaeda senior leader is now running operations in the United States. The car bombs in Charleston, the burning of churches and the attacks on infra-structure targets in South Carolina are his doing. We now believe he is in the Washington, DC metropolitan area.

"This man is skilled in the deployment and management of sniper teams. He honed his skills in Iraq. On a few occasions, I was part of a counter-sniper group to clean out the snipers operating in the Sunni Triangle. I don't believe this al Qaeda leader was operating in the field as a sniper. A highly talented sniper, who was the leader of the sniper teams in Iraq, is now in the United States. There is no guesswork here. Surveillance cameras and other information confirm their presence. Kathy was the first to spot this high ranking terrorist in Charleston. She saw and photographed him leaving the rug shop a few weeks before we destroyed it. So far, nothing I've said is conjecture or speculation.

"The rest of this brief is at best projected analysis of the above facts or conjecture based on experience. Make no mistake, the threat is very real. The man who sometimes provides our missions believes there will be attacks in the Capitol area within the next few weeks.

"Our role is to identify probable sniper targets, locate shooting points, and develop plans to deny the snipers success within an area extending from a few kilometers outside the beltway to the Capitol. Questions?"

No one said anything. They all just stared at Jack. Finally Kathy said, "There are only five of us. The search area is huge, and there is very little time. There is one more fact. I think we have a clue in the cars our terrorist picked to drive. In Myrtle Beach, he drove a Cadillac CTS. He left that car in Myrtle Beach and drove a Passat north to Richmond. His car choices were made to fit in with his cover and pattern of movement. He did not want his car to call attention to him. Guess what he deliberately bought in

Richmond? A used white Ford 150 4x4 pickup truck. He is not going to locate in an urban condo or in a downtown apartment with a pickup truck. True to his own internal security commandments, he bought the truck to blend in with his new environment."

Kelly said, "You mean this guy is going redneck on us and live in a rural area?"

"I don't know about the redneck part, but I'll bet he's now located in some relatively isolated rural area. Remember the four-wheel drive capability. He doesn't want to be blocked by road conditions, and we are now in an area where snowstorms can shut down travel as late as mid-March. We need to search for the white Ford 150, as well as sniper nests."

Jack said, "Excellent point, Kathy! You and Kelly allot some of your time to searching likely rural areas for the truck. The place would likely be within an hour of DC and I think to the west, areas like Leesburg and Poolesville, Maryland. He won't want to be caught east of DC because of the natural barriers to car travel. That logic also makes south and north of the city less attractive. Now to the resources issue.

"I'm sure there will be other teams working the problem. Our job is to limit the area to patrol and come up with innovative approaches to foil multi-sniper attacks. We'll have logistical and analytic support and special equipment. A helicopter for our sole use will be positioned at the Leesburg Airport tomorrow or the next day. There must be more questions."

Lou said, "I'm sure you have an approach. Tell us your ideas and our questions can be more to the point. So far the mission is overwhelming."

"You're right, I've got a basic plan for beginning, but I'll need help to flesh it out."

For the next hour Jack laid out his initial approach. A lively discussion period followed. Before midnight they had a plan that gave them a blueprint to start.

Jack designated responsibility areas. He and Lou made up one search team. Kelly and Kathy, the second one. Storm was given the responsibility for running their command room, coordinating intelligence, integrating search team reports and keeping track of searched areas. Jack and Lou would assign search priorities. They could sleep in tomorrow, but after that, breakfast would be served at 6:30.

The next morning breakfast was over by 7:30 and all, except Storm, were out of the house. She was in the command center getting familiar with the equipment and setting up databases to handle the incoming information and channel it into files to organize and retrieve search results. Jack and Lou left to pick up the equipment Frank promised Jack from a local storage unit business. Before going to pick up the material, Jack stopped to rent a pickup truck. He thought the Professor's logic made sense. For their search activities, pickups would blend in far better. He planned to get a number of magnetized signs to change the truck's appearance from time to time.

After checking for anyone following them, Jack drove back to the house and they off-loaded the equipment into the garage. The box of maps and declassified images were carried into the house for Storm to sort and store. Kathy and Kelly, following Jack's lead, also rented a pickup truck. Following Kathy's hunch about the Professor using a remote rural area for his headquarters, they checked the records in the Loudon County courthouse in Leesburg and the Montgomery County, MD records. Moving from Leesburg to Montgomery County, Kathy crossed the Potomac River at Whites Ferry. Kathy gave Kelly five dollars and told her to hold it out the window for collection. Kelly couldn't believe a ferry, dating back before the Civil War, was still the site for a major river crossing. Kathy pointed out the Chesapeake and Ohio Canal just east of Whites Ferry.

Kathy said, "Look, kid, while we're here I'm going to give you a bit of area knowledge. It will help put things in context tomorrow when we begin a serious search. Just ahead on Whites Ferry Road is a town called Poolesville. For a period in the Civil War, it was occupied by Confederate troops. We can get a quick lunch and then I want to browse a really good antique store, called Hearthside. The couple who run it know antiques. In my single days, I bought some things there. I was always treated well and never overcharged. Anyway, I like to mix a little fun and pleasure into our work. The man who owns the shop also does some work in real estate and may know if anyone bought a remote small farm in the past year or two."

Storm was swamped with the maps and DVD images Lou and Jack handed off to her. She asked Mrs. Minh to please bring her a sandwich and coffee. She didn't want to leave the windowless room Jack called the command center. She had now mastered the technology and swiped topographical maps, images and text from the iMacs to a series of monitors along the wall. She was ready to get on with the first search when Jack gave the word and selected a target.

Forty-nine

The Professor and Hasani were going through the plan for tomorrow, step by step. Meticulous detail was the Professor's signature. He knew the devil was in the details. Get the details right, and the plan will work.

His worry was over the timing issue and the transfer of the drivers of the car bombs to the getaway cars. Hasani ran three practice runs of the target bridges during rush hour traffic at the same time as he planned attacks. The first one was very poor. By the third run, it was much better. The bridge bombs would have been within the allotted five-minute window, and the drivers could have easily transferred to the getaway cars. The bridges would not be destroyed but traffic would be delayed for hours and damage repair would take a few days to a week or so. He wasn't after damage. He wanted terror in the hearts of every citizen. Let the authorities worry about who was responsible. No phone calls to claim credit from him. Tomorrow morning, a new phase of the war comes to Satan's Capital.

At 7:15 AM, the car bombs and their escape cars left the stable on the Professor's mini farm and turned north on Route 15 to the Leesburg bypass, where one set of cars then went east on Route 7 to Route 123 through McLean to

Chain Bridge. The second set of cars stayed on Route 15 through Leesburg to Whites Ferry and Poolesville, and then on to the Beltway southbound to the American Legion Memorial Bridge.

The weather, for a day in mid-February, had a taste of spring. A few crocuses were showing their muted blooms in protected areas. An intermittent sun shown through clouds that threatened nothing. John Asker, his wife and their two preteen daughters were crossing Chain Bridge heading to McLean to drop the girls at a private school. After that they were going to have a leisurely breakfast at the local deli and then do some shopping at Tysons Corner for birthday presents for the oldest daughter and Alisia's mother. It had been a while since they had had leisure time to themselves. They needed the two incomes but little time was left after attending to the essentials of married life with two daughters.

John saw the car coming toward him slow and stop. Wondering what in the world any driver was doing stopping in rush traffic on Chain Bridge, he slowed quickly and the green Ford Taurus tailgating him couldn't stop and slid into Asker's rear bumper. Asker thought, hell, a damn fender bender. We'll be here for at least 30 minutes. Asker got out of his car, telling his wife and daughters to stay inside. No one was hurt, and they would soon be on their way. He saw a man half running from a car behind the one he saw stopping. A police car passed him and stopped beside the stopped cars. The police officer walked over to the cars blocking incoming city traffic. Asker heard an explosion he knew was gunfire and jumped back in his car, with the thought he had to get his family out of danger. A clear lane lay ahead and he accelerated across the bridge. The exchange of insurance information could wait until they cleared the bridge. He was directly opposite the second stopped car when the car bomb went off. The Askers' car was blown off the bridge into the raging waters of the Potomac River. No one in the Asker car survived. Several cars were blown off the bridge. Others were burning. It was ten minutes before the first help arrived, and the first responders were too few to handle all the casualties and chaos. The Professor's men died in the explosion. The woman police officer prevented their escape but paid with her life. No one would ever know what she knew when she died. No eye witnesses survived. The bridge wasn't badly damaged, but it would be at least a few days before its soundness could be officially verified.

Five minutes after the first explosion, the second car bomb on the American Legion Memorial Bridge exploded. The Professor's men escaped just as planned but several commuters were killed and wounded among the bumper to bumper traffic. It was hours before the mess was cleaned up, and the bridge was closed until it could be certified safe. Commerce and personal travel on the western loop of the Beltway came to a stop. Tomorrow, alternate routes into and out of the city would be jammed for hours.

Fifty

Jack and Storm were putting the first search plan together when the TV monitor on the wall, tuned to Fox, interrupted programming with a news alert. Jack took one look and called the others over the intercom to come down to the command center. Kathy said, "No doubt the guy we are after is here. I'm only surprised he didn't hit more bridges."

In Iraq, snipers were often there to spread the chaos and kill the first responders. What is the plan here? Surely this can't be the end game.

Kathy said, "We know the mantra is 'the goal of terror is to terrorize.' This bridge stuff must be only a beginning or … it's a diversion."

Kelly asked, "A diversion for what?"

Storm said, "The vulnerability of all cities is their need for the movement of goods and services. Throughout history, population centers were attacked by shutting off supplies into the cities under siege."

"Storm, good approach," Jack said. "The terrorists involved here are led by a man who has a deep historical understanding of warfare and the role of terror. He knows he doesn't have the resources to block supply routes, there are just too many of them. His aim may be to spread chaos and terror among the people, just as their doctrine teaches. So what can he attack?"

Kathy said, "He can attack the streams of traffic that occur every day in hundreds of places. He doesn't have to stop the flow of goods and services. He only has to disrupt them. Attacks could be at a different place every day. It would drive the police units crazy. If the attacks could be sustained for a few months, DC would be turned in to a city under siege."

Lou looked at Jack and said, "You know what I'm thinking?"

"Yes! You're thinking he can't use car bombs to put the city under siege and spread chaos and terror through the population, because he couldn't keep it up. Not enough resources and widespread car bombing is very complicated. Preparations are critical and you need a safe area to prepare the cars and train the people who will not survive the attacks. So you need a steady supply of vehicles and people. They are not reusable. It just so happens that we know the answer. Teams of snipers. Snipers can escape after the attack. There is a need only for ammo resupply and transportation. Targets are everywhere and anywhere. Firing positions 500 or 1000 yards from the target are very difficult for fast reaction teams to attack. By the time we figure out where the attack came from, the snipers have moved."

Kelly said, "Makes sense to me. You told us a highly skilled al Qaeda sniper is in the country. Your analysis fits the intelligence we have."

Storm asked, "But why the car bombs?"

Kathy replied, "Because they wanted to start with a diversion. This guy knows no one could convince the security world that the real attack will come from teams of snipers. Even after the snipers begin, the security people will be worrying about car bombs and will not be willing to switch their resources to counter sniper teams. In a nutshell, that's why we were asked to take on this mission, because the very smart people tasking us know how security and law and order organizations think."

Jack said, "Okay. We ignore the car bombs and concentrate on the sniper threat. Storm and I will lay out the first search area. Kathy, wait until Lou and I come back with some lessons learned before you and Kelly work on your search pattern with Storm. Before we all get to work, did you and Kelly learn anything yesterday on your ground tour to the west?"

"Yes, we did. I already was familiar with the terrain but it was all new to Kelly. She can now look at a map of the area and have a better understanding of ground truth. Also, we checked county courthouses for small farm property transactions in the last three years. The badge helped with the record search. The clerks were very responsive. In Loudon County west of Goose Creek, there were 100 transactions. In western Montgomery County, 75 small farms under 20 acres changed hands in the same period. Kelly and I will work with Storm to mark these places on our maps. We'll need a little luck to get much from a property search. We also need something to narrow down the area. Kelly and I will ponder that problem."

Meeting over. People turned to their own tasks.

Jack went up to the master suite and called Frank. When he came on line. Jack said, “I know you’re swamped but give me a few minutes to tell you our thinking.”

Jack then gave Frank a full rundown on the meeting consensus.

Frank said, “That’s why I wanted your group up here working the problem. I agree. It will be snipers, probably starting tomorrow. The Professor won’t give us any breaks. He will feast on the chaos he caused today. What are your plans?”

“I believe the sniper attacks will take place in the areas of the two car bombs. I don’t mean the bridges themselves but the resulting traffic pattern from bridge closures or limited use. I doubt he has more than four or five teams. He won’t want any teams captured or killed. So Hasani will plan for long-range shots, probably nothing less than 300 yards. You know the closer the shooter is to the target, the more likely the target will be hit, but also closeness puts the shooters in greater danger. Good snipers are hard to find or train. He won’t want to lose any right now. So he will only want targets that can be hit with long range shots.

“I remember Hasani favored .50 caliber rifles, the Barrett specifically. There won’t be much if any sound suppression. My guess is that he’ll position a team upriver in the Potomac River Gorge where the shooter can be higher than Chain Bridge. Most likely on the ridge below the George Washington Parkway where there is a clear shot to the bridge area. The trees are still bare. Visibility should be good. He won’t want rain or high wind. There will have to be a good escape route. Probably have the snipers climb to the Parkway and get into a vehicle. At least that's the way I would do it. The attack could shift to the Parkway itself, if Chain Bridge is closed. The same kind of logic fits the area of the Cabin John Bridge or whatever it's called today. We'll need to know what the traffic situations on those bridges will be tomorrow. We need to be able to focus on the most likely target."

"Good. I'll call you about planned bridge traffic for tomorrow. The entire effort of all the security forces will be to prevent another car bomb attack. When one doesn't happen, they will say, "See, we stopped the terrorist car bomb attacks. I don't drink anymore, but they may drive me back to the bottle."

Fifty-one

Hasani finished briefing the Professor on the car bombing operation. The Professor sat silent for a few minutes and then said, "My friend, things went well. It's a good start. Our security is intact. There is no trail back to us. The cars and the bodies will reveal nothing. Even the license plates were stolen. Tomorrow, the fools will expect more car bomb attacks. Instead, you will show them the terror snipers can bring to the enemy. I accept your plan. Tomorrow, it will up to you personally. Take a good man with you. I need you. Your martyrdom is not for tomorrow. Rather, your outstanding skills will bring terror to the city Satan built. It is too bad we were not a team fighting the Templars outside of Jerusalem in the 12th century. Now get some rest. You won't be able to sleep once you get in position."

Hasani had scouted the possible firing positions he could use to attack the Chain Bridge area months ago. He knew just were to go and how to get there. At 11:00 PM, the driver of the white Toyota pickup pulled into an overlook area on the George Washington Parkway. The truck was stopped with lights out for less than a minute. Hasani and his spotter Ali were out of the truck with all their gear and starting down the steep slope of the Potomac River below Chain Bridge.

Hasani wanted to be east of the bridge to avoid shooting into the sun just at the middle of the morning rush hour. His targets were all within 400 meters, a range he couldn't possibly miss from. They had a long wait. Hasani wanted to have the pickup truck blend into the normal traffic. After midnight the traffic thinned to the point that individual vehicles might stand out, or a patrolling police car might wonder why a pickup truck was stopping on the Parkway, when hours before Chain Bridge was under attack. The killing of a police officer always increased the vigilance of all security forces. The killing had not been part of the plan.

A light drizzle helped muffle the sound of their movement. Even so Hasani enforced great discipline on himself and anyone under his command. No talking, smoking or jingling of equipment. Nothing that might reflect light. Their exit used different paths than the incoming. They had practiced moving on the steep slope many times, carrying fishing rods and proper licenses. They carried minimal equipment. His favorite sniping rifle, the Barrett M82A2, American made, but they know how to make and use weapons. This rifle weighed 27 pounds. He and his spotter carried a maximum of four magazine loads, 44, .50 Browning rounds.

The sniper nest was well concealed. He needed no night vision equipment to find his firing position. They were set up in ten minutes. The light rain and patches of misting fog might make it difficult to see the bridge and its approaches in the morning. He understood the necessity to be patient. He would wait hours for the right conditions. The Professor told him that the bridge might be closed or opened only for limited use, perhaps a lane for city-bound traffic. If it was closed, his targets were the workmen. The tactic wasn't to maximize casualties. It was to bring the bridge under attack. Spreading terror was the goal.

Fifty-two

After the attack on the two bridges, Jack and Lou went into crash mode to counter the sniper attack they believed would follow. They could only field one team. Kathy and Kelly weren't up to going against Hasani now. Jack didn't like not having the time to sight in and fire his rifle. Frank had his best people sight in the rifles but it was definitely not procedure to ever go hunting a sniper without a very thorough session with the rifle, ammo and sights. Jack accepted that emergencies often played hell with following the proper procedure. After studying topo maps and satellite imagery, they decided that their best chance was to work the Chain Bridge area. A deployment site area was chosen on the Maryland side of the Potomac and upriver from the bridge.

Just before first light, Jack pulled into a parking area at the Chesapeake and Ohio Canal park about 300 yards upriver from Chain Bridge. Jack and Lou made their way into a clump of winter foliage and high grasses. With camouflage suits they blended in well. Jack knew the site was not good for watching the bridge, but it did give them good views of the opposite high ridges on the Virginia side. If a sniper was set up on those slopes, Jack was sure they could find him, but probably not until he fired.

Dividing the search area into sectors, they began to search the opposite shore line and ridge. When the sun came up, Jack realized that Hasani would have spent hours scouting out the best shooting positions. For early morning shooting on a sunny day, it was better to be downriver from the bridge. Too late now. He could see some sections of the steep slope below the bridge. The distance to any probable sniper sites downriver was over a kilometer from their position and difficult due to the sun angle. He knew from experience hunting snipers took patience and extreme care to keep from becoming the hunted.

Two hours of constant searching turned up nothing. At 8:00 AM, the booming sound of a large caliber rifle fired from somewhere downriver broke through the sound of traffic. Nine more shots followed at almost exactly ten-second intervals. Jack had heard that sound before in Ramada nearly ten years ago when he had been hunting Hasani and his .50 caliber sniping rifle. Even the interval was the same. After 20 seconds of no firing, Jack told Lou to scan for movement. The shooters were on the move, probably up to the Parkway.

Jack said, “Even if we see them, we’ve no shot. No sense in tipping them off that we have figured out their strategy.”

Jack got his cell out and moving a bit away from Lou, asked for Frank. He came on the line instantly. Jack said, “I’m sitting in the brush upriver from Chain Bridge. A sniper has just fired 10 shots. I’m sure he and his spotter are headed up the ridge to the Parkway for their escape ride. Look for pickup trucks. Check both inbound and outbound lanes starting from the first overlook below the bridge. He picked that spot to avoid shooting into the morning sun."

Frank hung up. Jack knew he was firing off orders to begin the hunt.

Fifty-three

Butch Malone, supervisor of the eight to four shift, had just come on duty. He checked in with the traffic cops to make sure only the inbound lanes were being used this morning. Rush hour traffic was backed up for a least a mile coming down Chain Bridge Road, but moving orderly. His crew all had their instructions and he could see he was on schedule. He had a good crew and was proud of their can-do attitude. Many of the workers he had known for at least a couple of years. Butch was checking the Virginia end of the bridge when he saw the head of the cop directing traffic in the center lane explode. Butch had spent some time in the second Gulf War and knew a heavy caliber rifle sound. He dove behind a dump truck. The second shot boomed and the officer, who ran to the aid of the downed traffic cop, went down. She was hit in the chest. A large area of her back was gone. Blood was pooling in a low spot in the center of the bridge.

Butch used his radio to call for help. He yelled to his number to get the workers under cover now. With his cell he called 911 and told the dispatcher, "Gunshots on Chain Bridge. Two officers down. Send help. We are still under fire. Hurry."

Three more shots had been fired. Three cars moving on the bridge rolled to an out-of-control stop. Cars close to the bridge that could see the growing confusion and damage, sped up to get across the bridge to safety. Before they reached the center point, three cars were hit in their passenger windows and crashed into bridge repair equipment. Others turned right from Chain Bridge Road and raced up Glebe Road, jamming it. The next two shots killed workers on the bridge who hadn't found a protective place. Two minutes of no firing and people began to stir. Rescue and police vehicles couldn't get through the jumbled traffic on the Virginia side. The Maryland end was clear and help was soon on the scene. Two of Butch's workers were dead from head shots. In addition to the two police officers killed, four people in cars were dead and several other commuters were wounded, two severely.

Frank called Jack's cell and told him to get up on the bridge and look around, find the sniper's nest and see what we can learn for the next time. He said he would call the right people and for Jack to show his Pittsburgh police badge as an identifier. Jack yelled to Lou to pack up. He ran back to the car and slid to a stop near where he guessed Lou would emerge from the brush loaded with their gear. Lou dumped the weapons into the truck and Jack roared off to the bridge. A Maryland State Police officer was stopping traffic. Jack showed his badge and the officer waved him through. Parking in the first open area he found, they jumped out of the car and ran across the bridge to the Virginia side. Jack introduced himself to the lieutenant in charge. The lieutenant said, "I just got a call about you, telling me to give you anything you want."

Jack said, "The sniper fired from somewhere downriver. Probably less than halfway down the ridge and no more than five or six hundred yards from where we are standing. I want to see if I can tell the angle of his shots. Then my partner and I will climb the ridge and see if we can find the sniper's nest. One more thing, please tell your guys not to shoot at two guys in camouflage suits poking around on the ridge up there."

Turning to Lou, Jack said, "If I remember correctly a trail runs down to the river from this end of the bridge."

Lou said, "Yeah, I've been fishing along here and there is a way down."

Jack said, "You check this end of the bridge for anything that'll give us an angle of the trajectory. I'll check the wreckage in the middle of the bridge. Yell if you find anything. Wait a minute, maybe we have the trajectory data right here. Lieutenant, where was the officer standing when he was hit when the shooting started?"

"Right over there at the nearest blood puddle. He should have been standing with his back to the shooter and facing oncoming traffic. I see what you're thinking. He was about 5'11" or six feet tall."

"Lou, stand over here. This is about one yard from the blood marker and you're about the same height."

Using his spotter scope, Jack plotted the trajectory to a general area and marked a prominent tree as a location point 425 yards from where the officer was standing. It took them 25 minutes to climb the steep ridge to the tree. Once there, Jack said, "This is an ideal spot. Good cover, a distance that Hasani could easily manage on a routine basis, and a path back up the slope to a Parkway pick up site. Now let's find the exact shooting spot. He nearly always shoots from a tripod. The tripod marks will have been swept, but he will have left some mark. No one is good enough to clean up everything without leaving some track."

Moving in ever-widening circles around the marker tree, Lou found a skid mark where it looked like a boot had slipped going up the slope. Using the skid mark, Jack asked Lou to hold his position while he looked for a tripod site that would give line of sight to the Virginia end of the bridge. The shooting site would have to provide space for a prone shooter and firm tripod site or a sandbag. Jack thought it more likely Hasani kept to his M.O. of using a tripod. It only took him ten more minutes to find the site. There were signs of the cleanup attempt and disturbed leaves where the shooter and his spotter had set up. No brass was found.

Marking the location with his iPhone App, Jack called Frank, gave him the GPS data and asked him to check cell phone traffic from the area starting at 8:06 AM. Hasani needed the cell call to set up an exact pickup time. The shooting started at 8:00 and was over within one minute. He estimated Hasani took five minutes to clean up and would need another ten minutes to climb the slope and to cross the Parkway to the westbound lanes, because going that way provided better escape routes than going farther toward the city on the Eastbound lanes. Traffic cameras may show the getaway vehicle, probably a pickup truck. The .50 caliber rifle Hasani used weighed 23 pounds. The spotter probably had a weapon also but not a heavy caliber. They probably carried the weapons concealed some way, maybe disguised as fishing gear. Frank said, "Good work. We'll get right on it." Then hung up.

Jack said, "We're done here. Let's get back to the house and get ready for the next attack."

Fifty-four

Hasani called for pickup when he and Ali started up the wooded, sharply inclined slope. He knew they could be in position on the side of the westbound lanes in 12 minutes. Traffic would be heavy on the eastbound lanes. No matter they would get across. He didn't think the police would have stopped commuter traffic. The capitalist minions had to get to work. They didn't even know they were in the midst of a war zone. Next time they might be the targets.

Hasani was pushing Ali. Ali was breathing heavily and asked to take a one minute rest. Ali refused and pushed on. He should have known men like Ali don't keep themselves in good condition unless someone makes them. He had been so busy getting ready for the Professor's war, he neglected his men. Now it was too late. Using his immense strength and stamina, he surged past Ali and grabbed his jacket and pulled Ali up the ridge. In a few places he had to use a convenient tree trunk to get them up to the edge of the Parkway. He could hear cars moving swiftly down the Parkway toward the major river crossings into DC. Pulling himself up, he saw the cars were moving at least 50 mph and nearly bumper to bumper. He thought these are crazy people to be rushing to their boring godless life's work.

The white pickup had already pulled off the road and was impatiently waiting. The driver was waving his arm at them as Hasani, still dragging Ali, appeared on the edge of the eastbound lanes. Only the lanes of fast moving traffic with no breaks were between them and their escape.

At last Hasani saw a break in the traffic. Reaching back to grab Ali, he said, "Be quick. This is our chance." The break came and Hasani dashed into the break, almost dragging Ali. Crossing the second lane of rapidly braking cars, Ali slipped from Hasani's grasp and sprawled on the pavement. Hasani looked back, saw there was no chance of dragging Ali off the Parkway, and leapt off the pavement into the grass strip between east- and westbound traffic. He heard the sickening thud of a swerving SUV hit Ali who was trying to scramble to Hasani and safety. Ali was dragged nearly ten yards before his body rolled off the roadway. Hasani left his heavy pack by the road and raced to Ali. He saw that Ali still lived but was terribly mangled by the heavy SUV. Without hesitating, he pulled his Browning 9mm and shot Ali twice in the head. Then picking up Ali's rifle, he ran back, snatched up his pack and darted through the sparse traffic on the westbound lane. As the pickup merged back into traffic, Hasani promised to give thanks for Ali's support and his early martyrdom.

He told Asad, the driver, to get off the Parkway at the McLean exit and drive thorough McLean to the Tysons Corner shopping center. He knew he was seen getting into the white pickup after shooting Ali. In the day of everyone with a cell, reports of accidents and crimes flowed into 911. The pickup truck had to be dumped in the parking lot of the shopping center. He would call for a car from his other team members. He hoped he wouldn't have to abandon his favorite sniping rifle. True to his reputation. Ten shots, ten hits. With that rifle and God's will, he could not miss.

Fifty-five

Returning, Jack and Lou found the rest of the team busy planning a mission. They had seen the news, including the report of a man killed by gunfire after being hit by an SUV. Jack called Frank, who came on the line after a couple of minutes. He said, "Jack, the guy killed on the Parkway was one of the shooters. He was carrying a handgun and a spotter scope. No identity documents. We have several 911 reports of this man being shot after being hit by a car. He was hit twice in the head from very close range. Obviously, a case of making sure he didn't talk. The same reports said the killer jumped into a white pickup truck on the westbound lane. We have an APB out. I suspect they've already dumped the truck, probably in some big parking area. That's part of the Professor's M.O. Police are now searching all the parking areas between McLean and the Beltway. We should have the truck in an hour or so. Do you have anything?"

"Not much. Ten shots and ten hits from four to five hundred yards. Nearly exactly 10 seconds apart. Some of the targets were moving, maybe 20 mph. First shot was a head shot. Only a sniper with Hasani's skills would take a head shot from that distance when he didn't have to. The shooter was definitely Hasani. He never left any wounded behind. He always had them killed or he did it himself. He made a mistake, not realizing it is suicidal to cross the Parkway on foot when the traffic is moving fast and close. On the day or days he did his casing, the traffic could have been less dangerous. I have two suggestions. Circulate the Professor and Hasani's pictures. Second, they will need to replace the truck. Canvass for anyone buying a used pickup, panel truck or van and paying cash. Unless they steal a vehicle, they have to pay cash. Oh, one more. I know you have people checking all the relevant cameras, but please tell us if anyone gets a hit.

"They'll attack somewhere tomorrow. The same target should not be ruled out. If I provide some coordinates, can you have police or military counter-sniper teams in place? Tell them to set up only in the designated area and not to change positions. We don't want to lose people to friendly fire."

"Okay. I'll take care of it."

Jack rejoined the group. TV monitors covering major news channels were back to back with talking heads discussing who could be responsible, what could the motives be and what could the authorities do to make the roads and bridges safe for commuters.

Jack said, "I'm sure we'll have another attack tomorrow. We need a list of probable targets now. Let's cut the search area down with some common sense factors. I'll start. The sniper's target has to be worthwhile. Assume the target is the transportation infrastructure. Heavy predictable traffic, potential to cause major tie ups and spread terror. There must be an escape route the authorities cannot shut off with a quick road block. Drop offs and pickups require coordination and luck. Hasani would sooner have a place to park his transportation. Transportation could be one or two motorcycles. Okay. Give me some help."

Lou said, "The targets will be random. He doesn't have to search or wait for a designated target. Rush hour in this area is several hours long. He is not forced to meet a time schedule, so the sniper has an advantage. He can pick any few minutes to attack any of dozens if not hundreds of targets, while we have to cover targets 24/7."

Storm said, "Keep it coming, this is good stuff and I'm getting it all down. I think the coordination link with this sniper has to be a cell phone. Therefore, all the areas we pick should be monitored for cell calls that match any intercepts from today's attack. I suspect the cells they use are buy-and-throw units. Did they buy them all in advance or as they need them? Jack, your friends might check into their data banks."

"Noted."

Kathy said, "There are too many targets to protect. Even with a lot of help, they cannot all be covered. My suggestion is that we cover a few, say three or four with on-ground teams and the rest we cover from the air. Two helicopters with counter-sniper teams in the air during time of greatest threat. As soon as we get the first report of an attack in progress, the nearest bird heads to the attacked scene and drops the team astride the most probable escape route. Other assets swarm to the same area to set up roadblocks and deploy more search teams."

As Kathy finished explaining her approach, a news alert showed up on the monitors. Clear pictures of the

Professor and Hasani were shown as persons wanted for the sniper attacks. The men were described as committed Jihadists and were armed and dangerous. Do not attempt to apprehend. Call the authorities on the following hotline number.

Jack said, "Great, that should help smoke them out. Kathy, I like your idea. Storm, you and Lou pick an area for our helicopter to cover. Lou, you and I and Kathy will make up one team. I'll see if I can arrange for a few more. I'll need to tell them what area we are covering. Also we will need call signs and a cell or radio link to Storm and Kelly who will man this room. Kelly, don't look so disappointed. You need some long-gun training first. I'll try to work it in next week. Okay, everybody, you know what to do. Let's move."

Fifty-six

The Professor was just recovering from the shock of losing Ali. Hasani had done the right thing. He couldn't afford the CIA interrogating one of his people. Ali knew too much. An hour later he saw his picture and Hasani's on a news alert. How did they get a picture of Hasani? No one should know he was here. His entry into the country was perfect. Hasani lived his cover and never made mistakes. He was vigilant and carefully checked the details.

They could change their appearances somewhat but extensive disguises were difficult to wear constantly. He knew a safe place was required to make each change from one appearance to another. No, they would have to avoid close up exposures to people. One of Hasani's people would have to be their public face to buy supplies. Now they needed two more vehicles. They might have to steal the cars and trucks they needed and the license plates. Only the numbers on the license plates made individual vehicles of the mass brands identifiable.

He had no choice, multiple attacks had to be put on hold. Martyrdom was always a concept. Now it was real. His attack plans had to change. He would never get back to Pakistan. Tomorrow was the beginning of the last phase of his Jihad. He had to remember the purpose of terrorism is to terrorize. Terror was effective when it affected the common man. People expected terrorism to focus on embassies, airports, security infrastructure, landmark buildings and national treasures. They do not expect they will be involved, nor their property, nor their families. We must continue to pit Americans against each other and foster a lack of faith in their government. This will be a long struggle but one that is worth our treasure and lives. Hasani will be pleased that martyrdom is near. He never felt more alive than right now. Publication of their pictures complicated his plan. Just to keep the security forces scrambling, tomorrow the planned attack on the American Legion Memorial Bridge would go as planned. The attack team would not include Hasani. He needed Hasani with him to modify their plans.

Fifty-seven

It was mid-morning lunch before Storm and Kelly finished marking up the probable targets and the best sniper positions for five. Targets were limited to bridges and other rush hour traffic backup points. Jack grabbed the marked up topographical maps and called the Leesburg Airport to tell the pilots to get the helicopter ready for a flight over the western beltway. Westbound traffic was light, and Jack, Lou, Kathy and Shadow were airborne in the Bell 429 an hour and twenty minutes later. The side panels carried the logo of Global Surveys.

With marked up coordinates and the onboard GPS system, it was not difficult to check the proposed sites, photograph the positions and send the results to Frank before they landed. Once they were back at the airport, Jack called Frank and said, "If you agree, our team will react to any attack on the American Legion Memorial Bridge on Route 495. If there is an attack there, I believe it will come from the Maryland side. The ground is higher and escape routes are numerous."

"Good, I'll take care of covering the rest. The release of the pictures of the Professor and Hasani may delay the next attack. We still have to cover as many targets as we can today and tomorrow. You've been a great help in designing a reaction plan."

At four o'clock Jack told Kathy and Lou to check their weapons. He wanted to be on station over the target area at 4:15. Jack had a strong feeling that the Professor would give the go ahead for at least a limited attack to keep building terror.

When they arrived over Route 495 near the American Legion Memorial Bridge, the weather was ideal for aerial surveillance. Three to five miles of wind from the west, visibility was good, with little or no haze over the bridge. Jack thought, this is ideal for the sniper. There were several places where a sniper could set up with dozens of traffic targets. The inner traffic loop of Route 495 was already slowing across the bridge. The cliché of shooting fish in a barrel must have been describing a situation like this. Jack knew the chance of spotting an experienced sniper from a cruising helicopter was almost nil. But after the sniper started shooting targets, then they had a chance to spot the movement during the escape. Hit targets may give some insights into the sniper's firing position. Jack didn't believe there would be more than one shooter unless the sniper and his spotter had to defend themselves.

Then the spotter would take on the closer targets. He also doubted that the sniper would try for targets beyond 500 yards.

It was now 5:00 and the light was beginning to fade slightly. Jack alerted Kathy and Lou that the shooter couldn't wait much longer. He used the intercom to speak to the pilot to ask him to swing over the bridge to the Maryland side and hover over the high ground he pointed out. They were just crossing the bridge when a car on the bridge slammed into the cement bridge barrier. Then, a second and a third jumped lanes and crashed into cars moving from Virginia into Maryland. A massive traffic accident was occurring under them. The police radios they were monitoring reported shots fired and an officer down. Jack was looking for any sign of the shooting position when Lou said, "A white pickup truck just pulled off to the side of the beltway below us. I bet it's a getaway ride."

Jack told the pilot not to lose the truck. He used the chopper's secure radio to call Frank who came on line instantly. Jack told him what was happening and to get out a bulletin on the truck, a white Chevrolet Silverado on the inner loop of the Beltway just over the Bridge on the Maryland side. He also told Frank they would be in pursuit and he would call in as soon as he had anything.

Kathy said, "Two people just got in the truck and it's pulling out."

Jack said, "Sam, did you get that?"

"Yeah, I did. What do you want me to do?"

"Follow that truck wherever it goes. Go up a thousand feet, so we can see more. I may want you to go down quickly, if I decide we're going to be shooting. Be ready to land on short notice. There are at least two highly skilled shooters in that truck who will shoot as us without even thinking about it. One of the shooters will have a heavy caliber weapon that can knock holes in us from several thousand feet. So don't give them anything. As it gets darker go down low enough so we don't lose the truck. The shooting was timed so the darkness will help them escape."

Lou said, "I think they are headed for 270 West to Frederick and merging with the torrent of traffic coming out of Washington. State Police road blocks will be hard to manage. When they think a police search is coming, they'll split. Probably leaving the driver to create a diversion to help their escape."

Jack said, "Lou, I think you've got it. There already is one diversion. First responders will still be going to the bridge as fast as they can. Not everyone will believe we're following the bridge shooters. We have no real evidence for the law and order world. We saw no one shooting and we saw no guns. Only a pickup truck pulling over, and two people getting in. We can't be sure they were the men. So most, if not all, of the police will be focused on the bridge area and not on our truck. There may not be many road blocks and that may help us get these snipers."

Kathy said, "You know, I don't think they know we're following them."

Jack said, "They may be just playing it cool. Here we are west of Frederick into the rolling hills and mountains that extend into Pennsylvania. Where are they going?"

Sam, the pilot, said, "They're slowing down. I think they're looking for something. Look! They're pulling off. My map shows an extensive state park below us. If they get loose in those mountains on foot, we'll never find them from the air. It's too dark now, and I can only spend another hour searching for heat signatures before heading back to refuel."

"Take us down to 200 feet. We're going to stop that truck. Lou, Kathy, get ready for some shooting. We only have bolt action counter-sniper rifles, so we need aimed fire. Concentrate on the cab. Sam, if the truck stops, take evasive action. They'll come out shooting. If they start shooting find a nearby place and put down. Shadow and I will get out. Kathy call in and report. I have enough in my pack for three days. I'll carry the radio and my cell."

Jack secured Shadow's leash to a seat belt, so he wouldn't be thrown out the open doors by any violent maneuvers. The truck was maintaining a 50 mph speed on a gravel road, throwing up a tail of dust. The first few rifle shots hit the cab, and the truck lurched off the road into scrub pine trees. Two of the occupants ran out, sought cover on the edge of the forest and opened fire. The low-flying helicopter was an easy target for experienced shooters. Several rounds pierced the thin skin of the chopper before Sam could take evasive action and get out of the line of fire.

Kathy yelled, "Lou's been hit! Looks bad!"

"Sam, is the bird okay?"

"Yeah! Nothing I can see wrong."

"Good, get down now to jumping distance."

Jack was shrugging into his pack and getting Shadow's leash loose.

"When Shadow and I get out, get Lou back to Frederick. Kathy, you know what to do. Call the nearest competent emergency for gunshot wounds and do what you can with the onboard first aid kit. It doesn't look like a pumping chest wound. I have to go now. I'll be in touch. Don't worry! Come on, Shadow, let's go to work!"

Sam kept just above the tree line until they were out of range. Kathy took his kevlar vest off and cut up the center of Lou's jersey. The vest did not stop the bullet. The entry wound was high on the right side of his chest. There was no exit wound. She hooked up a bag of plasma, gave Lou a shot of morphine, and stuffed the wound with bandages. While she was doing this, she called Frank, who told her to get Lou to Frederick Memorial. He would call ahead. They had a helicopter pad and a good reputation for emergency care.

Sam broke in and said, “We’re losing fuel fast. I think we can make Frederick, but we have no time to waste. Make sure the pad lights are on. I’m tapping into the air control system and declaring an emergency. We can’t deal with any delays.”

Kathy said, “Frank, here are the coordinates where Jack and Shadow got out. Jack asked that reaction teams stop at the wrecked truck and do not try to pursue. Jack doesn’t want the friendly fire problem. He’ll get them. Shadow can track at night. The terrorists will not be able to rest. Monitor the area for cell phone or push-to-talk radio. I’m sure they will try to contact the Professor or vice versa. Tell the emergency care people, Lou is barely conscious. I’ve got the bleeding from the wound under control. He is having increasing difficulty breathing and some bleeding from the mouth.”

Sam said, “There’s the pad. Buckle up. We are going in hard! Fuel is gone! Hope fire crew is standing by. I’m cutting all power! Hang on!”

When Kathy awoke, Sam was sitting by her bed. He had a large bandage on his head. Kathy sat up and said, “How’s Lou?”

“He’s still in surgery. That’s all I know. You’re in bed because we hit hard, and you cracked your head on something. I did, too. The doctors said we could both leave when we felt okay. Minor concussion, they said. My head hurts like hell, mostly from the stitches. You should rest before trying to get up. Lou's daughter will be here very soon. The head surgical nurse swore she would come to this room with news about Lou as soon as she can."

"Damn it, my head's okay! It's Jack I'm worried about. He's out there hunting down three skilled killers, and he acted like he was going for a hike with his dog!"

"Ma'am, I wouldn't worry too much about your man. I've seen many tough men but Jack is the coolest and toughest of all of them. He thinks he has the strongest hand. I think so, too. I wouldn't want him and that huge dog on my trail."

"Maybe so. We've been living with this kind of stress for two straight years. I'm beginning to doubt my ability to continue. The worst is the waiting. People you love are doing incredible, dangerous things. And as good as they are, they don't always come back. We lost my best friend in a firefight last year. She gave her life to save Jack. Now she isn't there to help."

Fifty-eight

Jack told Shadow to heel and headed up slope to get above the wrecked truck. He glanced over his shoulder before entering the thicker bush and saw the helicopter speeding off to the East. Putting Lou's condition out of his mind, he concentrated on moving unseen to the truck. There was a chance one or more of the killers were in ambush nearby. He didn't believe the chopper had set down more than a couple of hundred yards from the damaged truck. Moving quickly but quietly, he and Shadow moved through the scrub pine growth. Either a past fire or logging operation had cleared the slope of the taller pines and deciduous hardwoods. The footing was soft, making it easier to move at night without making noise. The temperature was dropping. He was dressed for the weather and had enough gear in his 40-pound pack to easily survive the cold climate for a few days.

By his dead reckoning, Jack was sure he was very near the truck. An east to west wind carried the distinct smell of gasoline. He stopped, put his hand on Shadow and crept down the slope. He saw the gravel road first and then saw the truck. Settling down with Shadow curled against him, they watched the truck. Jack expected that one person wounded or not would be left behind to slow pursuit.

After 15 minutes, he smelled tobacco smoke. Shadow looked up at him as if to say, what took you so long? Jack couldn't believe a professional would do something as dumb as smoking in an ambush site, unless he was dying and needed the nicotine. Well, we can't wait any longer and,leaving his rifle and pack concealed, gave Shadow the hand signal to follow.

Using the excellent cover of the pine growth, Jack and Shadow moved closer to the truck. Jack now had a clear view of the front of the Chevrolet pickup truck. Its gray color blended in with the surrounding edge of the forest. His SOCOM automatic was now in his hand. Watching the windshield from 25 feet, he saw the ember of a cigarette. Jack swung up the SOCOM, fired three times and, keeping low, charged the truck. Reaching up from his position below the door, he ripped the door open and pulled the man slumped against the door out of the truck. Turning the man face down Jack felt for his carotid pulse. Finding none, he rolled the man over. The cab interior lights came on with the opening of the door. This was no Arab. This guy looked American all the way. His wallet held only a few hundred in cash and a driver's license that was probably false. Jack's three shots caught him in the chest. The windshield showed a tight pattern. He had another wound in the abdomen that had to be from shots fired from the helicopter. His companions knew he would not live to talk. He might be able to slow pursuit.

Making a final check with one eye closed to preserve his night vision, Jack found a cell phone on the floor. He put it in his pocket and motioned to Shadow who followed him back to where his pack and rifle were temporarily cached. Going back to the truck, Jack opened the passenger door and motioned for Shadow to check out the scent. Shadow knew the drill. He had hours of tracking training five years ago that Jack kept current with games for finding people and objects. Shadow found a pair of black leather gloves on the floor under the passenger seat. He spent almost a minute nosing the gloves before jumping out of the cab and waiting for Jack to tell him to start tracking.

Jack pulled Shadow's leash out of his pocket and motioned for Shadow to come over and get his leash snapped on. Jack knew Shadow wanted to run loose on the trail but tracking two snipers was different. They would see the dog as their main problem and set up for a long shot to kill the free-ranging tracking dog before his handler could get in position to cover the dog. While that wasn't a problem at night, it would be when the sun came up. It was better anyway to work a tracker on a leash at night. Shadow would help Jack keep to the same trail as the snipers.

After the first hour they came to a small mountain stream with steep banks. After watching Shadow for a few minutes and listening to the forest sounds, Jack was sure the snipers were not close by and shielding his flashlight he examined the stream bank. Sure enough, Shadow was right on the trail. He could see the marks in the steep bank where they crossed the stream. In a few places, their boots sank into the soft mud along the stream. Water was still seeping into the boot indentations. Jack judged they were less than 30 minutes ahead. After studying and measuring the boot prints for a few more minutes, Jack rubbed the Bouvier's head and said, "Okay, big guy, let's go." Shadow scrambled up the bank, tracking the snipers.

So far Jack had learned quite a bit about his prey. They must be using a light, for it was too dark to follow the narrow game trail they were using without some illumination. The trail led almost due west. One man was much heavier than the other. The lighter man with the smaller boot was leading. Using his mute flashlight sparingly, Jack had seen by the length of the strides that they were hurrying. Good, that would wear them out and, with luck, maybe a sprained ankle. They didn't appear to be woodsmen but might have some tactical smarts. Like doubling back to check the back trail and set an ambush. They didn't know a trained tracker dog was on their trail. Jack knew Shadow would alert him to any ambush. The snipers were moving west and downwind. Jack doubted Shadow even needed the scent from the trail. They were close and getting closer each hour.

The dead man's cell phone that Jack found in the truck vibrated in his pocket. When the vibration stopped, he snapped his fingers, and Shadow stopped and sat down. Jack checked the phone. The screen told him he had voice mail. He tapped the voice mail icon and tapped again for the message. Putting the phone to his ear, he heard a foreign voice saying, "You have a tracker dog and an American sniper on your trail."

Jack turned the phone off and thought, the plot is thickening fast. How could anyone know Shadow and I are following these killers? Only one way. There has to be a leak close to Frank and his organization. No wonder the Professor is so hard to pin down. I don't want to risk using my cell to call Frank. I don't want anyone to know just yet there is a mole lurking around. The good news is the bad guys we're tracking didn't get this message, so we still have the advantage. I'm sure they feel they have at least a six- or seven-hour head start on any pursuit. Wish I knew where they're going. Their steady pace tells me they have a destination. Pulling into this park was not a random turn. The question now is, will they bed down on the trail or keep moving in the dark. Checking his own iPhone, Jack noted he had climbed 800 feet since the start of the chase. We're still going up. The trail will probably get steeper and more dangerous to travel at night. Question, are these guys on home turf and do they know this little used trail? They must have a map.

There is a little moonlight filtering through. I can make out the trail. Okay, Shadow, let's take a break, drink some water, eat and then pick up the pace.

Fifty-nine

Storm had just arrived and was in Kathy's room asking questions about her father when Dr. Green came in. Kathy introduced him to Storm who immediately asked him, "Is my father okay?"

"He has a very serious wound. It will take some time for him to recover. His right lung was too damaged for us to save. His vest saved his life. The 7.62 round veered upward and smashed into his clavicle. He will need more surgery to improve shoulder function later. We got the bullet and fragments out. The bleeding is stopped. Your father is now in the ICU Ward. You can see him, but he's still sedated and will be in considerable pain for several days. He was lucky you brought him here. Including myself, we have two other surgeons and a few critical care nurses that have had experience with gunshot wounds from serving in the Iraq and Afghan theaters. Your father's wound was not a new thing for us. He's in good shape and will make an almost full recovery. I don't think he will be up to gunfights from a helicopter anymore."

Storm said, "Thank you, Dr. Green. How long do you think he will be here?"

"At least a week, maybe longer. Now wipe your eyes and go see him."

Kathy said, "What about us?"

"We like to keep patients with concussions overnight. You should be able to leave in the morning. I must say your group has some real clout. We've received several calls from an important National Security Officer who told us to spare no expense and to get you the best treatment possible. The Government would move you anywhere for treatment right now."

Kathy said, "I need my cell. The nurse told me I need your approval."

"You have it and whatever else you want. The weapons the crash crew took off the helicopter are being held for you. The man who called me at least three times said when you wanted your weapons to give them to you without any delay. So, when you check out, you can pick up your weapons. Your helicopter is not going to be able to fly out of here. As landings go, that one was hard. I'll check on you in the morning."

Kathy buzzed the nurse and asked her to bring her cell phone. When the nurse said, it would be a while, Kathy lost it She said, "Look, if that phone is not here in five minutes, I'm coming out to get it. You don't want that to happen. So move it now."

Sam, who was still sitting with Kathy, said, "Wow! I thought you were a laid back lady."

"Call me ma'am one more time, and you will see laid back. When my cell shows up, please go somewhere for ten minutes. Okay?"

"Sure. I think the nurse is coming now. I'm out of here."

The nurse came in and put the phone down on Kathy's bedside table and said, "You didn't have to be so nasty."

"It's a personality flaw. I can't stand pompous, unhelpful people. You are definitely in that category. If I want to talk to you again, I'll buzz you and we'll start over."

When the scowling nurse left, Kathy called Frank.

He said, "Glad you're awake. How are you doing?"

"I'll be better when I get out of this place. Just a slight concussion, bumps and bruises. Lou is in the ICU Ward. Doctor says he will be okay, if no complications. He lost a lung and his shoulder is messed up. It will require further surgery. Dr. Green is good. What do you know about what happened?"

"Start from the beginning."

Kathy told him the story and asked what he knew about Jack. Frank said, "The State Police found the pickup truck just where you said it would be. A dead man was on the ground on the driver's side. He was shot three times in the chest with a very tight grouping and had been hit earlier in the abdomen, probably when you fired at the truck from the chopper. I believe he was left behind because of his wound. Even with prompt medical attention, the State Police said he would have died. There were three bullet holes in the windshield on the driver's side and signs that the man was dragged out of the car. I assume Jack was the shooter. There were big paw prints on the seat. Again, I guess Shadow was acquiring the scent of the two men who left the truck. The state police said they found the tracks of the dog and a man moving swiftly after the fugitives.

Reluctantly, they followed my wishes and did not send their team on the trail. Is Shadow a trained tracking dog?"

"Shadow is incredible. He has all the tracking honors. Jack keeps him current by playing find-it games. By the way, Jack is also a very good tracker. I can't believe what he can tell just by looking at a trail. Change of subject. Have there been any intercepts in the search area from cells or radios?"

"None so far. Reception in that area is very poor. Maybe you could get a signal from some high points. I don't want to risk a call. It could be a distraction or give Jack's presence away."

"Frank, I don't think the pickup truck turning into the State Park was a random thing. Before the turn, Sam said the truck is slowing down, like they're looking for something. If that's the case, they may know the turf, have a cache of supplies, a hideout or a pickup point they are moving toward."

"Good point. I'll ask the State Police about cabins, camping sites and access roads they could reach on foot in two days. Call me tomorrow. I'll send Sam's partner in another helicopter to pick you up."

Sixty

The fifteen-minute break with some water, trail mix and kibble for Shadow was over. Now they were back on the trail at an increased pace. With Shadow following the scent of the snipers with ease and the faint moonlight helping him see the trail, the pace he set was as fast as they could move without making much noise. Jack was counting on Shadow's reaction to tell him they were getting close. Another hour on the trail and Shadow wanted to speed up. Jack stopped him and attached his leash. Their quarry had to be close. Were they stopped or still moving at a slower pace? The trail opened crossing a steep slope and Jack saw a faint moving light maybe 50 yards ahead. When he stopped, he could hear low voices and occasional footsteps.

Jack had no night vision gear and was thinking about shooting now. He was sure he could hit one but didn't want to give up the element of surprise for one kill. The other sniper would be a hard problem. You wouldn't find him strolling along a mountain trail using a flashlight. More likely, he would try to set up an ambush. He let the light move ahead and checked his cell phone. Signal strength was low but he had service. It was after 9:00 PM but he called Frank's office. No surprise! Frank was there and anxious to hear from Jack. He gave his coordinates and asked Frank not to act on them until he explained a problem.

Frank said, "Go ahead."

"We have a problem. I recovered one of the snipers' cell phones from the truck. At 7:25, I felt it vibrate. I didn't answer and the caller, with a foreign accent left a voice mail. I'm in a place now where I can play it for you." After playing the message, Jack said, "The most likely explanation, given the timing, is you have a spy or an electronic leak in your office."

Frank said, "I've been in this business too long to say no way. You're right, the timing is very suspicious. I don't recognize the voice. What other thoughts do you have?"

"My speculation is that someone with access to the results of our helicopter chase called the Professor. I doubt the Professor would pass on that kind of information to a couple of throw-away snipers. He's a pro and knows he could lose an invaluable source by passing the information over a cell phone and leaving a voice mail. No way he would do that. But, if he told someone else in his group with a purely tactical mindset, that person could have passed it on. Also the foreign accent was easily heard. You told us his American English was flawless."

"Jack, let's set a trap. Suppose I tell the same people who knew about the helicopter event that your dog broke a leg and you had to turn back, but we have the coordinates and are deploying teams. We know the snipers on the trail in front of you probably do not have a cell phone or radio. If the information is passed on, it will be to the phone in your pocket. I'll arrange monitoring of any cell phones from here and tell all my staff that I'll need everyone to stay for a few hours."

"I assume Kathy got Lou to a hospital."

"Yes, Lou is in the ICU Ward in Frederick. He's lost a lung and has other damage to his shoulder. The chopper was hit in the firefight with the truck people. It ran short of fuel and made a real hard landing near the hospital pad. Kathy and Sam are being held overnight for observation. Both had concussions. They are up and walking around. Kathy called me 30 minutes ago."

"She's tough, but I think she should take a break for a while."

"You know what she will say."

"Yeah, I'm afraid so. She won't like my current plan either. If the State Police can figure out where these guys are headed, they could set up a block and maybe ambush any attempt at a pickup along some highway. Just tell them I'm the guy with the black dog. Before we started talking, they were less than 100 yards in front of us and using a flashlight. Maybe Shadow and I will just keep trailing them to a State Police trap. I'll call if I can find another service window. Gotta go."

The trail was getting steeper and covered with areas of shale. The snipers were moving more slowly and Jack and Shadow rapidly caught up, maintaining a 100-yard interval. The trail reached its high point and ran northwest paralleling the ridge line. Cover was sparse and even with the cloak of darkness, Jack slowed their pace. He could have sworn Shadow looked back at him in disgust.

Concentrating on the party ahead, the vibration of the captured cell phone startled him. When the vibrating stopped, he checked for a message. Shielding the light from the cell phone and turning down the volume, he heard the same accented voice saying, "The man and dog on your trail have turned back. Several teams are entering the area to search for you. Before the man turned back, he sent your coordinates to the police. Change to destination B."

Jack switched the phone off and called Frank on his own cell. This high cell service was stronger. When Frank answered, Jack said, "I have a message I received in the last few minutes." He played the message for Frank.

Frank said, "Case is proven. We have a mole. He or she is very good. I haven't noticed any calls leaving here and no one has left the area."

Jack said, "Maybe it wasn't a cell call from your office. Could have been land line, text message or an email. Even a posting to some website or obscure Facebook identity."

Frank said, "With your permission, I need to borrow Kathy to help me with this mole. I'll hire her as a consultant to give her cover."

"Sure, as long as she agrees. Tell her also that Shadow and I are still safe and not going to do anything heroic, although Shadow sorely wants to attack. Oh, are you going to share the change in destination with the State Police? I know while the fugitives never got the message, it does indicate that they were heading to one destination and now are instructed to go to another. The pickup vehicle, if that's the plan, will now go to destination B, wherever that is. I see a light moving. Have to go."

The light was moving but very slowly. Jack settled down to watch. Shadow stretched out and was taking a nap.

Jack sniffed the air. He not only smelled cigarette smoke but wood smoke as well. He thought, well, our fugitives are hunkering down. They must feel safe and have decided hurrying over this terrain at night is not a good idea. In daylight they can safely move a lot faster. They believe there is no pursuit. They could have water. It was SOP to carry water on a sniper mission. Almost for sure, they have no food. Maybe a few candy bars. It's getting cold, and they don't have a big dog to curl against or a light blanket roll. I'll bet they won't even take turns staying awake.

We could easily sneak up and take them prisoner. Then we have to watch them, while traveling for several hours. I don't like that. Taking prisoners at night is not without risk. I could easily kill them and end this chase. The law would call that murder and these guys maybe are US citizens. While I'm carrying a badge, it won't cover the shooting of two citizens without giving them a chance to surrender and maybe kill us. There's a reason people on real world operations don't like a mission to take prisoners. Always more risk in capturing versus killing.

There is also more risk in following armed men in daylight. So, Shadow, we have to make a decision. I vote for giving them an hour to sleep then rousting them. Maybe we can get them to abandon some of their gear. If they shoot, we can shoot. Okay, in two hours, we move. Jack found a place to wait and rest 30 feet off the trail.

Just after midnight, Jack and Shadow crept up the slope to a point higher than the campfire. The footing was good, wet from a recent melted snow. He could hear the men talking. With his hand on Shadow, Jack stopped to see if he could make out the conversation. They crept closer.

Now the words were clear, especially one voice that was louder than his partner's. The louder voice said, "Tell me again where you think that damn helicopter came from. Man, it was right on us. They had some good shooters in that bird. Thank God, they only had bolt action rifles. I know we hit it and I think it touched down but then it flew off to the East."

"I think it was watching the bridge and when the shooting started, it searched for us. It ain't hard to see two guys jumping into a pickup truck near a possible shooting site and figure they should follow the truck. But they had to be sure to open fire. Another half mile and we would've been under a canopy. Jake was hit bad. Think he had a chance?"

"Maybe, if the cops got there in time. Hasani will be pissed. He told us never, never leave a live teammate behind. I just couldn't do it. I've known Jake a while. My worry is or was that the copter dumped off a team to run us down. I'm sure we're free and clear now. Tomorrow by lunch time, our ride will be waiting for us. I wiped the truck down before we left. The cops don't have a clue who we are. These al Qaeda guys are smart and tough."

Jack heard enough. He moved up the slope, behind a grouping of waist high boulders. Peeking over the boulders, he could see into the camp a good 60 feet down the slope into the camp. The fire was bigger than they needed for warmth and lighted the whole scene. Shadow relaxed and settled against Jack's leg. He decided to wait until they went to sleep.

Finally, the two men took their boots off and went to sleep. The rifles were kept close. Leaning against one of the boulders, Jack felt it shift slightly. He put his weight against the boulder and it moved a little more. Quietly, he went to work stacking boulders he could carry around the much larger loose boulder. When the pile looked big enough, Jack put his back against the key boulder and pushed. At first it budged and, pushing harder, he felt it begin to topple. Then it went with a crash, picking up speed as it bounced down the steep slope, gathering smaller rocks in its wake. The mass of the rockslide went right through the camp, smothering the fire and continuing down the mountain. As the dust settled Jack could see the men still on the ground begin to stir. Both rifles were gone. Charging down the hill with his handgun ready, Jack released Shadow who bounded past him and, with a growling roar, pounced on the nearest man. Jack had his handgun pressed against the head of the other sniper. Calling off Shadow's attack, Jack told him to watch. Shadow stood over the downed terrorist, growling softly.

In the darkness compounded by lingering smoke and dust, Jack knew the two killers couldn't see what was happening. He had his man securely tied with the nylon line from his pack and moved over to tie Shadow's victim. Neither man seemed to be badly injured. Jack, with his SOCOM pressed into the man's forehead, told him to be still and he might live. Shadow leaned in close to his victim's face. The man said, "Okay! Please get that bear out of my face. He was biting me."

"Yeah. Too bad about that. He was just getting started. Are you carrying any other weapons besides your rifles? Don't lie. You'll be very sorry. Now speak up!"

"We each have a knife and a 9mm Browning. But I don't know where they are."

"Never mind. Keep quiet and no talking." Jack dragged him 20 feet from his partner. Jack turned to Shadow and said, "Gun."

Shadow immediately began searching the area. Jack found two K-Bar military sheath knives inside the scattered boots. With both men securely tied, Jack helped Shadow search for the other weapons. Shadow barked softly indicating he found something. In a short time, he found both rifles. Jack found one of the Brownings partially covered by debris. After ten minutes of searching, he called Shadow off. With the rockslide, the second Browning could be dozens of yards down the slope. A nearly impossible search at night, even for Shadow.

Back at the campsite, Jack searched for identification documents. Neither man carried any documentation. He found two loaded magazines for each rifle, matches, cigarettes and a half dozen Snicker bars. Neither had a cell phone.

Kneeling beside the man Shadow had attacked, Jack said, "I'm going to ask you some questions. I don't want any questions from you, no pauses, no thinking and no, I don't knows. I'll know if you're lying and punishment will be immediate and severe. My dog is waiting patiently for his reward. One word from me, and he will make you very sorry. I may not be able to pull him off in time. Okay, let's start. Understand?"

"Who the fuck are you?"

Jack softly called Shadow and pointed to the downed terrorist. Shadow leaned in close, baring his teeth and growling. Even in the dark, Shadow's intentions were clear.

"Okay!! Call the dog off."

"I told you no questions. What didn't you understand? This is your last chance before we make an example out of you for your friend. What is your name?"

In the darkness Jack turned on the recording function of his iPhone.

"My name is Lawrence Parry."

"Place and date of birth?"

"Jacksonville, Florida, June 22, 1980."

"Who are you working for?"

"A Jihadist named Hasani."

"Who else?"

"Hasani is the only person who gives us orders."

"How were you hired?"

"I volunteered in a mosque in Falls Church, Virginia, and was trained in a camp in Pakistan."

"Where are you going on this trail?"

"We're going to a pickup place on Route 70 west at the intersection of State Route 295 just east of Hagerstown, Maryland."

Jack continued with the interrogation for another 10 minutes, then shifted to the second killer who was suffering from a broken or dislocated shoulder and numerous cuts and bruises. One of the larger boulders must have hit him. Beyond his personal identification, his answers contained nothing new.

Moving out of earshot, Jack left Shadow on guard and called Frank. When Frank picked up, Jack told him he was sending the results of a preliminary interrogation of the two bridge snipers. Taking a few minutes to listen to the forwarded information, Frank said, "You never fail to astound me. How you trailed and captured two killers without firing a shot is incredible. Too bad I must shield you from the media. Every once in a while, we need some good results in the public media. Actually, the two live jihadists makes it easy for me to keep you under cover. I've got the GPS data and will send one of my teams to take them into custody. I'll send them to Gitmo, if my management can stand the heat from the Attorney General. We'll also ambush the pickup on Route 70. Send me pictures of the two captives and I'll arrange for two 'lookalikes' to approach their ride."

"Question, how are you going to prevent your internal leak from finding out about these arrangements?"

"I'm going to use a team from outside my office. No one, except Kathy, will be informed until we nail this damn spy."

"One more question. Can you make arrangements to have me and Shadow picked up somewhere? If Kathy is wrapped up in an investigation, send Kelly. She's resourceful and the only member of my team that's not hurt or unavailable. Also, I won't be here when your team arrives. I'm leaving these men firmly tied. They'll be okay for a few hours but will suffer some damage, if they aren't untied before nine or ten o'clock. Also, it's cold here and getting colder. My weather data states a storm is possible before afternoon. Not that I care, but these shooters will die if a storm prevents a team from getting here. I'm leaving their empty weapons several yards below their position. I'll mark the weapons site with a white handkerchief on a four-foot stake. Incidentally, there's a missing 9mm Browning, Shadow and I have not been able to find. It may be buried under the rockslide that swept through the campsite. A metal detector may be useful. I'll hang out until you tell me about my pickup place. Phone reception here, on this high point, is good. See you."

Jack and Shadow ate the last of their food while waiting for instructions. Kathy called as Jack was getting ready to move out. He asked how she was.

Kathy said, "Other than worrying about you and Shadow, nursing a splitting headache, numerous bumps and bruises, and figuring out how to help Frank, I'm fine. Oh, I forgot. Lou is still in the ICU and Storm is worried sick. Jack, please be careful. We can't save the free world by ourselves. Tell me someday we can have a normal life."

"Kathy, yes, you are the love of my life and I will be careful. I never even fired a shot or struck anyone in capturing these guys. Please tell me how I get out of here. My battery is running very low and I need to save some for any emergencies."

Kathy relayed Frank's instructions identifying the meeting place along Route 70 and a direct azimuth to the site from his current position. She told him Kelly would be driving. She felt lousy and her headache was getting worse, reading the personnel files she had ask Frank to provide.

Jack knew Kathy was rattled but didn't know how to fix the problem. He was following the road he promised his father he would take. The risks were higher than he had counted on. Much worse than the Marine Corps or police had provided in his past. Mulling the problem over, he checked the tied up terrorists, gave them each a long drink, motioned to Shadow and set off toward his meeting site.

Sixty-one

Kathy had just left Frank's office. Being inside seemed different. Even though she had once been an inside player, she now felt she had little in common with the bureaucrats manning the work stations. They just didn't live in the world she and Jack lived in. The only risk here was political. Political correctness ruled the roost. When she told Frank her approach to finding his mole, even he swallowed hard. He did say that was why he needed her help. She had a ruthless efficiency that was increasingly rare on the inside. Anyway, he agreed, and gave her a small office and an assistant who was hired and given a clearance only a few weeks ago. She wanted no one else, especially someone that had been in the office for more than two months. Their heads were already screwed up. Kathy had been happy in the field but could barely stand working at Headquarters. It was without lethal risks, but the process was mind-numbing.

You can't ferret out moles by being afraid to break rules or correctness barriers – both can be real obstacles. Profiling was a no no. Kathy planned to use her own profiling system to narrow down the search for the mole in CTC. If she didn't tell anyone, who was to object?

Kathy shared her office with her assistant. She liked having the people she was working with to share the workspace. She knew only what the file told her about Jennifer Collins, a graduate of Connecticut College with a major in Criminology. She seemed to have a rare ability to eclectically extract the essence of information and to organize it quickly in her head. Her file alluded to this ability and, after talking to her for a few hours, Kathy agreed. You didn't often find personnel evaluation with such insight. Kathy was ready to start breaking eggs.

"Jennifer, wheel your chair over here. We're going to begin. Are you ready?"

"Yes, I now know what the problem is, but how do we start?"

"Any good investigator starts with a process to narrow down the search field. It means analyzing relevant evidence. First, we must collect the pieces. Only Frank can know all the areas we are poking into. All our requests for data are for his office only. We're merely helping him. That's our story. No deviations. Got it?"

"Yes. But why so much secrecy?"

"That's one of the reasons I picked you to help me. You're so new, you don't know looking for a mole is the most sensitive work any intelligence organization does. You don't want the mole to know anyone is looking for him or her. Also, no one wants to participate in such an investigation. A mole hunt is the same as a witch hunt. Often, innocent people have their careers ruined. In the intelligence business, it's better to punish a few innocent employees than to be so careful of individual rights that you fail to find the mole.

"In this case, we have a time and a date when a piece of sensitive information was created and when it was passed on to the enemy. That's a big deal. Frank gave me a list of all the people who heard him talk about the pursuit of a pair of snipers.

"We want all those personnel files. We want to find out where all those people were in the following hour and what they did. They are professionals and shouldn't have passed Frank's comments on to anyone. Let's hope one of them is our mole. Otherwise, we have to widen our search. That, I do not want to do.

"I hope we'll find our mole in the 14 personnel files on this table. These are the only people with first-hand knowledge. Get over any prejudices you might have about profiling. Profiling is what we do, but we don't call it that.

"You get half of the personnel files. Look for anyone who is an Arab or has an Arab name, anyone who is a Muslim, anyone with a spouse who is Muslim or Arab. Anyone who has made a trip or trips to Pakistan or Afghanistan, Iraq, Egypt, Yemen, Iran, Syria, Gaza, or any other Muslim country. Especially if they have family or friends from those places."

After two hours of reading files and taking notes, Kathy said, "C'mon, Jennifer, let's get a cup of tea or coffee. The stuff they make here is hardly drinkable. I'd forgotten how bad it was. Before we go, we put everything in the safe Frank moved in here. Only the two of us have the combination."

Over a corner table in a nearly deserted cafeteria, Jennifer said, "I only have two files to go, and I have three people with extensive travel to Muslim countries."

"I have four. I'll give you another hour, and then we'll start to compare notes. I plan on breaking at ten o'clock and picking up at seven in the morning. I hope I'm not messing up your life, love or otherwise. What we're doing is incredibly important and could end up saving a number of lives.

"I probably don't need to tell you this, but I will anyway. Do *not* tell anyone what you are doing or who you are working with. This is dangerous stuff, and I don't want to wonder what I could have done to protect you."

It was nearly eleven o'clock when Kathy pulled into the Brandon house. She heard Shadow using his happy bark and knew Jack was home. She met a bounding Shadow halfway to the front door, and Jack a few steps closer. Both gave her a welcome that nearly knocked her down. She hugged Jack and had a brief but good cry on his shoulder while Shadow leaned against her.

Kathy said, "Easy, big guy. I'm still sore and the headache is hanging on. Not as bad as it was."

Jack said, "If I had known about your helicopter crash landing, I would have dropped the chase and raced to be with you. It scares me to think I might have lost you."

"Give me your arm. I feel in need of a stiff scotch on the rocks, a long bath and a good sleep. I have to be in the office at seven tomorrow. And, if you think you were worried, I worried more. My man and his dog going after three armed and trained snipers. Thank God, Shadow was with you. That dog is your good talisman. When I learned about the leak in Frank's office, I was really angry. These missions are tough enough without the bad guys having access to our plans and actions. I'm going to find and fry that bastard. This is now personal, very personal. Be prepared to give me some slack, because you may not see much of me until I find and deal with this mole. What's the latest on Lou?"

"Lou is still critical but Dr. Green told me he will probably be moved out of ICU tomorrow morning. We need to find another recruit. Lou is through with hard action. I want both him and Storm to stay. Even so, we need at least one more experienced recruit. Kelly is coming on fast but needs time for more training. Relying on OJT is not only unfair to her but dangerous for us. Let's move inside. You need some food and rest. Until you find the mole, we are all at risk. You remember what happened once in this house. It ain't going to happen again."

Sixty-two

In his log cabin on the south slope of Mount Gilead, just outside Leesburg, the Professor was having a critical planning session with Hasani, who was devastated by the loss of three more of his sniper team members. Hasani was talking about his own martyrdom and trying to get the Professor to allow him to go into battle for the last time. The Professor said, “My most experienced and devout warrior cannot think of his own path to glory. We must make the Americans pay a much larger price for our lives.

“We are the first to bring a sustained battle to the Land of Satan. We must show the way for devout Jihadists to follow. Our ranks no longer depend upon warriors from the land of our forefathers. As the Muslim warriors of the past established the Muslim cultural center and stronghold in Cordoba, Spain, we must lay the ideological foundation for doing the same in America. By using American-born warriors in our battles today, we are placing the first cornerstones in that foundation. You and I and the rest of your American warriors will soon be gone. But we must not sell our lives too cheaply. The goal of battle is to inflict losses on the enemy, not seek ways for our own premature deaths. Now, how many men do you have ready to fight?”

“I have four more sniper teams.”

"The longevity of our campaign is now my major goal. By spreading out our attacks, we will continue to gather publicity here and in our world. The Arab Spring is turning former American lackey dictator nations into true Islamic lands governed by Sharia Law. We must provide a worthy example of carrying the Jihadist War to the American homeland. We will provide a way for others to follow. We will give hope, where there has been no hope.

"I want you to give me a plan that will keep our war alive for another two months. Use one team at a time. Your attacks do not have to be on high value targets where the Americans with their technology and rapid response can cause us such losses. I don't understand how they found, followed and attacked our last team so rapidly. They even captured or killed our men, while they were going into hiding. I hope to learn more about their response. I'm also concerned how one man and a dog tracked and wiped out the entire team of highly trained fighters on ground they knew well."

Hasani said, "Remember the Sunni Triangle and our sniper teams there? The tactic the Americans used there is the model for their destruction of our team yesterday. We learned that there was a Marine Lieutenant leading their counter-sniper operations in the Triangle who developed a rapid response attack strategy, using in-flight helicopters carrying counter-sniper teams over any sector where our snipers might be used. They cut off our snipers from their escape route. First, a rain of fire from the helicopters, and then the insertion of teams in pre-planned tactical positions. Once they had eyes on a team, it was very hard to escape. In Ramadi, they deployed in a few minutes after sniper action. I think they are now using the same tactic."

The Professor said, "I have a method to defeat this tactic. The helicopters with their hunter teams can hover over 10 or 20 potential targets. But not hundreds. We will attack small unprotected targets. To spread terror we do not need so-called high value targets. Terror can be brought to the people of Satan's capitol by hitting unprotected targets that no one could pick to defend in advance of our attack, and our attacks will be over in seconds, not minutes. Use this strategy to develop your plans. Don't worry, my friend, you will have your opportunity for everlasting glory."

Sixty-three

Kathy was in the office at seven. Jennifer was already working but had taken time to get a cup of coffee for Kathy. Kathy said, "Thanks, Jennifer, a hot cup of coffee is always better than an apple. Now I'll expect one tomorrow."

"You got it, boss. Every day, especially since Mr. Batcher stopped in and told me I was working with a legend."

"Frank's the legend. I'm just another worker bee. Okay, let's find the bad guy. I want him! Go to the whiteboard and write what I tell you and anything else you think should be on the board. We're going to gamble and take some intuitive short cuts.

"We have seven officers who have visited Arab countries. To keep anyone from seeing the board, the door will be locked at all times, and we'll use a simple code for the people of interest. Take them as I call them. First gets 'A' as an identifier and so on."

Two hours later, the board was covered. Of the seven, Kathy rejected four names and put them in a lower priority. Her top suspect had been to Pakistan three times, twice by himself. He had a long list of foreign national contacts. The names were all sent out for extensive investigation of databases. Her second suspect had family in Egypt. He, too, had a number of contacts that were also sent up for checking. By lunch time, 75 names had been forwarded for checking and cross-checking.

Jennifer said, "You asked me about the marital status of these seven officers. Five are married, one is single and one is divorced. What do we do now?"

"We check all the wives, lovers, live-ins, and significant others as far as we can. Anyone married to a foreign national, a Muslim, or to a partner with close relatives in any Arab country gets looked at. We don't have time to put surveillance teams on everyone. For now, we can only do data checks.

"I'm including bank accounts, debt loads and any off-shore accounts. Frank has someone that will take on the money stuff according to the priorities we assign. We need to look at three or four years of performance reports. They are usually not very revealing. We'll be looking for any dramatic changes in performance rating levels. There is always a reason for big changes. Finish your sandwich, and we'll get back to the whiteboard. I love working on a board. It seems as if a picture is being painted or the dots connected in a way that tells a story not there before.

"Tomorrow, I want you to continue to check the files for more names, check the bank data Frank should have by then, but don't take any action or ask anyone for information. I'll be late tomorrow. Probably come in after lunch. Oh, in case you're interested, quitting time tonight is six. I need some down time with my fiancé."

At dinner Storm gave a report on Lou. She said, "Dad is out of the ICU, eating well, and moving around with help. He is very tired and will be until his body makes the adjustment to the oxygen output from one lung. His spirits are good. He doesn't remember much, and I don't think he wants the full story yet. By the day after tomorrow, he can have visitors, and I think he'll want to see you. He's probably tired of my face and nagging. He wants to come back to work, but I don't see how he can. This outfit's missions are too tough for a man with one lung."

Jack said, "Storm, as long as he's willing to work, he has a job here. We need Lou for more reasons than his work as a shooter. He has an operational head that is one of the best I have ever seen. Kelly is stepping up to more field work, and we need Lou to take over the important support roles. Storm, you also have your choice of work. Your computer skills and organizational knowhow are impressive. Our inside guy was impressed with your work in identifying and laying out targets. We have more of that to do. The snipers aren't done yet."

Kathy said, "I have a job for Kelly tomorrow, helping me with some investigative work."

Kelly said, "Super, I need to get out of the house for things besides picking up a smelly guy and his dog from a highway crossroads. Both of them went to sleep in the car. I still don't know what happened."

Kathy said, "Jack, you like to tell stories. Let's hear it. The complete tale, no politically correct dodges. I thought it might make a good bedtime story but now is better. The floor is yours."

The next morning Kathy and Kelly met for breakfast at six. Kathy said, "Today we are breaking the law. Bring your weapon and your permit. Also, a change of clothing. We may have to do some surveillance."

The first stop was nearby, a small detached bungalow in Falls Church. Kathy pulled to the curb just before seven. Pouring fresh coffee into their cups, Kathy said, "The house across the street about a half a block from here, painted that hideous shade of hospital green, is our target. There should be only one person living in there. I'm a little suspicious of the occupant for reasons I cannot tell you now. This guy is either a loyal civil servant or something else. If he is something else, he will be dangerous and, in entering his house after he leaves, we have to be careful, very careful. The man should be coming out soon and going to work. We'll sit here for an hour after he leaves. If someone else comes out, I want you to follow them. Take the car if you need it. When the guy leaves, I'll call the house to see if anyone answers. If not, I'm going in. Stand by, I may call you to come in once I have a chance to look around. We have a search to do."

"Kathy, what can you tell me about this man?"

"Absolutely nothing. I don't want to influence your judgment and, if this man is innocent, I don't want to tell anyone who he is. Careers have been destroyed for less."

"You're looking for a mole, aren't you?"

"What do you know about moles? You're new to this business."

"I know from books and news reports that they exist and are very difficult to find."

"I'm searching for someone who has been leaking information to the high level terrorist we've been chasing. Yes, it is usually almost an impossible search. Many times when bad things happen, people suspect a mole is the cause. Sloppy tradecraft, a breakdown in security, careless talk and bad luck can also cause bad things to happen. Our search is much different. We have a tight timeframe when the leaks occurred, and we know the small group of people who had access to the information. Those factors make this a search that is doable in a time measured in days. We have to be careful the mole doesn't learn of our investigation. The stakes are very high, high enough for me to do a physical search of a few places without a warrant."

Kelly said, "Thanks. Hey! Look, a car is backing out of the garage."

"Yep. Right on time. Let's see what happens next. Another car is parked near the front of the house."

Kelly said, "A woman is coming down the porch stairs. She looks like she's dressed to go to work."

"When the car moves away from the curb, I'm getting out. Get ready to slide over and take the wheel. Follow her, carefully. I want to know where she goes, no more. Just note the time and the building. Do not follow her into any parking area or garage. Stay in the car on the street and keep your eyes open. Tell me immediately, if she heads back to the house. Call every ten minutes. Make sure you always have cell phone service. Okay?"

"Got it, Boss."

Kathy called the land line phone in the house. When no one answered, she walked around to the back of the house and found the back door was screened by some eight-foot yews. She quickly picked the lock, after checking for any traps like a small piece of paper placed to fall if the door was opened. Nothing. She eased the door open and stepped inside the kitchen. Checking for simple traps, she toured the house. Definitely, a woman was sharing the house and the bed. Female necessities in the bathroom and more than half the master bedroom closet held female clothing. Using her iPhone she photographed the medicine cabinet and closet before moving to the office. An iMac notebook and an IPAD were on a long table. Kathy knew the man could not take his notebook or IPAD to work and guessed the woman also worked in a secure environment. Both machines were pass-worded, and it took her several minutes to play administrator and get into the files. Inserting high gigabyte flash drives into the USB ports, she downloaded the files in each computer.

Her iPhone vibrated. Kelly was calling in. She told Kathy the woman drove into CIA Headquarters in Langley. Kathy said, "Okay. Come back here and pick me up. I'm done."

Kathy was walking down the street when Kelly pulled over and picked her up. Kathy climbed in and said, "Nothing there. Two more stops. I'll tell you where to go."

Fifteen minutes later they were in the midst of a development outside Vienna, Virginia. Kelly asked, "Where do all these people work? I thought Pittsburgh was a crowded city."

"This is where your tax dollars go. These people nearly all work for the US Government, either as employees or as contract workers. Now pull over here. At least half of these houses have someone in them. I don't want anyone to see me going into a house and have some good but nosy citizen call the police. Talk about embarrassing! My badge without a warrant would make the problem worse. Also, I think this man is hiding something. It's okay for him to hide his love life but not his travel or his foreign contacts. He, like our last suspect, lives 'alone.' I'll call to see if anyone answers. If not, I'm going in. You stay here and warn me about anyone approaching the house. Give me a heads up, even if you aren't sure. I don't mind warnings that turn out to be non-events."

No one answered Kathy's house-checking call. It was beginning to rain and the wind was picking up. No one was on the street when Kathy approached the house. From the front of the house, she could see an ancient door knob lock. She mused, why bother. She rang the doorbell while inserting her pick. She could do this lock left-handed with her eyes shut.

The doorbell didn't summon anyone and Kathy slipped inside. She paused to let her senses adjust to the house. The living room certainly didn't look as if this was a bachelor pad. More than decent furniture with a few good antiques and Oriental rugs. Moving into the kitchen, she noted it was full of stainless steel appliances and lined with granite counters. The counters were clean. She thought this guy must be well-trained. Even Jack, with all his discipline, was not this good a housekeeper. Going up the stairs, she took in the expensively framed oil and water color paintings. No masters but not bad. This guy didn't do this on his government salary. Family money or some other outside source was at play here.

You could always tell if a woman was in a house. Lotions, perfumes and a ton of cosmetics give off a distinctive scent. No question a woman lived in or was often in this house. The master bedroom confirmed her suspicions with the cosmetics and other necessary female maintenance implements. Several dresses, suits and blouses hung in an orderly manner. So the order in this place may come from the presence of this woman. Now, woman, who are you?

A search of the house and basement turned up nothing. Kathy downloaded files she thought relevant onto her flash drive and backdated the transaction. She thought, everyone has secrets but this house does not have what I'm looking for. She went out the front door and walked the short distance to where Kelly was waiting.

"Did you find anything?"

"No. Boring house, nothing to indicate he might be a mole. Onward to our last stop for today. This time it was a small dingy house in an old section of Arlington. The house needed painting and the landscaping shrubs had given up. Kelly said, "With the rain and overcast sky, this place would fit into the small towns I knew growing up. It certainly doesn't look like anyone with clean or dirty money lives here."

"I believe the kind of person we are looking for is not motivated by money. There isn't enough money to reward him for the incredible risks he's taking and the strain of daily living a complex false background, where one slip can be the end. Stand by here. The same protocol. I should be out in an hour and we can get some lunch."

No one answered Kathy's check call, and she was soon going up the slight out of kilter stairs with at least two shades of gray showing through the layers of peeling paint. Jack's house in Pittsburgh looks very upscale compared to this one. The lock, though, is good. I'll have to focus on this one. Two minutes later, Kathy stepped into the small living room furnished with early Salvation Army overstuffed furniture. Rag rugs covered the floor. Moving swiftly through the ground floor, she saw nothing of note. Like the outside, the inside was grubby and devoid of any touch by loving hands. This is a real bachelor pad. Upstairs, there was no sign of another person, man or woman, living with her third suspect. She took some photos, checked a number of possible hiding places and went down into the dimly lit cellar. Kathy knew from a previous case people believe the cellar is a good place to hide things. She had found a cache of information on another search, alias documents and cash hidden in the cellar wall. Using her small high intensity flashlight, she searched by dividing the cellar into quadrants.

The old house creaked with the gusting wind. Kathy reached back and touched her SOCOM .45 automatic. She often found it reassuring to touch the weapon. Hunting for leads to a mole in a cellar of an empty, creaking old house was beyond spooky. Come on, girl, focus. Search this place and get out.

No doors in the cellar walls. One dusty workbench that hadn't had any use for a long time. An oil furnace sat in one corner. When it suddenly started up, Kathy jumped and smiled at her nervous reaction. Focusing the light on the overhead to search between the joists, she noticed the hot air ducts radiating out from the furnace. The ducts were vintage. Many had taped joints. Noticing one of the ducts turned ninety degrees up to a ground floor register, she thought, it's the only clean thing down here. As she turned to leave, she wondered why the ten-inch elbow duct was clean and went back to examine it. With her height she was able to reach up and put her hands on the elbow joint. It seemed tight but she couldn't see any metal screws in the joint. Pulling down on the elbow, it separated from the floor register joint.

Kathy searched around for something to stand on. She picked up an old galvanized two-gallon bucket, placed it upside down under the exposed duct and stepped up, bumping her head. Muttering to herself about all she needed was to keep bumping an already aching head, she carefully moved her head between the joists and saw a long box-like object. Examining it with her light, she noticed very little dust on the container. Reaching in with an extended arm, she felt what seemed to be a light-weight metal box. Pulling the box toward her, she soon had the box in her hands. It wasn't heavy, and she was able to step off the bucket and set the box on the cement cellar floor. The box had no locks or traps she could see. Opening the well-oiled hinged lid, she saw a .38 special revolver and a box of shells, and two large brown envelopes. The envelopes were unsealed. The first one contained a large pack of big bills, at least twenty thousand dollars. The second had two sets of identity documents complete with passports, driver's licenses, credit cards and other miscellaneous cards to support the false identities.

Kathy thought, well, well. We've now found our mole. This is the man who Frank personally vouched for when he was hired, the son of a Princeton classmate. I wonder how he is going to take this. Now I have to put everything back, except for one set of identities with Mr. Richfield's picture but a different alias. Kathy used her iPhone to photograph all the documents and the hiding place before leaving by the back door.

Back in the car with Kelly, Kathy called Frank and told him she had his mole but didn't want to say anything more over the phone. Knowing Frank wanted to know the details immediately, she said, "I'll drop Kelly back at Jack's house. I'll be in your office in 30 minutes. Can you arrange for some uninterrupted time?"

"All the time we need. This is my top priority."

Kathy was a few minutes late, and Frank was waiting for her when she got off the elevator. Frank handed her a cup of coffee and led her to a small interview room. Once inside, before sitting at the table, he said, "Tell me."

Kathy motioned for him to sit down first and said, "You're not going to like this. Your mole is Sam Richfield."

"What!! Are you sure? That can't be right! I've known Sam and his father for thirty years!"

Kathy reached into her zipped jacket pocket and slid one of Richfield's alias passports across the table. Frank examined the document, turned white with anger, slammed his fist on the table and said, "I just don't understand how Sam could do this. The family is wealthy. He can't have become a traitor for money. Sorry for doubting you. I should've known better. Do you have anything else?"

Kathy leaned across the table and showed Frank the photos on her iPhone and told him about her search. Frank shook his head and said, "This is an open and shut case. The evidence wouldn't hold up in court due to the illegality of the search, and I don't want to tip off the Professor we know about his source. We'll have to handle this on our own. Sam's father and the Professor were close in graduate school at Princeton. I wonder if the father is involved?"

Kathy replied, "He must be! How else could his son have gotten involved with al Qaeda?"

"I can't argue. It looks bad for the Richfield family. We can't arrest them or even get a subpoena to search their residences. Any defense attorney will get the case thrown out on grounds of the illegal search. My plan is to use our mole to set a trap for the Professor. Whether or not the plan works, al Qaeda will suspect Sam and his father. They are not forgiving and will deal with them."

"What's our next move?"

"Ask Jack to arrange for another meeting in the Ritz. The three of us can decide on an approach for taking care of our mole and putting an end to the Professor and his campaign."

Sixty-four

The next day Kathy and Jack were waiting for Frank to arrive. The sandwiches had just arrived. Jack tipped the waiter and said to Kathy as the door closed, "Frank is never late. The guy makes a religion out of being on time. It's two minutes until twelve. Wanna bet he'll be here in two?"

"No way. If I thought he'd be very late, I'd try to seduce you in this beautiful suite. What is it, the honeymoon special?"

"No, the management just likes to take care of its bill-paying clients. I don't see why we can't stay for a few minutes after he goes."

"Make it a few hours and you might have a taker."

A few seconds after noon, a tap on the door broke up their banter. Jack checked and let Frank in. Frank greeted them and said, "Sorry, I'm a little late."

Kathy said, "Yes. I wanted to start without you, but Jack was sure you would come along."

Frank sat down at the table and poured himself a cup of black coffee. Looking up at Kathy he said, "I just can't believe you were able to find the mole so quickly. If this story comes out, you are going to be a counter-intelligence legend. That reminds me, give me your cell phone. It may be legally dangerous for you to have the images of the documents you found in Richfield's cellar."

Kathy dug into her purse and slid the iPhone over to Frank, saying, "It's your phone anyway. I'm going to pick up an iPhone 4 with my own brand of encryption."

For the next hour they discussed various plans for dealing with the Richfields and the Professor. When Frank left, they had a plan that should work. A minute after the door closed behind Frank, Jack hung out the 'Do Not Disturb' sign and said, "I could hardly wait for him to go."

He looked over at Kathy who was shedding her clothes. She said, "Come on, big guy. Don't keep your bride-to-be waiting."

When the passion ebbed, Kathy said, "Your trip in the wilds didn't hurt you any. You're still a fantastic lover."

"Only when my partner is a tall, sexy, shapely blonde who knows all my buttons. I forgot you're also a dangerous and intelligent lady. Now let's get a shower and order tea and some pastry. I have something we need to talk about."

Kathy poured the tea and asked Jack what he wanted to discuss.

Jack said, "Now, bear with me. I'm feeling my way. My father told me not to trust anybody all the time and most people not at all, when the stakes were high. I thought it was strange when Frank asked you to hand over your cell phone with the images you took in the guy's cellar. He could have asked you to destroy them which you would have done without question. Instead, he didn't trust you to destroy them. What legal danger could there have been?"

Kathy started to say something, but Jack said, "Let me finish. You found his mole. No question. The mole is the key to finding the Professor. The logical move would be to pick up Sam Richfield, interrogate him, and make him give up the Professor. Any time, any day, the terrorists led by the Professor could take dozens, maybe even hundreds, of lives. Yet, here we are developing complicated plans to take down the terrorists. And guess who is leading the charge? We are! We're good but not that good. The teams the Government can put together make us look like what we are. A very small team of specialists who can and have made contributions.

"We're not the A team. Frank is. In the plan we just discussed, if one thing goes wrong, we get wiped out. Given advance knowledge, the Professor and Hasani could ambush and kill all of us. We are the only people who even know about a mole. Does what I'm saying make any sense to you?"

Kathy was silent. She stood up and began striding back and forth across the room. She turn toward Jack and said, "It only makes sense if Frank is playing us and protecting the mole and the Professor. If you are even close to being right, we're in serious trouble. Our proof of the existence of a mole is gone."

"Not quite. I copied the images on to my iPAD just to be on the safe side, in case something happened to your collection. Right now, I don't see how that can help us."

"I'm going to run a little test. Give me your phone. I'm going to call the young woman Frank assigned to help me." Kathy called Jennifer's cell. She answered and Kathy said, "Where are you?"

"Kathy, I won't be able to help you anymore. I got a spot promotion and an immediate transfer to Afghanistan."

"Wonderful! Who told you about the transfer?"

"Mr. Batcher just told me. He said he had talked to you, and there was no further need for me to help you. The problem went away. He said my transfer was very sensitive, and I shouldn't talk to anyone about it. He said not even you, but I just couldn't go away without saying goodbye to you. I hope we have a chance to work together again. I'm sorry, but my ride to the airport is outside. I have to go. Bye for now."

Kathy had the iPhone on speaker so Jack could hear every word.

Jack said, "Okay. What do you think now?"

"I'm scared! You have to be right. Otherwise, nothing makes any sense. I think Jennifer might get killed for her role in helping me. Take her away, and only you and I know about the existence of any mole. We have photocopies of alias documentation, most likely done by the Agency, ostensibly for Richfield's use in a CIA operation. I do have Richfield's alias driver's license. I did not give it to Frank. What do we do now?"

"Frank's been in this business a long time. He knows we're a danger to him as long as we're alive. I believe he intends to make us the fall guys. We either get killed or arrested as traitors. We need some official help or we need to kill Frank and Richfield."

"I'll bet Richfield's house is now empty, and he's in the wind. A search of the cellar will turn up nothing. To get official help, we need real evidence. What we have is useless, a CIA officer working in counter-terrorism with three sets of alias documentation. Means nothing. You still have those recorded phone calls warning the sniper team you and Shadow were chasing. Again, nothing to convince any skeptics."

Jack agreed and said, "Now we know how the so-called mole learned so quickly about our activities. Richfield wasn't the mole. It was Frank who kept the terrorists one step ahead of us at every turn."

"Your father made Frank's reputation by helping him to track down and arrest members of KGB sleeper cells in America. There was no reason for him to double-cross your father. For twenty years, he was Frank's mentor. He never knew the real Frank. Did your father ever tell him about the mountain hideaway?"

"No. He told me no one knew about it. Maybe we should think about locating there for a while. I hate to expose Kelly, Storm and Lou to this kind of trouble. They didn't sign up to have their own government after them."

Kathy said, "I would bring Kelly to the cabin but not Lou or Storm. Lou's need for regular medical care will make him too easy to find. And Storm is not yet committed. Maybe in the future, but not now. I believe she resents what happened to her father and feels we had no business exposing him to such danger."

"I believe Frank is the problem. With him gone, we are all okay. He needs us dead, not arrested and talking to law enforcement. The problem is he knows we will quickly figure out what's going on. He knew asking for your cell phone and not having his own plan to pick up the mole you found, gave him away. Once we had those phone calls I found on the sniper's abandoned cell phone, he had to manufacture a mole.

"Putting you in charge bought him time and let him track our activities. Richfield is probably no mole. Frank arranged some way of putting those documents where you would find them. In the same way, he gave you a stack of personnel files. He wanted you to find Richfield and go away, believing you did a first-class investigative job. Case closed. Back to business as usual, continuing to use us to make himself look good. He miscalculated how little time it would take you to find Richfield and to smell a rat."

Kathy said, "The son of a bitch wants to set us up to get killed in action at the hands of the Professor. He can then either let the Professor disappear or kill him as well, depending on which option is the best for him. If we play it right, we can use his plan against him. If our deaths can be attributed to the Professor, so could Frank's."

"Exactly! Whatever the action, we have to keep that part to ourselves. We'll send Lou and Storm away. If they lay a good enough false trail, they should be safe. What do you think about Kelly?"

"I think we should include Kelly. She has good instincts and is totally committed. Besides Frank knows about her and could see her as a danger or a way to get to us. She's safer with us."

"Okay, I agree. She needs to know the whole story. Will you brief her?

"You got it."

"Starting now, we have to be super careful. Frank is a very dangerous man. He is entirely ruthless and a little sick. I believe he likes us, you especially. Still, he'll kill us at the first safe opportunity he gets. Okay, let's get out of here."

As they were going down in the elevator, Jack said, "Our car is in valet parking and is probably safe. I don't put it past Frank to put an explosive device or a beacon on our car. He knows the valet will be getting the car for us, so any pressure switch will be on the passenger side. Please humor me and get in the back seat. I'll check the car over back at the house. Until this is over, the car has to be checked every time it's out of our control.

"While I'm checking the car, tell Storm to get rid of her cell phone and take Lou to Hawaii as soon as he can travel. Get her a cashier's check for $500,000. Tell her to use cash. No credit cards. Their contracts will be honored for the next year and then we'll see about the future. Tell her the risk is real, but no details. Also, no contact with family or close friends. In Hawaii, she can get a prepaid cell phone and a new notebook using a different name or a variation of their names. Ask her to send a postcard to our lawyer, Lee Jensen, every month indicating their hotel. Don't scare her to death but impress her with the need to be careful. The sooner they are away from here the better. Tell her to make the plans but don't implement them until you tell her to go."

"Got it. Storm is not going to be happy."

"Being alive is better. This should all be over, one way or the other, in a month at the latest."

Sixty-five

Jack slowed and glided to the curb, just down the street from Richfield's house in Vienna. Kathy had briefed Jack on the inside layout. The house lights were on, and they could see someone moving around inside. Kathy said, "I was wrong. I expected the house to be empty and Richfield gone. You thought he was innocent and it looks that way now."

Jack knocked on the door and when a man meeting Richfield's description opened the door, Jack asked him if he was Sam Richfield. When he said yes, Jack showed him his badge and asked if they could come in. He and his partner had a few questions.

Richfield looked carefully at the badge and said, "I've never been to Pittsburgh."

Jack said, "We know. You are not a suspect of any kind, but we believe you can help us. May we come in?"

Sam said, "Okay, but I don't have much time. I'm expected back at the office. My boss called."

Kathy said, "We only need a few minutes. We won't keep Frank waiting."

Sam looked startled and said, "What's going on here? Who are you people with the Pittsburgh police badges? You should leave now!"

Jack said, "We'll leave when we're ready, and we may take you with us. So settle down, and let us tell you a story that may save your life and your father's."

"Okay! You have my attention."

Kathy handed Richfield the alias driver's license she took from the hiding place in his cellar and asked, "Is this yours?"

"My picture is on it. I assume you know where I work."

Kathy said, "We know more than where you work. Where did you keep this document?"

When Sam didn't say anything, Jack said, "We're not recording any of this. There will be no notes and no reports. Now please answer."

"I don't see any harm in answering that question. Documents are kept in the office. I check them out when I have approval to use them."

Kathy said, "Is that your answer?"

"Yes."

"Please look at these pictures."

She passed all the photos taken earlier in his cellar across the table. Richfield's expression was real. The wide eyes, breath catching and face color couldn't be faked so convincingly.

Jack said, "What do you have to say? Please be careful."

"I can't believe this. I'm not permitted to keep these things. Someone must have planted them."

Kathy said, "Now we're getting someplace. We happen to agree with you. Do you recognize the hiding place?"

"Yes, I made it to hold things I sometimes had to keep overnight."

"Did anyone know about your safe place?"

"Of course. Those places have to be on the record in case something happened to me."

"Who knew besides Frank?"

"Maybe Alice, his assistant."

Jack asked, "Why would these documents be in your cellar?"

"Honest, I've no idea."

"When are you expected in the office?"

"I should have been there 15 minutes ago."

Jack looked at Kathy who took the cue and went to the front window to watch the street.

Richfield asked, "What is she doing?"

"Unless we're very wrong, some bad people will be coming to see you very soon. Do you have a weapon and know how to use it?"

"Yes, but …"

"No buts. Just go and get it. Make sure it's ready to use."

"You're letting me go get a loaded weapon?"

"Yes. You're not a prisoner. You may not know it yet, but without us, you'll never see the sunrise tomorrow. Also, if there's trouble, another shooter is always a good thing. You've got one minute to grab your weapon and whatever else you want. Don't worry about clothes. Dump your cell phone. Now go!"

Jack moved up beside Kathy who was studying the street in front of the house. Jack said, "If anyone comes, they'll park right in front and come in fast. They'll either kill him right here or take him away to a remote place, ask him a couple of questions and then kill him.

"I'll stay here. Go to the back door. Check and see if the back way is clear. We're going out the back, behind a few houses to our car and then home. I've put the Minhs on alert. With them, the Vietnamese gardeners, and Kelly on guard, they should be okay. Frank won't want a shootout in McLean."

Sam Richfield came back with a 9mm Browning and a small bag. Jack grabbed the bag and said, "Let's go out the back door. You lead. Go right behind your neighbors' houses and right again to the street. Head for the black Cadillac SRX. Don't stop. Don't shoot unless I say so, or you see someone drawing down on us. Go!"

The way was clear to the car. Kathy slid behind the wheel and was getting ready to start up when a black Chevrolet Suburban braked hard in front of Richfield's house. They all ducked down to watch. Three men burst out of the car, up the steps and smashed through the door. When they were all inside, Jack said, "Okay, Kathy, let's go. Sam, did you see anything subtle about that? I don't think you called for that ride."

Sam said, "Holy shit! What's going on?"

Kathy said, "Sam, that was your execution squad coming for you. They'll place incriminating evidence in your hiding place and make sure someone finds it after you're dead. They must have been sure you were there, otherwise they would not have broken the door down. Leaving evidence like that is not good."

Jack said, "Here's the quick version. We've been helping Frank for the past few years. I discovered there was a mole when I was trailing the two snipers in the mountains between Frederick and Hagerstown. I captured one of the sniper's cell phone. When I checked it, I noticed a voicemail message. I played the message and heard someone warning the head sniper that a man with a tracking dog was after them. Frank and I worked up a trap message telling the snipers the tracking dog broke a leg and the man turned back. Frank said he made the test message available to a limited number of his senior staff.

"He brought Kathy in to find the mole. She was told to conduct an investigation, but very discreetly. He then gave her information steering her to you. You were to be the mole.

"Kathy found your cache of documents and showed photos to Frank, who confiscated her cell phone and transferred her assigned assistant to Afghanistan on short notice. Instead of immediately taking you into custody for interrogation, he did nothing. Later he met with us and sketched out a plan for using you to capture the ringleader of the sniper terrorists. My small team would be totally committed in the take-down. We believe Frank intended for the snipers and their leader, a man referred to as the Professor, to kill all of us in an ambush. Frank also said your father was close to the Professor, when they both were going to Princeton, and must be involved with his son, the mole. With all of us dead, Frank's position would be protected. How's that for a story?"

"Unbelievable, but you made me a believer. When you told me to go get my weapon, I opened my mind. The sight of those three hoods smashing into my house removed all doubt. Thank you both for saving my life. What do we do now?"

"We take you to our house for the night. I'll ask our attorney, as an officer of the court, to take our statements including the photos and records as affidavits. I'm not sure we want to go the legal route, but I want the option.

"Tonight, we call Frank and demand a meeting on our ground. We tell him to come alone, we want to go over our options. We have no desire to bring any charges against him. Our aim is to work out a win-win solution."

Later that night, lying in Jack's arms, Kathy said, "Did you notice Sam looking at Kelly? He did everything he could to get close to her."

"I noticed she wasn't running away. Romances can start anywhere. From what I see, I like Sam Richfield, but I feel like Kelly is our daughter. Maybe nobody is good enough for her.

"Another subject. Frank is the only person who knows my father was once a KGB officer and never became a US citizen. He will use it to make us back off. I would like to find and destroy that information. Our estate just went over the one billion mark. In some circumstances, the government could take all of it."

"The money doesn't worry me. Jack, have you ever counted up the laws we have broken? Never mind we were on the side of the angels, the law and order Mafia would lock us up in a heartbeat. No one would come to our rescue."

Jack said, "It's clear. Frank goes down or we do. I swear Frank will not continue his life of deception and death. He played us, big time. Now it's our turn."

Sixty-six

Secure in the isolation of his log cabin hideout, the Professor closed up his throw away, prepaid cell and called for Hasani. When Hasani came into the largest room in the cabin, lighted only by the flickering fire, he could tell his friend and mentor was worried about something.

Hasani said, "My friend, what is the problem? We will soon restart our sniper campaign. I have three teams ready to go. The glory of our martyrdom is close. I thank you for the opportunity of bringing our battle to the heart of the enemy. It is more than I ever dreamed was possible. Your wisdom, faith and courage have brought us this far. Do not worry."

"It's not the coming battle that worries me. My old friend, who has helped us for so long, needs us now. He wants us to delay our attacks until an internal danger is eliminated. A few people have discovered his role in working with us. He had to agree to meet with them tomorrow at 10:30 AM in a wilderness park along the winding road with the sharp curves you love to drive on the way to McLean. At the crossroads of Route 193 and Old Dominion Road is the entrance to Great Falls Park. The park is located on the Potomac River where the river is a racing flood, smashing through huge boulders and over sharp drops."

"Yes, I know the place. I met with one of my teams there last month. It is a beautiful place. The shot will have to be close. Less than 100k meters, since I won't know exactly where the targets will be. I don't want to move around to get a better angle."

"Good! I want you to be there to kill all the people he will be meeting. If something goes wrong, give my old friend the gift of death. He has served well and does not deserve to be dishonored. I'm asking you to go alone, because I don't want other witnesses. You know, I have never been sure of the true faith of our American converts."

"I will be there, waiting before the sun comes up tomorrow."

"Go with God, my friend."

Sixty-seven

Coached by Jack and Kathy, Sam negotiated a meeting place and time with Frank. Jack was surprised and a little alarmed at how easily Frank agreed to the Great Falls Park meeting site. Obviously, he was confident he could manage the circumstances. It was a one-on-one meeting. Only Sam Richfield and Frank would be meeting at the designated site. There was no discussion of guns or no guns.

Richfield would carry his Browning and Frank would surely be armed. Jack wondered if Frank would have the FBI or the police standing by to cover him, but decided that would be too big a risk for Frank. He had to get rid of the people that could compromise him, not arrest them. Their testimony would be damning. No, Frank was too smart to use the legal system.

Just after midnight Kathy dropped Jack and Kelly near the entrance to the park. They both carried Stoner SR-25 rifles with sound suppression and ghillie suits they would put on at their shooting site. Richfield knew where to stand to shield himself from shots coming from the angle Jack was sure any shooter, especially Hasani, would use. The sun angle at the time of the meeting would be a critical factor in the selection of a sniper sight. Jack expected there would be more than one shooter.

He had debated whether to have Kathy or Kelly with him to protect Richfield and kill Frank. Kathy wanted to be with him, but she was the only one who could take advantage of Frank's concentration on the meeting to enter his house and search for data incriminating Jack, his father and her. She knew Frank's habits, his thought processes, and had been in his house a few times when she worked directly for him. Kathy had experience in surreptitious entry operations and knew the methods intelligence operatives used to protect their hiding places.

Frank had been living alone for the last two years. He had no close neighbors and landscaping shielded the house from direct view from the street. Storm volunteered to be her driver and warn her of anyone approaching the house.

In selecting the second shooter, Jack's instincts told him, even with the limited practice Kelly had in using a rifle, she was a better reaction shooter than Kathy. Kathy still had the fatal killing flaw of thinking too much. Also, she had been one of Frank's prized officers. She once had great respect and admiration for him. Jack thought those past feelings might cause her to delay a shot for a few seconds. All the doctrine preached "to be tentative is to die." Kelly did not have a tentative bone in her body. She had shown her willingness to shoot quickly and with deadly efficiency.

By 1:00 AM, Jack finished positioning Kelly. She had her lines of fire and instructions on what to look for and when to fire. With her camouflage suit and nearly buried in dead leaves, an opponent would almost have to step on her to see her. Jack selected a position 25 yards to Kelly's right, a little closer than he liked for the mission, but he wanted to be able to support her quickly. Both were equipped with low-powered line-of-sight transceivers and night vision capability.

Jack knew, no matter what Frank planned, his back-up would be in place before sunrise. He also knew it was a job for more than one shooter. He had some doubt Frank would show up. If his back-up shooters could kill one or more of the people who had evidence he was a traitor, without exposing himself, why would he.

Sixty-eight

Hasani always followed orders. This time he couldn't. He knew the Professor was wrong. Even he wouldn't be able to protect the Professor's friend and kill all the other people. How many, he didn't know. At least three people with guns would be protecting their side of the meeting. He would have to move after every shot or two. Any sniper, no matter how good, is vulnerable when moving. He would play the main role but he needed help. Hasani, two of his trained snipers, and another recent recruit to drive the stolen panel truck, were now approaching the drop-off point.

It was 3:30 AM. If he was operating by himself, he'd have been in his hidden shooting position before midnight. He doubted his team members could get in position and stay quiet for seven hours. Numbers of players always affected the outcome. In this case, he had had no choice. As he defined the mission, the highest priority kill was the Professor's friend. The others didn't matter. If his friend had to agree to this meeting, he was already compromised. Hasani believed he was following the Professor's implicit order. His friend's usefulness to Jihad was over. Death would be his reward for past loyalty. Dead men cannot give up secrets.

Kelly was working on keeping her focus and trying to get to the state of mind Jack said would come. He said she would know it when it happened. He described it as becoming part of the environment. You were aware of everything happening around you. The noise of the night predators, the movement of insects, the flight of bats and owls and, worst of all, the sound of snakes slithering through the brush. Like her mother, Kelly hated snakes. Somehow she felt close to her warrior mother who must have spent many, many nights in a sniper hide, waiting for her targets to appear. Kelly knew Jack was counting on her to even the odds. She liked Sam Richfield and hoped he would survive the next half-dozen hours. If Jack didn't spot the back-up shooters before they were ready to shoot, Richfield wouldn't have a chance. Jack told her even experienced snipers sometimes expose their positions by being careless with the movement of their rifle barrels or being too aggressive in shifting to a better shot-making position. He told her to look for unnatural forms and lines. Straight lines weren't part of nature.

Struggling to hold her focus, she nearly jumped when Jack's quiet voice echoed in her ear. He said, "Be alert. A vehicle slowed and stopped on Route 193. I saw car lights pause and then move on. The action is behind us. The shooters may move through our positions to find their own shooting hides. If you think they have seen you, shoot and move and keep shooting. If you see them and have a sure killing shot, take it. I'd just as soon kill them before they get set and hidden.

"More than one shooter will be looking for a place to set up and wait. At least one will have some night vision capability. They will outnumber us. We will still have the advantage. We're already in place and know they're coming. The leaves are dry and no one can move at night within 30 yards of our position without one of us hearing them. We should hear something in the next few minutes."

Kelly thought, my God, this is really going to happen. Mother, I hope you're watching over me.

Jack shielded his watch dial, now on the inside of his wrist, and looked at the time, 4:00 AM. If Hasani is here, he will place the shooters, so I expect a fair amount of movement. He won't set up his own position, until he is satisfied with the others. Because of the short-range shooting, less than 70 yards, and limited targets, it will be one man to a hide, no sniper/spotter teams. He whispered to Kelly, "Unless you are in danger, don't shoot. I expect three shooters. We need to spot them before Richfield gets here. If we kill them when the light is good, the chief sniper won't have the cover of darkness to shoot and move. I think he will stay in his hide until Richfield and maybe Frank show up. Copy?"

"Copy."

Hasani could not believe his two men could be making so much noise. True, the night was very dark with overcast skies, and he was the only one with night vision optics, but they just didn't believe there was any danger in the park at this time of night. The paths would be quieter, but he didn't like the confining nature of a path. It was too easy to predict the position of an enemy if they followed a path. They were also very easy to trap with sensors or explosives. Making your way through the brush was safer, if noisier. At least these American Muslims weren't talking or smoking. If one of the US counter-sniper teams was in the area, these two men wouldn't be leaving the park alive. Their clumsiness would provide cover for him to do the killing. All he needed from them was a distraction.

Kelly heard something moving through the brush. She froze and slowly turned her head in the direction of the sound. Through the greenish world of her night vision optics, she saw three armed men 30 yards above and west of her position. One of them was wearing night optics. They were spread out at ten yard intervals. Waiting until the sound disappeared, she alerted Jack and gave him her report.

She could still follow their green forms slowly moving up slope and now north of her. Fifteen minutes later, she could make out only two men, moving higher on the slope above the parking lot. She couldn't be sure, but it looked like the two men moved 20 yards up the slope and then separated. Kelly searched with her glasses but could see no further movement. Kelly adjusted her earpiece and checked with Jack.

He said, "I was also able to follow them for a while. I lost them when it looked like they all paused for a minute or so. I believe the leader is Hasani. I've seen him before with my night vision gear. When they paused, he was placing one of the shooters in the point position. Guiding on his position, the other two will move up the slope and then split, forming a triangle of shooters above the meeting site. Keep a watch on the area. Especially locate the shooter in the point position. He is your primary target. Locate him when the light gets better and plan your shot. If you can find the man farthest from you, take him next. I think Hasani is somewhere near your ten o'clock position. I'll take him. I expect him to move at the first shot. Remember to compensate for the downhill shooting. If you move, move quickly and burrow into the leaves and brush, and stay still until you have a shot. Patience, patience."

Hasani settled into his hide and made some improvements in his concealment and view of the parking lot and picnic tables. He was glad he opted to leave his .50 caliber Barrett rifle at the log cabin. It was too heavy to move through brush and wasn't optimum for shooting at this range. He selected the Dragunov SVD. Half the weight of the Barrett, it had been a main sniper weapon in the Sunni Triangle. He was very familiar with its performance and optics.

Kelly now appreciated the discipline her mother and Jack developed by remaining motionless in a concealed sniper hide for hours, and even days, waiting for a shot that may or may not come. It wasn't patience that was required, it was super patience. For her, the hours dragged by. It was just after 10:00 AM.

An hour ago, she noticed movement in the area she had been searching since the light improved. Focusing on the area, she made out the outline of a body and a poorly concealed rifle barrel. Jack said, "Good. Plan your shots. I haven't found Hasani yet. So when you shoot, roll behind the log you're snuggled against and don't move. If you've hit the second sniper, stay behind the log with your head down. If not, I'll talk to you. Count on Hasani firing on your location."

Jack checked his watch. It was time for Richfield to show up. Using Google shots of the park, Jack had

Richfield set up behind a large tree trunk to shield him from downhill shots. Only when and if Frank arrived at the actual meeting site, was he to expose himself. When Frank got out of his car and into the open, Kelly would start shooting. In a perfect world, the snipers would all be down before Richfield was in the open. Jack thought, we might get two of them, but Hasani was a special case.

At 10:15, Richfield drove into the parking lot in one of the Brandon cars. A few miles away, Kathy was checking the back door of Frank's house. Storm and Kathy saw him leave five minutes earlier. Kathy took the time to examine the back door with a magnifying glass, searching for very thin wires or a hair across the door opening. Seeing nothing, she got her picks out and started on the dead bolt lock. It was a well-known brand and not difficult to pick. Frank knew if someone with professional skills wanted in, they'd get in.

Kathy wasn't hunting for a safe. She knew Frank's philosophy, the best hiding place was in plain sight. Something he could get to in a hurry and small enough to move if he had to. What she was looking for would not be on paper, but most likely on flash drives or DVDs. DVDs fit in with his theory about hiding things in plain sight. Frank had a large collection of DVDs on the bookshelves in his living room. There was a DVD player in his study, as well as the living room. The largest collection was in the living room. She would start there.

Sixty-nine

Richfield got out of his car, moved to the general meeting location and sat down behind a large oak tree. Kelly saw both of her targets adjust their positions to cover Richfield. The adjustments made them better targets. She heard Jack say, "Focus, focus. When this happens, it will be incredibly fast. No time for thinking."

Five minutes later, another car moved into the parking lot and stopped within several feet of the meeting site. Jack thought Frank is going to use the car as a shield. He figures we might be here and would be shooting from the high ground. Smart guy, but it won't work. We still have the angle we need. When Frank got out of the car, Richfield stood up and start moving toward the nearest picnic table.

Jack waited five seconds, then said, "Shoot."

Kelly fired and fired again. Just as she rolled over the log, a rifle slug knocked bark off the log. If I hadn't moved fast, he would have hit me. An instant later, Jack fired and said, "Stay still, I think I hit him but don't know how hard."

Hasani recoiled from the hit on his right hip and rolled into a protected area behind a huge white pine tree. The hip joint felt broken and an artery was spurting. He still had time. Gathering his concentration, he sighted on his primary target and snapped off two shots. His target went down. Frank wondered who shot him. His left ear was gone and his left arm was useless. Instinct took over. He crawled to his car and staying low, drove out of the lot.

Richfield started to get up. Jack yelled, "Sam, stay down."

"Kelly, what about your targets?"

"One is moving. The other one is on his back and not moving."

"Can you see their weapons?"

"Yes. The sniper that's still moving is holding his rifle. The other one's weapon is several feet away from him. He's still not moving."

"Okay, stay put. Hit the sniper who's still alive again. I'm going after Hasani. We need to get out of here fast. Switch frequencies and tell Richfield to run to the car and drive it down to where you can run down the hill and get in. Pick me up at the entrance. Wait five minutes, then go. I'll call for a pick-up later. All the weapons were sound suppressed and the wind helped mute the sound, but someone may have still heard the shooting. Most important, call Kathy on her throw-away cell and tell her Frank has been hit but may be trying to get to his house."

When Jack finished passing instructions to Kelly, he heard the muted sound of her rifle. Jack mused, she is her mother's daughter. Jack knew where Hasani went down. Keeping to cover, he raced up the slope and stopped behind a stack of deadfall. Looking through a gap in the deadfall, he saw Hasani pointing his rifle downhill. Jack, keeping the weapon in sight, circled behind Hasani and crept up close.

Without looking around Hasani said, "Good shooting, Lieutenant. You missed me in Ramadi. You are a warrior. You are too many for us now, but we will win, even if it takes a thousand years. I am finished. I've only minutes left. Can you see yourself granting me a few minutes of prayer before I die?"

Jack said, "Where is the Professor?"

"Give me your word you will kill him yourself, and I will tell you. Do not allow him to be captured."

"Okay. Now tell me."

"He is in a log cabin house on the west ridge of Mount Gilead just south of Leesburg. Near a shooting lodge called, Isaac something. I remember because Isaac is a name from the Book."

"You are a warrior. Die in peace but, first, throw the Dragunov down the slope."

Jack saw the rifle being tossed and left Hasani to his final prayers.

Running hard, he just made the pickup. Jumping in the back seat, he said, "Fast to Frank's house but no speeding tickets."

They saw no police cars racing to the Park and ten minutes later were approaching Frank's house in Langley Forest in McLean. Jack spotted Storm getting out of her car. Frank's car must have slid sidewise when he braked hard coming up the circular driveway. There was blood on the small front porch. The door was ajar. Jack, followed by Kelly, never broke stride crashing through the door. Both had their handguns out.

Frank was sitting on the floor with his back braced against the living room couch. He was holding a handgun pointed at Kathy. Jack's hand flew up. His SOCOM fired. The left side of Frank's head vanished in a red mist. Jack had Kathy in his arms, checking to see if she was hurt. Kathy put her head on Jack's shoulder and said, "I'm okay. The bastard was going to kill me. He wanted you to see it happen. You came so fast and shot him, I don't think he even knew you were here. I didn't see you or hear anything until the boom of the SOCOM."

"We have to get out of here. Do we need a wipe-down?"

"No. I wore gloves the whole time."

"Did you find anything?"

"Yes, I found his secret stuff on these three DVDs."

Kelly said, "I've picked up the brass."

Jack said, "Good, lock the back door from the inside. Don't touch anything."

Kathy said, "Everyone out the front door. It has a snap lock. This house is so isolated, I doubt anyone heard anything. We need to drive out of here slowly, just like we're admiring the neighborhood."

Jack said, "Kathy, come with us, we have one more job to do. Storm is back in her car, call her and tell her to go back to the house and monitor the news."

Getting in the car, Jack said, "Sam, let Kathy drive."

Kathy said, "Just tell the driver where we are going."

"We're going to Leesburg to kill a terrorist. I promised a proud warrior that I would personally kill him and not let him be captured."

Sam said, "Why did you make that promise?"

"Two reasons. He refused to tell me where the Professor is hiding until I promised to personally kill his friend, and Hasani was a proud warrior who was dying and wanted to spend his last minutes in prayer. I thought it was a good exchange."

Jack told them what Hasani had said about the Professor's hideout.

Kelly said, "Okay, what's the plan?"

"Get Storm on the phone and tell her what I told you. We need precise directions and images of the cabin and this Isaac-something shooting lodge."

Sam Richfield said, "That's easy. It's the Izaac Walton League, a lodge for outdoors people. It's got a shooting range but most people go there to trap shoot. I was there once with a friend. I'm not sure I could take us directly there."

"Storm can work her magic. No one has an iPhone or Droid, only prepaid cells, so she can't send any images but word-of-mouth instructions will work. Now the plan. A very subtle one. We're going to surround the cabin, and fire everything we have into the doors and windows. Then I'm going to charge one of the doors and toss in a couple of fire bombs. In the back of the SUV, we have a quart of oil, a siphon hose and some water bottles. If he comes out, we shoot him. Sam Richfield gets back into his counter-terrorism official role and does whatever he should do."

Richfield said, "It just might work. I have my house and job back, and all the bad guys are dead. Nobody knows just how Frank did what he did. He kept everything close, and I mean close, to his vest."

Jack added, "And we are totally out of it. Lou is out of the hospital today and will disappear with Storm."

"Kathy, pull into the empty soccer field. I have to get our cocktails mixed."

Following directions from Storm, Kathy found the Izaac Walton Lodge and located the hidden driveway leading up to the log cabin. Jack said, "Okay! Let's go!"

Kathy roared up the steep driveway, bounced over a cattle guard and slid to a stop beside a white Ford 150 truck parked at the top of a short flight of stairs leading to the cabin door. Kelly and Sam ran around to the back of the cabin and started shooting. Jack and Kathy opened up on the front door and windows. After a mad minute of firing, Jack gave Kathy a few seconds to reload and start firing. Jack raced to the front of the cabin and hurled gasoline and oil-filled bottles with lighted wicks through the broken windows. In the light of the growing fire, he saw the Professor scrambling from room to room and emptied his SOCOM. He was sure he hit him at least once. The fire raced through the old cabin. The Professor managed to get the front door open and was met with a hail of fire. He fell back into the burning house.

Jack called out, "Load up now. Let's go!"

Kathy had them on Route 15 south to avoid going back through Leesburg.

Jack said, "Good work, people, four minutes on site. Still haven't heard a siren. Hey, Richfield, it seems you've got to alter your cover story. On second thought, I don't think you want to tell anyone you were on site at any of the three killing areas. How you play the rest is up to you, just don't leave trails back to us.

"The rest of us are going back to our house. I think Kelly should take you to your house. You should get back in the game as quickly as you can. With everything that's gone down, your office has probably been looking for you."

Richfield said, "The reality is, Frank Batcher will never be charged with being a mole. No one even suspects it. Kathy's young assistant will never figure it out. She got a promotion and a transfer. Frank's dead, he can't harm her. He will end up being a hero. Killed by al Qaeda for his role in saving the city from the snipers. We just don't have enough evidence to bring any charges or suspicions. It doesn't seem right, but Frank did a lot of good work and, in a convoluted way, he did help save the city from more destruction and death by involving your team. Maybe American history has other cases of villains we honor today as heroes."

Seventy

Kelly was back from taking Sam home. She found the Brandon house full of activity. Kathy was gathering up all the weapons used in any of the day's events for dumping in the river. She hated to dump her SOCOM, but if any bullets were found at the cabin, they could match the SOCOM. Shadow was pacing around, sniffing everyone who came in, as if he knew they had left him out and wanted to know what happened. Lou was being discharged from the hospital tomorrow. Storm was taking him to Hawaii when he could travel. In the meantime, she rented a condo in Leesburg.

Storm was in the operational center watching several screens of news and commentary about the day's events. No one, it seemed, really knew what happened. Storm thought with all the shooting in broad daylight, you would think someone would have seen something. Even the talking heads were stumped, trying to find a thread to tie all the events together. Some were waiting for a group to claim credit. The CIA, FBI and the Pentagon all deferred comment until the investigations were completed. One commentator said she thought some deep national security issue would eventually come out to explain these strange and deadly events. Storm thought. I was involved and *I* don't understand everything that happened.

Jack went down to talk to Storm. He wanted her to know that both she and Lou had jobs with the Brandon team as long as they wanted one. He said, "We want and need your computer and organizational skills. Lou has a great operational planning mind. He doesn't need to be an active shooter. We need him. One lung won't be a problem. He will have to judge when it's time to lay up for a while."

Storm thanked him and told Jack she and Lou appreciated the offer. Please give them some time to work out their plans.

Jack and Kathy had a private talk with Kelly. Kathy asked her about her thoughts. Kelly said, "Everything happened so fast, I didn't have time to think. I now realize just how dangerous this work is, and I know why you pay me so much. If I'm going to keep doing this kind of work, I need much more preparation and training. All the action I was in, one of you gave me complete direction. On the hillside today, without Jack's move-by-move coaching, I would have been ineffective, dead or both. Sometime, I may not have one of you at my side. I need to be ready for being on my own. I want to continue with your training program and, at the same time, finish my degree at Pitt. When I'm ready I want to see where my mother was killed."

Jack said, "Granted. One piece of advice before you go back to school. Kathy, jump in any time. We both saw the budding interest between you and Sam. It is, of course, your business, but you should know the spouse or lover of an intelligence officer seldom can have a career of their own. A relationship between two strong career-oriented people seldom works out. The internal competition puts a strain on the relationship."

Kathy said, "Very true. I was married once to an intelligence officer. It lasted less than a year. I was glad to get out. Take your time. Get your degree or degrees and stay close to us. You've been wonderful. And Kelly, take the SRX with you. It may fit your lifestyle better. We don't want it in front of the house, in case someone might have seen it at one of today's violent scenes. I'll sign the title for you, so you can get Pennsylvania plates."

It was late, Jack had just gotten back from dumping the guns in the Potomac. Kathy was in bed trying to make her nails presentable when Jack got in bed and said, "You know I'm a traditionalist, and I have a serious question, Will you marry me soon? Here's the ring to seal my offer."

Kathy threw her arms around him and said, "Yes, I'll marry you, with or without the ring. I'll also stay with you, without the vows. I'm your woman forever and always."

Kathy opened the ring box, and Jack slipped the three-carat diamond on her finger. "Jack, I love it. When did you have time to get it?"

"We all have secrets. If you look closely, you will see even the diamond has a traditional 'mine' cut. And I have another request."

"It's yours, no matter what."

"Shadow is getting a bit long in the tooth. I want to get a puppy for him to train. It will be at least three years before the pup will be ready to work."

"Okay, as long as Shadow approves. I owe that dog my life. Now come here, and let me show my appreciation."

About the Author

Barry Kelly is no stranger to the world of espionage, counter-terrorism, weapons, martial arts, clandestine tradecraft, deep cover, black operations, para-military operations and the inner workings of the governmental security apparatus. Twenty-seven years of government service provided hands-on experience in all these areas. His immersion in the Cold War began with enlistment in the U.S. Navy during the Korean War. A magna cum laude BA from The University of Pittsburgh and a master's degree from Duke University, through the James B. Duke Fellowship Program, followed his discharge from the Navy.

Kelly's experience at CIA included deep cover operations, a wide spectrum of agent operations, overseas experience, primarily in South and Southeast Asia, a tour as the Station Chief in Moscow, TDY excursions to the Middle East and the Far East. A volunteer assignment in Vietnam resulted in the award of two medals by the Government of South Vietnam for service in the five northern provinces, one of which is The Cross of Gallantry with Silver Star. The author held command positions in three Directorates of the CIA. He was awarded the Certificate of Merit with Distinction, the Intelligence Medal of Merit, the Distinguished Intelligence Medal and the first Intelligence Officer of the Year Award.

After retirement from CIA, Kelly responded to a call from the White House to fill a position on the National Security Staff as Special Assistant to President Reagan in the last two years of his administration. He was responsible for all intelligence activities and operations, including counter-terrorism and covert action. In this position, he chaired the weekly meetings of the top counter-terrorism committee in the government.

Barry Kelly has had a lifelong interest in martial arts. He holds a first Dan Black Belt in Hapkido. Born in Western Pennsylvania, he now lives with his wife, Joan, in South Carolina, a true warrior state where service in the CIA is honored.

While this book is fiction, it could be true. The real world of intelligence operatives is stranger than fiction. Were we permitted to write about real world intelligence activities, no one would believe the tales.

Justice Beyond Law, Barry Kelly's first novel, is available on Amazon and through Prose Press. Read the gripping prologue below.

Justice Beyond Law

Prologue

December

Arthur Cohen, congressman from New York's 10th District, was anxious to begin his usual morning run. Everyone else in the Cohen house was still sleeping, at least in the case of his wife, Shara, who liked waking up softly, especially since their third child was expected late next month. Without his workout he had trouble concentrating on the minutiae of constituent problems. They invaded his time to work on new legislation. At 7:15 a.m. the world looked good. The weather forecast was for a bright sunny early winter day. The first rays of light made the forecast look good. The coolness of the night still prevailed and wafted around him like a cocoon as his ten-minute-a-mile stride carried him down the slope to the C&O Canal. The dirt path along the canal was the best place he had ever found to run. It was good for his over-forty knees. He often felt he could run forever along the canal. This morning he would run for exactly another twelve minutes and ten seconds, and his life would end.

Just before first light Jason settled himself into his shooting position and waited for his target to come striding down the canal path. It wouldn't be long now. In the distance Jason could see a few runners approaching. Runners all have distinctive styles. Jason saw the blue and white warm-up suit come in view. The second runner was his mark, but to be sure Jason used his binoculars to compare the runner to the photo his Control had given him. It was a match. For the last two mornings from his carefully chosen shooting position, he had watched the congressman run along the tow path. Jason liked punctual targets. He had one here. Right on time. The light was good. At one hundred meters he would fire one round into Cohen's chest. Then he planned to hit two more people among the cyclists, runners, and dog walkers to confuse the police and worry the local population.

Jason was concealed near the top of a steep bank. He had a clear view of the canal path. His getaway car was parked just off MacArthur Boulevard, a short walk from his ambush site. The weapon, a Steyr-Mannlicher SSG-69, when broken down could be concealed under his long dark coat. Although Jason was over sixty, he was a born hunter with steady hands and a keen eye. Jason's spare frame carried the same weight it had decades ago when he came across the Canadian border. Nothing about him stood out.

The perfect kill was always easier than the perfect escape. The target neared the stone he had placed to mark the distance. Cohen's left foot landed beside the hundred meter marking stone at the same instant Jason fired his first round. He hit Arthur Cohen in the middle of the chest. Cohen took one more half-step and fell on his face. No one paid any attention to the partially silenced first shot.

Jason held his position and selected the next target, a tall blond ponytailed runner with a near perfect stride, who had been gaining steadily on the blue and white warm up suit. Ponytail saw Cohen fall and broke her stride. Sighting on her upper right thigh, Jason's second shot knocked her down within three feet of his kill. As other runners and bikers seeing the blood and the downed figures scrambled for cover, Jason, secure behind a screen of dead wild grapevines, selected a young male cyclist on a silver racing bike and shot him high on the right shoulder. The bike swerved and plunged into the shallow canal, causing more chaos.

Jason picked up the three brass casings, smoothed out the impressions made in his ambush position, and then worked his way back up the slope, wiping out all traces of his movements.

Jason didn't mind killing. These people were all enemies, and the mission came straight from Moscow. He would just as soon have killed everyone on the canal trail, but he always followed orders. Jason did not hurry. It would be ten minutes before the first District of Columbia police car and an emergency medical unit arrived on the scene and by then he would be part of the morning traffic headed north around the beltway. In two hours Jason would be back on Tilghman Island on the eastern shore of the Chesapeake Bay, secure in his job as an owner-operator of a small marina. He would call his Control as soon as he turned off 495. This job was worth a nice sized bonus.

PROSE PRESS

The origin of the word prose is Latin, prosa oratio, meaning straightforward discourse.

Prose Press is looking for stories with strong plots.

We offer an affordable, quality publishing option with guaranteed worldwide distribution.

Queries: E-mail only.
proseNcons@live.com

CPSIA information can be obtained at www.ICGtesting.com
Printed in the USA
LVOW061155190612

286757LV00005B/3/P

9 780985 188917